The Barsukov Triangle, The Two-Toned Blond & Other Stories

Edited by Carl R. Proffer & Ellendea Proffer

Ardis, Ann Arbor

Ardis
2901 Heatherway
Ann Arbor, Michigan 48104

Library of Congress Cataloging in Publication Data

The Barsukov Triangle, The two-toned blond, and
  other stories.

  1. Short stories, Russian—Translations into English.
2. Short stories, English—Translations from Russian.
I. Proffer, Carl R. II. Proffer, Ellendea.
PG3286. B3 1984   891.73'0108   84-387
ISBN 0-88233-805-6
ISBN 0-88233-806-4 (pbk.)

CONTENTS

v

RUSSIAN PROSE 1961-1984:
ITS RELATIONSHIP TO UNION OFFICERS, BORDER GUARDS, AN EXECUTIONER, TESTS OF CHARACTER, THE DANGERS OF FORM, EMIGRATION, AND THE FUTURE

This anthology is a companion to our *Contemporary Russian Prose* (1982). The latter contains long works by only seven very well-known authors.[1] The scope of this new collection is broader and more diverse; we intend to complete this series with an anthology of postwar verse and at least one more prose collection, all part of our plan to make available in English a representative body of Russian writing from the early 1960s to the present.

This will become increasingly difficult in the future. As we learned in the mid-1970s when we tried to buy rights from VAAP, it has been an official policy of VAAP not to allow an approved Soviet writer's story to appear in any anthology which mixes official writers with Russian writers who live or publish abroad. Thus, Western anthologies can only choose freely from the pre-1973 works of approved writers (1973 being the year the USSR joined the Universal Copyright Convention). The strong trend toward convergence of the "two" Russian literatures (one abroad, one at home) which was characteristic of detente and the Brezhnev era has been attacked in numerous ways during the Andropov-Chernenko period. Soviet efforts to separate and compartmentalize writing will no doubt continue for some time, but it is doubtful that they will ever be as successful as Stalin was: the practices of the last two decades and the power of Russian culture abroad make this unlikely. While outside the USSR we are able to admit there are *some* good writers still living in Russia, inside the USSR it cannot be admitted that there is even *one* good writer living abroad—even if, like Aksyonov and others they were *required* school reading for young people until they emigrated.

This collection includes different works by three authors (Rasputin, Iskander, Shukshin) who are also represented in the earlier volume, but *The Barsukov Triangle* offers several writers who are less well known—in some cases simply because they have not been translated, in others because their work appeared only in samizdat and then abroad (Popov, Maramzin). There is no question that the lack of the support of the Soviet publicity machine, starting with the Union of Writers' powerful Bureau of Propaganda, is a serious obstacle for a writer who wishes to achieve an international reputation. Writers such as Abramov and Zalygin have had the full force of this machine behind them. Others have been supported—Grekova, Baranskaya, Rasputin but with serious critical reservations, and, very likely, internal "discussions" in the Directorate of the Union of Writers. Others have had serious problems with the authorities. Okudzhava was under investigation as late as 1972; his performances had always been controversial, and he began his prose career in the once sensational *Pages from Tarusa*[2] (1961). Maramzin's novella first appeared in 1975 when he was on trial in Leningrad, and among the items confiscated at the time of his arrest were Nabokov's *Lolita*, and the issue of *Russian Literature Triquarterly* containing the first English translations of two of his stories.[3]

But on the whole this anthology, which has obvious sociological as well as esthetic interest, represents accepted or "official" Soviet Russian literature. Of the fifteen stories, nine were printed in the USSR. Given propitious circumstances and the proper cuts, four of the other six might conceivably have appeared there in earlier days. Only Maramzin's work is unthinkable in the Soviet Union, and Katerli's might be considered dubious.

The anthology also represents different generations ("young writers" in the Soviet Union are those who are forty), from Nina Katerli to Grekova and Okudzhava (both in their sixties). Three of the best known have died within the last decade—Shukshin, Trifonov, and Abramov. Some of the writers are associated with the vague trend called "country prose"; a few, such as Iskander and Varlamova, deal with non-Russian nationalities; still others are resolutely urban in their concerns (Trifonov, Katerli). Except for Maramzin and, to a lesser extent, Katerli, they may all be called realists. Thus both in terms of long Russian convention and the modern forced marching called socialist realism, they fall into a tradition. Realism is a tradition which most Russian writers naturally find congenial, but one which is positively enforced by Union of Writers' privileges (special housing, special food, special medicine, and special vacations—not to mention medals) and negatively enforced by KGB sanctions (from "talks" and non-publication to barbed wire and guard dogs). While specialists will focus more on the things which the twelve writers have in common, non-specialists will probably be surprised at the relative diversity which these writers prove. Either way, as editors we will be satisfied. There is no period of Soviet Russian literature which it is harder to analyze than the period 1960-84. The warning that to generalize is to be an idiot has extra meaning. But we must say a few things. It is the first period totally dominated by truly Soviet writers, i.e., men and women born after the Revolution, educated in the new Soviet society, and brought up entirely under the new literary conditions. The shifts in official policies have been frequent and startling. Scarcely anyone would now dare say when exactly all the "thaws" were. What is publishable has varied spectacularly from journal to journal and year to year. One year Solzhenitsyn could get published; another year he was thrown out of his country. At the start of the 1961-84 period poets and singers such as Evtushenko and Voznesensky, Vysotsky and Okudzhava, performed before crowds of thousands (even though Vysotsky was never allowed to publish or even to have a poster of announcement, and Okudzhava never was allowed a book of music); but by the end of the period the two celebrated poets were obediently wealthy Soviet classics, while Vysotsky (who died in 1980) was first published in the illegal *Metropole* (1979) and Okudzhava, his only book of words and music published abroad by Ardis, was careful, comfortable, and kind when he travelled abroad as an only slightly suspect representative of Soviet culture.

In 1977 the Soviets staged an international book fair at which Ardis was allowed to display Russian books by Nabokov, Brodsky and others for the first time in Soviet history; the Soviet copyright agency, VAAP, was actively buying rights to Western books; tens of thousands of Russians were being allowed to leave the country and call back to their friends unhindered. But by the end of 1979 everything had changed. Ardis was the only publishing house banned from the next Book Fair, where the number and kinds of Western books confiscated grew markedly;[4] we and other American publishers were denied visas;[5] VAAP assumed a defensive position and tried to stop Russians from publishing abroad; emigration ground to a virtual halt; and a large number of the Soviet phones were unplugged.

A neo-Stalinist, isolationist position is the one held today. One reason country prose has many authoritative supporters, is because it at least makes people look inwards and to the past rather than outwards and to the future; and even better, it can foster xenophobia. Such influential literary power-brokers as Palievsky and Kozhinov, ideologues of the nationalistic Russite movement, help foster country prose—or foreign prose which they can interpret as showing the virtues of nationalism and the past. Isolationism is obvious on the political scene. The destruction of an international commercial airliner is the most obvious example, of course. But it is also clear from such things as (1) the restrictions on international (and even inter-city!) telephones, (2) restrictions on book export, (3) intensifying attacks on modern Western culture (everything from films such as *Star Wars, The Deer Hunter, Gorky Park,* and *Moscow on the Hudson* to rock music), (4) new customs rules, (5) the blithe ease with which Soviet theater authorities acting for the Central Committee, took away their greatest theater director's theater (Yury Lyubimov's Taganka) and gave it to a willing compromiser, A. Efros, (6) on December 9, 1981 *The Literary Gazette* reported in absolute seriousness on a Union of Writers' Secretariat meeting devoted to the theme of the relations between writers and border guards. A competition for works on the MVD was also announced. Because of the new climate of press vitriol and the successful creation of non-specific fear, rejected writers think less often of the option of publishing abroad. It used to be one couldn't take pre-1917 books out of the USSR without library permission, then it went to pre-war books—now customs agents are tougher coming and going: *no* books can be taken out without the laborious process of getting written permission. This is symbolic of the current Soviet attitude toward the movement of literature across its borders in either direction.

The reader must remember that we are dealing with a nation which can always find a large supply of willing writers and quickly manufacture new classics to take the place of those who leave Russia (Brodsky, Solzhenitsyn, Voinovich, Aksyonov, Maximov, Sokolov—just to name a few who have been widely translated into English). Not only do they do this, they also refuse to discuss it, and they ever so honestly proclaim in *The Literary Gazette* (July 15, 1981), that the two main centers of modern culture are Moscow and Paris! And this from a country in which *every* page of *every* proof must be signed and stamped in ink first by the editor and then by the censor before it can be printed—whether the page is instructions for a sausage grinder or the first page of another epic novel on the meaning of Soviet history from Yalta to the signing of the Helsinki accords.[6] It's no surprise, therefore, that copying machines are all in locked, windowless rooms. It's more of a surprise that even many emigre Russian writers insist that their modern literature is superior to American and other Western literatures now.

In spite of these phenomena, in spite of the new stringency of control, there are some counter-indications. This is comforting, because in all the past periods of relaxation or control, there were always things happening which didn't fit the pattern. Thus, a few new names are appearing in the literary journals, such as Dmitriev and Molchanov, whom even very suspicious emigre critics have praised; so there may be hope. Furthermore, most of the writers represented here are still active, and no doubt some of them will continue to attract interest.

If we return to the long period during which all the works here appeared (1961-84), we can make a few fairly safe generalizations about the themes, characters, and style which dominated in these works and many others. The two basic facts of these writers' and all Russians' existence were (1) Stalin, and (2) War. Equinanimously, an internal dictator decimated his enemies and his friends with the Great Terror; then an external dictator laid waste to much of the land and its population. Arguments are still going on about who killed more millions of people—Stalin or Hitler.

It is peculiar that one of these basic facts—World War II (called in Russia the "Great Patriotic War")—is the subject of a great mass of official Soviet literature, as represented by Abramov, Zalygin, and countless others. (War is a common theme in emigre prose as well.) The other basic fact, the archipelago of camps, is seldom mentioned in official literature, but is one of the main subjects of dissident literature. Stalin and his phantasmagoric system of camps are as vital to samizdat as patriotic war stories are to the Union of Writers. Although it may not always be obvious, many of the concerns and characters in the stories below are related to one or the other of these two basic themes.

Although there are notable and early exceptions such as Shalamov's tales,[7] the camp theme seems to be more prominent in long novels than in short stories. The military theme is not as restricted by genre. What about plot? Particularly among the dominant realist writers, the short story often tends toward the character sketch rather than the O'Henry-style plot construction. This, too, is traditional in most Russian literature. Who are the characters? Stories about country eccentrics, quiet rural heroes, strong old women, the "grabbers" and the conscious-stricken city bourgeoisie have been staples of Soviet literature at least since the early 1960s. Those writers who describe non-Russian life in such regions as Kirghizia, Abkhazia, or among any of the many tribes from the Urals to far Siberia, also tend to find analogous kinds of "little" heroes. The true positive hero of the Stalin era is rare. The exception is in the official Prize-winning novels; indeed, that hero is mainly a creature of the Union of Writers' authorities, such as Markov and other powerful secretaries who pen (or have ghost-written) multi-volume epics, dutifully bought and shelved by Party careerists and eagerly read by Soviet Petrushkas. (This is called "Secretariat Literature" by the cognoscenti).[8]

Thus the main characters of nearly all of the writers represented here do fight battles. They try to do things in the face of resistance, but it is seldom that their tests are anything more than the tests which everyday life and Soviet *byt* ("existence," the sum of things and customs in everyday life)[9] put before them. They are ordinary people trying to do something hard—live. Compared to the great character types and crucial tests of classic Russian literature (from Akaky Akakievich to Ivan Ilich), they are not universalized and their test is ordinary. It's as if *byt* were the central Russian problem and the main determinant of character.

This holds both in the city and in the country. Many of the main conflicts are at the family level (perhaps one reason that the developing child is so often prominent). The world of the characters is usually narrow. Soviet characters not only do not travel to different countries much, their radius of action for a whole life is ordinarily very restricted. (The war or a camp may make an exception to this rule.) They seldom know what's happening outside their home, never mind in the world at large. And since they live at a fairly simple, subsistence level, basic housing and when they will eat meat are central issues. Modern civilization does not provide many tests. Characters do not have their lives complicated by such Western problems as sudden fortune, who to vote for at the next election, falling in love with one's psychotherapist, computer burn-out, or even moving to a new house out of state. Such *bytovoi* (everyday) things as the German deciding whether to buy a second car or not, the American deciding which airline to take to Europe, or the Frenchman where to vacation on the Riviera do not concern Russian characters. Sex concerns them, of course, as is clear from the unpublishable Maramzin; but it is never the subject of detailed thought, description, or fantasy. The stories by Trifonov and Rasputin are more characteristic of the Soviet approach, even though each writer has original touches. The ultimately sexual slap the girl endures in "Games at Dusk" is as close as a Soviet writer can get even to that famous whip in *First Love*, so beloved by the Japanese in their numberless translations of the Turgenev story. Because of their use of fantasy in the broad sense (fantasy is one of the things that makes them suspicious from the Soviet point of view), one can easily tell Katerli and Maramzin from the others. But if we put the others, the more or less traditional realists, side by side without names, it would be difficult to tell *solely by style* who is who. City and country would help one to guess, but that isn't style in the narrow sense. By the Russian style alone, I suspect the only clearly unique one would be Trifonov (with apologies to Popov).

It is not very well known in the West that form is almost as likely to get one banned by an editor or censor as content. Most victories over the censors, violations of the taboos, which Russian writers and readers boasted about in the sixties and seventies were thematic victories. So-and-so said something that had never been said before, and it "got by" everyone. Since forbidden topics are myriad, the new truth, or portion of the truth, could be almost anything. Russian readers *lived* for this kind of breakthrough. They waited in line on Kalinin Prospect, Moscow Art Theater Lane, Kuznetsk Bridge or at the hundreds of kiosks for books or magazines that had—or were rumored to have—such new truths and semi-truths. However, the poet or prose writer who wanted to experiment with style alone was no less likely than the thematic heretic to get red ink in his face and bad comments on his work record (*kharakteristika*).

Poets were harder to pin down, especially if they were optimistic, patriotic, could describe a drill-press, or did the usual stultifying nature descriptions. But they had to watch their language, their metaphors, and their allusions. Colloquialisms, especially the really new ones, ones young people loved, were dangerous; metaphors had better be simple and comprehensible—none of that Pasternak mumbo-jumbo; the Encyclopedia of Myths didn't get published until 1983, so too many allusions to classical gods and goddesses were out. In short, nothing too "imaginative," nothing too hard—for those are signs of "bad" verse, poetry incomprehensible to the masses.

xiii

As for prose, there the form-censors no doubt felt surer of themselves. Read Sasha Sokolov's *A School for Fools,* and you'll see what got the editors' goat; in many ways it is an angry compendium of precisely all the things that cannot be done with form in the Soviet Union. Stream-of-consciousness is out; after all, they've had Joyce on the pillory for sixty years, the chief demon of Modernism (whatever that is). Proustian detail and self-analysis is impossible. The use of the grotesque and fantastic must be held to a bare minimum, even if the editor is a liberal; Kafka was not banned for so many decades on a whim. Chronology cannot be too disorderly, let alone obliterated; it is the first step to easy comprehension by Metro riders, pensioners, and *kolkhoz* workers of average education. Therefore departures from normal chronology must be reconstructable without much page turning, and even then it is allowed mainly for writers over seventy who have proved their loyalty, old men like Kataev, who had voted to throw Pasternak out of the Union of Writers in 1958, and dutifully attacked Solzhenitsyn a decade or so later.

As for language, here we get to a major and interesting debate. Ideally the editor and censor would like the diction to be unnoticed and unnoticeable. The language of everyday life; i.e., newspapers, Party decrees and informational bulletins, and the classics of the past, from Chernyshevsky to Chapaev and Belinsky to Lenin, should be the models. After all, these writers used plenty of words without the smarty-pants author having to go find different ones. Aside from warning articles in periodicals—*The Literary Gazette, Questions of Literature,* and even *Russian Language in School,* there was a powerful weapon used by authorities to insure linguistic conformity—dictionaries. While it is true the Soviets produced the largest multi-volume dictionary of the literary language (17 vols., 1950-65) and that other lexicographers like Ushakov did brilliant work, neither set was common on writers' desks after Stalin. Writers, like most Russians, instead used the acceptable 50,000 words of the dull, dreadful, ubiquitous *Ozhegov Dictionary,* which wordsmiths such as Nabokov have justly abused. For limited minds, the perfect Sovietese and nugatory definitions of numberless Ozhegovs were the ideal weapon. When the country prose craze started (since most writers didn't know much about real country speech), the good old *Dahl Dictionary* (1840s) was reprinted a number of times—naturally not its best editions supplemented by Baudouin de Courtenay, but the bowderlized ones. Even cut, it is a good lexicon which many serious writers have praised, but it is a century old (thus certain dangerous modern concepts and usages are safely absent), and the much more up-to-date four-volume Ushakov became very hard to get. In the seventies it was reprinted in America, and Sasha Sokolov was very happy when Ellendea and I made him a present of one.

The Soviet Union is the perfect vertical corporation, it controls everything needed to write, from—depending on the decrees of the latest Party Congress or Union of Writers Plenum— the subjects that need to be written about to the words that the authors should use. For example, one of the main features of the works of Vasily Aksyonov was the startlingly new language. Stories such as his "A Ticket to the Stars" and "Halfway to the Moon" were the Soviet equivalent to *The Catcher in the Rye* and more.[10] He wrote very much the way the young generation actually talked. Pieces such as "Surplussed Barrelware" drove sedentary translators to despair. And he continued to use that diction, indeed to expand it, especially when the West became his subject matter. Even when he was popular, he got the low payments that dubious rebels get. He was lucky that he had an editor who gave him fairly free rein (good old Kataev at *Youth* [*Iunost*]) and that he came on the scene during one of those lax periods that misled everyone, at least until the tanks entered Prague. But long before this, Aksyonov had Khrushchev yelling at him in public, and as time passed he noticed his money was gone and that he wasn't getting much published (eleven years of enforced silence),[12] and in the end, when he finally published the works that reflected his true, completely unfettered language (he recalls he had to "order" his writing hand to be free), such as his major novel *The Burn* [*Ozhog*], it was 1980 and his book was published not in Moscow but in Michigan. The censors had no work to do on this because the KGB and Union of Writers worked in tandem to get him out of the Union and out of the country. Quite apart from its subject matter, the novel could never have been published there on grounds of (1) language, (2) structure and chronology, and (3) the use of fantasy in characterization. One could do a similar analysis of Bitov's *Pushkin House (Pushkinskii dom)*[13] from the formal point of view and show that it too had to appear whole only abroad almost as much because of its form, beautifully symmetrical, but "too literary" and perhaps intended as camouflage, as for its content, which was relatively uninflammatory except for a few discussions about the aristocracy and Russian history in the year 1937.

Of course, if we talk about *another* kind of language—*mat,* dirty language—the case is simple. Soviet editors never print dirty words. When Solzhenitsyn got *One Day* published, the theme was approved by everyone from Tvardovsky to Khrushchev but the language was another matter. No matter how mild and realistic the language was, he had to clean it up, with the help of friendly editors.[14] And since he wanted to belong and be published in *Novyi mir,* he did; but even so the relatively gentle terms left caused great shock and some debate. It was the beginning of a new kind of language. Dictionaries of camp language began to appear all over in the West, some of the texts smuggled out of the Soviet Union. One former prisoner, now at Harvard, was already working on thousands of cards for a future dictionary of "non-normative" Russian. All the words that show realia which in theory do not exist, all the regional vernaculars, all the forbidden words will be in it.[15]

In the case of a writer who thrives on dirty words, whose natural narrative idiom is the unrestrained, colorful "filthy" language of the zek, such a writer would never bother to submit his novels or stories anywhere—the first page would do him in. The funny thing is that when just such a writer left Russia, he ran into the same puritanism here. Most emigre Russians fully agree swear words should not be printed, that here too the press should be pure. Thus, for example, Andrei Sedykh, chief editor of *Novoe Russkoe Slovo,* wrote me a letter rejecting excerpts from Aksyonov's *The Burn* on the grounds of his unprintable language—he said there would be nothing but dots left. And when Yuz Aleshkovsky[16] published something in *Kontinent,* the editors censored his language. When New York emigre publisher Russica published Eduard Limonov's *It's Me, Eddie* they put the name *Index Publishers* on the book so that they would not get the blame for the bad language and sexual description.[17]

Form, language—what does this leave us with? With one area of acceptable innovation. As already observed, when country prose came in, the pale, polluted bureaucratese, and the hackneyed plain vocabulary of the socialist realist classics were supplanted by something which was at least *realistic.* Indeed, the very fact that it was realistic and from the "folk" (*narod*) made it acceptable in principle. So for the first time in decades, the rich dialects of many areas of the Soviet Union were reflected in literature. Abramov, Belov, Mozhaev, Shukshin, Astafiev, Zalygin and many others—to widely varying degrees—did bring something new to the language of literature which bears Glavlit's stamp on every galley. This is one of the reasons Solzhenitsyn has repeatedly praised the country writers, although there are also ideological bases to his approval. Furthermore, Solzhenitsyn himself writes in a language consciously constructed to be "truly Russian" and avoid those city-Party bureaucratic cliches. [18] As far as it goes this is good. It does let fresh air in. It's good that so many writers rediscovered the old *Dahl Dictionary* with the thousands of colloquial and dialectical words and idioms the scholar recorded. When the writers actually knew the country and didn't *overdo* this new vocabulary mercilessly, it was not a bad thing to happen. Therefore, the editors allowed the lexicon to expand.

What, ultimately, did this get them? Well, the bad thing that it got them is provincialism—and this is still true today. Imagine that a large number of the important American novelists wrote exclusively on the basis of Mark Twain's dialects and using an 1840 dictionary for color and originality. This is not as bad as the Russian situation, but it is a rough analogy. While piling on the demotic—in the course of which country writers describe every old wooden utensil that ever existed—they often forget such things as interest, characterization, plot and so on. Writing degenerates into the kind of ethnographic reportage that typifies such dead Nobel classics as Reymont's *Peasants,* or into the dull historical instruction sheets that make up much of Solzhenitsyn's own never-ending *Red Wheel.* [19]

So our final answer is clearly, yes, form is a fact in censorship. The Soviet writer can tinker with chronological blocks or use the Archangel peasants' quaint words for turnips or boot-liners, but he cannot invent truly new forms, or, to look at the larger picture, he cannot write the kind of complex country prose Sasha Sokolov does write in *Between Dog and Wolf (Mezhdu sobakoi i volkom)* with language based on Volga experience, Dahl, and *imagination;* with chronology—and a whole view of Time as such—that leaves one baffled; with characters who may or may not be alive, and so on. Or, to take an example from this anthology, one cannot fracture form as Maramzin does, use a language so "artificial" that even the title contains an odd and untranslatable grammatical error. Even a fairly orthodox writer such as Katerli is suspicious, because she uses a lot of "narrated monologues" which can be a trick to hide the author's point of view.

Or, to look at the larger picture, you can't do any of the formal experiments, good or bad, laughable or interesting, boring or inspiring that typify Western writers such as Grass, Nabokov, Pynchon, Elkin, Spackman, Barth, Barthelme, Cynthia Ozick, John Hawkes or Gilbert Sorrentino, to name only a few writers whose works will not be translated by the world's most literature-loving nation. More revealing, is that the Soviet writing cannot and does not equal the accomplishments of our own so-called "realistic" or traditional writers. Such writers as Oates, Didion, Bellow, Roth, Updike, Irving, Heller, Tyler and Beattie do far more experimenting with form than most of the Russian writers in the USSR or abroad, even within works which fit traditional expectations.[20]

Once again it is worth noting that many of the same attitudes toward formal innovations are widespread in the Russian emigration, too. In emigre journals and publishing houses traditional realism is predominant. There is not much question of experimentation in the books published by Posev or YMCA; and the journals with the longest lives and most subscribers, *Kontinent* and *Time and Us*, for the most part publish poetry, stories, and novels whose form (but *not* content) would be acceptable in the USSR. Language restrictions, except for swear words, are much less obvious than in the USSR; but in any case most writers follow the standards they were brought up on. Journals more open to risk in form and themes do not last long—e.g., *The Ark (Kovcheg), Echo.* The great majority of prose and poetry published both in Russian and in English, even by Ardis, which has a reputation for being "modernist" or "elitist," has been traditionally realistic and unexperimental.[21]

Thus this anthology reflects the true state of affairs both abroad and in the Soviet Union. Even if we take one of the long tales which has not been allowed to see light in the USSR, Nina Katerli's "The Barsukov Triangle," in spite of the touches of fantasy and the narrative devices, it is one of the *most* realistic pieces of the collection. The lives of the people she describes are precisely the lives of all the Russians we have known for fifteen years. If when writing about the 1973 *Russian Literature Triquarterly* issue devoted to "Contemporary Russian Literature" even that old Moscow hand Robert Kaiser could tell readers to look at Trifonov's "The Exchange" to find out what Moscow life was really like, in 1984 we can urge the reader to read Katerli not only because her story is fun to read, but to find out exactly how different people live from day to day in the Soviet capitals. In Maramzin there is much more that is unexpected and even puzzling; because of some tricks learned from

Platonov and Nabokov, his work has special charm for the re-reader.

Okudzhava's story "Lots of Luck, Kid!" is the oldest, but still one of the best. It was published in *Pages from Tarusa,* a landmark of Soviet liberalism or laxness.[22] When he visited Ardis in 1979, he recalled discussing the tale with Nadezhda Mandelstam. She said it was so good, in fact, that for a beginning prose writer it could be dangerous. He might not be able to equal it in the future. Because of her prediction, he claimed, every time he sat down to write after that, he remembered her words and got very frustrated.

The stories by Baranskaya and the pseudonymous I. Grekova ("x") attracted much publicity when first published and were discussed by the critics. Grekova, in many ways a true liberal, had long been a specialist in the theory of probability; and when she began writing, it was a nice paradox. Indeed, Grekova's story was one of two recently brought out by another American publisher as a discovery,[23] although it had been already translated in 1973 and published then; the longer work published with it is an example of fairly uninspired moralistic Soviet prose. With Katerli and Varlamova—whose emotional story of love, betrayal, and Soviet mores appears here for the first time in any language—the varied contingent of women prose writers of the past twenty years is well represented. To note that their sensibility differs greatly from that of the male writers here is not to be sexist or condescending.

We have already mentioned Abramov, Shukshin, and Trifonov as modern Soviet classics. Two different translations of Abramov's country novel *Two Winters and Three Summers* appeared at the same time in 1984.[24] We naturally prefer the Ardis edition, mainly because of the translation, and partly because it is available in paperback, but also because the presenters of the Harcourt version either are afraid to admit or are blissfully unaware of the central facts about Abramov's life. It is no surprise that he actively persecuted Solzhenitsyn and others, and that he won both Lenin and State Prizes, because before he began writing he was a SMERSH executioner. He personally shot at least fourteen people (worse stories about him cannot be confirmed yet). Certainly no other Russian writer of any period—unless we count Ivan the Terrible (he wrote letters) can say anything like that. Even earlier his reputation was formed: his fellow students at Leningrad University, where he would become head of the Soviet literature faculty, called him "little Pilate" (Pilatushka).[25] He made an extremely short but memorable visit to Ardis (my memoirs of that meeting will soon be published in *The Widows of Russia*). Can a bad man write a good book, I always asked Russians. If you want to know if an executioner can write, read his story below.

The cult of Shukshin continues, probably more because of his subjects and his movie efforts than his writing. He seldom had the time to be as demanding as a Chekhov, and raw dialogue dominates his stories so much that he never invented a unique style of his own. The Soviets continue to publish him very actively in many forms for readers of all ages. Trifonov is a far superior writer with a far better sense of literary traditions, but publications since his death have been few and far between. Even during his lifetime he was published less than more favored writers such as Abramov and Shukshin. If we very sceptically (Soviet statistics are seldom reliable) accept the figures Mehnert[26] cites from the *Yearbook of Soviet Books* from 1967-79, all of Trifonov's books had run to 1,747,000 copies, plus one appearance in the cheap, high-run *Newspaper Novel* (c. 2,000,000 copies). In comparison Abramov's copies run to 2,629,000 plus two appearances (i.e., another 4,000,000) in the *Newspaper Novel*, and Shukshin to 2,744,000 plus one *Newspaper Novel* appearance. (Contrast the "Secretariat Literature" which Aksyonov described. The non-writer who is First Secretary of the Union of Writers, Georgy Markov, had 5,162,000 books, plus 8,000,000 more in four *Newspaper Novel* publications.) A variety of facts leads us to conclude that Trifonov, who was easily the most controversial and liberal of this group, and who made enemies among the authorities, has fallen even further behind Abramov or Shukshin since his death. However, the demand is so great and his work of such general interest that both his posthumous novel *Time and Place* and his incendiary *The House on the Embankment*[27] (where he, his family and many leaders lived, including the likes of Radek and Svetlana Stalin) have been reprinted in Russian in the USA.

Of the popular Soviet writers in this anthology this leaves Zalygin and Rasputin. This is the first time Zalygin has been translated into English (outside of Moscow), but his works are so varied and voluminous that we cannot vouch for its "typicality." On the surface, he is genuinely popular in the USSR. Mehnert, whose rankings of what Soviets read most we think are more or less correct (and give a depressingly gloomy picture of the average Russian reader's taste), puts Abramov, Rasputin, Shukshin, and Trifonov among the twenty-four most popular writers (the company they are in is the depressing part of the chart). Zalygin, Grekova and Iskander are put among the twenty-four runners-up.[28] Zalygin is also very old and reliable, and he is a Union secretary who signed the required letters attacking liberal writers, so he is able to get away with some devices and subjects off-limits to young writers, including the use of fantasy, positive pictures of old-fashioned characters and superstition. The sentimentalism and Sucaryl level are high. If he were not an officer of the Union of Writers, I might apologize to him for what follows (he is not directly to blame); we present here the complete birthday greeting to him from the Union of Writers Secretariat.[29] It will give the reader a clear idea of official style and the sorts of things which are of value to the officers of the main writing organization.

We Congratulate on his Jubilee: Sergei Zalygin, 70 Years Old

The Secretariat of the Directorate of the Union of Writers of the USSR has sent the following greeting to Sergei Pavlovich Zalygin: "We heartily congratulate you, a notable Soviet writer on your seventieth birthday.

You entered literature with rich life and workplace experience. You wrote your first works while working as a hydrological engineer, as a participant in the great constructive work spreading out across the wide-open spaces of Siberia.

In 45 years of creative activity you have contributed a great block of material to the development of our literature. In your work, devoted to the most important events in the life of the Soviet people, up-to-date questions about modernity, and to the heroic pages of the history of our state, you understand the big social moral problems, with talent you reveal the characters and fates of Soviet people—laborers of the city and the country. Your books are extremely popular among the readers of our country; they are published in the languages of the peoples of the USSR, in foreign languages.

Your original talent shone brightly in such works as the novels *Altai Paths, Salt Valley, The Commission, The South American Variant,* and the novella *On the Irtysh.* You are now publishing the new novel *After the Storm.* Your works serve to educate Soviet people in the spirit of patriotism, socialist internationalism, and humanism. For the novel *Salt Valley* you were awarded the State Prize of the USSR.

To your pen belong publicistic works devoted to the defense of our native nature, the sensible use of its riches. Your literary scholarship and critical works—*An Interview with Myself,* the essay on A. P. Chekhov, "My Past," and others—were met with interest.

You carry on active social activity, as a member of the Directorate of the Union of Writers of the USSR, a Secretary of the Union of Writers of the RSFSR, the Chairman of the Council on Prose of the Directorate of the Union of Writers of the RSFSR, and Chairman of the Council on Latvian Literature of the Union of Writers of the USSR.

For services in the development of Soviet literature you have been awarded the Order of Lenin, two Orders of the Workers Red Star, and other medals. You have been granted the title of Deserving Activist of Culture of the Latvian SSR.

We wish you, dear Sergei Pavlovich, good health, and new creative successes."

This leaves us with only one writer—Rasputin—who still publishes exclusively in the USSR, who is largely approved by the authorities, who has managed to produce four important novels, not only original and independent for the Soviet Union but also good enough to be translated into English and other languages largely on their own merit (I say "largely" because at the 1977 book fair VAAP made a concerted effort to sell rights to Rasputin and the American publishing house Macmillan, which already had close Soviet publishing ties, bought all of his best work). Born in the fateful and fatal year of 1937, he is the youngest of the Soviet classics offered here and also the youngest among Mehnert's "top twenty-four," having sold about 1,427,000 copies between 1967-79, plus another four million copies with two novels in that influential *Newspaper Novel.*[30] *Contemporary Russian Prose* contains facts and evaluation that need not be repeated here. His novels, especially *Farewell to Matyora* (1976), first published in *Our Contemporary,* are better than his stories, though both the long autobiographical story "Downstream" and "Rudolphio" have real interest. Two unusual facts about this quiet fellow are worth noting. In March 1980 he was viciously beaten in Novosibirsk, apparently for his jeans; he underwent two operations, and for a while his future was in doubt. But in 1982 he published a new story in *Our Contemporary,* currently one of the most powerful literary journals, one with a general reputation for conservatism. He is the best living Soviet writer who seems never to have had trouble with the official establishment. At the present time he is also the most prominent Soviet writer who has never been co-opted by the official machine. He has never voted to throw anyone out of the Union of Writers. He has never made statements or signed collective letters attacking writers in disfavor. He has never made political statements (condemning, say, nuclear weapons or American leaders). Finally, unlike Aitmatov, he has never provided the kinds of toe-the-line interviews or essays which are demanded of every well-known Soviet writer. (To our knowledge, the closest he has come was a patriotic piece on a great and ancient historical battle.) He doesn't dance, either. What we are to make of this, it is difficult to say. Soviet Russian literature has always had intriguing anomalies which suggest the ultimate strength of human spirit.

Evgeny Popov shares with Rasputin a love of Siberia. He is a true Siberian in everything from language to interests, and he is another one of those forty-year-old "young" Soviet writers. Short stories are his passion and forte, but the blunt realism with which he describes rural life in Siberia did not make him a favorite of Soviet editors. Popov was, with Aksyonov, Iskander, Bitov and Erofeev, one of the nominal editors of the *Metropole* anthology (1979, English translation, 1983), which led to a major scandal at the Union of Writers. Nearly every contributor was punished, but special heat fell on the editors. Popov's "devil's dozen" of short stories was repeatedly mentioned by readers outside the USSR, in three languages, as among the most important discoveries of *Metropole*. Undaunted, Popov then got involved in the *Catalogue* anthology, an effort by seven enterprising authors to start an officially sanctioned and supported club for experimental poetry and prose. This time it wasn't the Union of Writers that called them in: the KGB took care of things with immediate searches, confiscation, and temporary arrests. Fortunately (and justly, as it happens) no one went to jail, and the collection was published by Ardis in 1982. It has not been translated, and except for *Metropole,* the three stories below are Popov's main appearance in English.

Finally, there is Fazil Iskander. Again, *Contemporary Russian Prose* provides more information on him. In general he has been translated more widely than many of the Soviet authors in either Mehnert's top twenty-four or second twenty-four. Iskander's chief work, *Sandro from Chegem* could be published uncut only outside the USSR (Ardis, 1979 & 1981), mainly because of such things as the hilarious Stalin chapter. The American translation was also put into two volumes, the second part, *The Gospel according to Chegem* having just (summer 1984) been released by Random House and Vintage. But for the most part Iskander's unique prose is well beyond political concerns, and his fantastically comprehensive and amusing sagas of life in the tiny Republic of Abkhazia appeal to Soviet readers as well as American ones. In spite of his gentle moralism and obvious indifference to anything aside from writing, he was punished for his fine contributions to *Metropole*. However, the administrators seem to have at least partially relented, because his book *The Defense of Chik* was published by the "Soviet Writer" Publishing House (Moscow, 1983); it even contains a story first published in *Metropole*. "Grandfather," the little story included below, has never been translated before; it will give the reader just a glimpse of Iskander's original world.

Predicting the immediate future of Russian literature is rather perilous, especially as it relates to the authors who publish only in the Soviet Union. As has been the case since the late fifties prose is more important than poetry. Rasputin, Katerli, and Popov are the only three whose careers are relatively new; it is impossible to speculate how they might develop, except to say that previous examples are not very comforting. However, prose writers tend to do their best work in their forties and early fifties. Zalygin is well past this; and I suspect his reputation will fade because he overpaid his dues. Despite the praise Kataev gets even from many dissidents, I think time will do the same to all of his chameleon prose; what he writes has always been parochial, mendacious, and finely attuned to the social order, so his international reputation, never large, will disappear when he does. On the other hand, Iskander and Andrei Bitov may have their best work ahead of them. Now, and for the next few years most of the interesting activity will be among writers abroad. Maramzin seems to have abandoned literature, but this still leaves a number of prose writers—both traditionalists and "others." I purposely do not say "experimentalists," because the most obvious figures who are commonly pigeon-holed here—Sasha Sokolov, Andrei Sinyavsky—are, for all their innovations, traditionalists in the best sense of the word. The achievements and prospects of the "Third Wave" have been analyzed in detail by the poets, prose writers, critics, and editors themselves.[31]

Not a few Russian writers believe that in spite of marketplace tyranny, contemporary Russian literature is superior to American or other Western literatures. The editor of the most influential Russian journal, Vladimir Maximov, argues this case in a recent interview.[32] Since none of the Russian writers with whom I am acquainted know very much about American literature, this is a curious topic for debate. I suspect the nationalistic "Russia-Christ of Nations" notion from Solzhenitsyn's Harvard Speech is at the core of much emigre thinking and writing. I know what Nadezhda Mandelstam would say about this. Fortunately, it is not the central issue, and in the next few years we will find many more re-readable books from Aksyonov, Voinovich, Brodsky and others than we will see from the USSR. Many emigre journals are amateurish and have short lives, but *Kontinent* will continue to be more varied, diverting, and lively than *Novyi mir*. Sinyavsky's resolutely independent journal *Syntax (Sintaksis)* will continue to be worthy opposition to the politics of *Kontinent*. All the early signs are that in spite of the increasing difficulty of finding truly good material, Georgi Vladimov will improve *Facets (Grani)* markedly.

While emigre periodicals have their trouble, in the last few years the entire Soviet literary press has become a shambles. "Colonial novels" like Alexander Prokhanov's immortal *A Tree in Kabul* are not only given serious attention, but even get translated and discussed in the propaganda journal *Soviet Literature*.[33] *Novyi mir (New World)* is lucky to print something good once a year; without Trifonov *Druzba narodov (Friendship of the Peoples)* is dead; *Nash sovremennik (Our Contemporary)* does a little better, but the editors' applause for the government is a little louder than required. The newspapers are a joke. *The Literary Gazette* used to be interesting sometimes; but now the hysterical tone has spread to every column, and even the fabrications are done so idiotically that it's no longer worthwhile reading them for fun. The reports on various plenums and directorate meetings are beyond all imagination. The gobbledigookish messages these plenums sent (printed) to Brezhnev in his last couple of years were at least a polite goodbye, usually extolling his leadership of them and his skimpy (no doubt ghostwritten) Lenin Prize winning memoirs. Under Andropov and Chernenko the vigilance campaigns have become more shrill and ominous, and the directorate reports more servile as they explain how they discussed Central Committee Resolutions such as "On the Further Improvement of Ideological, Politico-Educational Work" (*Literaturnaia Rossiia*, June 1, 1979) or the especially menacing "On Creative Connections betwen Literary-Artistic Journals and the Practice of Communist Construction" (*Literaturnaia gazeta*, August 18, 1982). Admonitory dicta from the leaders are printed in set-off boxes, like Andropov's in *The Literary Gazette* (July 13, 1983): "The main method of influence on artistic words must be Marxist-Leninist criticism, active, sensitive, attentive and at the same time unrelenting towards ideologically alien or professionally weak works."

The names of the authors and the subjects of the works (*Lenin in Paris*) for which they have been nominated for Lenin Prizes, State Prizes and so on have become progressively more obscure and ludicrous. Lucrative but never prestigious west of Minsk, the awards have been steadily debased by cut-throat Union of Writers officials and a new generation of toadies. Those from the so-called "People's Republics" are multiplying. The example of Chingiz Aitmatov, who has something to recommend him as a writer, has had very deleterious effects. He is at least a writer *and* a mouthpiece (he also helped pillory Solzhenitsyn); the new ones are only mouthpieces.

I regret to say that in *The Russians and Their Favorite Books* Klaus Mehnert is generally right about the reading tastes and habits of average Russian intellectual.[34] Copies of Chakovsky and Bondarev will continue to be bought and read by the millions, and no doubt Russian readers will snap up more millions of the *Newspaper Novel* (each writer has appeared there six times, i.e., 12,000,000 copies) which reprints their novels. Ivanov will be just as popular, along with Pikul, Alexeev, and even poor, dumb—but mean—Stadnyuk. Semyonov's novels will continue to be serialized on Soviet television and seen by as many as 150 million viewers. There is no question that in a related vein John Le Carré's *Tinker, Tailor, Soldier, Spy* was immensely superior as a novel and on the television screen. For that matter even if we get past the hard-core buyers of books to TV and TV films the Russian blockbusters are infinitely inferior to *Holocaust, Roots,* or even the television version of such novels such as *Rich Man, Poor Man* and *Centennial.* Good, professional middle writers such as Shaw and Michener have never existed in Russia.

Soviet Russian culture is impoverished in all areas, and this is one of the explanations for the apparent book-hunger we have all heard so much about. The paper shortage is always cited by authorities as the reason for not having big editions of someone like Akhmadulina, but this is a transparent lie. They have plenty of their "good" high-acid content, sixty pound paper for political literature and "Secretariat Literature."[35] I am sure this is intentional in its relation to book-hunger, and that their UNESCO statistics on literary titles are sheer fabrications. If we consider the massive world of private and small press printing I am sure that there is more reading of good literature here than there (aside from the low quality which Mehnert proves), and that more new literary journals and books appear annually in America, not to mention England, even though many are unrecorded, since we have no real national yearbooks. Of course the paper problem has its funny side. When the KGB tried to persuade the poet Joseph Brodsky to cooperate with them in the sixties, the main reward they offered was a book of his poems "printed on good Finnish paper." An analogous proposition was made to Sasha Sokolov in 1975.

Fortunately, the Soviet readers will continue to be given a few moderately good things along with the vast warehouses of tendentious pseudo-literature. Nadezhda Mandelstam once told us of a conversation she had with the Union of Writer hack A. Surkov. She asked why "they" didn't go ahead and publish *Doctor Zhivago* and avoid all the international furor. He replied, "If we did that after all this time, then we'd have to start letting young people have books like that." "Young people!" she exclaimed in amusement, "after forty years!" And now it's been over sixty years, and the Soviet reader has still not earned the trust of his leaders.

Carl R. Proffer
Ann Arbor
June 2, 1984

Notes

1. Carl and Ellendea Proffer (eds.), *Contemporary Russian Prose* (Ann Arbor: Ardis, 1982), contains works by Aksyonov, Bitov, Shukshin, Sokolov, Iskander, Rasputin, and Trifonov, an essay on their works to date, and an extensive bibliography of works by and about them—and their period—in English.

2. *Pages from Tarusa*, ed. A. Field (Boston, 1964), is an abbreviated translation of the collection.

3. A photographic copy of the handwritten KGB "protocol" of the search and confiscation is in the Ardis archives. Maramzin's stories "Don't Steal! Directive to a Future Baby, My Slip-Son" and "Get Away from the Scene of the Accident" were published in *Russian Literature Triquarterly*, No. 5 (1973) and reissued in *The Ardis Anthology of Recent Russian Literature*, ed. Carl and Ellendea Proffer (Ann Arbor, 1975).

4. While his account is that of an amateur who knows no Russian, the most detailed record of most external aspects of the Second Moscow International Book Fair is H. Lottman, *Publishers Weekly* (October 1, 1979), pp. 26-33. According to Anthony Austin's report, Pankin, the head of VAAP, declared that the confiscations were "the highest affirmation of the freedom of speech" (*New York Times*, Septermber 4, 1979).

5. Besides us, Robert Bernstein of Random House and Winthrop Knowlton of Harper & Row were also refused. In 1983 we applied again, and all kinds of Soviet promises that American publishers would be allowed to come were broken. Ardis itself was not given an acceptance, no matter who represented it. We were told the Fair "had run out of space"—at the same time that the Soviets were trying to persuade the Combined Book Exhibit to expand their space—at no cost—as much as they wanted. The Soviets regularly withhold visas (or issue them a few days before conference openings) not only from individuals but from whole groups of people whom they dislike, notably the Israelis. Thus literary people are by no means special. The same isolationist policy has been applied to international conferences of the National Academy of Sciences, the American Physical Society, the World Psychiatric Association, the International Political Science Association, SRI International, and the International Congress of Genetics. Fascinating details on all these groups and on the Moscow Book Fairs are in *Soviet-American Exchange and Human Rights: A Conference Report and Nine Case Studies* (U.S. Helsinki Watch Committee, 1980).

6. This description is not a joke. It is a toned-down version of the descriptions from *Novye knigi (New Books)*, the central advance book announcements of the USSR, which describe Books 1, 2, and 3 of Chakovsky's forthcoming (1984-85) blockbuster, *Victory (Pobeda)*.

7. Many have been translated into English. See V. Shalamov, *Graphite* (New York: Norton, 1981) and V. Shalamov, *Kolyma Tales* (New York: Norton, 1980).

8. Aksyonov guesses there are about three hundred such Union of Writers secretaries all over the country. A number of the authors Klaus Mehnert finds among the forty-eight most popular of the USSR are many of these secretaries. Mehnert is astoundingly naive about the authors—seeing almost no propaganda in them and their readers (K. Mehnert, *The Russians and Their Favorite Books* [Stanford, 1983]). Of them Aksyonov writes: "For them there is a higher system of royalties and for figuring the number of copies in an edition, i.e., they are able to get the maximum amount of money out of their books. Essentially free country dachas and other goodies are set aside for them by the Literary Fund, an organization founded over one hundred years ago with the idea of its noble founders that it was intended to help "writers who are have-nots and drinkers." Now everything is turned around. It's only with great trouble that the poor average writer can get a pitiful loan that he must repay, while the richest and most prominent, that is, the secretaries, get solid nonrepayable stipends for moving, say several thousand rubles to move to a new apartment, to repair the garden benches at their dachas a few thousand. Not to mention the city apartments, secretarial comfort (in Moscow right now they are all moving into the street with the convincing name of Atheist Street)." Among the most valuable privileges of the Union's secretaries is absolute freedom from negative reviews anywhere in the press and the right to make regular Union-paid trips abroad. See Vasilii Aksenov, "Krivobokii uspekh," *Panorama* (March 2-9, 1984), p. 14.

9. *Byt* is notoriously hard to define. It means everything from the mores and realia that define daily life in a specific society to such a loose concept as "the daily grind."

10. It is characteristic of (1) Russian overestimation of their translators' ability, (2) their puritanism and (3) their relative indifference to precision of meaning that Rita Rait-Kovaleva's version of Salinger was praised and prized—while in fact she bowderlized the book, dropping precisely that level of shocking but normal speech that makes American readers see the truth of the language and its meaning.

11. Ardis was forced to reject two attempts to translate this tale, both done by people with no real experience in the USSR. However, a joint translation by an experienced young American and a Russian emigre will appear shortly: V. Aksyonov, *Surplussed Barrelware and Other Stories* (Ann Arbor: Ardis, 1984).

12. Aksyonov decribes all this in his series on post-Stalin literature in *Panorama* (No. 150-54, 1984).

13. Andrei Bitov, *Pushkinskii dom* (Ann Arbor: Ardis, 1978). Random House will publish Susan Brownsberger's translation of this important novel in 1985 or 1986.

14. See Michael Scammel, *Solzhenitsyn* (New York: Norton, 1984), chapter 23, pp. 449-52 (proof copy).

15. See Richard Bernstein, "Writer Tracking Russian as It's Spoken," *New York Times* (December 28, 1982), Arts, p. 25 on Kirill Uspensky's extraordinary work. A variety of dictionaries of thieves' jargon and Russian obscenities have been printed or reprinted, but only in the West.

16. Sedykh wrote Ardis August 7, 1980, on excerpts which were sent to him. He said they contained "so much coarseness, so much vulgarity, that I cannot use them."

17. See E. Limonov, *Eto ia-Edichka* (New York: "Index Publishers," 1979). Parts of the controversial novel had previously appeared in the journal *Kovcheg*. Its translation by Random House was largely ignored by reviewers, but Limonov got emigre periodicals so enraged that his very name was blacklisted by some.

18. Solzhenitsyn had carried part of the *Dahl Dictionary* with him even in prison. Afterwards he did regular exercises based on it, and went from there to Dahl's collection of

folk sayings. All this, and the often dubious folk wisdom, can be seen in his works. From his titles to his characters' speech one can see his experiments with the past.

19. Most of Solzhenitsyn's "experiments" strike me as disasters—from the rows of exclamation points and the all-caps hysteria of *Gulag* to the deadly Dos Passos film strips and self-conscious neologizing of the *Red Wheel* (the new title for the endless "nodes" or "knots" of *August, October,* etc.). His discovery of Zamiatin was most unfortunate. The *Red Wheel* is loaded with archaisms, folk obscurities, and forced neologisms, but for many readers it is a creaky mechanism at almost every level, from linguistic to structural. But even the *Red Wheel* has its unshakable fans. For some explanations and a balance-sheet on the critics, Russian and non-Russian, see Scammel, pp. 832-35 (chapter 43).

20. Except for Nabokov and a couple of others, most of the authors listed in *both* categories here are little known or totally unknown to Soviet readers. (A few have been translated, selectively and censored.) By means of inflated figures for writers such as Jack London, Dreiser, and Mayne Reid (!), the Soviets' regular line is that they print more American literature than we do Russian. However, the fact is that both nineteenth and twentieth century Russian writers are more easily available in English-speaking countries than American literature is in the USSR. (Indeed, *Russian* books are more widely available here.) See, for example, M. Friedberg, *A Helsinki Record: The Availability of Soviet Russian Literature in the United States* (New York: Helsinki Watch Committee, 1980). This report is just the beginning of what might be said.

The main thing is that Soviet knowledge of significant American writers is woefully poor. The same is true of Russians in the emigration. A few read a few new things, but essentially my experience is that no Russians know all these authors or the many others who could be added. Indeed, their language ability keeps them from finding out about the new literary milieu (outside of a few New York aspects). In spite of their ignorance, like most of their well-known Eastern European colleagues, such as Kundera, they continue to believe they live in the future (because of their suffering under Marxism), unaware that in fact they are living in the past, both in their irony-filled works and in their inability to recognize that Russia and the East *are* throwbacks to less enlightened ages.

21. There is also an amusing semiliterary and semiliterate kind of writing which has been set free by the emigration—stories and novels which are attempts at pure pornography. One can usually identify these immediately by the tacky—*really* tacky—home-made covers. Thus one of the apparently popular writers is Efraim Sevela, who puts out things such as *Men-Talk in a Bath-house,* in which the naked steam beaters tell in sequence stories of how he met a gorgeous ballerina (actress, university girl, etc.), how she invited him to a fantastic apartment with unheard of (by Soviets) luxuries, fell in love with his prodigious member, etc. Details follow. It's pretty crude stuff, like dirty Russian *chastushki* after witty limericks.

22. See Note 2 above.

23. I. Grekova, *Russian Women* ["The Hotel Manager," "The Ladies' Hairdresser"] (New York: Harcourt, 1983). We first published "A Lady's Hairdresser" in *Russian Literature Triquarterly,* No. 5 (1973).

24. The two are: F. Abramov, *Two Winters and Three Summers,* intro. by Maurice Friedberg, trans. Jacqueline Edwards and Mitchell Schneider (New York: Harcourt, Brace, 1984), cloth $17.95. F. Abramov, *Two Winters and Three Summers,* intro. by Carl R. Proffer, trans. by D. B. and Doris C. Powers (Ann Arbor: Ardis, 1984), paper $7.50.

25. Some of the unsavoury details about Abramov's life are given by V. Maximov in the editor's column, *Kontinent,* No. 37 (1983). A friendly but even more damning view is from V. Zavalishin, "Vtoroe litso Fedora Abramova," *Novosti* (New York), November 25, 1983, p. 5.

26. Mehnert, pp. 190-93.

27. Yuri Trifonov, *Another Life and The House on the Embankment* (New York: Simon and Schuster, 1983), pp. 187-350.

28. Mehnert, pp. 32-34.

29. Published in *Literaturnaia gazeta,* such birthday greetings and announcements of

medals being a primary feature of the newspaper.

30. Mehnert, pp. 36 and 368.
31. See Olga Matich and Michael Henry Heim (eds.), *The Third Wave* (Ann Arbor: Ardis, 1984) and Georges Nivat (ed.), *Odna ili dve russkikh literatury?* (Lausanne, 1981).
32. *Strelets*, No. 4 (1984).
33. The term is M. Geller's, "Sovetskii kolonial'nyi roman," *Obozrenie*, No. 6 (1983), 26-27. He traces the ignominious genre back to Pilnyak on Tadzhikistan.
34. Mehnert's *The Russians and Their Favorite Books* does not seriously contradict my knowledge of who the main names are (his opinions of them are another matter). Sergei Schmeman's article "What Russians Read and Don't Read" in the *New York Times Book Review* (February 28, 1982) follows the same lines and is basically accurate (except for the remarkable error of claiming Tvardovsky had discovered *The Master and Margarita* and that it was done in *Novyi mir*). He also agrees that the *samizdat* of the sixties has been weakened and supplanted by *tamizdat*, Russian books published abroad.

One final curiosity about the isolationism and paranoia of Soviet literary officials: new books are monitored with special care, but older books—the entire realm of second-hand sales—are also subject to controls so strict they are hard to imagine. Thus printed instructions to all second-hand book trade units (all government owned and run) naturally prohibit the sale of any book on the "Consolidated List of Books Subject to Exclusion from Libraries and Retail Stores," but they also establish a hierarchy of stamps to mark each book to show what special category of person can *see* it. These include: "Secret," "Not to be circulated," "For official use," "For CPSU members only," "For Komsomol members only," "Distribution by list," "Advance copy," "For treatment as manuscript," "For review," "For ruling," "Compulsory copy," "Publication permitted," "Control copy." So ashamed are the censors of their existence that it is illegal to sell even books bearing the censorship's stamp of approval! Finally, to insure the nonexistence of ex-persons whose books have been removed from libraries, such as Solzhenitsyn, Aksyonov, Voinovich, Maximov, and all other emigres (Baryshnikov, Makarova, Korchnoi, etc.), all "publications containing articles and pictures" of these, "or quotations from their works," are banned. See the *Chronicle of Current Events*, No. 65 for a more detailed look at the official restrictions.

Bibliography

Abramov, Fyodor. (1920-83). *A New Life*. NY: Praeger, 1963.
___. *Two Winters and Three Summers*. Ann Arbor: Ardis, 1984.
See Mehnert (below) for more translations of Abramov.

about Abramov:

Novikov, Vassily, *Artistic Truth and Dialectics of Creative Work*. Moscow: Progress, 1981, pp. 204-15.
Soviet Literature, no. 10 (1983). Rasputin and others on Abramov's death.
Svirski, Grigori, *Soviet Writing* (see below), pp. 277-85.

Baranskaya, Natalia. "The Retirement Party," *Russian Literature Triquarterly*, no. 9 (Spring 1974), pp. 136-144.

Grekova, I. (pseud. of Elena Sergeevna Ventsel', b. 1907). *Russian Women*. NY: Harcourt, 1983.
___. "A Lady's Hairdresser," trans. Larry Gregg, *Russian Literature Triquarterly*, no. 5, pp. 223-64; reprinted in *Ardis Anthology of Recent Russian Literature*. Ann Arbor: Ardis, 1976.

Iskander, Fazil (b. 1929). "Belshazzar's Feasts," trans. Susan Brownsberger & Carl R. Proffer in *Contemporary Russian Prose* (see below).
___. *Forbidden Fruit and Other Stories* (Moscow: Progress, 1972).
___. *The Goatibex Constellation*, trans. H. Burlingame. Ann Arbor: Ardis, 1975.
___. *Sandro from Chegem*, trans. S. Brownsberger. NY: Random House, 1983.
___. *The Gospel According to Chegem*, trans. S. Brownsberger. NY: Random House, 1984.
___. "A Very Sexy Little Giant," trans. Carl R. Proffer, in the almanac *Metropole* (NY: Norton, 1983).

about Iskander:
Burlingame, Helen P. "The Prose of Fazil Iskander," *Russian Literature Triquarterly*, no. 14 (Winter 1976), pp. 123-65.

Katerli, Nina. "Treugol'nik Barsukova," *Glagol 3*. Ann Arbor: Ardis, 1981. Other stories published in *Avrora* and *Neva*.

Maramzin, Vladimir (b. 1934). "Don't Steal! Directive to a Future Baby, My Slip Son" and "Get Away from the Scene of the Accident," trans. Carl R. Proffer. *Russian Literature Triquarterly*, no. 5 (Winter 1973), pp. 217-20; reprinted in *Ardis Anthology of Recent Russian Literature*. Ann Arbor: Ardis, 1976.
___. "The Story of the Marriage of Ivan Petrovich. A Narrative," in *Kontinent*, no. 1 (1976)[English translation of nos. 1-2], NY: Anchor Press/Doubleday, 1976.

Okudzhava, Bulat. *Nocturne* [Dilletantes' Travels]. NY: Harper & Row, 1978.
___. *65 Songs / 65 Pesen*. Ann Arbor: Ardis, 1980.

Popov, Evgeny (b. 1946)."A Baker's Dozen of Stories" in *Metropol* (see below).

Rasputin, Valentin (b. 1937). "Downstream," *Contemporary Russian Prose*. Ann Arbor: Ardis, 1982.
___. *Farewell to Matyora*. NY: Macmillan, 1980.
___."The French Lesson," *Soviet Literature*, no. 1 (1975).
___. *Live and Remember*. NY: Macmillan, 1978.
___. "Money for Maria," *Soviet Literature*, no. 1 (1969).
___. *Money for Maria*. Australia University Press.
See Mehnert (below) for more translations of Rasputin.

about Rasputin:
Brown, Deming, "Valentin Rasputin: A General View," in *Russian Literature and Criticism*, ed. E. Bristol (see below), pp. 27-35.
Dunlop, John B. "Rasputin's *Proshchanie s Materoi*," in *Russian Literature and Criticism*, ed. E. Bristol (see below), pp. 63-68.
Hosking, G. *Beyond Socialist Realism* (see below), pp. 70-81.
Schneidmann, N.N. *Soviet Literature in the 1970s* (see below).

Shukshin, Vasily (1929-74). *I Want to Live*. Moscow: Progress, 1973.
___. *Snowball Berry Red & Other Stories*, ed. Donald M. Fiene. Ann Arbor: Ardis, 1979.
___. "Snowball Berry Red," in *Contemporary Russian Prose*.

about Shukshin:
The most detailed biographical, critical and bibliographical information about him is in the book *Snowball Berry Red & Other Stories*.

Trifonov, Yury (1925-80). *Another Life and A House on the Embankment*. NY: Simon & Schuster, 1983.
___. "The Exchange," in *Contemporary Russian Prose* (see below), pp. 255-303.
___. *The Impatient Ones*. Moscow: Progress, 1978.
___. *The Long Goodbye: Three novellas*. Ann Arbor: Ardis, 1978.
___. *The Students*. Moscow: Progress, 1953.

about Trifonov:
Kustanovich, Constantin. Review of *The Old Man*, in *Ulbandus Review*, vol. 1, no. 2 (Spring, 1978), pp. 169-72.
Proffer, Ellendea. "Introduction," in Trifonov, *The Long Goodbye*.
De Maegd-Soep, Caroline. "The Theme of "byt"—Everyday Life in the Stories of Iurii Trifonov," *Russian Literature and Criticism: Selected Papers*, ed. Evelyn Bristol, pp. 49-62.
Hosking, Geoffrey. "Trifonov," in his *Beyond Socialist Realism* (see below), pp. 183-87.
___. "The Seach for an Image of Man in Contemporary Soviet Fiction," *Studies in 20th Century Russian Literature*, ed. C. J. Barnes (Edinburgh: Scottish Academic Press, 1976), pp. 61-77.

McLaughlin, Sigrid, "Jurij Trifonov's *House on the Embankment*: Narration and Meaning," *SEEJ*, vol. 24, 4 (1982), pp. 419-31.
Patera, T. *Obzor tvorchestva i analiz moskovskikh povestei Iuriia Trifonova*. Ardis: Ann Arbor, 1983.[Though in Russian, this is the only book on Trifonov. See also her English letter about *The House on the Embankment* in *Canadian Slavonic Papers*, 23, 2 (1981), p. 207.]

Varlamova, Inna (b. 1923). "The Fire on the Other Bank," trans. Joel Stern, in *Ardis Anthology of Recent Russian Literature* (see below), pp. 369-90.
____. "A Ladle for Pure Water," trans. Helena Goscilo in *Slavic Women's Fiction* (Knoxville: University of Tennessee Press, 1984).

Zalygin, Sergei (b. 1913). *The South American Variant* (NY, 1984).

about Zalygin:
Grigori Svirski, "On the Irtysh," in *Soviet Writing* (see below).

Histories and Criticism

Bristol, Evelyn (ed.). *Russian Literature and Criticism.* Selected Papers from the Second World Congress for Soviet and East European Studies, Garmisch-Partenkirchen, September 30-October 4, 1980. Berkeley, 1982.
Brown Deming, *Soviet Russian Literature Since Stalin.* Cambridge University Press, 1978.
Brown, E. J. *Russian Literature Since the Revolution.* NY: 1983.
____ (ed). *Major Soviet Writers, Essays in Criticism.* Oxford University Press, 1973.
Brumberg, A. (ed.). *In Quest of Justice. Protest & Dissent in the Soviet Union Today.* NY: Praeger, 1970.
Gladilin, Anatoly. *The Making and Unmaking of a Soviet Writer.* Ann Arbor: Ardis, 1979.
Hayward, Max & E. Crowley (eds.). *Soviet Literature in the Sixties.* NY: Praeger, 1964.
Hingley, Ronald. *Russian Writers and Soviet Society 1917-1918.* NY: Random House, 1979.
Hosking, Geoffrey. *Beyond Socialist Realism. Soviet Fiction Since Ivan Denisovich.* London: Granada Publishing, 1980.
Mathewson, Rufus. *The Positive Hero in Russian Literature.* 2nd ed. Stanford University Press, 1975.
Mehnert, Klaus. *The Russians and Their Favorite Books.* Stanford: Hoover Institution Press, 1983.
Mihajlov, Mihajlo. *Russian Themes.* NY: Farrar, Straus, 1968.
Novikov, Vassily. *Artistic Truth and Dialectics of Creative Work.* Moscow: Progress, 1981. [on Abramov, pp. 204-15]
Proffer, Carl R, "Writing in the Shadow of the Monolith: A Guide to the New Russian Writers," *New York Review of Books,* February 19, 1976.
Rothberg, Abraham. *The Heirs of Stalin: Dissidence and the Soviet Regime 1953-1970.* Ithaca: Cornell University Press, 1972.
Schneidmann, N. N. *Soviet Literature in the 1970s.* Toronto: University of Toronto Press, 1979. [on Trifonov, Rasputin, Zalygin]
Slonim, Marc. *Soviet Russian Literature. Writers & Problems, 1917-77.* Oxford University Press, 1977.
Solzhenitsyn, A. *The Oak and the Calf.* NY: Harper & Row, 1980.
Svirski, G. *A History of Post-War Soviet Writing.* Ann Arbor: Ardis, 1981.

Anthologies

Blake, Patricia & Max Hayward (eds.). *Dissonant Voices in Soviet Literature.* NY: Pantheon, 1962.
Bochkarev, Yuri (ed.). *Soviet Russian Stories of the 1960s & 1970s.* Moscow: Progress, 1977.
Field, Andrew (ed.). *Pages from Tarusa.* Boston: Little, Brown, 1964.

Glagoleva, F. (ed.). *By the Light of Day. Stories by Soviet Writers.* Moscow: Progress, 1968.

Ivanov, Y. (ed.). *A Treasury of Russian & Soviet Short Stories.* NY: Fawcett, 1971.

Kazakova, R. (selector). *The Tender Muse (Soviet Poetesses).* Moscow: Progress, 1976.

Kunitz, Joshua (ed.). *Russian Literature since the Revolution.* NY: Boni and Gaer, 1948.

MacAndrew, A. R. (ed.). *Four Soviet Masterpieces.* NY: Bantam, 1965 [Vladimov, Voinovich, Aksenov, Kazakov].

Massie, Suzanne (ed.). *The Living Mirror. Five Young Poets from Leningrad.* Garden City: Doubleday, 1972.

Metropol. Literary Almanac. Edited by Vasily Aksyonov, Viktor Yerofeyev, Fazil Iskander, Andrei Bitov, Yevgeny Popov. Translated from the 1979 *Metropol.* NY: W. W. Norton & Co., 1982.

Milner-Gulland, Robin & Martin Dewhirst (eds.). *Russian Writing Today.* Penguin Books, 1977.

Niyazi, Shovkat (comp.). *Voices of Friends. Soviet Poets.* Moscow: Progress, 1973.

Pomorska, Krystyna (ed.). *Fifty Years of Russian Prose from Pasternak to Solzhenitsyn.* Cambridge: MIT Press, 1971. 2 vols.

Proffer, Carl and Ellendea Proffer (eds.). *The Ardis Anthology of Recent Russian Literature.* Ann Arbor: Ardis, 1975.

Proffer, Carl and Ellendea Proffer (eds.). *Contemporary Russian Prose.* Ann Arbor: Ardis, 1982.

Reeve, F. D. (ed.). *Contemporary Russian Drama.* NY: Pegasus, 1967.

Scammel, Michael (ed.). *Russia's Other Writers.* London: Longman, 1970.

Whitney, T. P. (ed.). *The New Writing in Russia.* Ann Arbor: University of Michigan Press, 1964.

Yarmolinsky, Avrahm (ed.). *Soviet Short Stories.* Garden City: Anchor, 1960.

Periodicals

Kontinent. Anthologies made up from the best-known emigre periodical are regularly published by Doubleday. To date four volumes have appeared, containing both fiction and non-fiction.

Russian Literature Triquarterly, 1971-. Every issue of this journal contains translations of Russian poetry, fiction, and criticism, primarily 20th-century works.

Soviet Literature. Published in Moscow by Progress Publishers, the official Soviet propaganda publisher, the twelve annual issues of this magazine are the best place to see the conservative Party presentation of Soviet literature and politics.

Nina Katerli

The Barsukov Triangle

CHAPTER ONE: GHASTLY NEWS

I

As usual, Marya Sidorovna Tyutina got up at eight, had oatmeal for breakfast, and cleaned up the dishes after herself and her husband. Then she went off to the corner grocery, a half-flight down from the street, where yesterday they had definitely promised that they would have cod filet in the morning.

Marya Sidorovna didn't bother to get a receipt beforehand. She just took a place in line at the fish and meat department so they could weigh it out first.[1] After standing there half the day— half an hour, anyway—, she finally would up at the counter, and then the sales girl told her they won't serve you without a receipt. Marya Sidorovna begged her to weigh out half a kilo anyway, for an invalid, because she'd been in line there since they opened, and it was too crowded at the cashier; but the salesgirl didn't even bother discussing it, took a receipt from some man, and turned her back. Someone in line yelled at Marya Sidorovna to stop holding things up—they all had to get to work; so she went straight over to the cashier without even waiting in line, said she just had to pay a bit extra on her bill and took out several kopeks. But despite the receipt, they wouldn't let her up to the counter because she'd missed her turn, and the filet was almost gone.

When Marya Sidorovna said that she'd been standing there, one woman declared that personally she hadn't seen anyone. What people! Marya Sidorovna didn't want to get mixed up in anything, so she went to the end of the line and waited another twenty minutes; but three people ahead of her they ran out of cod.

II

Pyotr Vasilievich Tyutin, Marya Sidorovna's husband, a retiree, loved to read newspapers and socio-political magazines, since he was a veteran and member of the Party bureau at the housing office. When he left the house Wednesday morning, he took

3

sufficient change for the purchase of *Week* magazine and *Crocodile*,[1] plus two kopeks[2] to call the home-care office and get a
doctor to see his wife, who had suffered a nervous collapse after
yesterday's shopping trip. In the telephone booth, Pyotr Vasilievich, partly from absent-mindedness and partly from being upset,
dropped a ten- rather than a two-kopek piece into the slot of
the telephone. At the polyclinic they told him rather rudely that
neuropathologists don't make house-calls, and that for someone
over sixty it was simply ridiculous. Who cared anyway? And
when Pyotr Vasilievich got to the newsstand later, he was of
course short eight kopeks, so he had to go without *Crocodile*.

III

After graduating from middle school,[1] Anna Tyutina was
accepted by competitive exam into the gas and petroleum technical school, where at a dance she met hairy Andrei, son of
a professor from a cultured family. It was incomprehensible,
by the way, what sort of "intellectuals" they could be if their
sons couldn't even get their hair cut like normal people and
walked around like primeval man.

In their senior year Anna and Andrei got married. Andrei
went on to study further, in the Technological Institute with
his daddy, while Anna was forced to work at an abrasives plant
on a three-shift system in order to support the family. Tufty
Andryusha didn't get a stipend because of his grades, which,
despite his pull, were much below average.

Anna's parents, Pyotr Vasilievich and Marya Sidorovna,
as retirees, were not always able to help the young people financially. Andrei's father turned out to be a scoundrel and, though
he was a professor of chemistry, he didn't give his son a cent,
supposedly on principle—you get married, now support yourself—but in fact because he hated his daughter-in-law, and considered her and her parents beneath him. He probably had two
families too, like all the rest of them.

After graduating from the institute, Andrei, with his father's
help, managed to get into graduate school, while Anna continued
to break her back as shift foreman of the thermics shop. By this
time, she had two children between three and five.

4

Four years later, Andrei defended for his candidate's degree[2] and started getting two hundred and fifty rubles a month.[3] Just at that time they discovered that Anna had developed myocarditis from undernourishment and nerves, and then, by chance, they found out that the jerk was seeing another woman, a speculator and "colleague of his father's," that is, the daughter of another rich professor, as much a rascal as all the rest of them.

Marya Sidorovna and Pyotr Vasilievich had every reason to appeal to the authorities in order to preserve the family, but they had no connections anywhere, and they considered it beneath their dignity. Now Andrei is living in a new apartment on Tipanov[4] with that new broad who looks like a herring in a fur coat, and both professors are beside themselves with joy. But incidentally, he never would have seen a candidate's salary in his life if Anna hadn't paid for it with her youth and health.

As for Anna, left with her myocarditis and her two children, she now quite rightly thinks that, as her parents say, it's better to raise the children alone than to live with a scoundrel who didn't chip very far from the old block.

IV

Antonina Bodrova, who lived in the same building as the old Tyutins, told her Anatoly that if he would marry her, she would register him permanently at her place with 18 meters.[1] Anatoly objected to this and said that since she was fourteen years older than he, he would set his own conditions, to wit that he was not about to feed Antonina's son Valerik, whom he considered a bastard with Jewish blood.

Antonina had long suspected that Valerik's father was Mark Ilyich, head of the wine department, but she wasn't sure, and couldn't be more certain because Mark Ilyich was doing time in a strict-regime settlement for embezzlement and bribing an official.

Antonina herself had nothing against Valerik — it wasn't the child's fault, though the kid's nose and the color of his eyes hinted at his parentage. Under pressure from Anatoly, Antonina promised to set Valerik up in a full-time nursery; but soon after, Anatoly changed his mind, would not give his consent to such a thing, and said that a children's home was his final word as a patriot and citizen of his country.

Antonina applied to the Regional Executive Committee three times and to various commissions dealing with the affairs of minors, but everywhere they pointed out to her that it was just unheard-of for a mother to give up her child that way. Antonina cried for days and beat Valerik, but Anatoly ordered her to hurry up with her decision and threatened that Polina the yardswoman had promised to register him—Polina wasn't getting any younger but she was really built and unencumbered with offspring of any sort.

Then Antonina drank a quarter-bottle of vodka on an empty stomach, took Valerik down to Moscow Station, bought him a children's ticket, one-way to Lyuban,[2] put him on the commuter train, bought him an eskimo pie, and told him his maternal grandmother Evdokia Grigorievna would meet him in Lyuban.

The boy believed his parent, though he remembered that his grandmother had died from palsy last year in Leningrad and lay in the cemetery where the flowers grow.

When the train left with Valerik, Antonina returned home and told Anatoly that they could go to the Registry Office. They drank a half-liter and another quarter-bottle to the best of everything, lay down on the sofa, and fell asleep in each other's arms. At the same time Valerik was crying in the children's room at the police station in Lyuban. He just couldn't remember his home address, and said only that he was going to see his grandmother who was buried in the ground.

By evening of the following day, Thursday, the child was nevertheless delivered to his mother by a sergeant of the railroad police, but Antonina, in a less-than-sober state, declared that this was the first and last time she had ever seen the little kid, while Valerik stretched out his skinny arms to her and yelled, "Mama! Mama! It's me!"

Anatoly, who witnessed all of this, spat on the floor, called Antonina a bitch and went off for good to the yardswoman Polina and her fourteen meters.

By police order, Antonina was forced to take custody of Valerik. The whole building condemned her, and the Tyutins wouldn't so much as say hello. What's more, Marya Sidorovna told everyone that when the child grew up and understood what happened, he would never forgive her.

6

V

Natalia Ivanovna Kopeikina raised her son alone. Since she was a nurse, she worked extra half-shifts and often took bonuses in lieu of vacation time so the boy wouldn't have to do without what other children had, so he would have everything as good as the children who grew up in families fortunate enough to have fathers.

Thus, Natalia Ivanovna denied herself everything, wore the same coat for ten years, and by the time she was forty, people thought she looked fifty and called her Mom on the street. Her son was named Oleg, and when he grew up, he got an education and a good trade, a taxi driver. Oleg Kopeikin always dressed entirely in imported clothes, and once, Natalia Ivanovna noticed that her son seemed to be ashamed of his mother. For example, when she asked Oleg to go down to the produce store with her for some cabbage for sauerkraut, he said, "I can go by myself." And another time he looked at her old coat and said, "You look like a real sight in that get-up. If you don't start looking after yourself, people will laugh at you."

Hearing about these other people, Natalia Ivanovna immediately understood that her son had fallen into the clutches of some girl. And indeed, precisely two days later her neighbor Tyutina from number 8 dropped in and said that she'd seen Oleg near The Spark movie theater with a girl—and that dress!— she must be dead to sin—it didn't hide a thing!

That very evening Natalia Ivanovna warned her son in no uncertain terms that she would not permit him to see women of easy virtue, and that it was either his mother or her. But for Oleg, apparently, his mother was worse than I-don't-know-what, and he yelled back that, in that case, he was leaving home. He packed his things in two suitcases and a knapsack, said that he'd be back tomorrow for the record player and his records and walked out. The next morning he showed up with his prostitute and, without so much as a hello, said that he wanted Natalia Ivanovna to give her consent to an apartment trade, otherwise he'd get a court order for a forced separation.

Natalia Ivanovna burst out crying and reminded her son that she'd raised him without a father, grudged him nothing, that he and that trash could just put her in a nursing home and take the whole room and all the furniture for themselves. At that, Oleg picked up the record player and headed for the door, and told his girl that only a shit could get along with Natalia Ivanovna. Natalia Ivanovna had a fit right then and there, ran up to that hussy and spat right between her painted eyes. The girl let out a howl, sat down on a stool by the door and told Oleg to clear the hell out, because she had no use for a man whose mother spits and calls names; and that a guy who betrays his own mother won't respect his wife much.

Now Natalia Ivanovna and that girl, whose name is Lyudmilla, are in the same ward at Konyashin Hospital. Natalia Ivanovna has a concussion and Lyudmilla has a broken collar-bone and a displaced shoulder.

VI

For some reason there were always non-Russians living in apartment 17 on the fourth floor, right above the Tyutins. Of course, there are Jews, and then there are Jews. Some are real people, but then, if I may say so, there are the ones like the Freudkins, who betrayed the Motherland and went off to Israel for the easy money. They say those Freudkins took out ten kilograms of pure gold; and that's quite likely, otherwise why would they have dragged that mangy cat with them? Antonina Bodrova, though she is really a scummy broad, said quite plausibly that they most likely used raw force to make the cat swallow tsarist coins a half-year before they left, and then took him along, making out that they're so fond of Mother Nature.

To hell with them, those Freudkins! But then, the Katz family, who were moved into the Freudkins' apartment for some reason, are very intelligent and cultured people. Especially Katz himself, Lazar Moiseevich, a candidate of technical science. And his wife Fira too, a dental technician, is a decent woman. Not to mention the mother, Rosa Lvovna, who after she lost her husband in the war, managed to bring up her son, get a good pension, and still works in the library.

Life treats different people differently. Take these two women—Natalia Ivanovna isn't any worse than Rosa Lvovna, but for some reason one was lucky with her son, and you get upset just thinking about the other one. Evidently it's true: Jews make good sons and good husbands—they bring home their whole paycheck; everything for the home.

So, a week after it had been disinfected, Lazar Moiseevich was washing his Zhiguli in the courtyard and suddenly noticed that a ragged and dirty old man, very familiar in appearance, was sitting on a bench and watching him. Lazar Moiseevich, without stopping his washing, tried to remember where he'd met that old man, but couldn't. In the meantime the old man got up from the bench, walked over to him and asked, "Is that your car?" Lazar Moiseevich confirmed that yes it was, and asked the old man just what he wanted. Then the old man burst into sobs like a child, took out a worn permanent passport[1] and showed him that he was, in fact, Moisei Girshevich Katz—born: 1901; nationality: Jew—that is, Lazar Moiseevich's own father, presumed dead during the war. True, as it turned out, Rosa Lvovna didn't receive an official death notice, meaning she never got any help for her son. Some women are so slow! Lazar told everyone that as a child he'd seen a letter from a friend of his father's at the front, informing them that, literally before his eyes, the fearless Moisei had been blown to bits by an enemy shell, and since his papers had most likely been blown to bits with him, it made no sense for his widow to make any inquiries. So Lazar had always considered his father dead, and only now, after thirty-odd years, does he suddenly learn that, as it turns out, Moisei is alive and well, and has remembered that he has a son—as much like him, by the way, as two peas in a pod. The old man was just about to throw his arms around Lazar, but the latter neatly pushed him aside and turned away. He shouldn't have turned away though, but rather asked: Where were you, my so-called papa, when Mother and I were sitting in Gorky in evacuation, the family of a man missing in action? And where were you later, when Mother wore herself out to give me a higher education? And now, when I've reached manhood, you appear and hand me some papers. You've been no father to me. I'm no son of yours; and besides my mother, I have and will have no other parents.

And though Lazar, unfortunately, from lack of character, said nothing more to the old man, the latter sobbed even louder and asked, since that was how things were, for three rubles for the trip back to Shapki or Tosno, where he lived with his children by a second marriage. He also swore he wouldn't even ask them for ice in winter ever again. Lazar Moiseevich gave him two rubles, though from the old man's puss it was clear that he would immediately spend them on drink, and hinted that he should forget the road to this house and not traumatize his mother.

And indeed, though he didn't say a word to his mother himself, Marya Sidorovna Tyutina, standing with her wash pail by the cistern, heard the whole conversation, and told Rosa Lvovna all about it the next day, word for word; and consequently Rosa Lvovna took to her bed. But she already looks much better now. Pyotr Vasilievich yelled at his wife, "why did you tell her?" and she answered, "What do you mean, why? So she'd know."

VII

The Petukhovs live on the fourth floor in apartment number 18, next to the Katz family. Just three years ago, Sanya Petukhov was your average young man; he had a motorcycle with a sidecar, and one fine day he brought his wife Tatyana home from the Palace of Marriages in that sidecar. Later, something or other happened—he was elected, or appointed, or maybe promoted somewhere, it's not important—and now, instead of a motorcycle, Alexander Nikolaevich drives to work in a black car, and his chauffeur often carries a big cardboard box up to the fourth floor after him.[1] It's no one's business what's in that box, so, when Alexander Nikolaevich, accompanied by his chauffeur, walks from his car to the elevator, naturally no one who meets him in the entryway asks stupid questions. But then last Friday, Antonina—they should have deprived her of custody of that child long ago—caught Tanechka Petukhova in the courtyard and brazenly asked, "I always see you taking out empty cans of instant coffee and tins of salmon in oil. Where do you get it? I never come across anything but chicory and cod."

Tanechka lost her head, but luckily, Rosa Lvovna was walking by just then. Rosa Lvovna looked at Antonina and said that, "One should be interested, Tonya, not in empty tin cans, but what a person devotes his labor to. Alexander Nikolaevich is a top-notch worker. Much is demanded of him, and for that reason he's given more than we are. Do you know what kind of responsibility those people have? They could call him up at any minute and he'd have to make decisions on..."

Rosa Lvovna got mixed up with Antonina in vain, because the latter immediately started bawling, "De-ci-sions!—You've got a Zhiguli, so drive to hell in it—and your son too! You're all the same—they can beat you, or give you a Zhiguli, you'll still kiss their asses and smile like cats before a shit! The Freudkins, now, even they were better, they just left like honest folk. And took their cat. We're going to get a cattle prod and drive the rest of the Yids to Palestine!"

Rosa Lvovna, the poor thing, got all flushed. Her hands started shaking. She turned to Tanechka for sympathy, but she had just sort of sidled away over to the entrance. Who wants to participate in a scene like that, especially when your husband holds a high post? And when the door had slammed behind Tatyana, the shrew said to Rosa Lvovna, "you see, that's that, what did you expect? That's how they defend all of us. They pig out on their instant coffee and lox, get in their black Volga —and off they go to defend us! You're so naive, I can't believe it! Well, bye—I've got to go to the nursery for Valerka." And she left.

VIII

Dusya and Semenov, who lived in the same apartment as the Tyutins,[1] were not responsible workers like Alexander Nikolaevich, candidates of science, Georgians from the market, nor persons of Jewish descent,[2] yet they were no worse off than anyone else. They were simple people. Semenov was a metalworker in a factory and Dusya was the storewoman at the same plant.

Semenov was a teetotaler and didn't do slipshod work. He really dug in like you're supposed to—he worked overtime, on days off for double-time, and even on holidays. Naturally, he took in work on the side too—he can do anything, he's got friends, and his work is high quality.[3] Semenov was just a great guy. What else can I say? He was respected at the factory. If there was an assembly—he was on the presidium, if there were elections—he was off to the Regional Soviet of Deputies. He was hand in glove with the section foreman, and the plant manager himself always said hello. How are things going, Semenov? —How should they be going! It's a mess.—You're quite right, we'll get things in order, Comrade Semenov. How are things going with that apartment of yours?—The factory committee's working on it.—I'm sure they'll work it out in your favor, Comrade Semenov.

So the Semenovs weren't going to be stuck in a communal apartment for long.

What's there to say about Dusya? How things went for her at work is her own business. You can get an awful lot of stuff for your family working in a storeroom—soap, for example, rubber gloves for doing the dishes, and other little things. But Dusya wasn't about to steal. She and her husband were decent people—neither one of them drank, and Semenov was in good standing at the plant. Still it would be just ridiculous to go to the store for a bar of soap when you've got a whole box of them in the storeroom. Around the house Dusya was the sort of home-maker you don't often find, a real work-horse. Day and night she was washing, cleaning, scraping, dragging worn clothing down to the collection center, or hauling paper over to the pulp mill for coupons—they had to get a library together for their son.[4] Her guiding principle, as she herself explained to Marya Sidorovna, was this: "Whether it's an old rag or a stale crust—use it up. Just look—you take out the trash every day, and I only do it twice a week." For that reason the Semenovs had a set-up no worse than the Katzes': a Rubin-205 television, a piano, and they just bought a Moskvich—secondhand, but you can be sure that with his know-how, Semenov will put it in such fantastic con-dition like Lazar Moiseevich could never get under any circum-stances for all his money and his academic degree in technical science.[5]

And here's another example: Just the other day the Sem-enovs got a desk for their Slavik at the second-hand store. Before, Slavik did his homework at the kitchen table, but now that he's transferred to the English School,[6] it didn't seem right. The desk they bought was old and inexpensive, but no matter what you say, the Semenovs don't get junk. It was just that the green felt on the top had worn thin here and there. Naturally Semenov decided to restore the piece himself—to change the cloth and varnish the wood. Instead of the green felt, Dusya went to Passage[7] and bought a meter and a half of blue—to match the upholstery on the sofa-bed—in a synthetic-wool blend. On Sunday Semenov neatly removed the green cloth—Dusya wanted to make in-soles for rubber boots out of it—and discovered a sealed envelope underneath. It turned out that there were four fifty-ruble notes inside. Who hid them there is anyone's guess. Perhaps the former owner may have been an old man who put them aside for a rainy day, didn't tell his relatives so they wouldn't steal it, and suddenly died. The relatives, not knowing a thing about the money, put the desk out on commission and cheated themselves out of a cool two hundred. Or maybe someone on a booze-up stuck the money in there to keep his hands off it, and forgot about it once he'd slept it off. There are all sorts of possibilities, but now we'll never know. Dusya said to the Tyutins, "Just imagine, we could have kept that material on there another five years, and then all of a sudden, another currency reform.[8] Can you imagine?" But Semenov objected that that couldn't happen. And he's right. It couldn't. But the most interesting thing is that even with the moving and the blue material and everything, that desk only cost the Semenovs a hundred and twenty rubles. Can you imagine?

No, it's true: the rich get richer.

IX

And, of course, Barsukov, the old drunk, the good-for-nothing, got every last kopek swiped while he was asleep in the bus station on payday. It's only Grishka himself who thinks that he was robbed. Most likely his own pals took it while they were getting the old crank soused in the entryway, because he still had his papers and keys on him. Thieves wouldn't bother to investigate what was money and what was papers and keys. That's what Natalia Ivanovna Kopeikina thinks anyway, and everyone agrees with her—the Semenovs, the Tyutins, and Fira Katz. Tanechka Petukhova said that, mostly, it was disgusting that now Grigory Ivanovich would be knocking at the doors of all their apartments and begging for money and eau de cologne.[1] Personally, she wouldn't give him any, but Rosa Lvovna, unfortunately, would, and Antonina too—she likes drunks, she's one herself. And really, Tanechka is absolutely right, you've got to pity people within sense and reason; and an old profligate like that Barsukov will never have money or his health.

X

Natalia Ivanovna Kopeikina was a completely different person after she got out of the hospital. In the first place, she's living alone now. After a Comrades' Court hearing at the taxi yard where he worked, Oleg enlisted in a work project somewhere in the North and went off after the good pay—didn't even see his mother after she got home from the hospital.

In the second place, Natalia Ivanovna used to be plump and looked older than her years, but now she's on a French diet, lost weight, got a new hair-do at the beauty salon, and wears an imported trenchcoat. Lyudmilla—remember her?—the same—she took Natalia Ivanovna under her wing, and visits her almost every day. They go to the movies together, they go to Pushkin, to the Lyceum together[1]—in short, they're girl-friends thick as thieves. Lyudmilla turned out to be a very, very respectable girl. She didn't spread the scandal any further because of any trauma she suffered. She's a dispatcher at the taxi yard—works two shifts on, three off—and studies nights at the technical college. It turns out her parents are also very cultured people, not like the Tyutins supposed—parasites like their former son-in-law, the professor. The father works on a river shipping-line, and the mother is a teacher. Her brother's in the army. And Lyudmilla sews those fashionable little skirts herself—they cost her just kopeks—and she's always dressed like she walked right out of the television. You won't find a girl like that if you search in daylight with a candle! Natalia Ivanovna told everyone that Lyuda was like a real daughter to her, and if Oleg found some streetwalker up there in the North who was older than he was, Natalia Ivanovna would throw her down the stairs.

XI

It was summer. The heat was scorching, the rain came in cloud-bursts. Pregnant street-cleaning trucks dragged painfully down the dusty streets strewn with poplar down. The wind would sweep down, now stifling and hot, now heavy and wet, as if bound in a cold tourniquet. Was it so long ago that the Tauride Gardens[1] smelled sweetishly of lilacs and later of lime blossoms, and in early September of fading flox? The smell of flox gave way to the smell of rotting leaves and wet earth, the sky became higher and more remote. Nature, which had surged through the city with all its summer colors, sounds and smells, now receded. Like an ebb-tide, it went off far beyond the outskirts and will live there until spring, separate, and reserved; while in the empty forests, day after day, the dry leaves rain down, sail down from the trees. Night comes, and the leaves still fall, rustling in the thick darkness; and then the rain begins, stern, uncompromising. For days it beats down on the numb trunks and stooped black branches.

...November. The most urban season. The stone of buildings and parapets reigns alone, the gratings of fences, the haughty statues and columns. Straight lines, triangles, perfect circles, blacks and whites. The triumph of geometry.

November. The holidays were over.[2]

November. Alexander Petukhov was on a visit to far-off, fraternal Bulgaria on the still-warm Black Sea, where huge silver gulls pace the sunny shore and foreign tourists stroll in white trousers and fitted leather jackets.

November. A dark morning. Rain and snow. In the house by the Tauride Gardens everyone was still asleep, not one window shone.

Antonina tries in her sleep to pull the blanket over black-haired Valerik's bony shoulders—he'd been coughing since evening, so she put him to bed with her.

Natalia Ivanovna Kopeikina is sobbing because she has had a strange dream—that her footloose son Oleg was standing in the doorway, barefoot for some reason, without his hat, his coat all wet, and the water pouring on the polished floor.

Rosa Lvovna Katz is also crying in her sleep, crying quietly, with pleasure. She forgives someone for her widow's loneliness, for the hellish life of an evacuee with a child and no papers at a stingy Polish lady's in Gorky; for the fact that she's already an old woman—and come to think of it, what has she seen in her life? Tomorrow Rosa Lvovna won't even remember what she dreamed. She'll get up in a good mood, and on the way to the library she'll compose a verse for the wall newspaper: "... Our peaceful labors did not suit/ Our enemy and foe./ He planned a war to break our peace/ And bring us grief and woe." Of course Lazar would start laughing again. He thinks everything is so funny—that's just how he is.

The whole house is asleep. Except Grigory Barsukov. He's lying in his dark room, staring into the void, thinking. How can he sleep when he alone in the whole city—what am I saying, in the whole city?—perhaps in the whole world, knows what as yet has been granted no one else to learn?

We are all absolutely right: That poor devil Barsukov has neither money nor health. But as for brains—that, dear readers (excuse me, could you move aside please with your diplomas and candidate's degrees), *that* we shall examine further. Because, if any us discovered something like this, it's quite possible that we wouldn't just take to drink, but run away somewhere. Or commit suicide from sheer terror.

I

The triangle is located in the center of the city, in the Haymarket,[1] which now goes by the name of Peace Square, to be exact. Its apex happens to fall in the Ocean Speciality Fish Store, where every morning credulous herring fans jostle one another, never imagining just where they're standing. The other angles are: 1) the subway station, erected on the site of the Church of the Assumption of the Holy Virgin,[2] which was wiped from the face of the earth; and 2) the bus station. Last summer already—remember?—Barsukov's whole paycheck apparently disappeared there down to the last ruble. But you'd have to be awfully gullible to suppose that that was the first such disappearance, or that the money was spent on drink, or stolen. Awfully gullible! And now Barsukov knew that.

None of us, thank God, ever has, or, let's hope, ever will end up in the Bermuda Triangle, that turbid section of the Atlantic where, according to reliable sources, airplanes disappear without a trace, vanish clean away in broad daylight; where powerless, abandoned ships drift blindly, and no one knows where the people went to. On one of those ships, they discovered a howling dog once. But what good's a dog?—It just understands, but can't explain what happened. The only one who could have, a talking parrot, also just completely disappeared.

Luckily the Bermuda Triangle isn't anywhere near us. It's thousands of miles and dozens of well-secured borders away, so we don't have to give a damn about it. For us, it's like the Wicked Witch of the West, or visitors from outer space—we don't know anything about it.

But even without the Bermuda Triangle, we've got plenty to worry about: war with China, a serious long-term illness, muggers, amnestied political prisoners,[3] our immediate superiors, and another, mysterious someone who neither eats nor sleeps, but is on duty day and night in our telephone wires to find out what we have to say about the weather.

But then I'm sure that those who live right near the Bermuda

Triangle, or have business dealings with it, also worry about war with China and mad dogs, and about their own Bermudan gangsters and employers. And of course, about cancer. But I bet they seldom think about these ships and boats—and then unwillingly.

Barsukov had nothing to think about. What was there to think about? He didn't need to think, but to take action. And for that reason Grigory Barsukov, a man over fifty who had changed jobs so many times that for that alone, not to mention his external appearance, he could be considered a *wifipro*—that is, a person without fixed place of residence or occupation—Barsukov, the subject in question, as I was saying, lay in wait for Lazar Katz, candidate of technical sciences, in the courtyard one early November morning and presented him with an unscientific statement. He informed Katz that in the Peace Haymarket, as he called it, things and money, people and even chauffeur-driven cars disappear irrevocably, and that he personally, Barsukov, had witnessed this phenomenon repeatedly.

"I can give you a whole bunch of examples," declared Barsukov.

"Go ahead, please," Katz encouraged him. He got to be a candidate of sciences precisely because all his life he'd had this unusual curiosity about natural phenomena.

"Go ahead, go ahead," he repeated, and took a pack of cigarettes out of his pocket. But glancing up at his window, he immediately hid it again and suggested to Grigory Ivanovich that perhaps they'd better take a walk through the garden.

The sky above the Tauride Gardens was covered with thick, whitish clouds, and the sun was trying to come out through the gaps between them, It would recklessly plump down in the pond, quiver a second in the cold water like a spoon-lure and then disappear.

"... And let indifferent nature/ With eternal beauty shine,"[4] said Barsukov suddenly, without rhyme or reason, for Katz' edification. He looked Lazar Moiseevich straight in the eye. Being a tactful man, Katz displayed no perplexity, as if it logically followed that an uneducated *wifipro* would quote those immortal lines.

"Beauty. Eternal!" insisted Barsukov petulantly and, when Lazar finally nodded his assent, added, "Nature is eternal, but man in nature is nothing. Here today, and tomorrow it's the cookies. If they're not sold out."

"Man is, of course, mortal," Katz agreed.

Barsukov looked at him with pity, waved his hand, took off his little cap and started shaking it furiously, like a shoe with sand in it. He didn't shake anything out but said in a business-like tone, "Here are some examples of the disappearance of persons and objects: forty rubles, eighty-four kopeks belonging to me personally. Okay? Now: Vitaly Matveevich, an old man..."

"Vitaly Matveevich who?" asked the meticulous Katz.

"I don't know exactly," Barsukov answered pensively, "but a real shit, I bet... I saw him disappear myself. Last Wednesday over by the bus station he asked me for a ruble. I tell him, I says, 'I've only got a three-note.' He takes it and says, 'That's okay, I'll go change it.' He walked over to the ice cream stand, crossed the street—I saw him—and then a tram went by, and that was the end of him. The man just disappeared."

"Sure," said Katz. "What were the other occurences?"

"Then there was the time with the blue car. Empty. No one in it, with its headlights on in the daytime."

"Was it standing?"

"Right. Come on! It came tearing the hell over from Moscow Station, right through the square, and then over to Sadovaya. The policeman whistled like mad."

"I believe," said Katz, lighting up, "that this is all simply a series of coincidences. "

"It's okay for you," Barsukov was shaking his cap again, "it's okay for you to say. You're a fool..."

He pressed the stunned Lazar's hand—Lazar still had his trap hanging open—and withdrew with the majestic gait of a man who knows what he must do. The candidate of technical sciences stood much longer by the pond in the empty allée with a stupid expression on his intellectual face.

The evening of the same day, when the Katz family was sitting over tea, and they were showing figure skating on television, the telephone rang.

"Lyolik, for you," called Lazar's mother. "You really should tell him that it's not nice to disturb someone after work."

"Oleg, maybe I should answer," said Fira. "And you've gone out and won't be back till late. Huh?"

19

"In the first place, I asked you not to call me Oleg any-more..."[5]

"Oh, please excuse me, I'd forgotten about your civic courage on the homefront." Fira immediately took to sulking. "But incidentally, while you're making a declaration on the rights of man, the man is waiting."

The man was indeed waiting patiently, though as it turned out, he didn't have a moment to spare.

"Hello?" echoed Barsukov's distant voice when Lazar finally went to the phone. "Hello! Listen and record this for science. This is Barsukov speaking from the triangle. I'm dying. Sucked under. I'm unable to fix my position. I don't know the time either. There's no way out of this fog."

"Where are you? What fog?" Lazar yelled, looking out the window where the stars peered down ironically from the clear black sky.

"Ordinary fog. Solid. Whitish green. Visibility zero. I'm dying."

"Are you drunk? Listen, Grigory Ivanovich, I'm asking you—are you drunk?"

"To the limit. Record this for science: Grigory Barsukov came out of the subway at 7:03 pm." The voice became more and more muffled and faded away, just as if something had carried the *wifipro* off the face of the earth.

"It's dark and there's no way out. I die the death of the brave for the greater glory of..." These were the last words Lazar heard.

"Barsukov! Barsukov!" his voice yelled through the dangling receiver. Not a sound.

No one, not a single person on earth ever saw Grigory Ivanovich Barsukov again.

II

After his return from Bulgaria, Alexander Nikolaevich Petukhov started thinking. Falling into thought, he would be rooted to the spot in the kitchen with a burning match in his hand, or he would lift a cup of black coffee to his lips and forget to drink. And Tanechka suffered greatly, seeing all of this. One time, she dropped in on her neighbor, Marya Sidorovna, for a mayonnaise cookie recipe when, all of a sudden and quite un-expectedly, she burst into tears. This was really very malapropos since Marya Sidorovna wasn't alone and was sick on top of it. Dusya Semenova and Natalia Ivanovna were sitting in her room, so of course, even though Tanechka explained that she had a toothache, they had to discuss why she was crying.

"He's been fooling around," Dusya said about Petukhov as soon as Tanechka had left. "And why shouldn't he? He travels around Europe at government expense[1] —bought himself a leather jacket."

"But he brought Tatyana a suede skirt," the even-handed Natalia Ivanovna interposed.

"He's fooling around, and that's for sure—despite the skirt," Semenova insisted. "Yesterday I see him coming home at almost eight instead of six, and he's looking around like a cat, left-right, left-right. And as soon as he sees Firochka Katz, well, you know ... Yesterday they were coming through the courtyard and he was carrying her handbag."[2]

"Fira's an interesting girl," Natalia Ivanovna agreed. "Good figure and she knows how to dress."

"That's for sure. They know how to live, you have to give them that much. Marya Sidorovna, should I pour you a tiny drop more amytal?"

"No, thank you," said Tyutina quietly. And they all fell silent.

Marya Sidorovna had her own worries, and all because of her husband. Of course, old Tyutin had never worn a leather jacket in his life, and didn't have wandering eyes, but lately all his conversations came around to the approach of death. He even started to forget somewhat about his former son-in-law. Then he'd start discussing what should be done with his old blue suit after the funeral. (Thank goodness Marya Sidorovna at least managed to talk him into wearing his gray suit in the coffin, but then he'd harp: "The blue's okay," he'd say, " but the grey one is imported. It would be a shame not to take it down to the commission store, wouldn't it?") Or he'd try to decide whether Marya Sidorovna should move in with her daughter and grandsons and then come to conclude, "Don't you dare! Anna will up and marry some skirt-chaser, and her mother will wind up without a place to stay." And Marya Sidorovna would say,

"Petya! Tell me, why all this talk? To traumatize me? Raise my blood pressure?"

And he'd say again, "The end of life is the finals. Death doesn't ask you when it should come. Look at Barsukov— he was alive and now he's gone."

And she'd say, "That Barsukov's a drunk! No one knows where he got to. Maybe he's in prison, maybe in a psychiatric hospital for compulsory treatment."

"Oh, stop it! The police were looking for Grishka. They know their job. They couldn't find him anywhere and sealed his apartment. And you with your 'no one knows'! If no one knows, the law doesn't permit the rooms to be sealed. Barsukov's gone. And I'll be gone soon too," Tyutin insisted. And today he made a general announcement that he definitely doesn't want any sobbing or bitter words at the funeral, because at his age death was nothing extraordinary, but quite natural and even necessary, like marriage or induction in the army for active duty.

"I want you to sing songs at my grave," he instructed his wife.

" What kind of songs?" Marya Sidorovna asked in a whisper and sat down on the sofa.

Pyotr Vasilievich thought for a long time, looked out the window, and then said, "Army songs. Understand, Mother? I'm a veteran. Army songs, remember."

"Good Lord!" Marya Sidorovna burst into tears. "Let me die first, for Christ's sake."

Tyutin spat, shook his head and went off to the newsstand for *Week* magazine. Marya Sidorovna had to call Dusya—her hands were shaking so much she couldn't pour her medicine.

So it was quite understandable why Marya Sidorovna Tyutina wasn't ready for Tanechka Petukhova that day.

Unfortunately, Petukhov wasn't up to his wife now either. Two weeks had passed since he returned to his native land from Bulgaria, but he wasn't himself from the first day back, and he simply stayed that way.

It was as if vivid color slides blazed in his brain: A night-bar,[3] quiet music, dim lights, Chesterfields, a martini. An eloquent bartender—a friend, not a flunkey or a boor—bends toward Petukhov, flicks an American lighter, and says, "Here's a light." The foyer of the Ambassador Hotel at the international Golden Sands resort, where Alexander Nikolaevich stayed the last three days of his first trip abroad. That was the program—after the conferences, councils, and receptions, a vacation on the shore. The casino with a row of cars standing outside all night. And what cars! Mercedes, Chevrolets, Volkswagons, Toyotas, Fords... Lights, lights, lights... A crowd of foreigners inside the casino, around the slot machines—they're called one-armed bandits. Petukhov himself saw some gentleman with wild eyes, and blue, sunken cheeks drop a silver counter in the bandit's slot, pull the handle—and a whole heap of those counters spilled, ringing into the chute. But Mr. Petukhov, a trade-union big-wig, in a just-purchased black leather jacket and white trousers, with American cigarettes in one pocket and Turkish chewing gum in the other, he, coiffed at the best salon in Varna,[4] he, whom people here, abroad, addressed only in German, he hemmed and hawed in a corner, not daring to go up to a machine, constantly turning to look at the door: is Pavlov coming?—the leader of their group. And as for his playing roulette, he couldn't think of it. And why not? W-h-y n-o-t? They couldn't care less—those Pavlovs—that Petukhov is a man with a higher trade-union education, who reads two languages with a dictionary; that in the nightclub, the NIGHT-CLUB!, those cattle from their so-called delegation, those slobs, those sons of Saratov or some dump like Minsk, just barely waited till the orchestra finally stopped before they struck up their old "Moscow Nights."[5] Why drag them off to foreign countries? It's just disgraceful! And to have to sit with them in front of everybody in a restaurant, among their unmentionable double-breasted jackets and ghastly, synthetic, sequined dresses!—To have to smile, and drink to their toast that Bulgaria is beautiful, but Russia's best of all. Well, why don't they just sit in their Russia, up to their ears in mud and drear! But no—Europe is served up to them, and like a fool, you have to amuse yourself here, with them, catch the scornful looks of the West Germans across the table. Germans, by the way, even sit differently, they hold their cigarettes gracefully somehow, and they all have cultured faces. See—they've been drinking too, and not one of them is red or sweaty; not one is yelling or waving his hands.

And worst of all, you can't stand up and yell, "Comrades!" I mean, of course, "Ladies and Gentlemen! I'm not like them! I understand! I think they're as ridiculous and disgusting as you do! I swear, I don't buy rubbing alcohol in the drug store and get drunk as a pig in my room, and then start bawling through the whole hotel! I don't make an utter fool of myself in the lobby from morning til night! I don't do Gypsy dances to jazz in the restaurant or stomp through a slow tango like a Stalinist colonial sideboard! Not me! Not me!

The well-dressed Westerners smile thinly, and if it were possible, they would immediately pull out their Polaroids and movie cameras, to record the barbarians' behavior as a souvenir. But you can't, it's improper.

Our compatriots, however, have no such concept as "impropriety." For them, anything is proper. They shout so the whole hall can hear, stare at people and even crack jokes—"People dance better and dress smarter at home," they say. Cretins! Neanderthals! Peasants!

They were really driving him nuts out there in Bulgaria. And now—he's back in his native land. His homeland—the motherland. Supermama. Russia, composed entirely of them, of those...

The day after he got back he popped into the Sever[6] in the afternoon to have dinner, and right away: "Don't you have eyes? Can't you see the table isn't cleared?... Oh, you can? Then what did you sit down for?... There aren't any places? Well, we don't have any staff.[7] You want to work here?" Service!

Of course he could have fixed her, shown her she couldn't treat him that way, the guttersnipe. But it's unpleasant to get mixed up in things like that, especially since he wasn't alone, but with his boss. Thank goodness, at least now he doesn't have to stand in line for groceries. They're delivered to his home... Ah, just imagine: to his home! Benefactors! They bought him for a lousy can of coffee! Yes, but when it comes right down to it, he doesn't give a shit about their instant coffee and lox! Or about their caviar, for that matter! Not by bread alone! They yell all over the place that we have human rights, but there's not a single night-bar in the city. Only *valyuta* bars, for dollars. Even the glimpse I got of Bulgaria was the West to me—as many bars as you want! And girls! But no girls for the likes of us. We get group leader Pavlov, he'll really fuck you!... Paris is out there somewhere. And Switzerland. And the States...

I wish I'd never seen their stinking coffee.

"Sashenka, why so late?" Tanya asked timidly when Petukhov came home at half-past seven for the third time in a row.

"The bus broke down," he snapped out in proud sorrow.

"The bus?! Why the bus? Where's Vasily Ilych?"

"Let that Vasily Ilych of yours cart someone else's ass around! Got it?" Petukhov yelled. "A lot I need their filthy Volga. And there'll be no more rations, understand? We've had our coffee, and that's it! We'll get along on second-rate Krasnodar tea and local sausage!"

"What happened, Sasha! Are you in trouble?" Tanechka was already in tears.

"Pull your face together!" screamed Petukhov. "You're not a woman, you're a doll! I've had it! One must have principles! You want to buy me cheap, Comrade Citizens!"

Alexander Nikolaevich raged on and on, slammed doors, and yelled slogans about democratic freedoms, about how he wouldn't let anyone stifle or trample upon them. Then he lay down on the sofa with his transistor radio and tuned in Voice of America loud enough for the whole apartment to hear.

III

In mid-December, Natalia Ivanovna Kopeikina chanced to learn that on Saturday the Ocean Fishmarket would be selling canned herring in the morning.[1] The holidays were just around the corner, and so Natalia Ivanovna, Dusya Semenova, and the recently-forgiven Tonya Bodrova set off an hour before the store opened to get a place in line. Marya Sidorovna, whom they also asked along, said that she wasn't up to herring, she didn't feel well; and the women decided to get two tins and split them: half a can each for Natalia Ivanovna and Antonina, half a can for the Tyutins—they're old people, you have to help them out— and half a can for Dusya. Antonina could really use some good herring just now, since Anatoly had promised to drop by on the first anyway. About time. He hadn't called her once since summer, and now... well, it goes without saying—or thinking. The Semenovs were taking Valerka overnight.

They really were selling herring, and the line moved fast, so by ten o'clock all three contented ladies were standing with their cans at the tramstop across from the Peace Square subway station. The weather was clear, the sun was shining.

The trams weren't moving, and a huge crowd had gathered at the stop. They said someone must be coming in from the airport, either a king or one of our own big-shots, so the traffic was cut off. About ten minutes later, a police car appeared. They started yelling through the megaphone and drove everyone up on the sidewalk. There was an unbelievable crush. And in that crush Antonina all of a sudden felt her eyes growing dim, her legs stiffening, and a greenish fog rising all around her like from a large gas jet. She didn't know where she was or why.

How long this condition lasted Antonina could never even estimate, but when she came to, she found herself sitting on a bench near the bus station with Natalia Ivanovna and Dusya sitting next to her—both pale, unwell, and sans handbags.

"What happened to me?" asked Antonina in a weak voice, but they didn't answer. As it turned out, they couldn't answer because neither Semenova nor Kopeikina knew what had happened to them—how, for instance, they got over to that bench from the tramstop and, most important, where their handbags, money, and cans of herring were. Like Antonina, they had seen only that greenish fog, that mist in bright daylight.

"Unquestionably—sabotage," surmised Natalia Ivanovna, and the other women agreed with her.

After they had sat there for about half an hour, come a-round, and talked it over, they decided not to tell anyone anything about it—they wouldn't believe it anyway and would probably laugh at them—and to collect from their own pockets the money that Tyutina had given them for the herring and return it. As for the cans of herring, they would say the fishmarket wasn't selling any—just frozen cod with the heads.

IV

It was true—New Year's was coming up fast. It seemed the November holidays had just passed, and a week later there's another vacation. Everything goes by so fast in this life, so fast you can hardly keep up.

Pyotr Vasilievich Tyutin loved New Year's and always rejoiced: "Just look—lived through another year, and I'm fine. See, dragged the tree over myself from Nekrasov, or rather Maltsev

Market (what an idea some dolt came up with—naming a market after a great writer!). Dragged it in, decorated it, set out the presents, and now?—My grandsons are coming over, Daniil and Timofei."

Pyotr Vasilievich liked New Year's, but it still wasn't his main holiday; Soviet Army Day and, most important, of course, Victory Day. New Year's was more for his wife and daughter, but these others were his own special days.

On those days, Pyotr Vasilievich put on his grey uniform, pinned on his medals—Order of the Red Star, and Patriotic War, second class—and went to see Pyotr Samokhin, his namesake, friend, and comrade-in-arms. Samokhin had a big apartment, and that, as they say, started a fine tradition—gathering at Samokhin's on holidays. The boys came without their wives, drank moderately, sang songs and reminisced. If someone started to tell the very same story for the tenth time, no one ever stopped him or corrected him—"That isn't right. You're getting it mixed up, you old fucker, everyone in the house has heard enough. We've been listening to it since we were yea high, and even then it was a bore. Won't he ever stop? I'm sick and tired of it. The same thing over and over again."—But his friends, they listen. And if someone cries, it's just an old man's tears. They don't notice, don't make a scene, and don't immediately start ohing and ahing and running for the Tyleval. In short—the manly friendship of front-liners.

It's interesting that so much time had passed since the war—Tyutin was a foreman for more than twenty years at the factory. (He retired like you're supposed to, honorably: no one drove him out, he wanted to go himself), and he still had friends—but you see, all that's left of these factory friends is greeting cards on red-letter days. But these fellows he was with for no more than three years during the war—what am I saying, three years? Some he knew less than a year—these guys would stick with him till death, till the very last day. Why?

Pyotr Vasilievich now considered these meetings with his war buddies the sole and most important duty in his life. Only with them, with the guys, could he sense who he was, what he had done, what paths he had followed. Personal matters are just personal matters—that's for women. A man lives for something else. But each time, fewer and fewer gathered at Petka

Samokhin's on holidays. Last Victory Day only three came. All the rest were sick... They had been meeting rather often lately, but these meetings were far from festive. What meetings! — They were wakes.

So it wasn't from spite, or weakness of character, nor from cruelty that Pyotr Vasilievich tormented his wife with funereal conversations, but because he saw his time approaching, and death seemed to him the last task that he was to complete on this earth, modestly and with dignity. Only a fool would imagine that you can die any old way, and irresponsibly—'Let the relatives worry and fuss. All I have to do is lie down in a coffin, cross my arms and sleep, beloved comrade.'

Pyotr Vasilievich wasn't a veteran soldier for nothing. Perhaps he got through the war with no wounds, and only one contusion, precisely because he could, and always did, do everything like he was supposed to; whether it was digging a trench or cleaning his automatic. And now—this is no trench, he's got to make a whole series of important decisions: his wife's, I mean his widow's financial security, the future tenor of her life, the funeral arrangements... Naturally, Tyutin couldn't count on his relatives in these matters, but he could count on his combat buddies. He knew that they would help Marya Sidorovna and not abandon his grandsons. But you do have to take a hand in things yourself. Just this morning he started making up a list—the names and addresses of those who absolutely must be invited to see him off on his last journey. But when his wife saw the list she broke into such a howl, the old fool, that Tyutin got angry, wadded up the paper, stuffed it in his pocket and went out for a walk in the garden, slamming the door behind him. Honestly, that's a woman's logic for you! Silly old hen. Later she'll go running around cackling like a chicken with its head cut off—Who should she call? How can she get in touch? Where can she find them? She should enjoy it—good people come to say farewell to her husband. No one stands on ceremony. Over here are his war buddies, and there are the working class folks—his co-workers and his apprentices, I mean successors.[1] And there's the boss. Okay... He'll finish his list later, without her around. He'll finish it and hide it in the desk, in the drawer with his medals and papers. They'll need the medals, start looking for them and find the list.

28

... Pyotr Vasilievich Tyutin was just walking along the narrow path through the snow drifts in his big felt boots on Sunday morning, looking at the white, feathery trees, the clean-washed, clear sky, the silly, fat-faced snowman with an ice-cream stick for a nose. He rustled the crumpled list in his pocket, thought, and suddenly he just didn't want to die anymore. He was so scared and reluctant to leave his homey, comfortable world, and vanish somewhere into the dark, where there certainly wasn't anything good, that he pulled out the wadded-up paper with the names, threw it hurriedly in the trash barrel and shuffled off as fast as he could—those damned felt boots weighed a ton! He still had to buy some candy, and tomorrow there would be lines in the stores—how awful.

V

On New Year's Eve Fira told her husband that she no longer loved him. She really had to think about that one—to pick such a day for a conversation like that! But Lazar had suspected for some time, at least a month, that something was wrong. Fira was constantly held up somewhere. She suddenly found a huge number of errands to do. But that always happens when things are going badly for someone at home. Everything upset her and drove her nuts, but for some reason, especially Lazar's innocent request not to call him Olesha, Lelik, or Lyalik anymore. Earlier she wouldn't have paid any attention, or perhaps she would have respected his wishes, but now:

"Oh, Lazar? I understand... That's your form of protest. 'I'm not hiding a thing, I'm even proud of it.' Very, veerrry brave of you, you're a regular Joan of Arc."

"Why do you say that?"

"Because it's disgusting! You're giving them the finger in your pocket. The hero—the champion of an idea. Why don't you wear a yellow armband?"

"I should—and I will. You know, the King and Queen of Denmark did when the Germans..."

"I know. You've told me about that at least three times... maybe four. But unfortunately, you're not a king, and you don't have to wear anything—it is, as they say, written all over

29

your face."

"I don't get it." Lazar finally lost his head. "Are you an anti-Semite all of a sudden?"

"It's simply, my dear, that I don't like people who can be bought off cheap. Your name's Lazar? Marvelous! You're proud of your Jewishness? Bravo, bravo! Encore! You don't like it when they curl their lips at you behind your back? It's disgusting that any thug on the tram can, if he pleases, call you a Yid dog and nothing will happen to him? Well, just imagine, I think it's disgusting too. But what good is this 'Lazar' business? Be consistent. Leave!"

"Have you gone nuts, Fira?"

"Ha, now you're scared! There it is, the price of your civic courage."

"Wait a second, are you serious?"

"I am serious, I'm even veerrry serious, and here you are, yapping like a dog under the gate with your eternal 'I would have socked him right in the mouth!' "

"Do you really want to leave? For Israel?"

"That's a secondary question—where? Just away from here. Got it?"

"All right, Fira, let's discuss it... Though I never imagined you would... Something happened to you!"

"Actually, it's a state of being. 'Something happened to me'! But nothing ever happened to you, not once, right, Lelik? I mean—damn—Lazar Moiseevich? Weren't you the one who for some reason wasn't accepted once in the lit department, even with a gold medal from high school? And aren't you the one who's forever in a rage because your paper's being read at some symposium in London by an Aryan with a Party card?!"

"Keep it down."

"Keep it down?! There we are! I'm sick of it! They get their faces bashed in and they say, 'Keep it down!' Why not just slit your throat? And would you get rid of that cigarette. Your mother will see and start yelling!"

"No she won't. And you don't have to convince *me*, I can give you a whole bunch of examples of that kind of thing."

"Well, and then what?"

"But... it's no good anyway. Like in that story.[1] It's no good, Firochka. But I still won't leave."

30

"Are you afraid? Afraid that if we apply for a visa, you'll get fired and not get permission to leave? Is that it?"

"To be honest—that too. But that's not first or even second. First is that—don't you see?—this is my homeland. A mere trifle, of course."

"Homeland—motherland?"

"Whatever you like: motherland, step-motherland, auntie-land, or just homeland. You can't get away from it."

"What do you mean, auntie? What relation to Russia are you, Lazar Moiseevich, Jew, place of birth— a *shtetl* in the Pale. She needs you, with your filial affection, like Tonka Bodrova needs that illegitimate Valerik!"

"God, what is this! I think it's ridiculous that we, you and I, are carrying on a conversation like this. Personally, I don't believe in a genetic love for the land of one's fathers. Perhaps I don't believe in it because I don't feel it myself. Of course, if someone does feel it, let him go. I wish him all the best..."

"... But you're okay here."

"No. Not okay. But I'm afraid it's no better anywhere else. And why this mocking tone? Do I really have to explain to you that I grew up here, that I like their stupid faces, that Russian is my native language, that I, forgive my vulgarity, love the Russian land, love Russian literature, and don't even know Hebrew lit. What's your most important Hebrew classic?"

"Mine?! Now listen here!" Fira was standing in the middle of the room, arms folded on her chest. " This conversation is disgusting. And, forgive me please, so are you. That's the psychology of a slave and a coward."

"Oh, go to... you know where you can go!" Lazar was furious. "Just think, a dissident!... I'm disgusting—then just clear out. I won't stop you!"

Fira immediately dressed and went out for the whole evening. Maybe some Zionist had turned up where she works? There are lots of them now—heroes with inferiority complexes and long tongues.

Lazar stood in the kitchen for a long time, smoking by the window and blowing the smoke out the vent. Finally he decided that most likely, someone on the bus or in a store had called Firka names, she really has that look—no need for an armband; she's a regular Rachel. Of course it's offensive! Of course it's disgusting! Only there's no getting out of this situation. How is it she doesn't understand that, the idiot?! Jews have always been bad off and should be bad off.

"She'll settle down, then we'll talk," Lazar decided.

But Fira didn't settle down. And now on the night of New Year's Day, sitting at the holiday spread, she officially informed her husband, in the presence of her mother-in-law, that she intended to divorce him because of incompatibility of character and political convictions.

Rosa Lvovna immediately said that she had a headache and was going to bed. But Lazar was regaled with the following: "It's a good thing we don't have any children, though I know you and your mother always faulted me for it behind my back. I need the divorce immediately. You and I are like strangers. You don't condemn the weak, you pity them. But pity isn't enough for me—in order to live with a man I need to respect him too, and I have no respect for you."

Here Lazar asked quietly, "Don't you love me anymore? Is there someone else?"

"I don't love you," Fira snapped out, "and whether there's someone else or not—in this case, what difference does it make? Your assimilationist attitude doesn't suit me. I figure whoever doesn't want to go home to Israel can go work for the KGB."

"Can I wait til morning? They're probably closed now," asked Lazar, mechanically biting into a chicken leg.

"Wipe your chin, you've got some grease on it," said Fira disgustedly. "I'm leaving. I'll just take the most necessary things for now."

She got up from the table, and five minutes later Lazar heard her slam the door—obviously the most necessary things had been gathered in advance.

Lazar reached for his wine glass, which had some champagne left, poured some vodka in it, and slowly drank it down without tasting a thing. He drank, wiped his mouth with the back of his hand, and looked at his watch.

One thirty. Where did she go? But then, the trains are running all night.[2]

VI

Imagine, Tonya Bodrova didn't celebrate New Year's. She ran over to the Semenovs' at eleven, sat a while, wished everyone a happy holiday, left Valerka until the second of the month as they'd agreed, and went home. Dusya says "Oh, stay, stay." But Antonina says, "Really, I don't feel like it. No particular reason, just that sort of mood. Decided to go to bed kind of early so I look like a human being in the morning," because Anatoly had definitely said, "I'll drop by on the afternoon of the first." Generally, you can't really believe him. It had happened before. He'd promise, and say "Wait for me!"—then never show up. But this time it would be different. This time, why should he lie? Once he'd left last time, back in August, she didn't run after him, didn't call him up, though she knew he and Polina weren't getting along—a booze-up every day, and after the booze, a fight.

They met in the bakery on the evening of the thirtieth. Antonina, pretending not to recognize him, turned away. She took a hard-roll, but her hands, as if they didn't belong to her, dropped the roll on the floor, and she had to pay for it. The cashier there was really nasty. She'd blow up—the roll was all dirty. Antonina had just gone outside, when there was Anatoly, right behind her.

"Oh, citizeness, pardon me, could you give me the time?"

Every day, for more than four months, and not just once mind you, Antonina had tried to imagine how it would be, how they would meet again. She decided not to behave crudely, but so he understood that she did have her pride. Even if at one time she had howled like a madwoman and practically clutched his legs just so he wouldn't leave, now all that was over, and she would be, as they say, like a different person. Let him suspect that she has someone else. Let him think what he likes.

But it turned out somewhat differently. She forgot about pride and started jabbering some nonsense. "How's life?" she asks. And he says, "Pretty rough." "What do you mean, pretty rough. You've got a young wife." And he says, "First of all, she's my wife only for purposes of my residence permit, and second, just look at her puss sometime. To put it bluntly, she's got an ass like a Pioneer and a face like a pensioner." Antonina should have said that it's not nice to talk about a woman like

33

that, but she said just the opposite. "You should put a towel over her head," she says, and all sorts of things that are so awful it's embarrassing for me to repeat them. The main thing was, she kept on talking. She knew it was all wrong, but she couldn't stop. Antonina really does have a loose tongue; but Anatoly likes that, the old goat. He's laughing and happy. He was probably afraid that Antonina would make a scene, but why should she? If she'd wanted to, she could have fixed Polina's mouth for her last summer—she wouldn't have had far to go; they live in the same courtyard.

Anatoly said something else, and then says, "You're looking pretty good, gained some weight."[1] Apparently Antonina came up with some sort of answer, but all the time she was just thinking, "Now he'll leave. Right now. Say good-bye and that's it. And then I'll just be waiting again, looking out the window to see if he's going by, and waiting again. And those hellish nights when I dream things that make me break out in a sweat just remembering them the next morning."

Then suddenly he comes out with, "Why don't you invite me over for New Year's?"

"But Tolya, New Year's is a family holiday, you spend it in the bosom of your family. Do you think Polina will let you go? Or are the two of you planning to come by?"

"What am I saying?" she thought. "Now he'll say, 'I was just joking. Say hi to the family. See you later! *Ciao, bambina!*'"

"No, of course not, come on!"

"If you want to, drop by then. Either New Year's Eve, or on the first."

"The first? That's fine. If you don't drive me away, I'll come at two o'clock. Get a half-bottle ready."

So they came to an agreement. He'll come. Why should he lie? He suggested it himself. She didn't force the invitation on him. He'll come.

***

Antonina, of course, spit-polished everything in her room and bought herself a new dress cinched in at the waist and the color of a wave on the sunlit sea. She really had to look for it—a size fifty that fit. They sew clothes for fat people in our country, as if we were all old women. They're not dresses, but sacks! It's really a pain. On the thirty-first she went to a hairdresser friend of hers, and got a set and a manicure. Then she went to bed, just as she'd planned, right after the national anthem.[2] On the first, she was all ready by one in the afternoon—with her dress, as if she'd been poured into it, and a pendant on her breast. True, she did run her stockings a little when she was pulling them on, but that was because they were imported. Foreign broads have sticks for legs, but in our country women's legs are shapely—that's why the stockings were tight. Well, it's not important. So she laddered her stocking. He won't notice.

Then she set the table. Rather modestly—not a lot just to have a lot, because she wasn't about to buy herself a man for some ham and caviar. She put out little pickles, sprats, and Jewish salad (Rosa Lvovna taught her how to make it: cottage cheese, finely chopped garlic, greens—and you can add dill or parsley), and she had cheese, and three hundred grams of " Soviet" dry-smoked sausage which she finally managed to get out of the store. Katka and Valentina are really shits. When they need groceries it's "Tosya" this and "Tosya" that, and of course she puts anything they want aside. But you always have to ask them a hundred times, come crawling... [3]

In short, the buffet came out not exactly luxurious, but decent. And as he'd asked, she had bought a half-liter of vodka. That's enough. Let him booze it up with Polina. Tosya's no Polina. What happened before is past, and there's no sense bringing it up.

Of course, there was another quarter-bottle and two beers in the refrigerator in reserve, depending on how things went.

Anatoly arrived exactly at two. He took off his coat in the entryway, and Antonina was really stunned. She'd never seen him like that before. A beige suit, an irridescent tie, curly hair— she'd already managed to forget, apparently, what beautiful hair he had.

They went into her room.

Antonina said, "Wow, what a get-up! Like straight from abroad."

And he laughed, "Hit the nail on the head that time! My suit's imported, "Made in Poland."[4] Well, okay, now, you've seen the suit? You won't for long."

He takes off his jacket and hangs it on a chair; the tie too. Then he starts on his pants. Antonina just sits on the ottoman and keeps quiet. She doesn't know what to say. He takes off his pants and laughs like he's cracked or something.

"What's your mouth hanging open for, bumpkin? You've got to be a contemporary woman. This is your lover, not just anybody. Get undressed."

Antonina stood up, froze, and was silent. On the one hand, of course, it was nice that he considered her a contemporary woman and hadn't come just to drink. But on the other hand, maybe it was all right for them, but we aren't used to it yet.

So he's standing there in his birthday suit, with just his socks and ankle-boots on, smirking.

"What's wrong? Get undressed. Right now!"

Antonina just looks. He takes the bottle from the table and pours her a shot, him a shot, then says, "Have a drink, let's go, maybe you'll get up some courage then. But you always were a fool. Haven't you seen any French films?"

She couldn't very well swear at him, she hadn't waited six months for that. Antonina took the shot glass, and drank up. Okay. If that's the way the French do it—that's the way they do it. At least she put on a new slip, a nylon one. She took off the blue wave of a dress, and he said, "Take it all off, this isn't a dress shop or a polyclinic." And he poured himself another drink. Antonina wanted to turn off the lamp, but he said, "What else? How ridiculous! Or maybe you want to get married first? I don't remember that there's anything missing. You've got everything in quantity and in the right places." What can you do with this guy? A real card!

Anyway, she gets undressed and just stands there. She doesn't know what to do next. But Anatoly hadn't even looked at the bed. He sat down at the table. So, she sat down opposite and covered her stomach with the tablecloth. It was really cold.

And Tolka says, "What are you covering yourself up for? In the first place, a woman's body is beautiful. Haven't you ever been to the Russian Museum?[5] And you're as fascinating as Venus. And I," he laughs, "as that, what's his name... Hannibal."

Antonina immediately got drunk, perhaps from shame, or nervousness, or maybe because she hadn't put a thing in her stomach since yesterday. And she could not care less that she was sitting there like an idiot, naked, and that, of course, her bod wasn't in the best of shape, and there was a draft from the window. She was happy and felt good because here Anatoly had come after all, come all by himself, and he was sitting there like some baron, with freckles on his shoulders like a little boy...

"Tolik, aren't you cold? I'll get you a shawl."

"Get out of here with your shawl! Better pour another round! We'll warm up later."

...and those wide shoulders, so handsome! Yeah, really, just like Hannibal or Julius Caesar or somebody.

French-style—so she'll play it to the hilt! Antonina got up, walked across the whole room in her heels and turned on the television. They just happened to be showing a pop concert. And— what the hell!—she got the beer and the quarter-bottle from the refrigerator.

They drank—to love. Antonina felt that she was getting drunk and that she really should have a little something to eat, but she couldn't get a thing down, and that was that. And then Maya Kristallinskaya starts singing, "I've been on the road a long time, but it's never been smooth." Nothing special, really, but Antonina was in tears.

"Tolechka, darling, I'll do anything you want! Just tell me and I'll do it!"

"Look, you know I can't marry you, Tonka. Just get that straight, you nut!"

"That's not necessary. What for? I'll just do—whatever you want... I'll wash and sew for you. And money—what do I need money for? I make enough myself. I wouldn't take any of your pay... And you can come home any way you want, drunk or anything..."

"Quit howling. You're a good broad, better than Polka. But marriage is out."

"Tolik, when I go past the Chaika[6] where you and I ate that time, I always cry, like some madwoman..."

"I'm a man... Got it? You're a broad, and I'm a man... And that's it... You got any kerosene,[7] huh?"

"Everybody here thinks I'm the worst, the most awful I-don't-know-what because of what I did to Valerik that time... You understand, I'm a mother! I love my child. It's not the child's fault... But I love you more than my whole life!... If you got sick, I'd give my blood..."

"What is this, lemonade, right?! She couldn't even get two half-liters! I told you—wait for me!... I'm a man... Blechh... B-bitch! That's it!... Got it?!... I'm not getting married. That's it!"

"Tolik, why don't you eat a little something? Have some pickles..."

"Get away! I said get away! That's it!... One bottle... Stingy ... The bitch... I'm a man! Your tits are drooping, you cow...I'm a man, and you're a bitch... That's it... That's it..."

"Tolik, if you're not feeling well, I'll run out for something. Just calm down, darling! Tolenka..."

"Get your hands off me! Hands off! Don't touch me, b...! I'll kill you, bitch! I'll kill you!!!"

"Tolik! Don't! Don't! Please! Here—I'm on my knees... Tolenka! Ouuuu! Don't kick! Tolechka! Tolechkaaa!"

"Shut up, whore! Had enough?... Get up! Sprawled out there... bitch... Take that! And that! Shut up, I'll kill you! Shut up!!!"

It was a good thing no one was in the apartment. The neighbor woman was out visiting.

VII

Rosa Lvovna was getting ready for a rendezvous.

Why should she upset Lazar? She didn't say a word to him about it yesterday. The boy has enough problems of his own. To his mother he was still a boy, though he was forty years old. That's the most dangerous age for men, by the way—if they have a heart attack at that age, it's very, very bad. They say you have to look after men just then, make sure they strengthen their heart muscles, play some sports, engage in light athletics. Only fate doesn't ask how old someone is.

Real suffering falls into everyone's lot at some time, and now it was Lelik's turn. In Gorky, in evacuation, in the most dreadful years of the war, he was happy—he was little, he didn't understand what was going on. His mother was there, and no one had fathers then. Rosa Lvovna didn't let him go hungry. She wouldn't permit it. She got a job in a noodle factory—they gave her a worker's ration card—and she sewed at night. It was really funny—

before the war she couldn't do anything, but when she was forced to by need, she learned to cut patterns, and sew, and knit, and even resole shoes.

Later it went easier. Lazar did well in school, and his comrades loved him. He was a very talented and sociable boy. He wasn't accepted at the university,[1] and that was a blow, of course, but he didn't lose his head. He entered a technical college, though he had dreamed of becoming a journalist. A talented guy, talented in everything, always. He even made it in technical studies— a candidate of sciences, a physicist! That's how she is, and how she brought him up—don't whine, don't complain. What you have—you have; what you don't—you don't need.

Just for example: Did anyone in the family, she or Lelik, ever say one word about Fira not having children? Lazar never complained about his wife at all—good man!—and Rosa Lvovna never once took the liberty of doing so. They found each other and so they ought to live their own lives.

How could she leave Lazar? What did he do to displease her? He's no nebbish, just firm and tactful. Not awfully handsome? But beauty isn't the most important thing in a man, and Fira understood that fifteen years ago.

Love... You can't control the heart, and though that Petukhov is no better than Lelik, and in fact much worse, what can you do if they're in love? And Rosa Lvovna had noticed some time ago that Fira was in love. She watched horror-stricken as Fira ate nothing at dinner, gave irrelevant answers, and seemed to be listening to something which she alone could hear. She would blush, then smile for no earthly reason. And her eyes! God, what an expression! At first, Rosa Lvovna even thought maybe Firochka was expecting, but then she would have been gentler, more affectionate to her husband.

Lazar didn't tell his mother anything about the evening Fira left home. Rosa Lvovna left at the beginning of that conversation. She didn't want to interfere. Maybe she acted foolishly. Later, Lelik just said, "Fira and I have decided to separate." "Fira and I"! And not a word more about it. But Rosa Lvovna just couldn't try to worm her way into her son's confidence—it wasn't like her, she just couldn't.

But others could. Everyone always knows everything in that building. First, they gave her those looks. Then Antonina, that dissolute woman, says, "Rosochka Lvovna, Rosochka Lvovna, how are things going over at your place, ha?" And later Natalia Ivanovna Kopeikina dropped in and just set it all out on the table—Petukhov, Israel, and poor, unhappy Tanechka.

Fira is just crazy to decide to leave. But you can understand—once you decide to destroy things, you go all the way. And it doesn't make any difference where you live with the man you love, as long as you're together. I bet all those years of sleepless nights after the news of the death of her husband, Rosa Lvovna herself thought thousands and thousands of times, "Maybe it was a mistake? Maybe he's alive? I don't care if he's a cripple, I don't care if he's shell-shocked, or mentally ill, I don't care about anything—I just want him to come back! Even if he was captured and imprisoned,[2] I'd still be happy. I'd go any distance to take Lelik to his father, even to Sakhalin. But it's not likely. The Germans wouldn't leave a captured Jew alive, and Moisei wouldn't have surrendered anyway—that's the sort of man he was." Rosa Lvovna was sure of that. And then there was the letter from his pal at the front... But mistakes do happen!

And here's a paradox for you! Now, after so many years, Rosa Lvovna suddenly learns that Moisei is alive, and it's a blow to her! Grief, and hurt, and injury. If she loves him, she should be glad. Who was it who prayed to God, "Let him come back any way You like, just so he's alive"? Well, he's alive—and now what? It turns out, "Better he were a cripple, or a criminal, or even... what a terrible thing to say!... Better dead. But mine."

You can't explain, you can't understand, so you have no business condemning other people for falling in love with Petukhov, though it's a sure thing Fira will suffer an awful lot. Who knows, that Petukhov might be a drunk and an anti-Semite. He had everything he needed, he had a high position, and suddenly—off to Israel! Treason, if you think about it. He's a Russian!

... And Lelik made such a fuss about her.

Rosa Lvovna was thinking about all this, arguing with herself, wanting to be fair, and in the meantime, getting ready.

The most important meeting in a woman's life sometimes occurs at sixty. Of course, clothes and hair-dos aren't so important, but the new spring coat she bought in December would come in handy today. It was March.

Rosa Lvovna neatly put the photographs in her handbag:

Lelik joins the Pioneers, Lelik with his class on graduation day, and that's her on the Board of Honor in 1950[3] —young, with a medal... Wedding pictures, Fira like an angel—we'll put that away, have to hide them later. And I'll take his candidate's diploma, and all his patent certificates, all eight of them. Eight inventions—that's no joke. One even has a foreign patent. That's the kind of son Rosa Lvovna raised; raised him alone, educated him and helped him along in life.

Rosa Lvovna closed the catch on her bag, swollen with papers, and went to the mirror anyway. She had to put on some lipstick, a kerchief. To hell with it! She'd wear a knitted cap. And no one would think she was over fifty-five! She hadn't gone to fat, she took care of herself. And grey hair looks dignified. It's the fashion now. Even young girls wear grey wigs.

Why did she pick the Yusuppov Garden[4] for their meeting? You could probably guess. Because the last time all three of them walked together, she, four-year-old Lazar, and Moisei—it was there. It was Saturday evening, June 21st. And they lived right near-by then, on Ekateringof. But of course, when Moisei called yesterday, she didn't have anything in mind. She said the first thing that came into her head, and the Yusuppov Garden came to mind.

"Hello, Rosa Lvovna? This is Katz calling about your postcard," Moisei began their telephone conversation. "I received your card and decided to call right away."

His voice turned out to be surprisingly like his son's. Only he had an accent, and Lelik spoke perfect Russian, like a radio announcer.

She tried to speak with dignity, with no excitement.

"Hello, Moisei. Since it turns out now that you've been alive all these years, my son has to get the facts straight for the questionaires. In case he goes abroad on business."

There were no trips in the offing, especially now, after the episode with Fira,[5] but Rosa Lvovna continued, "Before, he wrote, 'Father died at the front.' Now he'll have to give your residence and place of employment."

"I'm retired," Moisei said sadly.

"Then your last position and your duties."

"If necessary, I can come now," he suggested. "I know the address, I got it at the information bureau..."

"It's pretty late for you to suddenly need your son's address." Rosa Lvovna pronounced the phrase she had prepared in advance. "There's no reason to came by. You have your own life, and we have ours. If you really want to, we can meet. Tomorrow. At four. By the entrance to the Yusuppov Garden."

"Good. I'll be there at four," Moisei humbly agreed.

He came twenty minutes early, maybe more. Rosa Lvovna herself turned up by the garden at quarter to four, and she immediately caught sight of him—from a distance, from the opposite side of Sadovaya. He was already standing there. It turned out that the old codger had nothing in common with Lazar except his voice, and maybe the color of his eyes—but their expression was quite different, like some old jade's. Just a skinny, little... Oh, Moisei, Moisei, maybe you wouldn't look like this now if you hadn't betrayed your wife and son!

"Rosa, you haven't changed a bit," said Moisei when she came up to him. "You're just the same. I'm staggered."

Now what? Tell him what you think, what he deserves to hear? What for?

"Let's sit down," Rosa Lvovna suggested, inspecting Moisei's worn-out shoes and his short overcoat, which was missing two buttons, the first and fourth. "Or are you cold? I could treat you at the café."

Without answering, he dragged himself down the muddy, uneven path to a small bench and sat down, pulling up the legs of his trousers, though they were nothing but wrinkles anyway. Rosa Lvovna took a newspaper out of her bag, spread it out neatly and sat down on it so she wouldn't get her new coat dirty.

"Well, go on," she said.

"What can I say? When I decided... I met this woman... Well, when we wrote you that letter... I thought it would be better this way, you're proud, and it'd be easier for you to mourn a dead man than find out..." Moisei muttered.

"That doesn't interest me—the woman, your lying," Rosa Lvovna interrupted him. "Tell me the last place you worked and the year you retired. I know your address. I got it at the information bureau too."

"I've been retired since 1965, and I worked in a retail chain."

"Position?"

"Sales clerk."

"But you had an education! A technical speciality!"

"Well, that's just the way it happened. The family..."

"It's possible to support a family and still do some honest work. Yes... So, you're a sales clerk... Well, I'm not retired yet. Senior librarian. And Lazar's a candidate. He'll go to Moscow soon, he's been summoned to the Ministry."

Moisei was silent. She expected him to start asking her about their son now, but he was silent. And just then it started to rain. It instantly grew dark, and tiny little drops fell on the bench.

"I'll be going now," Moisei said sullenly and got up. "I've got a train to catch at 4:50, and I have to do some shopping.[6] The vegetables are awful in Shapki."

But Rosa Lvovna couldn't contain herself any longer "You've got a train?" she yelled, jumping up. "Do you have a conscience? What about how your son's doing, what he's achieved in life—doesn't that interest you?"

"It does," Moisei growled, shifting from one holey shoe to another in the puddle where he stood, "and you said he was a candidate. And I asked the neighbors. You've got an apartment and a car. Candidates! The Ministry! Librarians! 'You had a speciality!' But when you've got three children and a sick wife?! When there's nothing to eat?! 'Support a family and do some honest work'! Thanks for the advice, boss! Of course, I wasn't sober when I came that time, no doubt about it. But why did he turn away from me like I had the plague? He's my son... Here..." He fumbled in his pockets with his dirty, stiff fingers, shoved them in his coat, then his jacket. "Here, give him that. Tell him thanks from his Dad! He lent it to me, so I'm repaying the debt! I borrowed it from him!" He thrust a crumpled ruble and some change into Rosa Lvovna's hands. She was dumbfounded.

"What are you doing..." she said, stepping back. "What's this for? We've got money, we're not in need..."

"You've got money—and welcome to it!" yelled Moisei. "You're not in need—marvelous! Well, I don't need anything from you. I've got a pension—for my work! Well-provided for!"[7]

All of a sudden he snatched at Rosa Lvovna's purse, opened it, threw the money in, turned and headed for the gate, nearly at a run. Completely dismayed, Rosa Lvovna set off irresolutely after him. Near the gate he slowed down, obviously out of breath, but he continued on his way out without turning around.

Thus they moved on towards the Haymarket, one behind the other. Some ten paces ahead, Rosa Lvovna saw the old man's back, the narrow, rounded shoulders, covered by the old coat, a yellow string bag with some packages—where did he get that? It was probably in his pocket.

Moisei didn't look back.

They passed the fishmarket, crossed Moskovski Prospekt. Now Rosa Lvovna had almost caught up with him. Where is he going? Towards the subway, of course. It's easiest to get to the train station by subway.

And so their last meeting had taken place...

"Moisei," Rosa Lvovna called, "Moisei, wait!"

Her voice suddenly broke off. A thick greenish fog dimmed her eyes. Her legs grew weak.

"What's wrong, lady?" a young voice asked sympathetically, and Rosa Lvovna felt someone firmly grasp her arm. "Are you okay?"

"It's nothing... Stop him... that man," she barely gasped out, trying to lift her arm. "Over there, the old man, with the string bag..."

"There's no one there, lady. You were seeing things. Just calm down. Can you stand?"

"Yes. I'll be okay in a moment. I'm fine. Thank you."

The green mist dispersed, and Rosa Lvovna saw an anxious face in glasses quite near. Just a boy, probably a high school student.

"I'm fine. You go on now, young man. Thanks very much. I'm okay."

She freed her arm and moved on. Moisei had disappeared. There were a few people nearby. She peered at them carefully. He was gone. He wasn't by the subway entrance, or at the tramstop, or at the store. Rosa Lvovna had sharp eyes, she didn't wear glasses, she couldn't have been mistaken. Moisei Katz had disappeared. He'd just vanished.

Rosa Lvovna looked around the Haymarket slowly and carefully one last time. And... he just wasn't there. He was gone for almost forty years, and now he was gone again. Guess it's only right. What can you do?—it's all for the best. Rosa Lvovna closely clutched her handbag and went off to the tramstop.

VIII

Finally, we can get around to talking a little about the Semenovs. Otherwise, to tell the truth, we'd get really sick of all this drama and tragedy—Antonina drunk, her eye all swollen, black-and-blue marks everywhere, Rosa Lvovna in tears; Lazar silent and losing weight. I don't have enough paper to list all their problems. And anyway, you and I are just like everyone else—things are unpleasant enough for us at home and at work without getting more here. For once in his life a person has some time free from business, housework, and the television to sit down and read a book, and all he gets are more horrors, divorces, tears, some weird triangle... And the characters, one and all, are either shits or completely depraved. One can only conclude, finally, that this so-called "literary work" is simply libel against Soviet reality. What did you think? That there were no happy, healthy, pink-cheeked people around? No sportsmen? That no one goes off to BAM or KAMAZ?[1] That there are no wise intellectuals walking around our city with their briefcases, portfolios, and creative ideas? The weather is always bad? And there are always lines in the stores?

Enough! Time-out. We're exhausted.

We're at the Semenovs'. Their family is tight-knit, harmonious. Their health is excellent—and that's not blind luck, either, it's just that no one drinks or lies around on the couch reading books all the time. They're always working, so they simply have no time to whine or get sick. Their room is warm and clean. Everything shines, from the varnished floor to the furniture and windows. Their son is an all-A student[2] at the English school, and chairman of the Pioneer cell in his class. The head of the Semenov family is a production leader, and his portrait hangs in the courtyard at the factory—not some photograph either, but a real portrait, done by a real artist. The Semenovs are all even-tempered and easy to get along with, they never even have any fights with the neighbors. Of course the Tyutins are pretty old already, and when it's Marya Sidorovna's turn to clean, she sometimes leaves dust in the corners in the hall and she doesn't clean the stove very well. But did they ever say anything to her? Not once. On the contrary, its always, "Marya Sidorovna, I'm going to the dairy. Should I get you some kefir?"

Happy people are seldom evil—that's a well-known, proven fact—and the Semenovs are, from any point of view, happy people.

But what exactly is happiness?

A certain not-very-respected person[3] has said that happiness is the maximum correspondence of reality to desire. If we ignore for a moment the old scores we have to settle with him, then maybe he's right. The whole thing is—what is desirable, and to whom? What is our goal? What if it's not a sheepskin coat, but Communism? That's just it!

But on the other hand, there's the view that the goal is nothing. The progress toward it is all. And it wasn't just anybody who thought that up, but some classic thinker—maybe even the theorist of permanent revolution.[4]

There are others who maintain happiness is when there is no unpleasantness. There is something to that. Somehow, lying for free in the Twenty-Fifth of October Hospital is... not bad. But the Semenovs' happiness lies in the fact that they don't seek any definition of or justification for their situation—why, for example, they're living well, and Rosa Lvovna is doing poorly. In general, they don't look for solutions to problems, but simply live. They know the answers to most questions. They know what they want and what must be done to make their dreams reality. And they go about their business. They don't wait for some rich uncle or fairy-tale sorcerer to turn up. So I figure that if we can rest anywhere, it's at the Semenovs', where, just now, the master is at home, sitting at the table eating borshch. It's eight in the morning. Semenov just got home from the night shift. His son is already at school—today is scrap-metal collection day, so he left early—and Dusya's on sick-leave. They were lucky again—she only ran a temperature one day, but the doctor hasn't discharged her after a whole week, and she's getting a hundred percent sick pay from the factory.

A clean oilcloth. A dish with a gold rim. Ukrainian borshch with garlic and sour cream. The light's still on. It's dark outside.

"I'm going to work two shifts on Easter—the night and the day," said Semenov, taking a bite of bread.

"Huh?"

"The foreman said I'd get double time and a May Day bonus. And maybe there'll be some real money. Quadruple time.

No one wants to work—they've all turned into believers."

"Easter isn't for a long time yet..."

"We'll live to see it. If the boy gets all A's, we're going to have to buy him a bicycle. We promised... You're going to church to get your Easter cakes blessed[5] too, I suppose?"

"Yes. Why, are we different from everybody else?"

"So you're a believer?"

"Okay, so I am."

"If you're religious, where's your icon?"

"You're crazy! We've got a son, remember? A pioneer! The kids from his class will come over and then tell Maya Sergeevna that their chairman's got religious propaganda at home."

"Agh, propaganda! I was just kidding. And where would we put icons, anyway. They'd spoil the whole room. But tell me something, what did Christ tell you about 'Thou shalt not commit robbery'?"

" 'Thou shalt not steal.' "

"And what did you put that blanket cover together from the other day?"

"Oh, cut it out! What nonsense!"

"No, really. Did you buy the material with your own money or swipe it from the factory?"

"That's not stealing. Stealing's if it's from people, and I took the material from the storeroom. Do you know how much of that calico is lying around there? I've been working there for nine years, and it's still just lying there. They'll send it in for salvage soon. *I* don't take anything, hardly. Other people drag away twice as much as I do. The State's not going broke. Everybody takes things, and nothing happens. Even the shop foreman, even the assistant director."

"Do you think it's honest?"

"What if you find something on the street and pick it up— is that honest? Enough of your jabbering! We're not at some assembly. Finish your soup and go to bed. I've made it up. You got into some conversation there, deputy!"

"Duska, calm down. I didn't mean anything by it. Just teasing you. The borshch is great, good job! It's nice to have your wife home."

"Of course, being home's better than work. Oh, I almost forgot! Those two are going to Israel."

"Who?"

"Lazar's wife and Petukhov, an executive no less. What are you goggling at? She ran off with Petukhov and they're leaving for Israel."

"So what?!"

"Here's so what. Tatyana's ended up in a psychiatric hospital."

"Well, I give up. I never expected it from Petukhov. He had everything—a State-owned car, free trips abroad. If you've got everything, it's never enough."

"But I was thinking, maybe he's a Jew? He looks like one."

"Okay, Evdokia, I'm off to bed. Fuck all of 'em. It doesn't concern us, thank goodness. I figure I didn't even know Petukhov—just hello and good-bye."

And it's true. Semenov's right, it doesn't concern him. So let him sleep, the crackajack metal worker from the shock crew of the sixth brigade. He was sleeping after his shift, not after some garden party.

And we'll sit a while longer by the steam-heat radiator, painted light blue just a week ago. We'll be quiet so we don't disturb him. We'll just move the stiff, starched curtain back and look out the window where the wet trees stretch out their branches in the dark, trampled snow.

It's thawing. It's been thawing since yesterday. Water runs down the roof, and drops hit the iron ledge.

CHAPTER THREE: THE HOLIDAY

I

If you looked down from a helicopter on May Day, the festive square would look like a laundry tub where someone was washing linen. The multicolored foam floats and heaves, the bubbles of children's balloons break in the air, and the crowd runs off into the street in turbid streams, wearily lowering their furled, worn-out banners, dragging the heavy portraits on the ground.

And if you looked down on Marsovo Polye[1] from a helicopter, that would also be a very imposing spectacle. Lampposts wrapped in red bunting rise like torches, arranged in special geometric figures, discernable and comprehensible only from the air. In the very center, a yellow fire blazes day and night in eternal flame.

Red flags flutter in the wind along the railing of Kirov Bridge,[2] red flags hang down from the walls of the buildings, red flags in the hands of the thousands of people who fill the streets, embankments, lanes, and gardens this holiday morning. Red streets, red embankments, red lanes and gardens. A red city, if you look at it from a helicopter.

And red bands on the sleeves of ruddy *druzhinniks*, arguing with a little old woman, so inopportunely and unpleasantly pale, dressed in a white smock, standing by a white car with a red cross on the hood.

"The road is closed. No thoroughfare. Not here," one of the *druzhinniks*, the chief, wearily repeated over and over again. It wasn't the first time he'd said that. He should have started bawling long ago. He spoke so quietly only because a well-brought-up person isn't rude to an older woman, and he didn't want to spoil his mood on a day like this one. But it certainly wasn't the first time, more like the tenth, that the stubborn, muddle-headed old lady doctor had insisted, had rasped back in her hoarse, cracking voice, "A man may have had a heart attack over there, can't you hear?! A heart attack, understand?"

"The road is closed," said the *druzhinnik*, exhausted, not raising his voice even now. "Do you see the trucks? Your car simply won't get through. What can I do?"

The trucks stood in sharp, close order, blocking off the street. The doctor fell silent, then suddenly rushed toward the wide, red-draped back of the automobile. The four other *druzhinniks* silently joined hands to block off the car. This duty had been entrusted to them, they had been instructed in it, and they would execute it. What could they do? There was no one to ask. And they couldn't break the rules.

But the doctor... There are such ornery, stupid old women around! She raced over to her paralyzed white Volga, snatched a small, dog-eared bag out of it, shoved the tallest, ruddiest *druzhinnik* aside with her shoulder and, slipping through a nonexistent gap between two close-parked red vans, ran across the empty street toward Marsovo Polye, moving along absurdly on her thin legs, shod in cheap rubber boots.

II

The Veterans' Council sent Pyotr Vasilievich Tyutin an invitation to sit on the tribune. They remember, the devils. They value, they respect an old soldier. Look here, it says "*soldier*," not "*foreman*," certainly not "*pensioner*," but "*soldier*"!

When he received the invitational ticket, the old man spent a lot of time going around the apartment with it. He showed it to his wife and Dusya Semenov, and then went out in the courtyard and showed it to someone else. And he even called Anna at work, and solemnly announced that he would take both grandsons, Timofei and Daniil, to the square with him. However, his daughter said that the long-term forecast promised cold weather and some precipitation, and that both boys were coughing, so they'd better stay home. Aw, what are you talking about! Typical female nonsense! As if it weren't absolutely clear that going to sit on the tribune with grandpa-the-frontliner was a hundred times better for any boy than some mustard plaster or nostrum! Pyotr Vasilievich wheezed, dug a pile of two-kopek pieces out of his pocket, and started calling all his friends. He wished them happy returns of the forthcoming holiday, asked about their health and whether he'd see them on Victory Day, and at the end, just by the way, informed them that whether he likes it or not he's going to have to go up on the tribune on May Day. The Veterans' Council requires his presence. They brought a ticket to the house. So whether he's well or ill—that's no one's business—Comrade Tyutin: Be so kind as to appear at 10:00 to review the workers' parade.

On the day of the holiday, the rain poured down from early morning on. Malicious, fat-faced clouds crept across the sky like the armies of the Entente on some old poster, and there was a sharp pain in Pyotr Vasilievich's chest that was so strong that he took nitroglycerine behind his wife's back.

Marya Sidorovna looked at her husband anxiously several times, but she didn't dare tell him to stay home. And she was right—why annoy the old man uselessly?

Tyutin got over to Palace Square quickly, and in good order. The rain had let up a little just then, and late-comers were running down the streets, which rang with loudspeakers. Many, of course, had already had enough. It was really bad—pouring since early morning. Who could blame them? What a day! Back in the court-yard Pyotr Vasilievich had run into Anatoly. He was wearing a leather cap pushed back on his head, an unbuttoned nylon jacket, and a white shirt with the collar wide open.

"Happy holiday, Pyotr Vasilievich!" roared Anatoly, and Tyutin got a whiff of raw vodka.

"You too," Pyotr Vasilievich answered reservedly. He didn't like Anatoly.

"You going to demonstrate?" He wouldn't give up. "Me too. I'm carrying the banner to Palace Square. At the shop they promised us two days off for carrying it."

"You should be ashamed, Anatoly!" Tyutin just couldn't contain himself. "What cynic thought that one up? I'm going to write a letter to the Regional Committee... And you're a fine one! It's an honor to carry the factory banner!"

"Don't kid a guy on his day off, Pops! An honor! That's a word from pre-modern times. You just take it with you into well-earned retirement. Give us money."

Tyutin wasn't about to stand there talking with a fool. He walked away. But the louse had just about ruined his mood, and his heart had started stinging again. How simple everything is for them, the devil only knows! A fellow like that will drag the cross around the church on Easter for you for a silver ruble.

51

He balks at nothing, just so you pay him. Completely unscrupulous. That's how that generation is—they never saw misfortune. To hell with him, the scum, there's a lot more good people around.

Anyway, it's nice to stand on the tribune among honored people, practically right next to the city leaders, and salute—hand to hat!—the wet, but still happy, rumbling columns passing by. The demonstration was still just entering the square.

"Glory to Soviet women!"

"H-u-r-r-a-h!"

That's for sure—glory!—how much our sweet broads have borne on their shoulders, and still bear! And here they come—well-dressed, pretty, as if it weren't they who ran the machines, drove the trucks, worked in the fields. No women in the whole world are as pretty as ours. I know, I've been around Europe, saw a bit in my time. None!

"Glory to Soviet science!"

"We're first in space, and now we'll give 'em Sayano-Shushenskaya..."[1]

"H-u-r-r-a-h!" the square roared.

Something seemed to get tight in Pyotr Vasilievich's chest, as if there weren't room for his heart. It squeezed against his ribs, pressed against his throat. He took out the nitroglycerine, but his hands wouldn't obey him. He already felt that he should leave, leave as quickly as possible. All he needed was to crash down in a faint, and they'd say, "They invited all those old buggers up on the tribune, and they can't even stand up any more." ... And his eyes grew dim... The atmospheric pressure must have dropped. For people with high blood pressure, that's the end. Hurrying, trying not to think about the dull pain in his chest, not think about it and not be afraid, Tyutin got down from the tribune and walked toward the exit, toward Khalturin Street.

However, the pain in his chest did not subside. It was different, not the same as usual, but unfamiliar and threatening. It grew. But now he wasn't scared. There was Marsovo Polye already. He'll get over to Liteiny[2] somehow, and then he can catch a bus or stop a car or something.[3] Just so he gets home, home as soon as possible. It's getting dark. Is it going to rain again? The air is like wet cotton wool—you breathe and breathe and it doesn't help.

The pain was huge and red. And the whole city streamed down.

***

They were partying already on Marsovo Polye. The masses, battered and ejected from the square, had been thrown up here, everywhere—on the benches, on the paths, on the lawns—pieces of a crowd dispersed. A red calico banner was spread out, right on the damp earth, on the grass that was just coming up. Along the white sign reading *PEACE AND SOCIALISM ARE ONE*, there was a battery of beer bottles, two half-liters, and a pile of *pirozhki*[4] and cheese sandwiches.

"Happy holiday, old man!"

"Lots of luck!"

The paper cups were raised and knocked together.

"Hurrah, boys! Bottoms up."

"Hey, look! That old guy just keeled over. There, on the bench. He's lying there like a corpse. How'd he manage to get drunk that fast?"

"Years of practice."

"Practice—and years of it!"

"Well, Valera, come on! You're the specialist... He's not moving. Did he feel that bad all of a sudden?"

"Uh-huh. Just wait a minute. He'll be okay."

"Let's go have a look..."

"Go on, go on, Galochka, jog on over. Man's his brother's keeper, his comrade."

"Mister! Mister!... He unbuttoned his coat like it's summer. And all those medals and decorations... Citizen! Hey!... Kolka! Kolka! Valerka! Boys! Here, call an ambulance! Valerka! Look how he's breathing... Give me scarf, put it under his head..."

III

Finally, she came running over—the old, muddle-headed lady doctor. She was out of breath herself. It wouldn't be a bad idea for her to take a Validol right now...

"Some, ambulance! Just disgraceful! We called forty minutes ago. A healthy person could die in the meantime! Free medical!... Over here, over here, on that bench... At first we thought he'd been drinking... Faster, doctor! The way he was breathing, wheezing almost! But now..."

She was quite out of breath. She ran over to the bench, bent down, gingerly took the heavy, limp hand... Well, it was all very clear, very clear. But the young people were standing there, waiting. She unbuttoned the new grey jacket, the shirt... "Help me, young man. Open the bag. There's a stethoscope in it..." But what good was that stethoscope now? A little earlier... Just half an hour, maybe fifteen minutes... just fifteen minutes or so, and...

"Doctor, why are you just standing there?! Give him a shot! Let me run and get one of those heart-attack units."

***

The sky over Marsovo Polye was now a quite deep blue, piercingly bright. From the bushes, through the bare branches, a pink-cheeked face painted on plywood watched, gloomy and offended. Straight hair parted on the side, a dark shirt, a star on his chest.

And Pyotr Vasilievich had a star on his chest too—the Order of the Red Star, which he had pinned on, on account of the holiday.

Looking out from the bushes where someone had thrown it was the portrait, nailed to a stick. Looking up into the festively blue sky were the fixed eyes of Veteran Tyutin. They no longer saw how, far off in the cosmic heights, the irridescent bubbles of children's balloons flew above the city and burst.

IV

Natalia Ivanovna Kopeikina didn't go to the demonstration. At seven in the morning, the alarm went off. It buzzed happily for some time, then ran down. It was pouring outside, the wet loudspeakers were screaming, and she thought that on a holiday a person should be happy, and that being happy is when you do as you please. She looked guiltily at the alarm sitting there, pursed her lips, then turned toward the wall, snuggled down, and put her head under the covers.

Because everyone else had to get up and wander around in the rain, and she was just lying there in her warm bed like a queen, Natalia Ivanovna felt quite cosy. She fell asleep to the march music, which carried in through the window.

At half-past ten, she opened her eyes and thought how nice and clean everything was. She'd polished the floor yesterday. The dishes gleamed in the sideboard. And there was that *pirog*. And a whole day ahead of her which she could spend as she pleased. Then she remembered that the day before yesterday there'd been a letter from her son. He was fine and had a job as a mechanic. Maybe he'll turn out to be a decent person after all? It's true that Lyudmilla had dropped by very seldom lately. What if she's fallen for another Oleg again?

In no hurry, Natalia Ivanovna had some tea and *pirog*, dressed and went out for a walk, because, as far as she could remember at least, she had never just walked down the street with no errand, as an adult. She had walked in the garden with her little son, but when he grew up, it was only to buy something, to return something, to go to the doctor, to a parents' meeting, or to work, home, to work, home... True, this winter, Lyudmilla had dragged her to all kinds of places. She couldn't complain. To museums, to the Musical Comedy Theater, and to Pushkin, to the Lyceum. But those were really all activities for her cultural betterment—that is, more concerns: come, see what you're supposed to see, learn as much as you're supposed to learn, and leave. No. Today she would go off by herself, wherever she wanted.

"Happy holiday, Marya Sidorovna! Health and long life! Pyotr Vasilievich too."

"Thank you, Natashenka, the same to you. Pyotr Vasilievich has gone off to the tribune to wave his arm around. I didn't hear on the radio—is the demonstration over?"

"Not yet. It's still early."

***

The whole city's probably out on the street today, walking arm in arm, in threes, or even fives... Why is it that a person is

55

happy only when he can do what he wants, and he can do what he wants only when he's alone?... There are still a lot of single women in this country, and you can spot them instantly. A family woman walks along and doesn't look around, but those three over there, all healthy girls, look at all the men. Their smiles look unreal, their faces, unmarried... Funny women, latched on to each other like the three bogatyrs in that painting.[1] The fattest one is Ilya Muromets... No. Anyway, you absolutely have to walk by yourself sometimes...

Past the old women selling windfalls, past the slightly sauced invalid with a bunch of flaccid balloons, Natalia Ivanovna went up to a hawker's stand and bought herself a chocolate bar with brown filling for thirty-three kopeks. She hadn't eaten chocolate for a long time, so why did she just up and buy herself that chocolate bar all of a sudden?... There were more and more people out on the street. The demonstration was probably over already... And over there, a red-brown dog was being photographed with a small flag between its teeth. It stood still, as if it understood— head to one side, tail up. The guy with the camera was just a little boy... with no hat... He'll catch cold, and his mother will be in a tizzy, take time off work. Some little girls were standing nearby and laughing. The flag was all dirty, flapping in a puddle. Those are our young people for you—what an idea! We would never have dared to... We were painfully quiet, submissive, not like these... God, what was that? A scream. A really awful one. As if someone were being murdered.

There was a crowd by the entrance to the grocery. A harsh, hoarse, desperate woman's scream rushed about and beat against the walls, against the people.

"What are they doing?"

"They're drunk."

"Call the police! They're never around when something..."

"They went for the police."

With sweaty foreheads lowered, shoulders hunched, they advanced. Slowly, like in the movies. Natalia Ivanovna, of course, pushed through to the first row. In their hands they held—you won't believe it!—banners. They held them horizontally, like rifles. The sharp brass ferrules gleamed in the sun like No. 86 pen tips for school children—but now they don't write with those any- more, now it's fountain pens...

"Stop it, boys! Stop it!"

Natalia Ivanovna just latched on to one of the combatants' sleeves and pulled him away.

"Stop it! Do you hear me? Stop it! Are you mad?"

"Get back... b-bitch... bitch... I'll kill you! Get away!"

"Heavens! Tolka! You drunken beast!"

"Bitch!"

Natalia Ivanovna would have fallen hard on the asphalt, but she was driven into the crowd, and they caught her.

"Ah, you clod! Well, just wait!"

"What are you doing, lady? Are you crazy?! He'll stab you and not bat an eye!"

"When two dogs are fighting, don't make it three!"

What an idiot, and in glasses yet! Grabs on to my sleeve and won't let me go.

"Let go! What business is it of yours? Let go, I tell you! What are you picking on me for, four-eyes? Why me!?"

"Lady, have you been drinking, or what?"

"What are you getting in on this for?! You're the one who's drunk, you damned fool! Let go, you scum, or I'll let you have it in the goggles!"

But Anatoly and the other fellow, the shorter one, as if on some signal, cursed and threw their spears, aiming straight at each other.

And again some woman in the crowd screamed, squealed in fright.

Two ferrules like pen tips. Two shafts. Two pairs of hands, gone white from strain. Where are the police?!

And suddenly a waltz poured down from the silver loudspeaker over the heads of the crowd, like a summery, sunny, scattered shower. It rang in the street, muffling the screams. And the combatants moved closer and closer, their faces darker, their eyes narrower...

"Lady, cut out the hooligan routine! You want to get bumped off too?"

"Let go, idiot!!!"

"You've really cracked up! Hey, watch your hands!"

"Did she break your glasses?! Where are the *druzhinniks?* There's a drunk woman here starting fights!"

Natalia Ivanovna broke away and, holding her arms out in

front of her with fingers spread wide, pressed through the crowd, blindly, stepping on people's feet—to get away. Just to get out of there, to get home as soon as possible... home! Behind her there was music, a piano... And—a howl! That was no woman screaming. Faster, faster, stepping on paper flowers, on the dead shells of broken balloons... Faster... Just so she's farther from that crowd, from that place, where now, most likely, the rough stone wall is streaming with thick, red blood.

V

Evening. Warm, festive lights were lit over well-set tables, over white tablecloths. Light in all the windows. Happy holiday!
"Happy holiday!"
"Have a happy holiday!"
"Happy holiday!"

***

"Ah, some grandpa we've got! A real hooligan! We're all sitting here waiting for him—his daughter, his grandsons Timofei and Daniil. And him? He's gone off to his buddy Samoshkin's, no doubt. Probably met him on the tribune. Well, when he gets home..."
"It's all right, Mama, he'll come. Don't bother the old guy. Let the veteran have a good time."

***

Strings of multicolored lights burn bright, illuminating the contours of the warships.
"A battle ship. That big one over there's a battle ship. See it, Slavik?"
"What do you mean, Papa? That's no battle ship, it's a rocket launcher. They don't build battle ships like that anymore."
"Fine, the egg's teaching the chicken... Did you hear that, Dusya?"
Well, it's only natural! What kids we've got! They know more than we do!

"Lelik, what are you sitting there for like you've been struck dumb? 'His shoulders hunched, his legs like lead, he seems to be asleep while on his feet.' No backbone. Why don't you go somewhere? See your friends. You're still a young man, and you're moping around the television on a holiday. Show some courage, my boy! I raised you alone, endured all kinds of hardships, but I never lost heart. Not like you. Show me that you're strong..."

"All right, Mama, I'll show you. Want me to lift you up in your chair?"

"Always a gag! Just go over to the window and see how beautiful it is."

***

And she was right. It was beautiful. A crimson glow from the lights blazed above the city, spilled across the bright spring sky.

A salvo roared, rockets burst over Nevsky.

"Oh, how splendid! I never paid any attention to it before. Sasha, I don't know, we'd go crazy someplace else. There's no other city like this!"

"All lyricism, Firochka. A salvo is a rather barbaric spectacle, especially in combination with a crowd of drunken primates. I assure you, the carnival of Venice is not a bit worse."

"I know... but still, when you know that you'll never..."

"Hurrah!!!" they cry from the embankment.

"Now they're yelling hurrah, and tomorrow they'll be ordered to yell 'Kill the Yids!' And they'll all, to a man..."

"Sasha, you're right! You're always right, and I'm a stupid, sentimental fool."

"You know, it's not too late. You can go back to your patriot Lelik, to his mama and his Zhiguli..."

"Don't Sasha. Let's just sit down. There's a bench over there. How dark it is here! The lamps are in red shrouds of some sort."

"Shrouds—that's it exactly. And really, Marsovo Polye is a cemetery, if you think about it."

59

"Oy!"

"What are you oy-ing about? It's just a portrait. One of the members of the laboring class was too lazy to carry it and threw it away."

Another volley. Rockets. And—another volley.

***

"Hur-r-a-a-h!" rushed above the buildings.

"Hur-r-a-a-h!" Jiggers, wine glasses, tumblers, pewter mugs struck and clinked against each other.

A holiday. It's nice when there's a holiday. The people have fun. Thank the Lord. Hurrah.

EPILOGUE

What awaits us wherever we end up, when all of our business is at an end? No one has ever given a definitive answer to this eternal question. Pyotr Vasilievich Tyutin could now, in his capacity as eye-witness, but he is silent. He's probably silent because he knows something the living aren't supposed to know ahead of time. And he's silent, most likely, to put the impatient in their place—dead people's faces are always so arrogant, enigmatically aloof.

Alien and stern, Pyotr Vasilievich lies with hands folded on his chest. He is dressed in his old blue suit. As it happened, the grey one was all covered with paint from the bench.

Wreathes of spruce branches smell of New Year's. Bouquets of lilies-of-the-valley smell of spring, and of damp, shady ravines. The funeral bus moves through the rainy noonday. Drops flow down the steamed-up windows. The mourners, relatives and close neighbors, sit silent.

The front-liners went in another bus, a regular one. And they did the right thing—they are all old men. For each of them the funeral of a friend is a rehearsal. Let them ride separately, and talk of irrelevant matters. Let them. They have some time yet...

Marya Sidorovna was silent in the front seat shuddering to the bumps in the road. Her daughter, with her face so swollen from crying that you couldn't recognize her, had her arm around her mother's shoulder. Along the aisle, sitting up uncomfortably straight were Rosa Lvovna, Lazar Moiseevich, Semenov—he was the one who helped with the funeral arrangements, a wonderful guy!—Dusya, and Natalia Ivanovna. Antonina wasn't there. She hadn't been herself since the day they took Anatoly away. She understood nothing, listened to no one, ran around who knows where for days at a time. They say that she found him some special lawyer. Rosa Lvovna tried to talk her out of it. "Gangsters like that should be—excuse me, Tonya—shot on sight. He crippled a man, could have killed him."

A lot of good it did! She got all kinds of food together, and went off to the Tombs.[1] But prisoners under investigation aren't allowed packages, so she came dragging them back in tears. And the same thing the next day. She lost weight. Her eyes were so sunken she looked like she had two shiners, and her stomach was already sticking out—she was in her fifth month. What are women like that thinking about?! She was going to have another child. Again, the father wasn't around, and she was over forty herself. She should have been thinking about Valerka— a sickly little boy, weak as a potato sprout—and here she's pining away over that gangster! You see, she was expecting his son!

As for Polina, she couldn't care less. "That's how a parasite should be handled," she says. "He'll be convicted, and I'll get a divorce and have the fucker kicked the hell out on his ass!" She's always drunk. She and Anatoly make a real pair.

They had a long way to go—out Sadovaya and Stachek Square to the "Red" Cemetery[2] where, with great difficulty— his high-ranking war buddies had gone to a lot of trouble—they had managed to get permission to bury Pyotr Tyutin. Now they were going to lay him to rest in the grave that his father had occupied these forty years and more. This is called "conserving dying-space," but by the time you wring all the necessary papers out of them, your feet are shot.

Marya Sidorovna didn't cry. She was cried out. This morning her daughter had already given her some tablet that numbed her insides, made her hands disobey her and the thoughts in her head seem not her own. The widow Tyutina was trying to remember something and just couldn't. Something important, urgent— some duty, she thought.

Houses, trams flashed past through the rain. Other people were riding in those trams, and most likely many were unhappy— What the devil do I have to drag around in weather like this for?! They don't know how lucky they are that the day hasn't come when they have to ride in a bus just like this—going to a funeral for...

The ghost of some idea wouldn't leave Marya Sidorovna alone. It tormented her. They had gone a third of the way and she still couldn't remember what it was. Here's the Haymarket, the bus station where she and Pyotr left for Volosovo[3] last summer... And there's the metro, but it was a church once... the Church of the Assumption of the Holy Virgin... And suddenly her eyes swam, things turned dull, dirty-green, black.

Where is she? It's so peaceful, quiet. I don't want to wake up, don't touch me. What are they waking me for? Why are they shaking my shoulder?

Marya Sidorovna didn't want to come back. She'd rather stay there—in the peace and darkness, where there was no funeral bus, no heavy smell of wilted lilies-of-the-valley, no coffin; where it wasn't him lying there, not him. Yesterday she had screamed, called his name, begged him every way she knew—but he didn't answer.

She had to come back. They made her. They poured some sort of medicine down her throat. Her daughter cried and said something about the grandchildren. Natalia Ivanovna was rubbing her hands. And those three, the kids from Marsovo Polye, look how frightened they are, quite pale. Kolya, Valera, and the girl—what was her name?—Galya... As soon as they found out the address they came running over, and then stood on the stairs until ten o'clock. They were afraid to come in.

The bus stopped at a traffic light.

And then the green fog completely dispersed, her memory grew clear, and Marya Sidorovna said, loud and sternly, "We've got to sing. Those were his orders. He wanted a song over his grave."

"Mommy, calm down. Mommy, don't..." her daughter started wailing and creeping up on her with some phial.

"Shut up!" Marya Sidorovna shoved her hand aside. "I haven't gone crazy yet. I'm telling you, those were his orders. We've got to obey them. He'll never ask for anything again. He said he wanted a song, an army song because he was a soldier."

"Mommy," her daughter tried again, "what do you mean, sing at a funeral?!"

"Absurd!" Dusya Semenova was horrified.

"And when a living person dies—isn't that absurd?!!" yelled Marya Sidorovna.

"All right," Semenov decided, "why argue when the deceased himself gave the instructions? What do we sing?"

"An army song," Marya Sidorovna insisted.

Everyone was silent. Rosa Lvovna looked out the window as if what was going on didn't concern her. And anyway, she didn't know any suitable songs. Lazar was little during the war and never saw active service, so he didn't know any either.

Natalia Ivanovna looked at the widow and wiped away her tears —an old woman, what an idea... Dusya just shook her head, shrugged her shoulders and leaned back in her seat.

"How about 'Zemlyanka'?" Semenov timidly suggested, but his wife looked at him angrily, and he fell silent. He fell silent and looked guiltily at Marya Sidorovna—first guiltily and then frightened, because she had gone pale again. Her eyes were huge, and her lips trembled.

And then Kolya, the little fellow who'd been first to come into the apartment and tell what had happened to Pyotr Vasilievich, suddenly said, "Marya Sidorovna, don't worry, when we were in the Pioneers... Just a minute... Valerka!"

> *If I could only have a word from those I love,*
> *I'd learn each line they sent me,*
> *And when two winters and two summers all have passed,*
> *I'll serve my time and see them.*
>
> *And when two winters have passed,*
> *And when two springs are gone,*
> *I'll serve my time and see them.*

Oh, if it were true! Even if it weren't two, but five, or even ten winters—just so he came back alive! I don't care if he's wounded, or an invalid, or a criminal! I don't care if he's old and feeble, just—alive!

You understand that, don't you, Rosa Lvovna? And you too, Natalia Ivanovna, because your son is far away now. Who knows how he's doing out there. And you don't care about anything. You don't care if he's a bad son, an egoist. You don't care if he's crude. You don't even care if he's a hooligan and a loafer. Just so he comes back, just so he comes back!

Well, what about you? What are you biting your lips for, Lazar Moiseevich? You didn't even know your own father, so is it worth getting upset over her, the stupid thing, when she stopped loving you, when she wouldn't even bother to bear you a son? No, it's not. Sure, she's stupid. She stopped loving you and traded you in for riff-raff, for a career man, for an unprincipled shit. She lost her reason. She doesn't see that Petukhov has no need of her, just a visa to Israel, and that if he stayed here in that executive position of his, he wouldn't even deign to spit on a Jewess like her. She's a crazy fool, but... let her come back!

Let them all come back, all those whom we lost through our own fault, through thoughtlessness, blindness, cowardice, or indifference, those whom we did not wish to understand in time, whom we were not able to protect or forgive, whom we could not hold back. Now they're already caught, whirling, sucked down into the black whirlpool of the past.

How many such black holes are there on the path that each one of us follows? They're not overgrown with grass, or strewn with sand, or covered with snow. They do not heal, or become scars. But then, old-age isn't far away. Long winters pass faster and faster. Short springs flash by. The long sleepless nights come more and more often. Soon it will be too late.

Let them all come back. We're waiting. We haven't forgotten them and never could. Let them come back!

Anna was crying, howling at the top of her voice. Dusya crossed herself quickly and furtively, looking warily at her husband. And Semenov—he's wonderful!—he remembered the refrain on the way and had already caught up the melody. He has a loud voice, and he always sang well—on the stage or in the ranks. And Natalia Ivanovna sang out fine and clear, in harmony.

The widow Marya Sidorovna Tyutina sat frozen, dry-eyed. No, it can't be that everything should end like this—with this coffin and the rain outside the windows. After all, they weren't singing for that cold, deaf corpse, foreign and silently hostile. He can't hear them. And Pyotr Vasilievich Tyutin would surely hear.

Marya Sidorovna didn't cry. Now she knew for certain— Pyotr wasn't in that awful box.

They went through Haymarket Square.

How much more time did she have to live? Maybe a year yet, maybe two... When two winters have passed... That's nothing. She'll wait, she'll be patient. They waited longer than that during the war. That's nothing... But for now, everything's right. That's how he wanted it. Those were his orders. She's done everything. Carried them through.

... And when two springs are gone...

August-November 1977

NOTES

Chapter One, Section I

1. The Soviet shopper stands in three different lines for each purchase: in a given department to make his selection, at the cashier's for a receipt marked with the amount of the purchase and the department number, and at the department again to have the merchandise weighed and wrapped.

Section II

1. *Week* and *Crocodile* magazines. Weekly publications dealing with current events and political satire, respectively.

2. Soviet pay phones are for local calls (long-distance calls are placed from telephone/telegraph offices) and take only dime-sized two-kopek pieces, which are in chronically short supply.

Section III

1. An eight-year Soviet primary-school program is followed by one of three tracks, of which the normal secondary-school education (ending at tenth grade, eleventh in the Baltic republics) is the most prestigious.

2. Candidate's degree. In the USSR, the first graduate degree. Requirements include a short thesis published in an academic journal.

3. The average wage for a factory worker or young professional is about 150 rubles a month; however, Andrei's "pull" (*blat*) is likely to be more important than his comparatively large income in acquiring an apartment, a car, good books, Western medicines or even meat and vegetables.

4. Tipanov Street is in one of the desolate new high-rise apartment complexes on the outskirts of Leningrad, inhabited, the author implies, by the nouveau riche. The name of the street is as undistinguished as the buildings in the region—no one seems to know who Tipanov was.

Section IV

1. Anatoly is in search of the elusive *propiska,* the official authorization required for residence in the privileged cities of Leningrad and Moscow. Without such permission, staying in these and several other urban areas for more than three consecutive days is illegal. A *propiska* may be inherited or married into, and there have been cases of provincials paying several thousand rubles to Muscovites and Leningraders willing to agree to a marriage of convenience. Living space, measured in square meters, is allocated according to the number of persons in a family unit, and is limited by law. It too is a tradable commodity.

2. Lyuban. A town south-west of Leningrad on the railway line to Moscow.

Section VI

1. Soviet citizens over 16 years of age are required to have permanent passports for identification and travel within the USSR. For purposes of ethnic classification, Jews are regarded as a nationality, rather than as a religious group.

Section VII

1. High party officials like Petukhov are entitled to shop at special stores, closed to the general public, where scarce and imported goods are sold at prices well below cost. The privileged classes receive part of their salary in chits good only at these stores and marked in ruble denominations representing the state's limited supply of foreign

currency (*valyuta*). The chits sell for about eight times their face value on the black market. Leningrad's "special" food store is just south of Peace Square, site of the Barsukov Triangle.

Section VIII

1. Communal apartments, still common even in Moscow and Leningrad, consist of three or four rooms, each housing one family unit, and a common kitchen, bathroom, and toilet. Neighbors normally post a duty schedule indicating who is responsible for cleaning during a given week.

2. Four privileged classes from the narrator's point of view. In Soviet bureaucratese, a "responsible worker" is anyone in an administrative or executive position. Georgians, and other Soviet southerners, fly to Leningrad and Moscow with suitcases full of fresh fruits and vegetables from private plots to sell in the market. The prices cover plane fare, expenses, and still net the dealers a tidy profit. Jews are the only Soviet "nationality" allowed to emigrate.

3. Because it so often involves pilfering materials or tools, personal use of factory time, side-stepping regulations, or payment in kind (again, pilfered goods or extraordinary services), taking work on the side is regarded as a suspect, if not illegal, activity.

4. Although book prices in the Soviet Union are subsidized, the editions of literary classics, art books, and even basic reference tools (dictionaries, atlases, grammars) never quite meet the demand, boosting prices in the used book stores and on the black market. One reason given for small editions is the chronic paper shortage; so many hard-to-get items are available only for coupons from scrap-paper collections. Desperate Soviet literary students have been known to purchase sets of the complete works of Brezhnev (always readily available) and turn them in for the much more desirable coupons.

5. Used car prices in the Soviet Union are much higher than those for new cars. The buyer pays for the covenience of circumventing a bureaucratic application process and a two- to three-year wait. A good deal on a used car will often include the previous owner's collection of spare parts, another category of "deficit items" in the Soviet market place.

6. The English School, on Vasilievsky Island, is one of several specialized primary schools for gifted children in Leningrad. Approximately one-third of the instruction is in English.

7. A department store in an elegant nineteenth-century arcade running from Nevsky Prospekt to Rakov Street off Arts Square.

8. There was a major currency reform in 1958, the new ruble equalling ten old rubles.

Section IX

1. Barsukov would presumably be interested in eau de cologne for its alcoholic content.

Section X

1. The village of Tsarskoe Selo was renamed for Alexander Pushkin in 1937. It is the site of Rastrelli's enormous Catherine Palace, pleasure gardens, and the Lyceum for the Sons of the Nobility where Pushkin and other early nineteenth-century poets were once students.

Section XI

1. The Tauride gardens surround a palace (built in 1783) presented to Potemkin, the Hero of Tauris, after the conquest of the Crimea. From 1906 the building was used

for the Imperial Duma. The characters in *The Barsukov Triangle* live in a building opposite the gardens.

2. The anniversary of the October Revolution, November 7.

Chapter Two, Section I

1. The Haymarket, with its narrow streets, blind alleys, girls, drunks, poverty, and filth, was one of Dostoevsky's favorite Petersburg haunts. Disappearances were common there even in the nineteenth century. The name of the square was changed in an effort to alter the character of the neighborhood.

2. The Church of the Assumption was built during the years from 1753-65, and demolished in the late 1930s as part of a modernization campaign.

3. Despite socialized medicine, a Soviet family can be financially ruined by a serious illness. Costs may include black-market prices for Western medicines (even penicillin, common anaesthetics, and silver for tooth fillings are regularly unavailable), unofficial payments for access to specialists who work only in hospitals for the elite, tips to nurses and other hospital staff for basic services, and high prices for scarce meat, fresh fruits and vegetables to supplement the inadequate hospital diet.

Soviet cities are comparatively safe by American standards, but there are several areas of Leningrad that one is wise to avoid at night. The official press recognizes a persistent problem with "hooliganism," but individual crimes are not reported in the newspapers as being unrepresentative of Soviet reality. There are no statistics available.

Amnestied victims of Stalinist purges had the inconvenient habit of returning to face their accusers, many of whom had built their careers on the ideological deviations of others.

4. The final lines from Pushkin's lyric "Brozhu li ia po ulitse shumnoi" ("As down the noisy streets I wander") (1829).

5. Lazar's name is obviously Jewish to Russian ears. To alleviate any problems this could cause, he has been using the more Russian name Oleg, apparently since childhood. The diminutive forms of Oleg—Lyolik, Lyalik—are phonetically reminiscent of Lazar.

Section II

1. Trips abroad—even on business, even to Eastern Europe—are a special privilege. The prospective Soviet tourist must pass an examination in political philosophy and prove that he has traveled extensively within the Soviet Union before being granted a visa abroad, an ordeal from which Petukhov's high position exempted him. Spouses and children do not normally accompany the Soviet traveller abroad.

2. A gallant Russian will carry his girlfriend's handbag, and even the flowers he buys her in the course of the evening.

3. Bars are not a Russian tradition. Drink is sold in restaurants, at buffets in clubs and concert halls, in beerhalls and specialized jigger shops (*ryumochnye*) selling vodka, and at beerstands on the street. Leningrad bars are in hotels for foreign tourists, and accept only hard currency. They offer the best domestic and imported liquors, multi-lingual bartenders, suspiciously savvy prostitutes, and bizarre mixed drinks.

4. Varna. An important resort center on the Bulgarian Black Sea coast.

5. Moscow Nights (*Podmoskovnye vechera*). A Soviet hit from the 1950s popularized in the West by such exuberantly Russian singers as Yulya, Liudmilla Zykina and Ivan Rebroff. The song's sentimental nationalism ensures enduring popularity among Russian tourists abroad, or even in the republics, once they get drunk enough to be homesick.

6. Sever ("The North"). A popular restaurant on Nevsky Prospekt featuring rock bands and elaborate ice-cream desserts.

7. When a Russian waiter goes on vacation, his tables go on vacation too.

Section III

1. The smart Soviet shopper develops a network of acquaintances to learn when and where scarce goods might go on sale, since stores do not advertise. Shipments of virtually anything unusual are invariably sold out the first day, and the lines can be enormous and slow moving, so early arrival is advisable. Soviets carry at all times expandable string shopping bags (appropriately called *avoski,* from *avos',* 'perhaps') on the off chance that they may run across a promising-looking line. Etiquette and common sense require that you get a place in line first and find out what is for sale later. Semiprofessional line-standers will keep your place for a small fee while you run other errands.

Section IV

1. The usual word for trainees in the skilled trades, *uchenniki,* was dropped, in official pronouncements at least, for the more ideologically correct *smena* 'successors'.

Section V

1. The reference is to Nikolai Nekrasov's *Komu na Rusi zhit' khorosho?* (Who Lives Well in Russia?) (1870-74), dealing with the adventures of seven peasants who travel across the country trying to find out who lives in happiness, peace, and prosperity.

2. The trains, buses, and metro in Leningrad normally stop at 1 a.m., but run all night on major holidays.

Section VI

1. A Russian woman with a good figure is termed *polnaya*—'full', 'complete'. The adjective 'thin' (*khudoi*) is derived from the comparative form of 'bad', and currently has connotations of strange Western diets, ill health, or simply not enough food.

2. Soviet radio and television stations play the national anthem at 1 a.m. for sign-off.

3. Low-skilled jobs like Antonina's may offer better access to material comforts than professional positions do. As a clerk in the produce department of a comparatively well-stocked central Leningrad grocery, Antonina can set aside fresh vegetables for her acquaintances, trading the favor for concert tickets, records, admission to a popular restaurant, or the unusual dress she bought for this occasion.

4. Eastern European goods meant for export bear labels stating the country of origin in English, but printed in an adaptation of the Cyrillic alphabet.

5. The Russian Museum, housed in the Mikhailovskii Palace (1819-25) on Arts Square, contains the largest collection of Russian art after the Tretyakov Gallery in Moscow. Anatoly was apparently interested in the neo-classical collection, which includes a large number of nude sculptures.

6. Chaika. A restaurant on the Griboedov Canal off Nevsky Prospekt.

7. Cheaper, but more dangerous than either medicinal alcohol or eau de cologne, kerosene is the desperate man's drink.

Section VII

1. Admissions to Soviet universities try to reflect the ethnic geographic balance of the republics in which they are located. Today, a modest affirmative action program gives preference to students from working-class and peasant backgrounds and those who have served in the military. Both policies tend to work to the disadvantage of Russian Jews, who are classified as a distinct nationality within the RSFSR, are concentrated in large urban areas, and tend to be from professional or intellectual families. Since

entrance exams to the various institutes and university departments are given simultaneously, Lazar may have applied to a technical college where he was sure to be admitted, rather than wait another year to retake the exam for the literary faculty.

2. Large numbers of Soviet POW's were imprisoned upon their return to the USSR, under suspicion of being Nazi collaborators. The island of Sakhalin on the Pacific coast has had prison colonies since the mid-nineteenth century.

3. Soviet factories, institutions and governmental bodies honor outstanding employees by placing their portraits in courtyards, squares, and parks.

4. The Yusuppov Garden runs from Sadovaya to the Fontanka Canal, just west of Peace Square.

5. The implication is that Lazar would not be granted a visa abroad unless he left a wife or child behind.

6. Since distribution of consumer goods is centralized, the selection is much greater in large cities. It is not unusual for Soviets from remote areas to book tours to Leningrad or Moscow solely for the purpose of going shopping for food and clothes.

7. Pensions are at best an income supplement. Older citizens are often forced to find low-paying jobs as janitors, watchment, or cafeteria workers after mandatory retirement.

Section VIII

1. Acronyms for the current Soviet show-case construction projects. Such sites attract idealistic Komsomol volunteers.

2. The Soviet grading system runs from five (A) to one (E).   ·

3. Joseph Stalin.

4. Leon Trotsky.

5. Traditionally, Russian Easter cakes (*kulichi*) are brought to the church to be blessed on Easter morning before breaking the Lenten fast.

Chapter Three, Section I

1. The Field of Mars, where the great military parades were held during the nineteenth and early twentieth centuries.

2. Kirov (formerly Trinity) Bridge, completed in 1903, leads from the foot of Marsovo Polye across the Neva to the Petersburg side.

Section II

1. Sayano-Shushenskaya Hydroelectric Station, the largest in the USSR, was built during the years from 1975-78, on the Enisei River in the Krasnoyarsk region of southern Siberia.

2. Liteiny Prospekt is the major thoroughfare of the old Liteiny quarter, on the far side of which is the house on the Tauride Gardens where Pyotr Vasilevich lives.

3. Owners of private cars will often stop to pick up paying passengers.

4. *Pirozhok,* a pastry filled with meat.

Section IV

1. V. M. Vaznetsov's well-known painting of three heroes from the Russian folk epos, in the Tretyakov Galleries, Moscow.

Epilogue

1. *Kresty* 'crosses' is the nickname for the X-shaped prison (1892) on the Vyborg side, almost within sight of the Tauride Gardens.

2. The characters are driving southwest to the very end of Prospekt Stachek, to an old cemetery on the edge of town. The graveyard is surrounded by a red brick wall,

whence its name, recently made official.

3. Volosovo, town southwest of Leningrad in the Izhorsk Highlands.

Vladimir Maramzin

The Two-Toned Blond:
A Reciprocal Tale

"The soul is poisoned through the ear..."
St. Francis of Sales

My dear friends,

Thanks to you I received this August of a temporary ray of light which in all probability will soon be obscured again by circumstances. I don't know whether people in general ever do for each other what you have done for me, each in his own way, but if they do, then that means that He exists, and that obliges me to write a very joyous tale—but I can't do that now, it's turning out to be painful, bitter, even evil. Forgive me this.—

V.M.

I

THE DISINTEGRATION OF RUSSIAN CONSCIOUSNESS
(BY WAY OF AN INTRODUCTION)

This unfortunate's notes found their way to me almost by accident. If a woman wants to come back, she'll use everything: she arrives at the moment you least expected her; takes advantage of your embarrassment; wrapping an arm around your neck and burying her aging nose in that area between your underarm and neck where you once upon a time wore a long-sleeved waistcoat to weep into, she tries to galvanize, in the region above your stomach, your sufferings which she once inspired so skillfully; she's ready to run, stumbling and slipping, after your streetcar... in a word, she brought them to me and left them, hard as I tried to return that folder. With a pitiful effort at irony she handed him over to me, just as she had once tried to hand me over to him—now that's something I never engaged in, in spite of my imperfect morality.

Yes, you'll understand perfectly: the person he calls "the great man" is me. I won't pretend to be exceptionally modest, I know my value as an artist, but—a great man? Hardly. Only in his head could I grow to such proportions. Possibly the reason here is the similarity of professions, for he stubbornly considered himself an artist, too, and even gave to my wife's poor relatives some imitative pieces of cardboard, his share of the contribution to their ugly new life. Good Lord! The necessity of touching up a few things from time to time forces the authorities to spoon-feed a herd of decorators—note that the word isn't mine, he himself calls himself, in the style characteristic of those people, "a decorator of my beloved country." Designing ice-cream wrappers which any person, scarcely having looked at them, dispatches into the toilet; producing a poster, mounting a theater production, where as a poet said, our socialist virtue triumphs against a back-

75

ground of contemporary furniture—these are their concerns, and also of many others like them, the enumeration of which requires the accumulation of much more irony that there is in my whole system (I'm afraid the influence of style—their style— is much stronger than one might think). Irony, by the way, is also their invention. Stealing our by-products (there's no other way for them), they are forced to produce irony directed at us, and there's even a point to that: in certain respects this wall-, street-, fence-art is a much spicier dish than canvas painting. An artist makes things that are as natural as nature itself. If, let's say, my beloved Duccio* had not been born into the world, Nature (or whatever its name is) would have had to place that very same brush into another hand, but it's impossible to imagine humanity's not having seen a picture by Duccio at all, just as it's impossible to imagine its not having seen, for example, Mount Ararat, a variegated Russian forest with mushrooms and berries, a cumulus cloud, or golden sandy beach dotted with youthful, deftly undressed female sunbathers. A decorator skims nature, and it doesn't matter to him that tomorrow it will fade and shrivel —because, on the other hand, today it stinks and entices. That's just what leads them to consider themselves artists; well, to hell with them, my usual thoughts are distracting me.

Knowing that my painting was close to literature and had always been nourished by it, she wanted to interest me in the notes, deftly mocking—to my advantage—the person with whom she had lived the last five years. (It's not at all out of desire to pass over a sore spot in my soul that I don't name him: I have never been able to remember those simple last names—the Ivanovs, Antonovs, Smiths, Shapiros—they aren't even names, they're a sign of the absence of inborn grace; in addition, he has a namesake in town, who, though inconspicuous, is an absolutely real artist, and confusion might arise.) At that time I wasn't even about to look at them, but later, when this business was absolutely finished (by death), he sent me a strange telegram, and with it the full text of his notes. It turns out that I had only the first chapters, but that's understandable, after all, at that time the subject matter had not yet been exhausted, it was still flourishing.

*The author probably has in mind Duccio di Buoninsegna (ca. 1250-90), the founder of the Sienna school of painting. *V. M.*

Later I read them nevertheless (the title was astonishing), and I was overcome by acute pity for the author. No, he's not right in regard to the woman, he didn't break my heart, the heart of a "skirtchaser of a passing erotic muse" (a quotation from him —but the quotation is essentially accurate), I myself parted from her and was almost happy for the circumstances that fixed her up with someone and relieved me of care (for me this meant, in addition to everything else, the opportunity to stop working— that was so much better, so much energy was freed for painting). I won't conceal it—there was a time when I poured forth non-figurative tears—what could I do, I was used to it!—after all, I had once loved as few in life have been fortunate enough to love. The only thing that I couldn't understand at that time and that seemed really offensive was the strangeness of the betrayal! Never before could I have imagined myself replaced by that creature with a light blue suit and dull, no-longer young hair that covered his ears—an infallible sign of their well-known order, soldered together with "hind feeling" (as he puts it). But that's nothing, there's something worse: just think—my wife married a party member! It really is true, how little we know them while keeping them... She is nervous and sickly, concerned only about herself, ceaselessly playing Lolita ("such a Lolita," as she admitted herself)—it's unlikely that that's successful at age thirty-six... A certain role was played by disagreements "during the tender bed" (again a quotation, but really, it's well put!)— that is, during those mutually complicated actions which St. Francis of Sales considered "a duty which may be declined only by mutual consent"—beautiful is the vocabulary of saints, not to mention the meaning! True, now I unfortunately know why she used to avoid them so stubbornly and unilaterally: rare is the woman who can withstand a double assault for a year (all the more so longer)... but in general I admit honestly that that's the only thing I could forgive her entirely, and after all, I am sinful myself... it's easy to rip us apart and throw us away, but you can't forget us... that's a song, just a song... farewell, my darling, we shan't see each other again... and she was very talent-ed, but cut off since childhood from all principles... but now, when she's not here, I don't feel anything for her except infin-ite tenderness.

And the novel about Dolly Haze really appeared in our

story most inappropriately—well, what would it have cost the great American Russian to write it a dozen years later! For novels never teach anyone anything, but on the other hand, they impart to analogies a revolting conjecture: it's as if we live following an already prepared rough sketch, whose outlines, moreover, we constantly slip off, as if we were acquiring an elementary education: the result is a mass of messy inkspots and drips, not a single human figure... No, that's absolutely right: our story is just a caricature of the Lolito-Humbertian drama. Even the murder of a theater person plays a role here—and it's also reduced to a couple of blows on the head that cast our hero into a state of constant fear, true, as a result of which he turned so gray in a single year that he ceased to be announced by his name, the blond (I maintain the name nonetheless). The only serious difference is in the child; I loved the child most of all, I really suffered for it—but what could I do at that time? and later? and what can I do now? perhaps I won't even decline his insane proposal: what aren't we ready to do, all for the sake of what we so grandly call art... Everything else was more than humorous. After all it got to the point that in an insane telegram he offered to buy me off with two thousand (I think I even remember the text: "Leave off decrepit art comma departure of beloved woman of support comma partly to blame but let's shake hands of good wishes..."). I ought to have been offended, yeah? Shove the money order in his ugly mug? Be amazed, shrug your shoulders, but with the help of the post office I tidily turned this vile piece of paper into hefty red ten-ruble bills, while regretting only one thing: why only two? not four? five? seven? Yes, I took those rubles that are not really very large from a person who is well compensated by the state, and that gave me the opportunity to paint two pictures that crossed the border with great difficulty and now hang at the Guggenheim; the pictures, I must say, are among my best.

A few comments for those who live on the other side of the curtain—that is, in the auditorium of our iron world theater, as was remarked by a certain not incapable writer,* in whom I especially appreciate his biting humor, though I like it little in others: he has a new system of humor, and the latter is an in-

*I have to admit that the expression is mine. *V. M.*

strument of cognition, where the cognizing subject is included into a cognizable whole, while in the majority of people humor serves only to allow the author to place himself above a problem. But even this writer, in the last analysis, is trash, and he only treats minor details, and he's buried up to his knees in our joint experiments (what's more, they say he's started drinking like crazy), and in general, only painting can explain this world... but if I ever took it upon myself to publish this sad story, he's just the one I'd ask, no one else, to bring it into line with the requirements of contemporary journalism.

So here it is, the promised commentary. This strange, twisted language, this decomposition of consciousness, please note, is in principle that of one of the intelligentsia, but a consciousness that is no longer capable of being governed with the aid of logic, that stubbornly returns to two or three themes, to two or three thoughts, on which he stands amazingly firm: what is this? The delirium of a sick head? Subtlety of style? Do people nowadays really talk like that?... It goes without saying that this is a literary work—not in the sense of its being intended for our thick journals, but in the sense of its giving expression to what transpires inside this person (ivanov? antonov? grechko?—I constantly forget and all these names constantly seem to belong to him simultaneously). From this point of view, we have here simplicity, even utmost bareness. We, with our grammatical phrases, express ourselves much more poorly. In view of the insanity of the contents of that head, one can't help admiring the brevity, the arriving at the essence in three words or so, and sometimes fewer: "a grave epitaph"—really, isn't it clear? is it really necessary to expand this—an epitaph copied by me (indeed, here you can clearly hear personal participation) from an old grave? His unconscious slips are almost always full of content: for instance, "two-toned"[1] —that femasculine gender that flashed by awkwardly, like a skirt hem that flashed by near a Party big wig's dacha, where a casual female guest is not allowed in, she'd be trampled, and therefore it gives away the owner's life style, to whom she gets through by stealth, some rural schoolteacher from a suburban school—that feminine gender in the title (he doesn't even hide it later) gives away a certain duality of character, or more accurately, a non-monosemanticity, that is, I think, clear (after all, it's not the color, but the gender that's two-toned). But what are certain aphorisms worth? "Man—that sounds bitter..."[2] Why, if I didn't know him so well, I would presume here an outstanding wit, which so profoundly and concisely replaced the Gorkian "proud" (presumptuous and blasphemous), at the same time instantly reflecting the very history of the question. And note: he is absolutely serious, even tragic, he tries to the utmost to disclose himself—but after all he doesn't laugh, doesn't grimace, doesn't clown for us, and although at times it seems funny to us, behind this laughter gapes the desolation and abomination of the panicky terror familiar to every fellow countryman, the fear of perishing unambiguously to the sounds of "the non-stop holiday happy childhood"—oh, how distinctly audible it is, always and to everyone, our hero too, "that best state terror, full of the horror of our epoch" (a quotation).

Let's look at the other side—love, artistic creation? On the "allowable" side, as he says. These pitiable, greedy points of contact with alien manhood that he admits to! This compulsive, forbidden searching... Don't be in a hurry to turn away: it's a phenomenon. His Baltic contacts, much freer than in our northern capital,—after all, they didn't confirm him once and for all. He wasn't looking for the simple bread of sexual pleasure, even if it was somewhat daring... He doesn't need the European province that prides itself on its closeness to Sanskrit[3] (and which adapted itself to the regime as easily as if to a minor inconvenience in the kitchen), it didn't free him from the anguish of fatherlessness, he's looking for real support, that certain *alter* that wanders around in search of an *ego* in order to unite in the Latin formula, attempting thereby to maintain itself near culture. Note yet another point: by trying to substitute the authorities for a father, he remains all the more dissatisfied. He understands the sterility of a management which can pet, but is incapable of impregnating (what on earth is going on? I'm slipping into the blond's vocabulary). No, he needs members of the intelligentsia (forgive the word), this fatherless country needs them in general, ugly as the forms its mutilating attraction to them may take. The disintegration of consciousness,* yes, but this is the

*I cannot agree with the author. After reading the blond's notes, it isn't the disintegration of consciousness you see, but on the contrary, a very tenacious consciousness, one adapted for survival, although undoubtedly a tragic one. Yes, if only these problems were resolved on the mental level (as is said more and more often). Unfortunately, it's especially on the mental level that they aren't resolved. *V. M.*

disintegration of Russian consciousness, this Russian fatherlessness which concocts fathers out of any rogues, hoping to lean on ideas and thus keep from falling down. It is the disintegration of language,* yes, but it is a disintegration and a new collage, of this language, Russian, one that knocks against things in the dark— you don't care for "a pimple on the thigh of love?" So what do you think, maybe in the newspapers, in the personnel departments, in the propaganda bureaus, in vile stories with thieving cashiers and filthy butchers, or in correctional institutions which have been bred everywhere, maybe there you hear every moment a great and powerful language? Alas! as he would say and I'll say too. All around us editorial censorship, governmental power, conformist consciousness, and the declassé and drunken hinterlands make a monumental effort to deprive language of life, to deprive it of content, to turn the enormous labor of any article, speech, or conversation into a never-ending loss of power, into pure form deprived of any meaning whatsoever. I have never read newspapers—but I find it impossible to read them! Only by juggling in your head the everyday newspaper porridge and subtracting one thing from another can you bump up against crumbs of meaning, and that process is called "you have to know how to read a newspaper." An absolutely superfluous skill! Wouldn't it be simpler to use language? No, viewed against this background the blond is an abnormal phenomenon, but nonetheless a living one. And one needn't play the hypocrite: it's hardly likely that he's any worse than all of us. As a certain Anglo-saxon, a singer of plantations, expressed himself in a similar regard: the stench from him is no more pungent in the Lord's nostrils than that from other mortals (I think that's how it goes). And that pathetic, insistent Freud, with whom the notes are permeated, who is so typical for today's proletariat of mental labor

---

*Nor do I see the disintegration of language in the blond. To a member of the intelligentsia the language of the village, thieves' language, the language of the urban masses, and that of specialists in general often seems a deformity, although one not deprived of charm. I will remind the reader just of two ways of using language. One, strictly semantic and rational, when only the meaning of words is important. The other —when words are needed only for tuning the soul of the person that one's speaking with, and after that the communication proceeds beyond language, from heart to heart. Such is the folk use of language in Russia. It is said that the prophets used it that way. V. M.

who have heard about him only in the retelling—he's really much more interesting in the hands of our blond, because he got to him all by himself! thought him up himself, completely on his own (decorators don't read books): and this is no longer Freud, but he, himself, our hero, this is his study, the study of his name (oh Hell! once again, a name would be nice, but really, I'm afraid of being mistaken—Petrov? Sidorov? Amfiteatrov? the Petrov married to Ivanova—that reeks of science fiction, but in the future I see only that, nothing else; but no, in our case there were only initial vowels, that I remember well, and my poor wife with just as simple a last name as his, hers of course I haven't forgotten, you haven't caught me—and in his name there are only those unfortunate screaming vowels of initials which give you nothing to grab onto, which join together convulsively, seizing hold of whatever they can, but they don't know how to hold out next to hard consonants, and attracting a couple more burping, ahing, unctuous ones—the wicked irony of the case!—finally form something unbearable, something unstable on this earth, something that turns into a despairing cry—OAEEEE... EEEEEOA... EEOEEO... OEEAEE... a cry that is essentially horrible, but absolutely donkey-like)—

Nikolay the Painter (let it be like that)

II

THE TWO-TONED BLOND
(THE NOTES OF THE BLOND HIMSELF)

1. In His Own Way

Working since childhood as the favorite son of an actor father, I was the blond of patriotism, never without deviations, attained some gray colour with age: don't stand out against a background of population of industries.* My name and surname match the grayness, don't want to reproduce them on the page—ivanov all around. Coarseness is a secondary sign of a sexual male, alas, I couldn't envy, my feelings being too tender. If I were a worker-domino, then I easily went stale, like the second heel at the work of my production: in our calling of master of the brush what on earth can you achieve! Only the ecstasy of observation nearby. At school I went around shaved bald for three years and another nine months of childhood, it didn't help. Tenderness for coarse members of the same-aged sex lodged in me forever: they beat your head with something big but even soft, it turned out to be a fist. From childhood on I never took for girls, they wink come and get it in various directions, instead

---

*There is no self-denigration here: an undisinguished outward appearance was always considered good tone. This self-restrained tradition is being continued in our own time. It's enough to read through a police announcement somewhere in Upper Volochok: "Sought—a middle-aged man, gray suit, white shirt, when under the influence his neck turns red." The mistake of the author of the notes lies elsewhere. He places too great hopes on the tender color of his person (without knowing that even without that sympathy for him is guaranteed). Meanwhile, Grigorovich wrote over a hundred years ago: "It is said that the faces of blond people are always softer and more pleasant than those of brunettes; I do not agree with that; one meets fair faces too, on which coarse human qualities seem to have concentrated their residence" ("A Winter Evening"). *V. M.*

83

of "no" they say "maybe," it's absurd, a crooked knee in a skirt short, the hem of length is no better: suspects slovenly filth. No, no, never! Even a dream of childhood: athlete of sports of scarlet T-shirt of honor, the bottom half of the sport uniform sometimes not put on. Sell your home, sell the last pants of the shamelessness of poverty, sell your mother's daily bread, but never, even in extremity, sell your native land—that's my slogan of the up-bringing of life... My actor father, almost one foot in the grave, also trained us, the young inheritance, for the labor of incon-spicuousness; labor turned the ape into Soviet man, including the decorator of the beloved country. Even the great man, more about him later, doesn't deny—of course, in his own way...

2. The Postal Muse

I, beginning my biography, my actor father suddenly died, real grief. To seek a replacement, temporary urgency, I can't go on without a father, a feeling has developed, I sniff a paternal smell wherever he appeared—public bath, street car, public cafe, although you can't imagine each one, another one eats so fast, I wouldn't go reconnoitering with him on a single skillet, and he doesn't chomp: untimely, nice reminiscence of my lost parent. Where can you find real coarseness today? With father's death an example of fatherland was lost, and that's the boy's second birth.

I left the brushes, already sunken in diluted paint, travelled especially rush hour. Seek—and they'll give it to you, said a philosopher of ancient Greekhood. On the bus I immediately made my way to the back, there crowded together substitute men of excitement I inhaled a strong odor of rotgut, downed with onion, that's what they call wine of the rise of vodka, which is now too expensive for three representatives. A female passenger is afraid to the exit, makes her way higher, shielding herself a half-purse, not for anything can you safeguard not only the gentle secondary ones, but the faraway primary ones can get it from underneath two pairs of underwear, and you can't tell: the masculine virtue of strength surrounds, labor hasn't calmed half of it, a metal worker of a factory by a scientific system, having smoked up the toilet all day, and you'll never force him:

the basic advantage of victorious fate. Lenin was a formidable man, turned the wheel of history back in a single (taken separately) country—labor from now on isn't necessary, other than the power of leadership, likewise of most representatives of the arts: a full hall of incredibly fat-assed meetings in the course of the day.

Where I omit articles and prepositions, please forgive, note that I'm long since used to sending a telegram, to whom and why, I'll tell with the development of consequences, there our brevity will be paid for by the postal muse.

3. Stupidity

Why do I so seek to an indispensable father?

Not everyone can understand, only the delicate looks of the blond by way of illustration of mine. I want to lean on forever, somebody tell me responsibly: what am I to do with myself in this world of possibilities? Oh, it's so hard to start a sheet of paper, take for instance artist: it's terrifying to step on an empty pasteboard box, such an innocent space of the first dot, then you can't erase, in a white space, is contained the genius of any masterpiece, I'm afraid of being in the way on his path: which side should I start? Where should I draw my line to? The old ones listened to God, he spoke to them, then instead of God—reality, now—alases all around! God has been abolished, there's no reality, everybody drags stuff to himself, all that's left is man, and what's he? Amateur activity! Man—that sounds bitter, women were the first to lie down before the party.

Once at work called up by the personnel department,[4] fat and jolly, of excessive power. At first, of course, not very pleasant, then I looked around: the room stern, the man himself, in any eye a stick and carrot of coercion. He asked in detail what I read in bed, I told him, had to invent as fast as possible: everybody likes outgoing interest. He even asked who gave it to me, promised just between us, obviously strong love of interesting reading matter. I wanted to talk with him about the goal of life and death, but he refused, doesn't trust anybody. For today he explained what's forbidden in our joyous life, and what's allowable—we'll leave for a second visit. At the second, true, he couldn't explain either, and here's what he thought: on the side of "the forbidden" an iron room always helps us, a big Russian thanks for it, without "the forbidden" one couldn't create a popular masterpiece with a brush hair; but where the other side is, there's the rub! He doesn't know, the "allowable" side is omitted to look for yourself personally...

I won't tell anyone these thoughts of course, so as not to destroy the foundations, but I can't search, I necessary the help of an example, that is the lost personality of father, even if only an actor of minimal service, but not complete stupidity.

4. Passing Thoughts of the Mind

Beginning from and ending up to, everyone says: actions!... I'm a person who is careful and now beaten up as a preliminary. I know that actions make the visibility of life, but what do they decide? The soul flows out a drop at a time into an action, how much can you strain off of it? If you're going to act, stop, feel down under your shirt for your heart, that's my rule: check whether it's there, but it will turn out not to be. Perhaps only under communism will leakage be stopped up collectively, then you can act as you wish, from the belly. But that's a far-off dawn, communism the common future papa, and under communism even the very last Jew will become a Russian.

On the holiday of the revolution a preliminary snow has fallen, the streetcar screeches, doesn't want to wrap up in the rails, a gray light, dispensed from the sky, the wind falls from the roof, swept along the pavement, and again mounts up the wall opposite, hanging flags wait out the last section of the burning out day: a red flag and digressing it, a blue one. The first years only red, that is of the blood of dangerous workers, now having added blue, the livening up of its appearance, well and of course the departure of initiality, to both tastes: both the people on top can, for now, and the lower ranks like it, that is, they want to live the old-fashioned way again. Why don't I see a landscape, who said? Here, if you please, is the inclusion of a landscape into the fundamental passing thoughts of the mind.

5. Incident

I won't tell the detail—a long searches after a lost father...
the public streetcar doesn't work, lightly touching the flexion
of a posterior muscle, my arm is covered with goosebumps of
happiness, alas, not for long: a stop and they move exclusively
further on, not everyone likes it for some reason. Once I held
a half hour, got a response of closeness, and know what? Turned
out to be a woman with her head shaved, a dump-truck driver,
which still doesn't give her the right to become a full-fleged man,
all by herself, had to accompany her home and she didn't let go
until morning: a lover of big hickey kisses of mine.

In the morning I came out and noticed a picture: every dog
of a cheerful breed had a faithful, reliable master, the exception
being I.

Much attracted by the already-described man of the department a fierce last name of meaning— Lysovol,[5] that name is
widespread everywhere that we former Russians have to command and direct, expecially the police, the expert behind the
wall,[6] sergeant and sergeant major, and also the national super-
vision of police searches. I noticed that everyone is drawn to his
own bosses, but we can be misunderstood, and one thing is
quite certain: men of the personnel departments are unsuitable
for this—But why! Running ahead! Again attracting attention!
In the downtown of a street of the city! Scarcely having caught
sight from a distance! Attacked! With his fists out front! Instead
a sharp wallop between the eyes! No pity for the poor personality's personal looks, including sunglasses of the new fashion!
But a student of a personal course of my decoration might come
by! What kind of authority will I have! Toppled! He should have
pity on his biography too! Shouldn't stand out from his co-
citizens! The police might take *him*! No ifs or ands! The great
man of the art world of the epoch! Knocking me off my feet,
that's even nice! Take note, bread-winner of his own personal
daughter! So you don't understand now, I'll explain later! If
they take both of them, where will the family be left?!... One
thing I'm sure of, getting up off the ground: artists don't knock
each other's eyes out, we live on the tree of culture, such a tree
as hasn't yet been described, in the former incident.

6. A Grave Epitaph

I never entered into the distant inflammation of the mind, I live on real asphalt, I don't let myself be torn away, the exception only perhaps thoughts about the cosmos: The Cosmos is now written with a capital letters, it's the highest sphere of authorities, the party bows to it, I'm just a member. All the same I realized I'd leave my city of welcome for a time; it spread out over all four banks of the Neva, where my childhood and creative work began: nearby are the countries of the Baltic Coasts, it's almost an entrance-hall Europe, where views on the hind feeling are quite different.

In general I can't understand: why has it been forbidden? People of different nationalities, in ancient grecian Rome, lived with each other in their caracallas by it and it alone, it was a rule not to refuse any citizen, and whoever refused—to him forever the charity of the stables, woman served only for appearances of a classical beauty. Now there's the progress of further feeling, big demand for happiness— and right away the barbarous law of the denial of manhood.* If they're afraid of disease, I'll answer: and is the female organism immune? and your everyday street glass? That's even much worse. If you're afraid of the wolf, don't go sticking your nose into the human forest at all, it always smells too dangerous.

The Baltic met affectionately, and that's understandable: a specialist of its profession. Right away one turned up, although not of the local breed, a Jew of the Ukrainian persuasion by the last name of Brut, took me under his documentation and that night drew me close to the common body. Alas! My question consists two unequal little halves, and which is more difficult,

---

*As early as this point I noticed that the blond's main topic is the correlation of the masculine and feminine in the world. This is not such an easy topic. It is well known that humanity in general is something feminine in regard to the Universal. One need only recall the Scriptures: the Church as a community of believers is Christ's bride. At the same time we distinguish a masculine and a feminine principle within humanity, and not just biologically. We link the feminine, perhaps, most often with mercy; the masculine with the courage to be, to resist non-being. The boundaries of these qualities do not coincide with the biological boundaries of gender. After all, why does he, our blond, take upon himself this difficult role, why does he attempt to realize in himself the feminine—isn't it because it is lacking? But then he has all the more reason to demand from others the fulfillment of the masculine. Alas, he doesn't find it, everything has become neuter, the poles have decayed, polarization is not prized. *V. M.*

I can't say: you want to obtain the great personality of life's direction, you have to begin the stale bread of mastering sex. But what can you do? After all, this isn't a feminine pasture of good fortune, where each one goes around with a ready answer, even a modest bookkeeper of warehouses of electricity, not counting actresses, lie down right in view of the hallway, true, it's the top story of a communication commutator, choose whichever one it's not repulsive to love, but you mustn't make a mistake if the place is already taken, but even then the help of a ring is offered. No! Our thing is more complicated, responsible selection, we're not held back by a pimple on the thigh of love, but on the other hand we need a real engineer of the humanity of souls.[7]

All these years no one has placed his trust that I trusted, you won't find even the trace of a great personality in our country, they say everyone has left for the relativity of physics, but I'll never understand it there: the language of higher formula! With the poor arithmetic of personally me. Then I sacrificed myself for a long time, making up my mind a woman of manhood, with a loud voice of substitution, but then I didn't reach it. I searched unsuccessfully to the border of the republics, thought I'd search until death itself, and then even shuddered.

I can't understand it at all: why are death necessary? An unpleasant word! A simple Soviet man, by the name of fifty years, can't live without it of course, the continuation of the product is in short supply, we're something else, a separate representative of an outstanding power. In the future, I'm certain death will be done away with entirely, why then does one need to study science? The enlightenment of the masses? Agriculture, the mail? The newly-presented corpse, not having had time to give up the ghost, will be taken away unharvested by an enterprise of organs, returned in form of fine aromatic powder of fertilizing flowerbeds: having vanquished life with a life.*[8]

---

*In connection with some matter or other I was rummaging through regional newspapers and read in *The Voronezh Commune,* 16 January 1921, under the heading "The Burning of Corpses": "Petrograd, 12 January. The crematorium set up for the burning of corpses is functioning efficiently. By 10 January 109 corpses had been burned, in accordance with the wish expressed before death." One senses the state's great concern: each planned corpse is to be surveyed about its wishes for after death. One can't say that our blond is inarticulate. *V. M.*

Yesterday I buried our former wife, more about that later, a sad meditation of feeling is left: a grave epitaph!

7. Eating

Sent it! The ruble owed! Equal, of course, to two thousand new ones! Which he was getting ready to propose, couldn't make up mind, as an alcoholic avoiding you! They deserved completely the arts acquired by happiness! If he weren't ashamed could have sent it even earlier! Now some legal basis! Depriving favorite wife of support! Joint whirlwinds are hovering over us! I never appreciate! The decorator is paid by the native land! We're not sorry! A ruble belongs to the person drawn from behind his back! We can only use for mutual help, I'll wait two weeks, after the deadline I've made, then let's shake hands of good wishes, the mutual wife has left, taking the remainder, I shouldn't refuse, not having means for the continuation of eating—

8. Will Not Be Recognized by Anyone

He stands approximately and looks at me by the store, his white forehead is dry, in spite of standing in the very sun; the feeling of a razor grew blunt on his face approximately long ago, the periphery of his hair is approximately an underfur of grayness; in his eye the absence of any sexual reponse, as if he approximately of the holy virgin of beauty; a nice face, crossing a suit from abroad, approximately dirty; it's clear that he'll never be a respectable old man, his eternally right hand holds a book pile, and by name Volodya the Lacerated, though himself a servant of the study approximately of the muses—thus began my happiness, but you'll understand incorrectly.

I'll never meet him in the course of life, he's simply a trumpeter of ascending fate, which is exiled the Russian land to abroadness, like a flea exists in the everyday groin. He was selling three hundred rubles a book underarm, I took it immediately, I'm forever not sorry: a viviparous genius! Bone and conscience of the epoch! Even a name of intellect—Nikolay the Painter, not like mine... With that book begins the aim of my life, published, of course, somewhere over there, it never could here, though the author lives inside the borders, where he paints pictures that exceed the frames as well, and that's the meaning of a really great man: it will do! And if I try, be arrested forever, might perish in basements of a palace of pioneer and student, where upstairs is the unrelenting holiday happy childhood, a scream of your blood will not be recognized by anyone.

9. Our Difficulty of Life

The sun was shining, birds of unknown breed were singing, the city near the Baltic strolled along its prospect, reaching the conservatory, then back, cafes and parks were open, like the legs of a girl, baring to passerby her shy crotch, alas, men are strongly forbidden that by society, and it's too bad, I'd like to see such a picture of a walk, the only thing that's left is the Russian bathhouse of togetherness, just a dirty gang,[9] the best people don't go, where to observe them? And in the course of such remarkable weather of spring I stood, leafing through the sudden book of pictures!

My bast soul became calm: youths of all generations of the country can stroll in their widened pants of contemportaneity, throwing each other mutual peaceable glances of art: I'll give wide publicity this book, by means of the adaptation of attached frames. A genius can't do that, that's our problem, we're a buffer between the frame and the freedom of danger. We'll insert a little bit any poster of remote lanes, the pillar of a big road, each incident of a nice old house, a candy wrapper—a completely cultured person, who participates to the hilt the everydayness of movies and the newspaper, also eats higher foodstuffs of price, will get out case of a masterpiece again a whole view, that's even nicer: a hint of intelligence! The artistry of guessing!

Thus we'll replace the need of illegality, afterwards can do away genius entirely—as excess of style of our difficulty of life.*

*Told in Soviet terms, this story does not cease being serious. After all, don't we know about the harmfulness of genius, about its duality? Naive Russian thinkers believed that they would resolve this question of genius among themselves, amicably: the harmfulness of one thing, wrote Kireevsky, is counterbalanced by the appearance of another, antipodal thing. The blond gives a simpler, more pragmatic solution for the problem. And the main thing is that then one need not strangle genius in the cradle. V. M.

10. Thought of the Last Time

I taught myself manual talent a whole year, although an egoist of my small health, but I literally would forget, feeding the breast by chance: only one old roll of a store. I again became like one washed again in living water in this book, where my tension of the brush was tempered, peeling off like metal, a dull surface ideological hue: a tint of oxide in the direction of my former soul, an impossible luxury! And so from morning to evening of sundown I was wholly a do-getter, the brush painted itself in my exhausted hand, I repeated each picture of the fifth time, and considered as if I myself had made it up in my infant childhood. I don't want to delude the frank goal: it's only my life I've already painted in its entirety, poorly. I urgently need to steal a new one somewhere, even a loan, thus to achieve the moment when the recognition of you of the world will come to pass, if only modestly our distributor the populace, in the neighborhood.

I'll describe the detailedness of these pictures, for the time being I won't, because my talent—in part, alas!—has been closed for the week on account of illness after a certain particularly successful blow to the ear of the thought of the last time.

11. Colorflower of Fantasy

Yesterday I had a terrible dream of abnormality, on awakening I told it to my new girlfriend of the bed, she couldn't explain what such a thing meant, she was frightened for the future substinence of our united fate, but I think she needn't, it's not a hint, just a female exile of the everydayness of life. I watch dreams in form of words printed by a type machine, probably I'm used telegraph tape, why never a color picture? I could translate onto canvas early in the morning, before I forget it, sell that evening to bossdom by name of Venikov, give my father-in-law of culture, even that's denied me, and why? Maybe I'm really to blame, punish me even worse! But never take away the last dreams from an unfaithful soul, that's too much... I'm looking to exchange this dream with a fiction writer of print, if he sees without use: in exchange is needed the most colored flower of fantasy.

DREAM

just as it was dreamed, I never dream of punctuation
with marks, I also dream a bad
mistake of grammar

A   long time I couldn't leave the house I know perfectly
well to town where I lived a long time the republics released
me to town too long but notalone with me was first aid taken
fromamuseum of our times I cried when I see everything had
changed it was painful to walk around the town inwhich I had
lived a time went by and I the living deceased was a corpse that
was selected for them and like a live doll the doctors called it
achemistry experiment an antediluvian rabbit taken simply in
order for samples of chem powders to test the solution I was
amazed how everything changed but onthesecond day I was
taken away to a little town from one city section with a movie
house was slapped together hastily slapdash took me a long time
to assimilate the atmosphere although it was the year 3221 the
meter showed 1970 everythingelse was inorder was crea... (the
dream didn't finish the word) such an atmosphere the smell
as in our time I willnot describe my ordeal I was put onaplane
of that time but that one was taken out of mass production I
asked no four of them from the 21st century were left as a memento ofthose distant times in twenty minutes Iwas in a city
where all the atmosphere was created and up to the end of 1999
we bombed Moscow news city of ancient invention I asked whether this cost a lot the sets* he smiled andanswered taken from a
museum everything we were seeing was only made to divert the
husbands attention lets reveal to his memory of me two years
of truth one abortion of my reason I don't think disease but
he wasnt used to should have done it inthat atmosphere in their
time that didnt happen well she can getmarried even in our time
no she herself wouldnt want a wedding and license... (here it
broke off completely, without an end)

*It is obvious how life and fantasy turned inside out intertwine even in his dreams.
I think that at this point the name of the play *We Bombed in New Haven,* which was
playing the theaters in those years, flashed through his mind. I wonder whether he didn't
have occasion to paint something in it. *V. M.*

12. Record

Listen everybody—betrayed wife, daughter dropping ears, even the local director of introduction because of: I'll never get to there is a well-known subject, an international film of poisoning "Mozart and Solaris," no! His continuous good health is dearer to me than the beer hall of contemporaneity—I'm a one-time only lover of my record...

13. Wants To

So, a small man of nudity has been painted, but he lives not on a cloud, his head the shape a light hatchet inclines downwards, so, under the left a toppled technicolor woman, lying permanently stuck of objection and under the title "Group Portrait with Mama"—true, there's no mama close by, but her presence exhudes going out far beyond from under the frame, and so here's what I think: a little Soviet man, like that dwarf in the joke chasing the girl, runs the surface of the Russian land exclaiming: "Oh-oh! is it really all mine? Is it really all mine?"— but not doing with the girl what she needs. That's the first thing.

The second: a certain Kirghiz girl of central asia of the east, but I'll skip, I think, ready passionate a destructive kiss, but not a name. I call myself personally everywhere, with him it's relatively worse, contrawise you have to fail to understand, yes, not a single average ploughman of the people: never reflected the variegatedness of an oak, the suffering of a birch, or other trees of weepiness other. But of course! Who can comprehend the wealth of an external idea, that elephantine tower of art: to identify the adequacy of the reaction with the immanency of texture... I read in an article of gratitude, I'll forget never that smart, that dark little author of a wife: after all I moved back to the second capital of a residence permit only with help! One artificial critic from the elevation of his height... without him I'd still be rotting in the café of semi-Europe, not further.

And finally, that sweet masterpiece of the preacher of paint: "Poor Mona Liza"[10] (again the name is mine, but everyone likes it too much)—no, I immediatley telephoned across three-hundred lakes, the urgency of an immediate link of ecstasy, but the phone was incessantly busy, merry buzzes of catching-up along... So, a picture of ruin the statue of the husband of the knout and sling, the branching of muscles, a large target in the lower part of the body (I'd definitely put in the target, but it doesn't matter that it's not there), in the face add a sour look of disintegration, forward-looking fingers of widened hands, it's always more interesting like that: the comic god Academ! Many critics consider that the content is intelligent, it answers the latest arrangement of reality, as it should be, in light of the latest development of dead matter, but a secondary alas! The wrong colors, a lower color than needed, a slight presence of light shades, and that's all—it'll immediately enter the ranks perfectly: a thrice millionaire of the soviet union! It's not yet enough to be soviet by birth, you have to prove it forever, though not everyone wants to.

14. Possessor of a Man's Reject

I'm happy to live at the same time such artists as especially Kochergin! A master of fantasy, bast birch bark all around the trenches, not to mention our great man, the canvas painter of the epoch, about which I'll never tire repeating every day of the all-national tribune ATS and UA. And note especially, there shows through them, rising instead of the usual east to the left of the west, a remarkable sun, a first-class Salvatore, having hundred rubles new, it's possible to go right up to your death and not create: he's created a whole mess for you, you need only to select from his personal book. True, I have another one, selecting from there, just finished up describing for all the future, I attach a picture.*

---

*I've kept the pictures, but—it's strange!—though the person doing them thought he was copying N. P., in fact the pictures have nothing in common with that master. Before me are several well-known subjects of our art, carefully, crudely transferred to paper: "Cobblestone—The Weapon of the Proletariat," "Walkers with Lenin," "The Morning of Our Native Land," "A Letter from the Front," "Hands off Korea," "Let's Forge Swords into Plowshares," and so forth. True, in certain personages some little doors are open, you can see through them the anatomical equipment of the celebrated heroic organisms. I don't know whether that can be considered a creative contribution. Until I clear up that question I can't make up my mind to publish them.—V. M.

I came back my native Leningrad, soon achieved an unexpected meeting, birthday someone (Venikov, I think), our
canvas painter came late with his taste, I'd despaired of waiting.
Sat down near him, asked two painful questions of testing: how
should one work on one's own creative works? And is there a
god? Smiled as to a school age of an idea, I listened with an
acute wide-awake ear, the first question he still answered somehow: when you feel inner tension going, under the burning frontal
bone, then you can begin boldly—you won't paint anything
forcibly bad. From there on he expressed himself coarsely, it's
not seemly for such a talent, memorized figuratively: "suddenly
you notice that it's as if someone were rubbing your snout along
the white primer of the canvas." I don't have any tension other
then the tension of the wind on my face, a storm of the pressure of external weather, the evening autumn, and nothing is
aflame in my forehead, even my eye is lusterless toward the end,
nobody rubs my face along a poster, all myself! Everything
and always exclusively me... but after all, I also do personal
art, if you please. Hence the conclusion: he told me an incomplete
truth, probably not wishing my competition, that happens with
talent, answer declined.

I proposed we look over together a public book of Salvatore,
where there's in abundance everything that we artists of the
contemporary wall and immortal fabric need, but he again declined: he's afraid from the power of imitation of the brush.
Of course, he said his delight about his book too, there weren't
words, nothing but ellipses, he modestly passed over an answer
in silence, just tensed his wisdom vein on his forehead and somehow became stronger with his whole face, but not long. Then
the final attempt: I put the hand of good wishes on his knee,
alas, the knee collapsed specially, as if the weight of my regard,
almost fell to brilliant feet... I'll always remember.

Then the left hand, under my observation from below,
danced!... The foot strikes the parquet!... He smiles, rolling
the young teeth of his organism!... Musical ecstacy!... Inspiration
of the body!... Throw out the fingers!... Feminine presence
already moved aside... Don't need it! In his beard glistens a gypsy
grin, mixed in a drop of some tribe, I'll figure it out later... All
right! But later on showed himself a skirt chaser, embraced corridor unwilling guests, even the recurrent freshness of the hostess,

I wouldn't for anything, saw accidentally on the way to the kitchen... Then, they say, he was a master of sexual advance and attack, wasn't used to observing delicacies, still the abolished streetcar conductor was right in saying: the more they're in a hat, the more brazen they are...now, alas, of completion! He's weakened under my circumstance: can't satisfy more than three full-weight women coarsely and visually in the course of a day.

And at just the last moment I noticed that the personal spouse of his very own was looking interest at my direction, the modest blond!... Of course, a short woman of stature, without a waist of a figure, let's call her a girl, it's all the same to me— I'm now the unfortunate possessor of a man's reject!...

15. The Same Place

Now, when our common wife of art... I love to caress her scar of an upper lip, formed through the participation of him himself, by means of the falling of a hotel lamp the passionate moment of completion. I put the eye of this poor generalized spouse in my art of the street, as well as her hand and nose, various parts—except for the places of indecency—of the rest of the organism, which I had to study from bottom to top, providing her the local caress of a man, to which she was accustomed ... even a horse—I gave her features in the form of a symbol, I contrived to put in one arrangement of her burial mounds of breasts, scarcely covered by a cup of iron, concert pity... the mounds are especially dear: that's where my former youth is buried, worn down completely by the great man... he always participates with us during the tender bed—like a spirit between organs! I can't allow myself coarseness of the bed, not well brought up by childhood, but I always ask her to tell me how he could: a lovely reminiscence, which is exactly what I hold for... Oh, how much I wish to tell later! I'm not about to write now... how I tried to make his initial daughter, a child of love of a haulted marriage... a cheery grown maiden of darkness, she'd be a sweet comrade of the undeclinedness of feelings, but of course only on reaching the legal age of blossoming, we don't break the law of criminal morality, in its principal features, not counting the obsolete points of habit... I confessed to her a common school of musical childhood, it goes without saying, I broke off... but all the same I let him know obliquely!... The warm substance of my adoration! When I reached the period of a wife, but she asked for it herself, I was the last of those who had already been loved earlier... at first she didn't know, forgave ahead of time, maybe I'd turn over a new leaf: that habitual disease of the first step amorous place, everyone has it who has experienced our secret, the sexual forbidden organ of a posterior man, the baton of the great relay race moves in forever, the inconvenience of the tendency of our circle, I gave it to him precisely as a gift... that's exactly the representative of the substance of my unfortunate love... ugh, and gave her a glazed butterfly of a rainbow... in exchange she gave me a kit of foreigners, their silver ruble, and the inside not so simple: an engraved nail file and Turkish scissors—a bright manicure of all extremities of me... no! About that later... they slipped him a girl of a basic abroad, he accepted only for a time, then rejected, was offended by the western habit of the absence of feminine innocence... about that later!... I very much hoped the further actions of our lady of betrayal, if she would act, as the beginning with me, then she'd always bring into the nice home from the direction of production the aroma so dear to me of he higher man of the possession of support... but of course! I give up everything for a single quiver from him himself!... Oh, don't remind me, it's painful: with the same end, the same place...

16. On This Earth, Comrades!

Heroes of the Field of Grain   Workers of Farm Folk

TWO AT THE HELM
(Remarks on Our Years)

For Dmitri Fomich a grain field is total spiritual agitation. The sun blazes, its rays caressing the ears of grain—the heart rejoices. A heavy wind, accompanied by a heavy rain, would come up, tear up the field, crush it down to the earth—his heart would contract.

"Well why did it have to let itself go right here? Overturned everything, twisted it up, trompled it down." Jumping down from the cabin of the combine, Dmitri Fomich straightens up the felled grain. And he repeats over and over: "They've been flattened down and are afraid to raise up their little heads from the earth. Ears of grain are like little children—they can't stand coarseness, they want tenderness."

He looked to the side: there, among the lush grain, the combine had swung around and headed off toward the far edge of the field. The grain nowadays had turned out to be super...

"A man tries," Dmitri Fomich said approvingly. "And it clean wants to take the red banner away from me..."

And he pondered...—but why did he ponder, why did he ponder! There's nothing to ponder here, don't give them the banner, don't give it up to anyone, don't give the banner to the maternal mother of age, be always first! Ready to attack! I read the newspaper's good spirits, an honest pravda for issue No. 20116—there's been more than enough pravda[11] accumulated on this earth, comrades!

17. A Person of Indistinguishedness

Though a great and impossible talent, I easily bested him as a teacher of students, on that count my firm ideas, easier for him and more useful for the matter at hand, I can explain. A genius of the brush you won't learn anything, in the first place, and a decorator colleague only I can train, excluding the Armenian element of self-taught people, better to leave them without any pay at all. The great can't know our clever little ruses, not to mention the absence of firmness with personnel, I'm another matter: even if my grandfather was the founder of the poster, occupied the previous place, everyone studied from him, including I, but you yourself are a loafer of great stature—you'll always be remote my courses. A future colleague should be a special, stinging type, not too lazy, thoroughly healthy egoism to tread someone else's throat of success, but only the spiritual method of figurativeness, never entering the brawl of dangerous realism, going out the ramp of Nevsky Prospect, the brush and decor don't await a cheerful lanky fellow, just a small, but concentrated person of indistinguishedness.

18. Body and Technique

Finally I got the everyday togetherness of a spouse, but not only a chance in the office corner of distant dacha, where she wept the proximity of potential betrayal: let her now prepare for me his broth of the soup of everydayness, from me the help of the pestle to the mortar, nothing more. If it weren't for his lady of many years, I would never have enlisted my domesticity, lies around twelve hours out of twenty-four, too lazy even to wash out a glass of repetition... in the toilet everything leaks, everything's changing, would never bother to call a man handy at stopping up... supper exclusively only in sausage form, and that's fraught!.. And all the same she's better than the regular cafeteria, I can't smell the cooking of disgust: a little roll with a hoof, a meatpie of filling unfresh udder, no! I know her udderly not at all and at my age don't want to recognize that udder of poison. True, I've long since not gotten used to eating much, which only give the strength of sustenance in sitting of a chair instead of sustenance of work of the mind. At one point they cut out a quarter of my stomach, but now it's grown back again to its full length, they even accepted it into the party: a member lacking normalcy can't get in.

I asked her to bring photographs of him personally, beginning a little boy, I'll assign half the wall, to admire forever!.. I also insisted taking his books under the guise of property; I'll buy the remaining cupboard, the decorator's never offended in foreign currency, and I'll literally inhale the books, especially the ones where there are pictures of wits... To close my eyes and imagine him sitting down a deep chair of masculine quiet, an afghan across the appropriate place, smoking a pipe of doubts (although he doesn't smoke), his beloved parrot resting on his shoulder (there's no parrot either, but I'd like it there), and does he read in a row two hours or how many? I personally never read, except to the program regulations, I don't know... here enters me, and guess what?—the unexpected movement of the effect on him of my gay figure: the afghan rises all by itself, the lower edge of his absorbing book achieves a cone shape... the big index thumb of love!.. Ah, the dream of imagination! So much easier to live if I weren't a rising artist.

Yesterday I snubbed our mutual daughter again: I won't

let in my house to throw out a completely uneaten bit of grocery. In general I have a firm rule of food: after breakfast—ciao! My actor father didn't recommend any extra liquid. Finally I achieved everything that I planned, I'll describe it right now: (1) the era of universal togetherness! (2) the city of togetherness, which was difficult: all around the blossoming of samples of the writing of our personality; (3) the students of togetherness of the continuation of the course! (4) a wife and daughter of togetherness too! only one thing is left: that inaccessible man of togetherness ... I know that the skirtchaser of a passing erotic muse doesn't know where to pour in the energy of feeling, but he can't loan his temporary muscle to a colleague of lifelong gratitude of his talent, even though he sees that I love immortally his hefty body and technique—[12]

19. Hideousness

Again! Exiting from my job! In spite of the gift sent! How much is possible! You should beat someone up only the first time! Excuse the rest! Nonetheless the absence! Where's the nobility of holders of the brush! They haven't gone over in our russian history an excerpt of the dog-knights! They say it helps! But what for! It hurts! Fell at the glass door of a store! If the glasses shatter, it's impossible to get such a haze! How am I to blame! Wife of her own motion, be offended her! Or more accurately, yourself! I feed on the leftover of the table of genius and I'm always grateful! I can't resist myself to art! Adoring that thumping hand, but that's enough! In sight of our mutual wife, it's unseemly! It'll be necessary to soothe by means the local director, many-yeared experience of serving a sentence! I shake my fist! I lock it on a hook! Where are the people! Lead him away! Drag him off! Only don't make great pain—don't hit a hen sitting on golden eggs[13] —he'll still be of use to my personal brush— as well as to our country, by the name the former once-upon-a-time Russian—what will they say about me then—we live on the tree of culture—as I already stated, but they always remember that—I'm an exception, and for that I suffer—the main thing he struck my head of poorness, one sketch of greeting a team leapt completely out, can't think it back, turn it in the same sort of urgency of a fire: it must be ready before out temporarily peaceful life catches fire. No-no! It's time to take up some actions: but he can remove himself from the heights of the ivory tower of the west to our soviet life of hideousness.

20. Causing Him Something

Alas! It still remained to tell the circumstance of grief, calmly dying of my hairless chest, but I won't go into details. Yes, everything is possible in this world, comrade!.. No, I don't pity on myself. I don't need a woman,* you know very well that I regret only one thing: Why didn't I bear me a son of the continuation of the species, instead an unfortunate daughter of an orphan? How I would love a son of his similarity! Of course, I carressed his adolescent... I even wanted to return him the lady for temporary accouchement, then take the expense on myself, as always, I'm willing to live by two different children of his breed... Ugh, now it's old and decrepit and covered with ashes...

I stand alone among the big road of our art of what to do. I can't love a woman, a man... I've thrown the artistry of the brush in dried-up paint... even edible happiness is denied me forever: tortures of the stomach... my unscientific life has collapsed!.. and yet I'm a person with all the ensuing therein, for instance, tears of vexation... everything around has been grabbed up, like a quick fish of the store, where to?.. I'm living with my back to my backbone!.. A huge planet is rushing passed me... I know that I'm being punished for great him, for causing him something...

21. Life From Here On

I recall his basic passing thoughts, the wife expounded them in our short years. He taught her to love his absolutely alien personality, and though it's strange, I can't use it. Even

*Note again: a woman has appeared here only in order at last to die. There are no women in this story, and that is typical. We do not know why she left the one and attached herself to the other. What was going on in her is unknown to us, and now always will be. *V. M.*

if you don't believe in a single god, wear the true cross on your chests, it won't hurt. Under the thickest sweater of wool something live might suddenly stir, for instance, I ran on the bus, I remembered. You need to not love the flaws of yourself—fed up. Every day he repeated the learning process, the teacher himself groveled before an old woman of short party stature. But it wasn't for nothing he was a great man, expounded his views: don't love a flaw, but don't it very calmly, without unneccessary alarm, don't embarrass your thoughts—of course, I memorized it. What you can't correct in yourself and in others, just put up with, that's clear: I've put up with his dear hand of a blow to my eye. Neither seek a world of calm, you're born for toil, even I know that, but I try to avoid: attain cardiac peace, if you can. There was all the rest, too, unfortunately!.. You need to strain your head, but I can't say when I'll be able to... But the main thing he taught was there will be a day and there will be a morning! That's what you need to remember for life from here on.

22. A Ray of Light Among the Clouds of Ghastliness

The burial was in the center of the day... they gave a car two minutes beforehand, a miracle of a happening... in the neighbors they're playing a melody full of cloudless grief... although outside there's rain... the beer of freshness is selling at the corner notwithstanding the utter absence of a customery line... ice cream smiles on every lawn, the first time at the end of the summer, when it sells like hotcakes... in town there are still lots of trees... we walked along, stepping through the waters of light blue asphalt... everyone looked up: a gesture of impatience for better weather... her lone mother, abandoning for a time her profession as a hulling mill... in my proximity... she stumbled with a weak, suffering foot in her last high overshoes of fashion in her lifetime... at the cemetery the rain stopped sowing... a bird of coloration flew... a white cloud strolled around on a walk, or the spirit of uncertainty... displayed pleasant shapes: a furry white chrysalis... the happy irrevocable baby of the sky, a fleeting winged cupid of a kiss... a woman holding a mirror of a view... a hole suddenly appeared in the mirror... into the hole appeared a beautiful flower of the seventh color, then it was removed... as well as layers of a seven-layered cloud of translucence... into it flew an airplane of the merchant marine... it released a stream of its own transcendental traction... but the stream spread, melted up... a hole of pureness was left... there a pale female face whirled around for a while, the diurnal moon of removal, but it stepped away... and then began to frown: a temporary ray of light among the clouds of ghastliness.

23. Christian

I sent it! The last telegram! I can't wait for the answer! Leave the younger daughter in my care! You don't have to with the older one, I realized! The will of our common spouse of the grave! She looks so much like you, a comfort for my life that didn't happen! You! Why do you need her! Only be in your way! The great russian canvas painter of the pen! Well at least for a time! Under the care of a cooperative grandmother of a pension! As long as the latter is alive inside her disease! I can promise anything you want, I'll even leave the membership! The native party hasn't helped in any way! Only you! In the face of a family of your blood! I'll love her as I didn't love even my sick mother! Imagining myself your former wife! The fruit of our passion! As if born inside my poor womb of intestinality! That little hand! That little leg, covered with a blotch of childhood! Her crafty eye! Already knows how to read and write! Colors any scrap of second-hand paper! I won't give her up for anything! I'll raise out of her a remarkable stater-on-paper of the epoch! I never mince words, don't you! You can kill! Trample with your dear foot of a factory sole! I don't care! I'll take to the baltic countries! Don't ask for her back! Don't chase after! Money is nothing! Complain to the court! Or police! Security organs! CC UN CPSU! in the beginning was the word—now it's obsolete—replaced with the all-powerful letter—UA-SS-SS-EANE* —vanquishing life with a life—but take heed! I, just as every posthumous christian!

---

*Everything has finally gotten completely jumbled in this poor head. He undoubtedly means the letter of the law, which he would like to observe, if it existed. Instead of that, abbreviations that have become habitually lodged in our today's hearing come off his teletype tongue. As a reminder (everything flows) I'll decipher the abbreviations mentioned in the blond's text:

ATS	All-Union Theater Society
UA	Union of Artists
CC	Central Committee
CPSU	Communist Party of the Soviet Union
SU	its latter, but not worst part
SS	State Salvation, which is inevitable
EANE	Exhibit of Achievements of the National Economy

You see that there is little sense in these citations, and seeking any would be a futile labor. *V. M.*

III

AFTERWORD
(WRITTEN, HOWEVER, FIRST OF ALL)

Of course, it might seem to anyone that there cannot exist such separate people, in whom a single separate characteristic is so prominent, just as there can't be a person with a prominent ear, an ear that covers his whole head, spreading out like a cauliflower ear, lying on his shoulder and hanging down along his arm to his elbow. In just the same way there can't be such a person whose eye takes up his face, roams in the middle of his physiognomy, bugged out, from left to right, revolves rapidly, absorbing the surrounding—in all their colors and shades, in all their insignificant shifts. Yes, as you correctly noted, there don't exist such people whose organ of perception expands excessively, in order to take in everything it can. But at the same time there do exist—who hasn't heard a lot about that?—people with intensely acute hearing, there are people with sharp vision—though to judge by appearances, by ear and eye, they don't look any different from any other people. So here too I want to introduce myself, whose organ that senses my connections and people's seems to be made more acute. It doesn't have any external signs, there's nowhere it can suddenly peep out imperceptibly, but I have that organ, just as everyone does, although often everyone's is weak.

I undoubtedly always wanted the organ to be visible on everyone, like a nose or a mouth, like an ear growing on his head, into which you could scream in despair, you could blow into this snail, even the weak in spirit could move close to it and blow enough. Or tender, like an eye that doesn't tolerate extraneous dust specks in it, but envelops them, washes them out with a warm tear, in order to remain perpetually clear. Yes, sooner like an eye, so that its loss, like the loss of obvious sight, would be apparent to everyone's pity, so that it would be recognizable, so you could see by the cane: anyone working, selling,

106

singing—was a person who didn't have it.

Perhaps all this has nothing to do with the matter at hand, you're thinking, but no, it does, soon there will be a portrait.

Once I was washing in the bathhouse, and at the end, as is customary, I was sponging down under the shower. The shower, partitioned off by little walls, between which one person could fit, supplied water at one and the same time for no fewer than five people. Each of them, separated by a short partition, had two encrusted brown knobs on the wall that he could turn independently, summoning his own rain out of the showerhead for himself. And with a little difficulty, but everyone managed it, having turned in both directions, about fifteen minutes each, adding some hot—obviously too hot, perhaps scalding his palms with the sizzling water that sprayed out from the axle when it was turned, and then if necessary, each added some cold too, unexpectedly getting a stream in his gut that would make him shudder, shiver, cursing the defects in the bathhouse plumbing system. The point of telling all this is that although it was with minor difficulties, which needn't have been there, each bather, within the limits of his strength and patience, was certain he was adjusting the water for himself. I was certain too. But then I noticed in a nearby stall a man washing with soap at a frantic pace. He splashed his underarms energetically and wiped there; he dug his fingers into his hair, clawing and pulling it; he bent over, running the washcloth down his smooth, even side, and ran it back up, immediately straightening up. His frail member, for some reason permanently stripped of its natural little dermal sock, slapped against his bare thigh. Lather seethed and splashed to the floor around such a quick and lively personality, aimed perpendicularly to himself. This personality didn't fiddle with the knobs, but having turned them on, let them run full force, in a flash exchanging his shower for the opposite, and he would leap out, panting, only when he couldn't stand it.

From the other side I saw a completely different person. He was pensively trying to get himself some warm water, he constantly turned the knobs, turned them some more, listening to the stream of water as it ran over him. More then anything else he wished for stability overhead and it was stability that he was so patiently striving for. A third person, at whom I was able to glance only when I came out of my kennel, and then to walk a little bit next to and brush against his water, the third one was constantly changing it, handling the tap. At first he washed with barely hot—he adjusted it exactly: then he changed it from warm to cold, maintaining each level for as long as he wanted. Having shivered under icy water for the sake of invigoration, he would then retrace all these steps back. There was still another who gave up his place quickly—all in all, there were all different kinds of people, each of whom has his own personality, his own habits with regard to warmth, his own theories about health and what's good for you, which were thoroughly scientific for him himself.

And, returning to my shower, I noticed that it was always changing, constantly, even if you didn't touch your own separate, personal tap. When an energetic person, turning the knob, released water, when a stable person turned the knob back and forth, when a gradual one changed his regime, when they superimposed one on the other, they came together to form, for example, in the sense of the release of warm water, or vice versa, the expenditure of cold, when they fluctuated identically or discordantly, counterbalancing in this case each other's water, then mine changed imperceptibly, grew warm, grew cold in the showerhead above me, so that I had to take my knob too, twirl it a long time, sometimes to no avail, then unexpectedly everything came back by itself, exactly in my beloved even warmth, through which cool streams could break through along the edge, and washed that even me, though changing slightly, but not losing the possibility of control—when suddenly a massive and cold stream would lash me, scald me, signifying that somewhere people had taken all the hot water at once for themselves, returning cold water in exchange, not thinking at all about the other bathers around them.

And I saw that through this simple mechanism, this shower above me, this rain of wet water, I felt the essence and strivings of remote people, neighbors not of my acquaintance, that is it wasn't the water I felt, but their changes, in their instantaneous characters, in their systems—that is, this shower had become a link among us. Having laughed a bit at myself, noting ironically the similarity of the words "soul" and "shower"[14] as is appropriate for a contemporary person who says "soul" in the poetic meaning, I nonetheless did not forget the shower—and here I am now drawing it into my tale.

My unfaithful brother, the so-called blond! Many waters flow through us, sinking in and then again falling on the earth— but marvellous is the Dniepr in calm weather!.. There lived in a certain remote corner of Russian two inhabitants... it's not exactly painful, as people will be dissatisfied with the hero... mind is asleep, perhaps would having found a sudden of distant relations of great means... what quotations! Unfortunately, it sinks in and falls with the water, but a person can't satiate another person... even if he does remain a blond, have it so that people don't find out about it from me, make it not be me that gave him away.— The blond, my brother! accept my last water, but honest! Be happy, blond,—or at least be gay, if it's impossible for you any other way.

V.M.

Leningrad 1973

1. The Russian title of the story, *"Blondin obeego tsveta,"* uses a feminine pronominal adjective to modify a masculine noun, a clear but suggestive violation of Russian grammar.

2. A play on Gorky's oft-quoted "Man—that sounds proud." Gorky's name, a pseudonym, means "bitter"—hence the additional irony of which the author speaks.

3. Lithuanian is generally considered the closest living relative of Sanskrit.

4. The personnel department in any Soviet institution has very close links with the KGB.

5. The name suggests a bald castrated bull.

6. *Za stenkoy* literally means "behind the little wall," but if read as a single word, as it appears in the tale, it means "torture chamber." The play suggests "the expert in the torture chamber behind the wall," perhaps with an additional allusion to bugging.

7. A play on Stalin's apocryphal identification of writers as "engineers of the human soul."

8. A play on an Orthodox Easter hymn: "Christ has risen from the dead, vanquishing death with death."

9. An untranslatable pun, *shayka,* meaning both "gang" and "wash bucket."

10. Russians grow up with N. M. Karamzin's notoriously sentimental tale "Poor Liza."

11. *Pravda* means "truth." The newspaper *Pravda* is the official organ of the Communist Party of the USSR. Hence the author's play on words.

12. The Russian word *kist* means both "hand" and "brush."

13. Russians normally avoid the word "eggs" because of its association with "testicles."

14. *Dusha* means "soul," *dush* "shower."

Valentin Rasputin

Rudolphio

Their first encounter was on the trolley. She touched him on the shoulder, and when he opened his eyes she pointed to the window and said, "This is your stop."

The trolley had already come to a halt. He pushed his way through and jumped off right after her. She was just a girl, maybe fifteen or sixteen, no more. He knew it the moment he saw her fluttering eyelashes and round face, which she turned towards him, waiting for thanks.

"Thank you," he said. "I could've missed my stop."

Sensing that that was not enough for her, he added, "What a crazy day. I'm exhausted. And I'm expecting a call at eight. So you sure did come to my rescue."

That seemed to make her happy. Together they ran across the street, watching out for a car speeding past them. It was snowing and he noticed that the windshield wipers were on. When the snow is like this—soft and fluffy, as if somewhere above fantastic snowbirds were being plucked—it's hard to go inside. "I'll wait for the call and then go outside again," he decided, turning to her and wondering what to say, since it would be uncomfortable to prolong the silence. But he had no idea what he could and couldn't talk about with her. He was contemplating this when she herself said, "I know you."

"Oh, really?" he asked with surprise. "How?"

"You live in building number 112 and I live in number 114. We ride the trolley together twice a week on the average. Only you, of course, never notice me."

"That's interesting."

"What's interesting about that? Absolutely nothing. You adults only pay attention to other adults. You're all terribly egotistical. Wouldn't you say so?"

She turned her head to the right, swept her eyes to the left and looked him up and down. "Hmm," was all he said. He still wasn't sure how to behave around her, what to say and what not to say.

She looked straight ahead as they walked in silence for a while. Without turning her head she declared, as if nothing had happened, "Well, you haven't told me your name yet."

"Must you know?"

"Yes. What's the matter with that? For some reason certain people think that if I want to know a person's name, I must have some abnormal interest in him."

"O.K.," he said. "I get it. If you must know, my name is Rudolph."

"What?"

"Rudolph."

"Rudolph." She began to laugh.

"What's the matter?"

She laughed even more loudly. He stopped for a moment and stared at her.

"Ru-dolph," she said, rounding her lips; then she burst out laughing again. "Ru-dolph. I thought only elephants in zoos were called that."

"What?!"

"Don't get angry." She touched him on the sleeve. "But it's funny, honestly, very funny. What can I do?"

"You little kid," he said, offended.

"Of course I'm a kid. And you're an adult."

"How old are you?"

"Sixteen."

"And I'm twenty-eight."

"That's what I say: you're an adult, and your name is Rudolph."

She broke into laughter again, playfully looking him up and down out of the corner of her eye.

"And what is your name?" he asked.

"My name? You'll never guess."

"I'm not going to try."

"Even if you tried, you wouldn't guess. My name is Io."

"What?"

"Io."

"Say that again?"

"Io. You know—*ispolniaiushchii obiazannosti*. Io."*

Vengeance immediately followed. Unable to control himself, he fell into a fit of laughter, rocking back and forth like a bell. All he had to do was look at her and laughter consumed him.

*ispolniaiushchii obiazannosti means literally, "carrying out the duties (of someone in a managerial position)" or "Acting Director," "Acting Manager," etc.; abbreviation: I.O. (title). *Translator's note.*

"I-o," he gurgled. "I-o."

She waited, looking from side to side. Then when he had calmed down a bit she said, offended, "Funny, is it? Not at all. Io is an ordinary Latvian name, and I'm Latvian."

"I'm sorry." Smiling, he bent toward her. "But it really did strike me funny. Now we're even, right?"

She nodded.

First came her building, then his. She stopped by the entrance and asked, "What's your phone number?"

"You don't need to know that," he said.

"Are you afraid?"

"That's not it."

"Adults are afraid of everything on earth."

"That's true," he agreed.

She drew her small hand out of her mitten and offered it to him. Her hand was cold and serene. He shook it.

"Run home now, Io."

Again he chuckled.

She stopped by the door.

"So now you'll know me on the trolley?"

"Sure, of course I will."

"See you on the trolley," she said, waiving good-bye.

"... which we'll ride together," he added.

* * *

Two days later he went north on a business trip and didn't return for two weeks. Here in the city one could already feel the spicy, sharp scent of the coming spring which blew the winter vagueness and indistinctness, like ashes, away from him. After the northern fog everything here was brighter and clearer, even the trolleys.

At home his wife almost immediately said to him, "Some little girl has been calling you every day."

"What little girl?" he asked, tired and indifferent.

"I don't know. I thought you knew."

"I don't know."

"I'm tired of it."

"That's funny." He smiled reluctantly.

He was taking a bath when the phone rang. He could hear

through the door how his wife answered: he's back, he's bathing, please call later. And he was just about to go to bed when the phone rang again.

"Hello," he said.

"Rudie, hi! You're back!" Someone's happy voice resounded in the receiver.

"Hello," he carefully replied. "Who's calling?"

"Don't you know? Come on, Rudie... it's me, Io."

"Io," he recalled at once, and chuckled automatically. "Hi, Io. I see you've found a more suitable name for me."

"Yes. Do you like it?"

"They used to call me that when I was your age."

"Do you have to be so stuck up about it?"

"Why, no..."

They lapsed into silence. He couldn't hold out, and asked, "So what is it, Io?"

"Rudie, who is she—your wife?"

"Yes."

"And why didn't you tell me you were married?"

"Excuse me," he joked. "I didn't know it was so important."

"Of course it is. You, uh, love her?"

"Yes," he said. "Listen, Io—please don't call me anymore."

"You're a-f-r-a-i-d," she pronounced, sing-song. "Rudie, don't make such a big thing out of it. Go ahead and live with her if you want to; it doesn't bother me. But don't be like that, telling me not to call you. I may need to call you on business sometime."

"What business?" he asked, smiling.

"Oh, any old business." She came up with, "Say... say, for example, I can't figure out how fast water from one reservoir flows into another. Then it's O.K., isn't it?"

"I don't know."

"Of course it is. And don't be afraid of her, Rudie. After all, there are two of us, and there's only one of her."

"Who?" he didn't understand.

"Your wife."

"Good-bye, Io."

"You're tired, aren't you?"

"Yes."

116

"Well, O.K. Say good night and go back to sleep."

"Good night."

"And don't even talk to her."

"Fine," he laughed. "I won't."

Still smiling, he returned to his wife.

"That was Io," he said. "That's that little girl's name. Funny, isn't it?"

"Yes," she said expectantly.

"She couldn't solve a problem about two reservoirs. She's in seventh or eighth grade, I don't remember which."

"And did you help her with her problem?"

"No," he said. "I've forgotten everything... reservoirs—that's really difficult."

***

In the morning the phone rang at the crack of dawn. What dawn?—there was no light out there; the whole city was having its last dream before daybreak. As Rudolph got up he glanced at the building across from him. Not a single light was on yet; only the stairwells, like harmonicas shining with metal, were lit up in four even rows. The telephone rang incessantly. As he went to answer it, he glanced at the clock: 5:30.

"Hello," he said angrily into the receiver.

"Rudie, Rudie..."

He blew up. "Io! What the devil..."

"Rudie," he was interrupted, "listen, don't get angry. You don't know what happened yet."

Cooling down, he asked, "What happened?"

"Rudie, you're not Rudie anymore, you're Rudolphio!"—it was triumphantly announced to him. "Rudol-phio! Isn't it terrific? I just thought it up. Rudolph and Io—together you get Rudolphio, like in Italian. Well, try it out."

"Rudolphio." Despair and rage mingled in his voice.

"Right. Now you and I have one name—we're inseparable. Like Romeo and Juliette. You're Rudolphio, and I'm Rudol-phio."

"Listen," he said, coming to his senses. "Next time you give me a name, couldn't you do it at a more suitable hour?"

"Don't you understand?—I couldn't wait. There! And besides,

117

it's time for you to get up. Rudolphio, remember: at 7:30 I'll be waiting for you at the trolley stop."

"I'm not taking the trolley today."

"Why not?"

"I'm on *otgul*."*

"What's that?"

"*Otgul*—it's a special kind of day off. So I won't be going to work."

"Oh-h," she said. "What about me?"

"I don't know. Just go to school."

"Is your wife also on *otgul*?"

"No."

"Hmm... how 'bout that. But don't you forget: now our name is Rudolphio."

"I'm glad."

He put the receiver back in place and, swearing, went to put water on for tea. He couldn't sleep now anyway. Besides, three windows were already lit in the building across the street.

***

At noon he heard knocking at the door. He was washing the floor and as he opened the door he held a wet rag which, for some reason, he hadn't thought to leave somewhere along the way.

It was she.

"Hi, Rudolphio."

"You!" he exclaimed. "What happened?"

"I also took *otgul*."

Her face was like a saint's—not a single trace of what they call remorse.

"I see," he replied in a strong voice. "So you're playing hooky. Well, as long as you're here, come on in. I'll finish the floor in a second."

Without taking her coat off she sat down in the chair next to the window and began to observe how, bent over, he moved the rag along the floor.

Otgul—compensatory leave; time off given an employee for working on a Saturday, Sunday or holiday, as demanded by the employer. *Translator's note.*

"Rudolphio, in my opinion you're not very happily married," she declared after a minute.

He straightened up.

"Where did you get that?"

"It's very easy to see. For example, you're washing the floor without any enjoyment whatsoever. And it's not like that when a person is happy."

"Don't make things up," he said, smiling.

"Would you say you were happy?"

"I'm not going to say anything."

"There you are."

"You'd better take your coat off."

"I'm afraid of you," she said, glancing out the window.

"What was that?"

"Well, you are a man."

"Oh—so that's it." He laughed. "How did you dare to come here, then?"

"Well, you and I are Rudolphio."

"Yes," he said. "I keep forgetting about that. That, of course, imposes certain responsibilities upon me."

"Of course."

She stopped talking and sat quietly while he banged the bucket around in the kitchen. When he came out, her coat was hanging on the back of the chair and her face was sad and pensive.

"Rudolphio, you know, I was crying today," she suddenly admitted.

"Why, Io?"

"Not Io—Rudolphio."

"Why Rudolphio?"

"Because of my older sister. She had a fit when I decided to take *otgul*."

"In my opinion she's right."

"No, Rudolphio, she's not right." She got up from the chair and stood by the window. "It's O.K. to do it once, can't either of you understand? You know, right now I'm so happy talking with you..."

Again she fell silent, and he looked at her attentively. Through her dress her breasts were gently pushing forth, like two little nests being shaped by mysterious birds for the raising

119

of their young. He realized that in just a year her face would lengthen and become beautiful, and he was saddened by the thought that in time she would have her own boyfriend. He approached her, took her by the shoulders, smiled and said, "Everything will be alright."

"Really, Rudolphio?"

"Really."

"I believe you," she said.

"Yes."

He began to step away, but she called out, "Rudolphio!"

"Yes?"

"Why did you get married so early? You know, just two more years and I would have married you."

"Don't be in such a hurry," he said. "Someday you'll marry a very nice young man."

"I'd rather marry you."

"He'll be better than me."

"Well... yes," she said doubtfully. "You think there are better men than you?"

"A thousand times better."

"But he won't be you," she sighed awkwardly.

"Why don't we have some tea?" he suggested.

"O.K."

He went into the kitchen and put the teakettle on the burner.

"Rudolphio!"

She was standing by the bookshelves.

"Rudolphio, we have the most beautiful name. Look—not even writers have better names." For a moment she was quiet. "Maybe just this Ex-u-pé-ry. Beautiful, isn't it?"

"Yes," he said. "Haven't you read him?"

"No."

"Take it home with you and read it. Only no more *otguls*—agreed?"

"Agreed."

She started to put on her coat.

"What about the tea?" he recalled.

"Rudolphio, I'd better go, O.K.?" Her smile disappeared. "Just don't tell your wife that I was here. O.K., Rudolphio?"

"Fine," he promised.

When she left he felt himself becoming melancholy. He

was full of some inexplicable yearning, a feeling as yet undiscovered but existing nevertheless in nature. He put on his coat and went out into the street.

***

Spring came rather suddenly, almost without warning. People became more pleasant in just a few days; and those few days seemed like a transitional period from a season of expectation to one of fulfillment, for spring dreams had predicted happiness and love for them with the skill of an experienced fortuneteller.

On one such day, in the evening as Rudolph was returning home, an elderly woman stopped him.

"I'm Io's mother," she began. "Excuse me, your name is Rudolphio, isn't it?"

He smiled. "Yes," he agreed.

"I know about you through my daughter. Lately she's been talking about you a lot, but I..."

She faltered, and he realized that it was difficult for her to ask what a mother must ask.

"Don't worry, " he said. "Io and I have the nicest friendship and nothing bad will come of it."

"Of course, of course," she replied quickly, embarrassed. "But Io is an impulsive girl. She doesn't listen to us at all. And if you could influence her... You understand, I worry—she's at an age when you have to worry—she can do a lot of foolish things. Besides, it frightens me that she doesn't have any girlfriends from school or among girls her age in general.

"That's bad."

"I know. It seemed to me that you have some influence on her..."

"I'll talk with her," he promised. "But in my opinion Io is a good girl. There's no need for you to worry."

"I don't know."

"Good-bye. I'll talk with her. Everything will be alright."

***

He decided to call her right away and not put it off, espe-

121

cially since his wife was not at home.

"Rudolphio!" It was obvious that she was very happy. "It was so nice of you to call me! Rudolphio, I was crying again."

"You shouldn't cry so often," he said.

"It's all because of *The Little Prince*. I feel sorry for him. Isn't it true that he visited us on earth?"

"In my opinion it's true."

"And in mine also. But we didn't know. Isn't that terrible! And if it weren't for Exupéry we never would have found out. It's no wonder he has a name as beautiful as ours."

"Yes."

"And do you know what else I think? It's a good thing he remained a Little Prince forever. Because it's terrible—suddenly he would have turned into just an ordinary person. And there are much too many ordinary people here."

"I don't know."

"I know, and that's for sure."

"And have you read *Man's Earth*?"

"I've read everything, Rudolphio. I think Exupéry is a very wise writer. It's amazing how wise he is. And kind. Remember how they ransom Bark, give him money, but he spends it on little shoes for children and is left with nothing?"

"Yes," he said. "And remember Bonnafous who pillaged and destroyed the Arabs, but they hated him and loved him at the same time?"

"Because without him the desert would have seemed so ordinary to them, but he made it dangerous and romantic."

"You're a smart girl if you understand all that," he said.

"Rudolphio." she fell silent.

"I'm listening," he reminded her.

She said nothing.

"Rudolphio," he said, uneasy for some reason. "Come over now. I'm alone."

***

Glancing around, she crossed the room and sat down in the chair.

"Why are you so quiet?" he asked.

"Is she really gone?"

"My wife?"

"Of course."

"Yes."

"She's a bitch."

"What?"

"A bitch—that's what!"

"Where did you get that word?"

"From the great Russian language. There's nothing there that suits her more."

"Now Io, let's not talk like that."

"Not Io—Rudolphio."

"Oh, yes."

"Awhile ago I called and got her. Do you know what she said to me? 'If you're calling about reservoirs,' she says, 'then you'd better ask your teacher.' I think she's jealous of me."

"I don't think so."

"Rudolphio, isn't it true that I'm better than she is? I know my figure hasn't developed yet as it should... everything is ahead of me."

He smiled and nodded.

"You see? In my opinion it's time for you to divorce her."

"Don't talk nonsense," he cut her short. "I'm too permissive with you."

"Out of love, right?"

"No, out of friendship."

She scowled and stopped talking, but obviously not for long. "What's her name?"

"Whose—my wife's?"

"Of course."

"Klava."

"Oh, what a name!"

He got angry. "Stop it."

She got up, closed her eyes for a moment, then suddenly said, "Rudolphio, I'm weird, forgive me, I didn't want..."

"Just don't start sobbing," he warned.

"I won't."

She stepped away and turned to the window.

"Rudolphio," she said, "let's say I wasn't here today and never said any of this, alright?"

"Yes."

"Pretend it was 'good-bye' that I said to you over the phone."

"Yes."

She left.

In five minutes the phone rang.

"Good-bye, Rudolphio."

"Good-bye."

He paused, but she hung up.

* * *

She didn't call anymore. He didn't see her for a long time, for he left again and was gone until May, when summer had finally outweighed spring on solar scales. At this time of year he always had a lot of work; whenever he remembered her, he'd put off calling: I'll talk to her tomorrow; the day after tomorrow... but he never did.

Finally they met by chance—on the trolley. When he saw her he began to push his way through impatiently, afraid that she would get off—for she might get off at a different stop, in which case he probably wouldn't dare jump after her. But she stayed and he caught himself being happier about that than he should have been, probably, considering their friendly relationship.

"Hi, Io," he said, touching her shoulders.

Startled, she turned around, saw him, paused and nodded happily.

"Not Io—Rudolphio—like before," she corrected. "After all, we're still friends, right?"

"Of course, Rudolphio."

"Have you been away?"

"Yes."

"I called once and you weren't in."

"I've already been back a whole week."

The trolley was crowded and they were constantly being pushed. They had to stand very close to one another, her head touching his chin. When she lifted her face and he bent forward to listen, they had to avert their eyes—their faces were so close.

"Rudolphio, want me to tell you something?" she asked.

"Of course."

Again she lifted her face so very close to his that he felt

124

like blinking.

"I'm always bored when you're not around, Rudolphio."

"Silly little girl," he said.

"I know," she sighed. But I don't miss boys at all; I have no need for them whatsoever."

The trolley stopped and they got off.

"You're going home to your Klava?" she asked.

"No, let's take a walk."

They turned toward the river and entered a vacant lot. They made their own path as they walked, jumping over clumps of grass and heaps of debris. He took her by the hand, helping her over each obstruction.

She was silent. It was unlike her but she was silent, and he sensed that she too was full of emotion—strong, droning, and uncontrollable.

They ended up by a steep bank. Still holding hands they looked at the river, then somewhere beyond it, then again at the river.

"Rudolphio," she said without restraint, "I've never been kissed before."

He bent over and kissed her on the cheek.

"On the lips," she asked.

"Only people who are very close kiss on the lips," he forced out in torment.

"And we?"

She quivered and this frightened him. The next moment he suddenly realized—did not sense, but literally realized—that she had hit him; she had given him a real slap in the face and had torn off, back through the vacant lot, through the clumps of grass, through the emotion, through the anticipation.

He stood and watched her run away, and didn't even dare call her, didn't dare run after her. He stood there for a long time—devastated, hating himself.

***

This happened on Saturday. On Sunday early in the morning, her mother called him.

"Rudolphio, excuse me, please... I woke you up, didn't I..."

She sounded confused; her voice trembled.

"I'm listening," he said.

"Rudolphio, Io didn't come home last night."

He should have said something, but he didn't.

"We're desperate. We don't know what to do, what steps to take... this is the first time..."

"First of all, calm down," he said at last. "Maybe she spent the night at a girlfriend's."

"I don't know."

"More often than not, that's how it is. If she doesn't show up in about two hours, we'll start searching. Calm down, now. In two hours I'll call you."

He lowered the receiver, thought a moment and said to himself: "You calm down, too. Maybe she spent the night at a girlfriend's." But he couldn't calm down. On the contrary, he felt a nervous tremor building up inside him. To soothe it he went to the closet and, whistling, began to rummage through his old, old schoolbooks. His algebra workbook had gotten lost somewhere, and while looking for it he became a bit distracted.

The telephone, lurking, didn't make a sound. Rudolph closed the kitchen door behind him and started thumbing through the textbook. Here it is: if water from one reservoir flows into another for two hours...

The telephone rang.

"She's come home." Unable to control herself, her mother started to cry.

He stood and listened as she wiped her eyes with a handkerchief.

"Rudolphio, come over here, please."

Again she started to cry. Afterwards, she added:

"Something's happened to her."

Fyodor Abramov

———————————

Olesha's Cabin

We had set out for the forest early, through a thick white fog, and hadn't seen the plank road-bed with its traffic of heavy lumber trucks.

But at this hour, lit up by the evening sun, it was right there in plain sight. For five or ten miles the two wooden rails ran straight ahead, like a gleaming wedge, into the blue sky on the horizon. But on either side... on either side, war had been raging. Countless stumps standing like tank traps or lying in porcupine snags, the earth scraped and heaved into embankments, birches and firs, shredded and split into fibers, lying side-by-side and piled one over another, like soldiers fallen in battle....

A young engineer, Promoinikov, nodded out the bus window time and again as he recounted to me, heatedly, the building of the road. He knew it all by heart, and spiced the story liberally with figures: where how many blocks were placed, how many cubics of soil moved, how many piles sunk.

"But as for our construction battalion, well..," he added, taking a playfully solemn tone.

Here the driver suddenly stopped, gave the horn a stacatto blast and called out:

"Olesha's cabin! Ten minute rest stop!"

Whooping and shouting, the passengers—bear cubs, every one of them—poured out of the bus.

"Let's get out too," Promoinikov suggested with a grin. You can't come all this way and not see Olesha's cabin."

The bus had stopped at a dry, pleasant spot. Thick, springy underbrush smelling of juniper, rose bay as tall as a man, shaggy old pines with wandering branches, like a herd of woolly mammoths, white moss underfoot... but where was this cabin?

"It's here, sure enough," Promoinikov winked at me, joking again.

"Yes, yes! Find the cabin!" We were surrounded by the young men and women. Pava Khaimosov himself, the good-natured, blue-eyed bear in whose brigade (famous, renowned throughout the region!) I'd spent the day, came over to us, grinning from ear to ear.

I was sure they were fooling me, because there was no cabin, not even the simplest shed anywhere around, but finally Promoinikov took pity on me.

"That's it, Olesha's cabin," he said, pointing to a tall pine on a distant knoll.

I stared at it—a sort of platform, something like a hunter's blind, was visible in the crown of the tree, the remains of a rope ladder dangling down from it along the trunk...

"Believe me, a cabin," Promoinikov assured me. "Someone actually lived there. Olesha Riazansky."

"That's the kind of people we had, comrade writer!" Pava Khaimusov broke in, with delight and, it appeared, envy. "Soaring with the clouds and the birds. You could write a novel about it."

"No, make it a film," a long-haired fellow corrected him.

"Why not? Make a film too," Pava agreed. "Once there was a pair of crows living there. Whenever you drove past they'd be sittin' up there, one to a side, like, say, they was keeping guard."

"When workers use to drive out here in the morning," another excited voice chimed in, "he, that's Olesha, would've just gotten up and he'd still be shaking the clouds out of his head."

"Who'd you say, who was just getting up?"

The cook, Kapa, flew up to us. In a flash she shoved and clawed us apart to muzzle the speaker.

"What rubbish! Just getting up! When the others were going to work he'd 'a already worked up a sweat. He'd make five quotas or more—you think he'd have the time to sleep?"

"Still, he must have slept sometime."

"How do you know, you know-it-all! When did Olesha live, anyway? You were just kicking in your mother's belly then, and now you're out makin' speeches about him."

Disconcerted by their laughter, the young fellow didn't open his mouth again. Nor did any others try to interrupt the cook. Toothless but for two canines in front, she'd always get in the last word. I'd tried to strike up a conversation at lunch, but nothing had come of it—she had everyone under her thumb.

"Oh yes, Olesha had a way with the stumps and snags around here," Kapa rattled on. "Like a wood-devil! Other men used tractors, bulldozers, weren't fools enough to break their backs, but he'd use a crowbar and a sledge. 'Olesha, don't overwork yourself, save your strength!' they said. But he'd just laugh, 'My blood gets clogged up at the wheel. And I hate the smell a' gas!' All by himself he'd polish off five quotas. And when payday came, good money! Stuffed his pockets. He'd go to the store and say 'gimme a case of wine!' "

"A whole case?"

"Now there's a thirst."

"And why not? Buyin' it by the bottle'd only mean more

130

leg-work. For him, one bottle was like a nipple to a baby. I've seen him drinking. He'd twist open one bottle, then another, then one more, pour them all into himself like a bucket, then he'd get up and go... Stand a wineglass on his head and it wouldn't jiggle. He could walk down a chalkline."

"But they say wine did him in..."

"Did who in? Olesha? You it might do in! It was her, that black-eyed bitch ruined him. Ksanochka from the Ukraine..."

Just then our driver impatiently signaled the end of the rest stop, and Promoinikov, obviously under the spell of Kapa's story-telling, shouted in an affected voice:

"All aboard!"

There was a new passenger waiting for us on the bus, a bald, red-bearded old man, the watchman of a fuel depot somewhere nearby in an old sand quarry. We'd hardly sat down before he started in:

"Kapa, ya ain't taken up tour guidin', have ya?"

"What's that?" Kapa rolled her eyes in disbelief.

The old man chuckled. "An' I figured, what with yer carryin' on about Olesha, ya'd got a new profession."

Here they ganged up on him from all sides: Hey, shut up! Don't spoil the story!

"That's how it is here," Promoinikov turned to me. "You can't touch Olesha." He gave Kapa a nod. "Go ahead, Kapitalina. Tell us the rest."

Kapa snorted even at that trifle, but it was beyond her power to stay quiet. Evidently this Ksanochka, the "black-eyed bitch" she'd touched on back in the woods, aroused some personal grievances.

"I remember how she showed up," Kapa frowned disgustedly, wrinkling her thin, angular face. "She came for the big money, figuring it was like twigs you could sweep up with a broom. Then, seeing you had to freeze in the forest and walk through snow waist-deep, she started to look around her—whose shoulders could she get a ride on. And there he was, Olesha. Bags full of money and simple-headed. So she started making an orbit around him."

"She sure was a sharp gal, alright. Had a fetchin' pair of eyes." This was the watchman's voice again.

"What was so sharp about her?... Those eyes of hers were

like black torches"—Kapa's own eyes were piercingly bright, with bottle glass color patterns—"with those eyes, if you want the truth, she swallowed his whole. Just like she was looking out of a cellar. You never could tell what she was scheming. Well, she got her way, dragged Olesha over to her place. She didn't have to drive through the woods no more. She could sit by the window and crack nuts. That was work enough for her. And Olesha—he spent one month in her paradise, then he ran for his life. He couldn't take even a step out of line—she kept an eye on him all the time. He didn't drink, didn't go out with his pals. She'd wait for him every night by the trucks. Straight out of the cab and into her hands. She took him home like a prisoner in a convoy. And as for the money, it couldn't have been worse. She took everything down to the last copeck. Didn't even leave him enough for a smoke. Well, Olesha put up with it for awhile, then he took off to the woods, and up a pine tree."

"What do you mean, up a tree?"

"Didn't we just show you his cabin? What would he be doin' in a tree if he could live on solid ground? It was all 'cause of dear Ksanochka... Could he really hide out from her in the dorm? No, she'd go to the party committee, the labor committee, the director, saying 'bring him back! He's got no right, after taking up with me!'"

The old man cut in again:

"Now really, Kapa, you're makin' this up. Ya' know when he built that treehouse? When they was pullin' stumps up here. To get away from the 'skeeters...'"

"Cut the crap! Who could ever get away from mosquitos in a tree? Everybody'd do it! Ksanochka black-eyes, she drove him to it. She knew all the ins and outs, let me tell you. She must have twisted more than one around her finger before Olesha. There he was dashing about, here and there—to the dorm, to a friend's place, but always intercepted, he never could get away from her. 'O.K., then,' he tells her, 'catch me up in a tree!'"

"Found the answer didn't he!" Pava Khaimusov rumbled cheerfully.

"You'd find one, too, if your life depended on it," Kapa snorted. "But all the same she wore a path into the woods, running back and forth to that tree. She'd bleat like a sheep: 'Olesha, let me come up to you...' But he only laughed from overhead:

'You've done damn plenty to me already!' Or else he'd scream down like a crow: 'Climb up to me on the winds if you can't live without me!'"

"Just like in a legend, by God," Promoinikov remarked.

Through the bus windows, reddened by the setting sun, the outskirts of the settlement were swinging into view: the usual smithy with its tall iron chimney, the service garages, the first houses... Then, out of nowhere, a big open truck came toward us, and a darkness of dust and exhaust enveloped the bus.

I was getting seriously interested in Olesha, and I decided that same night to go talk with old-timers. With those who'd known him personally.

2

In our time, people of the provinces make much use of the word "model." A model apartment, a model house, a model settlement...

Just so, I would call Semyon Mikhailovich Kovrigin a model pensioner. In perfect health, with a strong constitution and good color, not at all fat and without an old man's leanness, a non-smoker and non-drinker, a social activist and first and foremost—a physical worker. I found him trimming his lawn, already flawlessly combed and manicured.

A well known man in the region, Semyon Mikhailovich was accustomed to attention and honors, so when I told him that I, a writer, was interested in Olesha Riazansky, he was not a little surprised. He then asked me, in a quiet and businesslike tone, what organ I represented, and how I planned to address the given question.

"Well, I still don't know exactly how," I honestly admitted. "I'm just interested in him as a person."

Semyon Mikhailovich clearly did not expect such casualness from a representative of the Soviet press, and he took the matter, as they say, into his own hands from the very first.

"Well, first of all," he began didactically, "one must break with this myth regarding Titkin"—he said it exactly like that, "with this myth."

"Excuse me, but I'm interested in Olesha Riazansky, not Titkin."

"But there never was any Olesha Riazansky here. He was Olesha Titkin."

"But how could it be Titkin?" I couldn't believe that the man I'd heard so much about today could have such a stupid name.

"Yet it was Titkin. He even worked under me once. I was his superintendent. It was only later that they adorned him with the name Riazansky." Semyon Mikhailovich frowned and waved his hand impatiently. "It's all bungling with us. No one remembers the true organizers of production and Stakhanovites, but hooligans and drunks are memorialized." He muttered, then continued, more firmly, "It's an oversight of the social organizations. I put the question to the party committee last spring, when they were working out plans to combat drunkenness. I say we should tear out this cult of Titkin by the roots, hold meetings with the youth, otherwise all our conversations about combating drunkenness will remain just conversations."

I finally collected my thoughts and said, in defense of Olesha, that some of the old-timers had a somewhat different opinion of him.

"Which "some" do you mean?" Semyon Mikhailovich asked sternly. "Ah, so it was Kapochka who enlightened you! While you were driving in from the woods. Well, that's the one thing she can do—hasn't a care in the world, so long as she can wag her tongue. Her father fed on fairy tales, too. Everyone else went to the woods with their axes and saws, but he'd go empty-handed. His business was telling stories in the evenings. The first buffoon in these parts. But this Kapka... if she'd work harder with the ladle in her hand, her food might not stick in your throat. As it is, a hungry dog would think twice before swallowing one of her cutlets."

I thought that Semyon Mikhailovich might be right about Kapa's cooking, but I objected once more, saying there were other judgements about Olesha Riazansky, as I insisted on calling him.

"For instance?" Kovrigin asked, again in a judge's tone.

"For instance, Chief Engineer Promoinikov."

"Valery Loginovich? Regarding his productional qualities

I must abstain, since I myself spent only seven years as an engineer, and that with the technical school. But in the leadership capacity, comrade Promoinikov is lacking. This was pointed out to him at the party committee, and I would not advise you to rate him favorably."

"Well, O.K., O.K.," I was starting to get annoyed, "we'll leave Promoinikov in peace. But what about Olesha? You knew him yourself, he worked under you... they say he could fulfill five quotas..."

"He did," Semyon Mikhailovich said flatly.

"Well, what more do you want from a worker?"

"It's true, he did have productional qualities. But moral ones? On the moral side he was a minus. And if moral qualities aren't at their best," Semyon Mikhailovich concluded, "it should show up in productivity." And further, with characteristic thoroughness, Semyon Mikhailovich began to tick off on his fingers Olesha's sins: drunken sprees that frequently involved the whole dormitory, family problems, disgraceful pranks played on his fellow workers and on officials of the supervisory staff (Kovrigin's words) alike...

And I didn't doubt it. He was right, Olesha probably did have all this in his history, yet for some reason I didn't feel like listening to Kovrigin any longer, and when he excused himself to go inside and take his medicine, I gladly said goodbye to him.

3

So many new settlements have sprung up in the northern forest over the last twenty or thirty years! You can't count them all. But everywhere they are one and the same—surrounded by a wall of woods, the settlements themselves are dusty deserts. The pines and firs are pulled out down to the last seedling before the houses start going up.

Ropsha, unfortunately, was no exception. When I walked out the gate of practically the only green yard, it was as if I'd stepped into a scorching sahara, so hot was the air on the street.

But somehow this oven revived me. I began to breath deeply again. And everything seemed pleasant and in its place at that evening hour: someone blowing fiercely on a harmonica off in the outskirts, the resounding thud of a volleyball, the dirty and shedding stray dogs who lolled around the plank causeway that I was walking along. And I was walking aimlessly, without a single thought, and probably would have gone straight through the village that way, had I not been called out to, suddenly.

"Hey, where to? Stop in for a breather!"

I turned toward the voice and saw this picture: a smiling old man, lit up by the setting sun, sitting on a low front step. One leg over the other, a tube cigarette in his mouth, and ribbons of blue smoke, as if from a steamship chimney.

I didn't wait for a second invitation. I love people who enjoy life!

Lipat Vasilyevich, as he said himself, was watching the wonder of nature, the sun, which was just setting into the flaming pine forest beyond the village.

"I'm doing a 'speriment," he explained more concretely. "It don't seem to meet up with Petrusha Lapsha's house." And with that, to include me in the activity, he pointed it out: "There, you see. That's the house."

"What are you up to now? What new 'speriment is this?"

Out of the passageway, rumbling a pair of buckets, came an old woman, tall and stout, with a good-natured expression.

"Oh, it's you, ol' woman." Lipat Vasilevich made a wry face. "Save your nervous system, I tell ya. It won't regenerate itself."

"And don't you start gettin' me sidetracked. You've got to water the onions. Lord knows ya eat and drink your share too, day in and day out."

"I've had it with those onions," the old man groaned. "They say we've got a great science. Well, what're those scientists down there thinking for? Why not just take this onion and cross it with somethin'... if only with a pine...." The old man blinked in surprise—even he, apparently, hadn't expected such a twist of thought.

"I see, so ya wouldn't have to water 'em. But what would you do then, chaw on a pine tree?"

"So, what kind of a pine'd ya think I meant? A full-sized tree? The kind ya chop into firewood?"

Lipat Vasilyevich glanced about him, then jumped to his feet and pulled up a half-dried horsetail by the cowshed—there was a good crop of them there—and held it up for his wife to see.

"Here's the size of pine I meant. Got it? But you'n your female foolishness were gonna go overboard, go pull up a telegraph pole, I suppose...."

Lipat Vasilievich's visual method of justifying himself must have done the trick. At any rate, without her former categoricalness, his wife said, "Rubbish."

"Rubbish? Whadda'ya mean? People've been roostin on the moon, and you make trouble right here.... Too bad Michurin's[1] gone," Lipat Vasilievich suddenly shook his head in deep thought. "He'd have taught 'em a lesson long ago, a guy like him. Now here's what's going on this evening, right at this minute: all of Russia is rattling its buckets in the kitchen garden. Just like it was under Tsar Gorokh.[2] Well, so what, we'll manage. It sure was harder to produce a new species of cattle, though."

His wife stared at him and asked, uncertainly, "What kind a' new species?"

"A milk-bear. They crossed a bear with a cow. So ya wouldn't have to feed it in winter, when, ya' know, there's never any hay...."

"Oh, go on, you old hick!" The old woman was angry now. "And here I am, askin' for it... as if you'd ever hear a serious word from the liar." And, picking up her buckets, she went out to the kitchen garden.

Lipat Vasilyevich followed her with his gaze to the wicket gate out back. Then, with a sigh, he pointed to the sunset, and the red slate roof behind which the sun had hidden.

"And I've forgotten about the 'speriment again. Well, next time, I'll be on the lookout. Tell me," he fastened his eyes, dulled by time, yet lively and inquisitive, on mine. "Tell me what's goin' on in the world. I sit here and fiddle with the radio—my son-in-law came on vacation this spring and left it—but the batteries wore out.... I live off listening, whatever someone can tell me.... But maybe you'd like some tea," the old man suddenly switched thoughts. "I'll have it in a minute. You have to start with tea. With refreshments. That's the way they used to treat guests in Russia. First drink, food, spend the night, and only then ask questions."

I turned down the tea and shifted the conversation to Olesha.

"Olesha, you ask? Was there ever an Olesha around here?" The old man stared dumbfoundedly. "Next you'll be askin' me,

137

is this the U.S.S.R. or America?"

"I've heard different things," I answered evasively.

"From who? Aha!" he guessed, and frantically sputtered, "Don't listen to him! Kovrigin! If he had his way he'd not only blot out Olesha, but the sun itself. For shinin' too brightly!"

"And did Olesha shine brightly?"

"Who needs to ask? He was flesh and blood, sure, like everyone else—natural substance. But he spread so much good nature and cheerfulness around him. Even if he had to pull up stumps.... Who'd wanna overwork himself, crawl around in the swamps all day. But doin' it with him, Olesha, it was like a holiday. Where the roots were thicker and tougher, he liked it better. More challenge. The pines and spruces would topple. We'd work in twos and threes, heave-ho them all together. But he did it all by himself. 'All I need's a good grip and solid ground under my feet.' Like Mikula Selyaninovich."[3]

"Sturdy, eh?"

"Sturdy. You know Pava Khaimusov? Just like him, like two peas in a pod.... Only the other one's a little shorter. Ah, no." Lipat Vasilyevich waved a hand disdainfully. "What am I sayin'. Here's a good comparison—a telegraph pole and a sack a' potatoes! Pava... who needs Pava? Any fool can iron out a forest. And you live to enjoy life, to leave people somethin' to remember you by. But Olesha, ya' know.... Just imagine, It's in the spring, the first of May's coming up and there's no booze, it's all run out over the winter. Could we call ourselves men, with dry throats on a holiday? 'Come on boys,' he tells us, 'sail the high seas.' And they really were high seas. Everything overflowing—rivers, streams, swamps. To a town twenty miles away—you better forget it! But he gets through all the same. Nothin' stops him. Crosses this river on a log, swims across that one...."

"And it was drink, they say, that killed him," I remarked.

"Who, Olesha, killed by drink? Why're you listening to this nonsense? By drink.... Ksana Grigorevna, now, she did him a bad turn, the lad couldn't work things out with her."

Just then the old woman came back into view, and Lipat Vasilyevich, clicking and smacking his tongue like a mating grouse, sang out:

"Why, woman, you're just like a little red flower to me, like a beautiful daisy! Come over and tarry with me."

"Sit down!" His wife shook her fist at him from a distance, but came up to us willingly, pacified. "Waggin' yer tongue again aren't ya? I don't know what it is with him, that his tongue don't ache from waggin' day and night."

"Ah, but there is, there is a slight ache in my tongue, you must have noticed it. But the conference ain't finished, not all the truth uncovered...."

"Truth outta you!" the old woman laughed, "the truth avoids you like the plague."

"This time you haven't guessed it, Maria Tikhonovna. It's Olesha we're talking about."

"That drunk?" the old woman asked, surprised. "Well, you could talk on all night and not dry that one up."

"Now why do ya say that, Maria Tikhonovna? You know that you're golden to me, but all they'll take ya for is rust."

The old woman didn't take that as a joke, though. She stood up, picked up the buckets she'd brought from the garden, and went inside. Still in a playful mood, Lipat Vasilyevich called after her:

"Hey, old woman! Put on the samovar or we'll look uncivilized, underfeedin' our guest like this."

I was about to decline a second time but the old man stopped me.

"All right, we won't force you to the table. But I'm dried out like a dried-up stream in summer, myself. And as for Olesha," he started again without any reminder from me, "it's all a lie. When did we ever get a chance to drink? A quota in those days—you know yourself! With an axe and a bow-saw, we gave more cubics than today with all their fancy tractors and technology. Healed the war wounds that way.... Well, naturally, when we got our hands on it, we'd raise a hullabaloo. And Olesha, he was Olesha, first in everything. On payday he got a bundle. He made a lot, doin' his five quotas. And payday came only once in three months, 'cause there'd be nothing in the bank. But how could you spend all that dough? Today, maybe, you'd buy a T.V. or a car, right? But back then? 'Gimme wine!' He'd buy cases and stack 'em in the dorm. Well, that rubbed the directors the wrong way. Made the time table fall behind. Yes, sir. If, let's say, he drank it all by himself, that'd be different. But he was just so companional.... If he's out havin' a good time, so's the whole damn brigade, the whole dorm. He was one heck of an easy-going fellow, that one! Never grudged a thing. He'd give you the last shirt off his back.

So then they started hounding him: 'that's enough, Oleksay.' They told him once, twice, and the third time they had the militia-men telling him to clear out of the dorm. 'Who clear out?' he told them. 'Me? Well, I don't give a damn! I'll build me a place like the world's never seen.' So, angry and drunk, he set out for the woods and shinnied up a tree...."

"So, it all began with drink after all," I interrupted the old man again, for there was no mistaking that he too was climbing that tree, along with Olesha, and if he got all the way up, that would be the end to sober conversation.

"Come on now," Lipat Vasilyevich waved me away, disappointedly. "With drink, with drink. They always say it's drink. Obviously he didn't climb the tree sober, but I'd say it was more to show off, and there was a real sore point between him and the directors on another line. He just couldn't find a common language with gasoline."

"With gasoline?"

"You know... after the war it was all axe and backbone, right? And then, for the first time hereabouts, a tractor. 'Take the wheel, boys!' was the command. But who needs your strength behind the wheel? Does anyone notice it? That's why Olesha stepped outta line. Resentment of that. Used to being first in everything, at the forefront, but now there's some little snot—all he's gotta do is turn the wheel—at the top of the Honors chart. That's why Olesha went downhill."

"And Ksana Grigorevna?"

"What about her?" the old man honestly wondered. "Ah, as to their not getting along. There were scenes, sure there were. But that's nothing! When's a hen ever made an eagle cluck? If you're so interested in this woman question, go see Klimentevna. The old woman who she lived with. She can paint you the whole picture just like it was."

"Isn't it late now?"

"Meanin' you think she's asleep. Not a chance. She has blood pressure, keeps her up. She only starts to live at night. She also keeps a goat, so how can she sleep? But, ya' know what, tell her Lipat sent you and she'll open right up. She's a relative of mine.

But listen, no one can tell you better about Olesha than I can. Why, whenever he'd go past he'd give a whistle. Even in the woods, up in his pine tree. He'd start to whistle like a highwayman. It'd send the goosebumps up your spine, by God.

It was pleasant sitting with Lipat Vasilyevich; I could have sat till morning listening to his playful speech. But I also wanted to listen to others who'd known Olesha well.

"Well then, all right," the old man reluctantly agreed with me, "Go ahead. The course is charted. Go straight along the walkway to the very end and you'll run smack into Klimentevna's palace."

4

Only a word-twister like Lipat Vasilyevich could call Klimentevna's place a palace.

The houses I passed were ordinary—one-story, two-story, single, communal, built of logs or squared timbers. Then, all of a sudden, a hut on chicken legs, with a green meadow all around.

Where was this from, I wondered. From what fairy tale had it flown there?

It turned out to be simple: the hut was a survivor from the old village, in whose place the new settlement had grown. The residents of Ropsha had gladly given up their delapidated old houses after the war, but Klimentevna, a solitary and feeble old woman—what could she do? So to this day her antediluvian dump stands at the edge of the modern community.

The white northern night, already rouged by morning rays, was settled over the crooked little bungalow. In the yard, haphazardly enclosed by a rail fence, a white goat was grazing. A stork-like wellsweep, raising its old head, looked forlornly out at me from under a ramshackle wooden roof with a bed of thick green moss.

As Lipat Vasilyevich had said, Klimentevna was up and about. She was sitting on her rickety porch binding aspen branches for her goat.

At first the old woman regarded me warily, and no wonder, for what sort of travelers come paying visits at midnight? I referred to Lipat Vasilyevich, which didn't help much. But as soon as I mentioned Ksana Grigorievna's name the bolts fell open in front of me.

"Come now, there's no need to be standing. Sit down and chat with an old woman." A thin, stiffened hand cleared a place for me opposite her. "And how did you happen to know Ksana Grigorevna?" She cautiously began to sound me out. Meanwhile the old eyes behind her glasses were sizing me up as best they could.

I didn't beat around the bush, but told her plainly that I planned to write a history of the local lumbering operations and so was interested in Olesha, because there were all kinds of true stories and tall tales being told about him.

"Oh, you're one of them," the old woman quickly lost her enthusiasm, "who writes in the newspapers. Well then, I'm not the one to help you."

"And why not, grandmother?"

"I'm not used to holding folks up to shame, sir. I never said a bad word about anyone in my life. And Ksana Grigorevna, she was like a heavenly angel to me. A natch'ral-born daughter wouldn't care so much about her old mother...."

"So she was a good person, then?"

"Others, talk with others, sir." The old woman backed away from my probing again. "Someone who's educated and clear in the head."

"But you know what the others say? They all say that Ksana Grigorevna's to blame. That it was she who ruined Olesha."

And with that an honest conversation began. Ksana Grigorevna had been closer than a relative, dearer than anyone in the world to this woebegone creature who'd never had children of her own—how could she listen to such criticism?

"Liars, liars, all of them!" Klimentevna menaced them with both hands. "Whoever spreads such slander, their tongues should shrivel. How she suffered from him, poor thing! After the care and the kindness and I dòn't know what else she enchanted him with. I know, you see, I watched it all with my own eyes. They lived here with me."

"Olesha lived here too?"

"That he did. Nowadays they'd say 'Give the young folks some living space, a room or apartment. They were both in good grace with the higher-ups: Ksana was a cook, he the best in the region. But in those days they'd be glad for a cot in the dormitory, family-living behind a curtain. Well, they come to live here with me. Ksana Grigorevna came dashing in once, she'd been to a dance. 'Auntie Grunya,'—that's what she called me—'light the samovar, I'm getting married!' 'To who,' I say, 'to Oleskay Mikhailovich?' He was a local boy, from a good family, he worked in an office. He was seeing her home. 'Yes,' she says, 'to Oleksay, but to the other one, the one who's stronger and handsomer than all the rest.' 'What do you mean, girl!' But I guessed right away who she meant. I'd seen him, he used to come up close to my house too. 'This Oleksey,' I said, 'he's not your kind, with him it'll be nothin' but drink and his friends on his mind....' But she shook her head: 'Don't worry, with me he'll forget all, both drinking and his friends.' And she flings open the door and, lo, there he is, the bridegroom. Well, what could I do—who was I to yell at her? Not her own mother. And that's how my Ksana Grigorevna put the yoke on herself...."

Up to the porch came the white goat, stretching out its neck and fixing its green eyes on me, inquiringly.

"What is it, Milka," Klimentevna asked. "Have you come to look at this stranger? Or to hear about Ksana Grigorevna, who your goat's heart is pining for? Sure'n we loved her now, didn't we? She practically set us a place at the table...."

My eyes popped open—how old was this animal anyway, if it could remember Ksana Grigorevna herself?

Klimentevna gave a heartfelt laugh.

"No, the creature's not immortal. Ksana Grigorevna came back to us three years ago, just as Milka was cutting her horns, sharpening them on everything in sight.... She hadn't been here for twenty years. She came back to look at the grave. And not by herself, but with a husband and grandson. Still, people started talking.... And she was all in tears, crying 'Oh, Auntie Grunya, what've those vagrants done to his grave?' Well, what don't they do? They drink there, and all around it there's broken glass. I go there myself, much as I can, and clean it up, but after every Sunday it's covered with broken bottles again. They all drink his health, the drunkard."

"Olesha?"

"Who else?.. Klimentevna frowned, chewing her toothless gums. "But I don't praise her, either. She's got a respectful husband who won't take his eyes off her, and a grandson—'Granny, granny!'—she's a self-made lady. And look, here she's grieving over God knows what. 'I live well, Auntie Grunia,' she says, 'I've got no complaints. My husband doesn't drink, my children are grown, well-educated, but,' she says, ' I left my heart in these woods, I can't forget Olesha, ever....' "

"So, she really loved him," I observed, and I asked whether Klimentevna had a photo of Olesha and Ksana Grigorevna, or of Ksana Grigorevna herself.

"There was one, somewhere, there was," the old woman tried to dodge my request. "Only where is it now? Maybe I took it to the barn, or maybe Paula Vasina took it—she asked for it time and again, she worked with Ksana Grigorevna in the cafeteria...."

Clearly the old woman didn't want to show me the picture; the idea suddenly seemed hostile to her favorite, so I turned to the past again.

"They lived, on the outside, pretty well, I can't say bad. He brought everything home, down to the last copeck. They brought a chiffoneer, bought a bed, I still have it here, they decked each other out in nice clothes, started sending money to his mother—it seems he had a mother, born down in the southern parts. And then once he went out drinkin' with his friends, then again and again... on and on this went, till he forgot the way home." Klimentevna thought for a moment, then gave all this the fitting judgement: "His whole life spent in dormitories, freedom, wine, friends—what good could come of it? My Ksana would cry, not sleep at night. She was ashamed to see people, she had to go home—her parents were waiting for the newlyweds. But he had drink and a good time on his mind. Drank up everything they earned. He was left in nothing but an overcoat, not even a shirt, they say, barechested.... Yes.... Then something snapped, once after nonstop drinking he ran off into the woods. He made a platform out of boards up in a pine tree. 'Go home, girl,' I told her. Olesha won't come back to you now, no more'n you can bend the tree down.' She cried. 'I'd go if I could,' she said 'but I'm afraid for him, he'll die of hunger.' And so she'd cook and bake and carry the food to feed him in the woods. But Olesha would only mock her. He'd shout down for the whole forest to hear: 'Go away, I don't know you, away with you!' Still, angel that she was, Ksana Grigorevna excused him. 'It's not him, it's the sickness screaming....' He died in the fall. Some say he fell out of the tree drunk, some that he froze, others that his friends were involved. Ivan Martemianovich, a hunter here, heard him: all night, he said, someone in that area was screaming...."

I stayed in Ropsha for over a week. As for the editorial assignment, I quickly, in a day or two, put together a sketch on Pava Khaimusov and his brigade, but I spent all the rest of the time tracking down Olesha, questioning more and more people. And the most diverse people, even those who had never even known him, spoke of him with delight and excitement. As if about their greatest hero.

Notes

1. Michurin, Ivan Vladimirovich (1855-1935). A landowner and self-trained botanist who attempted to adapt warm-weather fruit crops to the climate of northern Russia, with little success. He is nevertheless credited with founding the Soviet school of genetic engineering.

2. Tsar Gorokh. A Character from Russian folklore, here simply a euphemism for the distant past.

3. Mikula Selyaninovich. Another folk hero, a man of legendary strength, not unlike the American Paul Bunyan.

Vasily Shukshin

Makar Zherebtsov

This whole week Makar would go from house to house and continuously and caustically teach people goodness and patience. He taught them how to live—as far as possible happily, but sensibly.

He delivered letters to his fellow-villagers. He rated his work most highly and was not ashamed that at fifty years of age in good health, he was carrying letters and small papers, as well as the pension to old people.

He walked down the street calmly, concentrating. People called out to him: "Makar, nothing?"

"You can see—I'm going past you, so—nothing!"

"Why nothing? It's time already. Cursed devils!" Makar would go up to the paling, hang his satchel on a peg and begin to smoke:

"How many people do we have in the Soviet Union?"

The old woman didn't know.

"Devil only knows how many. Lots, I dare say."

"Lots."—Makar also didn't know exactly how many.—"And all of them have to be paid a pension."

"Why all? Everybody gets wages."

"Well, I didn't make myself clear. All those get a pension who should. That's so?"

"Oh come on now! Why you again!"

"Calmly now! The State delays your pension only one day and you already begin to raise your voice. You're in a bad temper and it's sickening to look at you. And the State has millions such as you. One asks oneself, do you have a conscience or not? You can't be patient for just one day. Try to put yourself in their place..."

Old women would be offended. Old men would tell him to go to hell! Makar would go on further.

"Semyon! You went to see your son?"

"Yes, I went..."

"Well? How did it go?"

"So-so!—Drinks as much as ever. Thrown out of his job again, the loafer!"

"So you jumped on him of course. Called him a few names!.."

"Well, what d'you think I should say to him? Peter, my dear son, please put an end to your drinking?..."

"Stop all that! You don't even know such words. You lash with your tongue like a whip. From childhood they taught you with the stick and you think, you old fool, that this is the way

149

it should always be. Nowadays it's quite a different life..."

"Before, did they drink like he does? A different life..."

"Put yourself in his shoes. He's young, finding his feet, gets some money... then needs strength to abstain—the strength of a horse! On the other hand, loneliness gnaws at him—away from his family. You go off to the city for a week and you're homesick, but he's already been away for years. Probably goes off to a movie, and they show a village—so he goes out and drinks. Everyone just has to understand this."

"You idler, you can talk well enough, but if it was your son you'd sing a different tune. You go to the village and gossip—old windbag!"

"I'm teaching you—you old fools! Go and see this Peter of yours, sit down and have a drink with him. . ."

"Your head's a jumble of ideas like a village council!"

"I'm telling you—have a drink with him, and then slyly, get through to him and tell him: cut it down, my son, cut it down—but gently! After all, we all drink on holidays... Holidays come along and there's drinking, but holidays come to an end and it's time to get back to work, and no more drinking. So that's it. There's no other way. Got to talk to him—persuade the fellow! Kind words, you'll see, 'll get to him sooner!"

"Have to get through to his head with a birch log, not with soft words!"

"Just as I say, you're all like rams—horns grow on the forehead and they're eager to butt—but you're human beings—given brains, the patient word!.."

"Get off with you!"

"Oh, what's the use!"

Makar would go on further.

At Ivan Solomin's house, his wife, Nastya, had given birth to a son. Ivan was arguing with Nastya as to how they should name their newborn baby. Ivan wanted to call him Ivan... Ivan Ivanovich Solomin. Nastya wanted him to be called Valerik. The married couple had been quarreling seriously. And just at this time Makar brought them a letter from Nastya's sister, who lived with her husband in Magadan and wrote in her letter that they were very well off and had just about everything except the

Fountain of Life, "but everything, you understand, comes in cans because the climate is so harsh."

Makar congratulated the parents... And they, of course, set to arguing again, trying to prove to him their own point of view.

"Ivan!.. There's only a few Ivans left today—you and the fairy tale, Ivan-the-Fool. I'd rather die than let him be called Ivan! You're like Ivan-the-Fool yourself..."

"You're the fool! Now in this matter they've gone back to the old days. Look at the cities..."

Makar was all prepared—ready to pounce—wits sharpened—his victim perceived.

"Calmly, Ivan!" he said. Don't call her names like that. Even if she is your lawful wife, you don't have the right to call her a fool. Suppose she does call you Ivan-the-Fool, you should call her 'My little silly,' or something of that sort—tenderly! She will be ashamed, and she will be quiet. But if she won't, you should stay quiet. Control yourself, and be silent."

"Get out of here, you peacemaker!"

"You don't have to send me away. Why do you tell me to go? Send me away if you like, but first try to understand. After all, I didn't come to you to quarrel—I didn't come as an evil-doer, but lawfully, as your friend and comrade. And I want to give you some good advice: call your little son Mitya, in honor of your brother-in-law. After all, they even send you parcels, and throw money to you from time to time... Write to him and say: Dear brother-in-law, in your honor our son is named Mitya!... And where he would have sent one parcel, he might think of sending two. Naturally he would think: they have named their son in honor of me—this is a great compliment... For such esteem people pay back esteem."

For some reason Ivan snarled at him.

"Get out of here! Why do you poke your nose into what is not your business!"

Makar laughed mildly, tolerantly, kindly. He knew well e-nough the quarrelsome nature of Ivan.

"So you want to make a bit of noise?.. You really are a blus-tering fool... At the same time, Ivan took the postman by the scruff of the neck, hauled him to the door and gave him a kick.

"Take that for your advice!"

Makar went further along the street. He rubbed his sore neck and muttered: The devil has a hard foot—as hard as a horse! And began to recount the proceedings to anyone he met: "Ivan Solomin... Went to his house—they were kicking up a dust! Couldn't decide on a name for their son—I have suggested to them Mitya. He has a brother-in-law in Magadan—Mitya..."

But nobody wanted to listen to Makar: there was no time. And there were few people on the street in the village in summertime.

And now it had come to Sunday. On Sundays Makar didn't work. He waited for Sundays. In the morning he drank a glass—or two, no more, had breakfast, and went to the small bench near the gate... He had a bench with a little table, a neat and tidy bench, and here he would make himself comfortable, crossing one leg over the other, smoking, and waiting with bright shining eyes for someone to come by.

"Mikeevna! Good-day to you, Mikeevna! I wish you a good holiday!"

"What holiday is this?"

"Well, it's Sunday!"

"Good Lord! Some holiday!"

"That son of yours not writing? For quite a long time I haven't had to come to you."

"No time, I dare say, to write anything. Also—it's not a health resort you know—these are mines!"

"All of them, the scoundrels, never have any time. They can all guzzle vodka—always time for this. But to write a letter to their mother—no time for that. Why don't you complain to the Director of the mines about him? If you like, I could write something. Send a registered letter..."

"What a stupid idea, Makar! To complain of one's own son to the Director!"

"It's possible to do it cunningly. Can send a telegram, say— 'Worried—Is he ill?' They will call him out and bring him to task..."

"Pah! What the devil. You've got nothing else to do but sit there making up things!"

"But you have to teach the scoundrels, teach them!"

The old woman, irritated, vexed with her son, went further on her way.

"The fat hog," she muttered. "Have your own children first, and then complain! Then would you deal with them like that?"

"Until a man is given a knock—up to then he doesn't understand," Makar said to himself... We are offended by Fate, but it teaches us, Mother, it teaches!

People still continued to pass by, and Makar would start talking to them all, and all in the same spirit—the Sunday mood! He would suggest how, if possible, they might spite their mother-in-law—and how they might force the Directors of the State Farm to respect them... It's only necessary to be more daring, to speak out at all the meetings, and each time—against. At first they snap, then try to subdue you somehow, but you speak out about it at the next meeting. It's important not to give way, and when they understand they can't do anything to you, then they begin to respect you. And then they become a little afraid?—something to hide, perhaps? Who is sinless?..

"But if you do this, then they kick you out..."

"Where will they kick you to? Somewhere further off?—It's not like in the factory..."

Some time at two in the afternoon, old man Kuzma arrived at Makar's. He never had any money for drink.

"Give me something for a bottle? On Tuesday I'll go fishing with my son-in-law and bring you some fish..."

Makar gave him twenty roubles for fruit wine but only asked: "Come here to drink it.—There's no one to talk to."

The old man brought the bottle of fruit wine and poured a glass.

"Yesterday me and my son-in-law had too much—he's lying down and suffering too."

"Take him a little glass."

"No need—he's young—can get over it alone. There's only a little left for me."

"Greedy."

"No," the old man said quickly.

"And I suppose he doesn't have any money either, your son-in-law?"

"Noorka has some... But would she part with any?.. Not if you were dying! How's that wife of yours?"

"She's ill."

"Perhaps you beat her?.. Why is she ill all the time?"

"Never once raised a finger to her in all this time! She's just a febble person."

"Strange fellow you are, Makar.—Don't understand you. I understand everyone I've seen growing up around here, but you there's no way I could ever understand."

"What seems ódd about me?"

"Well, how shall I put it... On Sundays you just sit all day with arms folded. People wait, not to lie around on a Sunday, but to be busy doing some sort of household work, but you seem to have nothing to do."

"But what do I need it for—this household work?"

"Well, that's just what's strange... Where are you from?—or have I already asked you that?"

"Not far from here. What is it to me, this household work? Will I take it to the grave?"

"Well, you still have time before the grave... Work won't beat a lay-about.—And you're not even ashamed!" The old man was truly amazed. "Are you really not ashamed?"

"Not even that much..." Makar gestured towards the end of his little finger."

"But why, for example, do you tell some people one thing, and others quite the other way around? Why do you confuse them so?"

Makar began to think, looked at the street, then said: "It wasn't for this kind of life I was born, old fellow."

"For what then?"

"Don't even know myself. Here you are, saying I confuse people. I myself don't know why I do this. Should I feel sorry for them, or have a laugh at them? I walk around and look—want to help them with some kind of advice, and then change my mind and think: Go to hell, the lot of you!"

"Hmm!"

"So here one is—going around every week, poking one's nose into their business. Then comes Sunday and I'm fond of resting. 'Rot further, you devils!' I keep thinking, and suggest some dirty trick."

"What a stinker!"

"Really!.. But tomorrow again I shall go from house to house, again I shall get into their business, and even though they don't listen to my advice, I can't stop myself from giving it. I really should give advice on a big scale, without having to face them. And I would be good at it! Of course, I would have to learn some more—that's only natural—but I have the urge to give advice—the desire to teach—and that's it, even if I had to die."

"You should be teaching one thing only, but somehow you jump about from one thing to another."

"Yes, that's what I want! But after all, I tell them one thing and then they curse me!—and not only that, they knock me around as well! That fool over there—Solomin—pushed me from his porch—the dragon!"

"Well—that's the kind of a fellow he is."

"But I was telling him for his own good: Name, let's say, your little son 'Mitya', in honour of your brother-in-law, and this brother-in-law will lay himself out for you!—What difference does it make to him, the fool, whether there'll be a 'Mitya' or an 'Ivan' growing up in his house? But it would make his life a little easier. The brother-in-law there, in the North, handles thousands of roubles!—But really, I don't dislike people! On the contrary, I feel sorry for them."

The old man drank up the remains of the wine and pulled himself up.

"But for all that, you're a stinker!" he said, without malice.

"You going already?.. Sit down—I'll give you another rouble."

"Got to go... Son-in-law'll be coming to himself now—probably digging up the cellar—have to help him. I'll bring two kilograms of fish—on Tuesday!"

"Fine! That's good...I love fish soup."

"Thanks for coming to my help."

"Don't mention it."

The old man went off. But Makar stayed sitting on the bench, looking at the village, and smoking. Sometimes his sick wife came out of the house to sit close to him in the warmth of the sun.

"And just how many houses are there here," he pondered, not looking at his wife. "And in each house—his own! But this—this is only one village. How many such villages in Russia?"

"Lots, agreed his wife."

"Lots! sighed Makar,—Lots!"

Yury Trifonov

Games at Dusk

We knew them all by name; not one of them knew us. We were simply, "Hey, little boy! Bring the ball!" Or else we were, "Thanks, little boy," or "There it is, behind the bush! More to the left, more left!" They played from four until dusk, while we sat on a bench carved by knives—my friend Savva and I—turning our heads from right to left, right to left, right to left. Our necks hurt. This continued for hours. Neither hunger, nor thirst, nor any earthly desire could distract us from this remarkable occupation. From right to left, right to left darted the small, right to left white, right to left tennis ball together with firm resonant strokes which were evenly right to left, right to left hammered into our brains, made us dizzy, cast a spell on us, and hypnotized us, we were like drunks, unable to leave, to stand up, even though at home a bawling-out awaited us, we continued to sit stupefiedly, turning our heads from right to left, right to left, right to left.

From the other side of the court—if someone happened to glance at us!—we resembled two little bowing Chinese idols, so tirelessly and smoothly did we move our almost crew-cut heads. And truly, we were like little Chinese idols. But really, not little Chinese idols, not at all Chinese, but very real, suburban Moscow, eleven-year-old summer residents, idlers who wasted their July evenings turning their heads from side to side.

Nearby was the river, a sandstone slope, a sandbar, barges—the odor of the water and yells of the swimmers reached us without penetrating deep into our consciousness. These were the odors and noises of a distant and superfluous world.

At dusk our chance came. The first player to give up was a lanky spectacled guy whom Savva and I called "The Trembler."[1] The Trembler was very nervous on the court. At each unsuccessful stroke he would yell, "Oh hell!", seize his head, look around with amazement at the rim of his racket, shake his head and mutter something like, "What's going on? What's the matter with me?" But nothing particular ever came out of it. He always played the same. The best player, Tatarnikov, an aristocrat, the owner of an Erenpraiz bicycle, a model in everything for Savva and me, who played almost at the same time as The Trembler, would stop the game. He was silent and ironical, and wore elegant striped shirts, hair sleekly slicked down—for such a haircut he was nicknamed "politcut."[2] Tatarnikov treated his partners so scornfully that he could get away with stopping the game whenever he felt like it, even in the middle of a game—if he had fewer points. He would suddenly raise his racket with the words, "That's it, folks! This has no class—an eyesore," and would walk off the court, and no one dared to argue with him. Everyone swallowed this boorishness silently as if in their minds they thanked Tatarnikov for the fact that he came to play at all. After all, Tatarnikov had once played with Henri Cochet himself and the latter had said about him, "A fine fellow."

Tatarnikov would get on his Erenpraiz and ride away, and immediately Anchik would get ready to go also. She wouldn't throw down her racket right away, but it was clear how uninteresting everything became for her. She would stop trying, miss the ball, and bicker. Anchik was dark-complexioned, like an Indian. Sometimes she could be very merry, laughing loudly and lifting everyone's spirits, but sometimes she was gloomy and irritable. Poor Anchik! I pitied her. And Savva did too. Although Savva once said he didn't like coquettes, I saw that he was lying. I noticed how he would tense up and how his face would flush in spots when Anchik addressed him in her soothing though completely indifferent voice. "Little boy, would you mind..." With sullen haste he ran after the ball much faster than usual. I, on the contrary, sat silently and haughtily. Just as soon as Anchik stopped her game, the Professor and Gravinsky usually accompanied Anchik to her dacha on Line 3.

A small, dark-faced little man in square glasses, the owner of a Japanese racket, would remain playing longer than the others. Savva and I suspected him of being a spy. A husband and wife, a disgusting pair for whom tennis was necessary only to lose weight, would hang around the court even longer than "the spy." They played very badly, but long and persistently, until dark. I noticed that the worse the players, the more avid they were for the game. Savva and I detested them. They deprived us of the last, precious seconds because the real players did not permit them, like us, on the court. But late in the evening they didn't permit us, insolently using their prerogative as adults. "Children, children! You've been hanging around here all day...." But finally they too would clear off. I would take my twelve-ounce Dynamo racket from its case and Savva his marvelous German one—with steel strings—and we would run out into the empty court. There were no people happier than we at that moment.

The court was cement. It became white in the dusk, like an open and spacious meadow. We really hurried. In the dark we often missed. We wanted to serve with all our strength. Every now and then the fast balls which we missed would strike against the wooden wall with a drumming noise. The back line and the serving courts were no longer visible. The flying ball would fly out from the dark so unexpectedly that I instinctively held up my racket in self-defense. We enjoyed ourselves for twenty minutes, until Nikolai Grigorevich, the net manager, returned from swimming and took it down and left. We continued to play for a while without the net; actually, in the dark, it made no difference, with or without the net.

And then for a long time we would talk about all sorts of things and meander home along the bank. On the other side of the river, in the meadow, hung layers of fog. Someone was swimming in the river and someone stood on the bank and yelled, "How's the water, eh?" Someone would run, warming himself after a swim, along the smooth, sandy strip by the water. The patter of bare feet along the gray sand resounded clearly and softly, like the slaps of palms on a naked body. One could hear this person with his patter of bare feet saying, "Br-br-br!" And the superfluous, starry July world lie around us amidst the pines and beyond the river, where on the horizon, the fires of Tushin shimmered through the warm air. That was a long time ago. It was back when people used to wade across the Moscow River, when people used to ride a long, red Leiland bus from Theatre Square through Silver Forest, when people wore silk tolstovkas, pants made from white linen, and canvas shoes which were rubbed with tooth powder in the evenings so that in the mornings they looked freshly white and with each step released a cloud of white dust.

***

It is difficult to say now who these people were, how old they were. They disappeared from my life and at that time I didn't pay any attention to such things. I only knew regarding Gravinsky that he was the son of some worker of the Comintern. The Trembler and the Professor may have been students, but perhaps not. Tatarnikov worked somewhere, but it is possible that he worked nowhere at all, because he often came to the court during the day. Anchik was a high school senior; that, however, is not sure either, and it's quite possible that she was a college student. I knew that her father drove a black Rolls Royce. Once I saw the black automobile stop outside a house on Line 3 — there was a terrible downpour and I had been sent to the corner for milk; I was soaked to the skin and plodding along the street, hurrying nowhere—when Anchik jumped out of the car, took off her shoes and, squealing, splashed along in her bare feet toward the gate. Right after her came a man in a black hat. Suddenly he stopped right in a puddle, took off his hat, exposing his bald head to the rain, and stood several seconds in a strange pensiveness, looking at the ground.

Anchik was tall and slender, *with a wasp's wisp of a waist*, with *jet-black hair* and big black eyes, as black and deep *as the night*. I liked her very much. Of course, not in the same way I would like a girl, for example, Marina, my classmate. Anchik I liked platonically—as a woman. I liked her husky voice, her clothes, sarafans and *maikas*, which apparently were last year's—a little too small and tightly cutting her body. I liked the way she walked, swinging her arms and swaying like a sailor. I liked her habit of joking about everything and talking in a haughty manner. I liked the way she picked up the ball from the court, not stooping, deftly and quickly by the rim of her racket and foot. I could pick up the ball like that too, but only with the help of my left leg. Anchik did it with ease with either leg. The ball seemed to stick to her racket. And she never dropped balls on the court. But Savva and I dropped them often.

I don't know, maybe it was because of Anchik that we hauled ourselves to the court each evening. That didn't occur to me then, but now I think that that's the way it was. Because of Anchik and because of Tatarnikov, whom we also liked. After all, we could have come during the day, in the heat when no one was playing, but the empty court and the empty benches didn't suit us—we wanted the public, noise, passions, struggle, beautiful women—and we wanted to see it all, as in the theater.

In the middle of summer Savva's father died, and his mother took him to Leningrad. He left me his racket with the steel strings. He promised to return at the end of the summer, but he didn't. Never again in life did I meet Savva, nor hear anything about him.

And he didn't see me when I played doubles with The Trembler or see what happened the following summer when the Moscow-Volga Canal was opened: the river was made navigable and ships began to go up it. New players appeared on the tennis court, but Tatarnikov remained the champion of Silver Forest and environs. He played some people for money. He would spot them four games and still win.

At the beginning of that summer—when the first ships came— it was very hot, but later it rained constantly. It was a kind of light, fleeting rain which broke out suddenly and did not last long. But we had to wait half an hour or an hour for the court to dry. The tennis players would gather under an awning built next to the court, play chess and other games, or simply sit, telling jokes. I loved to sit on the bench among them and listen. One day we're all sitting together, myself, Tatarnikov, the Professor with Gravinsky, Anchik and someone else—when this Boris came and said that an acquaintance of ours had drowned. Boris had appeared at the court not long ago, he didn't play badly, but sort of flashily and arrogantly. He argued after every ball. His father was the director of a factory and they used to live in Tbilisi. So he came and said that an acquaintance of ours had drowned. It later turned out that no one had drowned, he had concocted it all, but, of course, at first everyone became alarmed. Anchik even screamed and then this Boris stepped up to her; he was stocky, not tall, shorter than Anchik, with very memorable, round, knee-like cheekbones. He always spoke clenching his teeth, and this made his cheeks move. And he said, clenching his teeth, "Take this, you trash," and hit Anchik in the face with the edge of his palm—a violent back-handed blow. At this point everyone began to shout.

"Hey! What's that for?"

Boris didn't answer and looked angrily at Anchik while she stood covering her face with her hands. She neither cried nor moved. The way Anchik was struck and the way she *took* the blow was so unbelievable that in astonishment I froze on the bench, while everyone else was jumping from their places, jostling one another and yelling. The Professor or Gravinsky or perhaps both seized Boris around the chest. But he brushed them off and quietly said:

"Butt out! Get away! I'm telling you, get away! Or else...."

"Wait," said Tatarnikov. "Did anyone drown or not?"

And at this point Boris again struck Anchik on the hands covering her face, but with such force that she was knocked off balance, staggered back like a branch, and almost fell. Then she started walking quickly, almost at a run, and Boris kept up with her. They went through the pines and the bushes, not glancing at each other, paying no attention to where they were going, business-like and straight, and each was isolated, but something terrible and simple bound them together. They were like one person, flashing for a moment amidst the pines, going away from us.

The court dried and someone came out to play, but I couldn't stand to see the pale face of Tatarnikov with his "polit-cut." The tennis players were filled with indignation and, as I heard, agreed not to play again with Boris, with this beast. "Striking a woman! Sinking so low! It's a pity that he left. We'd have stomped on him!" But I felt they were indignant at something else.

After this, life on the court somehow began to quickly and irretrievably change. Some people completely vanished, stopped coming, others moved away. New people came. Many new ones. They say that Anchik with her younger sister, brother and grandmother, was living at Elk Station. But Tatarnikov came just as before on his Erenpraiz; sometimes The Trembler and the man whom Savva and I considered a Japanese spy would come. They built a volleyball court next to the tennis court and in the evenings a noisy crowd gathered there to play. There were forty people who waited to play, the losers yielding to those left and the winners staying on. The hubbub was like at a bazaar.

The beast Boris came once on a Sunday with a friend as if nothing had happened. Both were wearing jockey caps. Boris asked, "Who's next?" We didn't answer him. There was a foursome on the court and another foursome was waiting in line. Boris and his friend sat waiting for half an hour, then began to make a scene. There would have been a real fight had there not been a strange noise from the riverside. The woods cracked under the feet of a hundred people. A huge crowd was moving to our side with music and songs, and in front ran little boys who informed us that a ship had docked, that the crowd was coming from there, with a tin-pan band behind them. The tennis players continued to play coolly. In a moment the horde surrounded the court; several of them were noticeably merry and sat down on the grass.

Some danced, others played leap-frog, an accordian was playing, several people entered the court and started to demand that the tennis players take down the net. They, understandably, refused to do so and said they were going to call a policeman. The Trembler became particularly excited and yelled,

"We're going to complain! Tell me where you work?"

A thickset man in a panama also yelled, swinging his arms.

"But you want to play in fours so that four hundred people watch you, right? Is that what you think?"

"You're disturbing us!"

"Comrades, where's a policeman...?"

"We have an arrangement with the resort administration!"

The band came out onto the court and made themselves comfortable by the wooden wall while they argued. Someone had already stripped off the net and the first couple began to shuffle along the cement, even without music. But then a waltz broke out: "The blue globe spins, turns." I saw how Boris, his cheeks puffed out, dragged along a thin ugly woman, a total fright in a shawl, and began to dance with her. The tennis players were still aroused and were trying to break up the band. Only Tatarnikov was not excited. He got on the Erenpraiz and rode off.

The wooden fence was broken down and burned for heat during the war. Once, after ten years, I went back there and walked up the hill in order to see the place where began so much of what my life later consisted. But at that time there were only promises. However, several of them were fulfilled. On the top of the hill I stumbled across a majestic, summer movie theater whose thick white walls glimmered. All that remained of the court was a cement area on which people were bumping into each other, arm in arm, men and women from the dachas waiting for the beginning of a performance. How could you call them people from the dachas! This was Moscow. It smelled like Moscow, with gasoline and dusty foliage. I asked a man in a red pullover made half of leather, half of wool if he knew where the cement square had come from. "It's from the war," he answered with confidence. "There was some sort of fortification here. When the Germans flew to bomb Moscow, it was from here, over Silver Forest, that they were shot down. Yes, it's from the war."

I went up to the river and sat down on a bench. The river

had remained. The pines also creaked as before. But dusk was somehow different. I didn't want to swim. In the days when I was eleven, dusk was much warmer.

1. In Russian, *drozhashchii.*
2. A haircut that was typical for officials in the government, for bureaucrats.

Inna Varlamova

A Ladle for Pure Water

Elena Dmitrievna Khatanzeyeva, dressed in a festive Khant national costume with varicolored cloth ornaments along its hem, walked down the middle of the street. She walked along like a proud duck, swaying from one foot to the other. She was small, swarthy, and had flashing black slits for eyes. On her head she wore a splendid turquoise kerchief with red roses. Its fringe was long and silky. Her young husband Nikolai, a tall pole of a man, bounced along at her side. Everyone they ran into bowed respectfully to them: "Good day to you."

Elena Dmitrievna had been promoted up the ranks even before the war, and was an active member of the woman's section of the Party local committee, a deputy to the village regional council, a former distinguished kolkhoz wild-animal keeper and huntress, and a rich woman. Fifty of her deer grazed in the tundra along with the kolkhoz herd.

Husband and wife were going to a lecture at the community center. Elena Dmitrievna had mastered her public role well and she respected it. She conceived of it as the necessity of setting an example for her neighbors, always and in everything. That was why whenever there was a lecture or meeting in the village, she would dress up and make her way to the community center with measured steps. She would seat herself up front, usually in full view, so as to have easier access to the presidium. On the presidium she would sit motionless. Her face would be enigmatically immobile, while the black slate of her pupils glittered with the coldness of mineral. Her small hands, which were unusually beautiful, tapered, and untouched by age, would lie in her lap.

When the need arose, she would get up and boldly deliver a speech. Actually, it was always the same speech, whatever the occasion. The tongue-tied and almost incomprehensible phrases, nevertheless, would turn into something indisputably patriotic. And her audience would grasp what was most important—the sincere feeling, and Elena Dmitrievna had no doubt that they would grasp it, and didn't worry about choosing natural, clear words. Even she often failed to understand what the regional and district superiors were saying from the rostrum; all that mattered to her was to hear the familiar words "socialism," "Party," "the people," "competition," "the plan"—and wasn't it really all the same how they were interwoven? And when her time came, Elena Dmitrievna would rise, move forward to the proscenium (she didn't stand behind the rostrum, since she was too small and knew that a person looks funny if he stretches his neck in order to be seen), and in a high, forced voice she'd shout out:

"Comwades,[1] we awe justifying the twust of the Pawty! Socialist competition is a pledge, comwades! We awe the fishewmen and weindeew bweedews of the wondewful nowth, comwades! The Pawty and the govewnment have established a happy life fow us! Education, and fwee medical aid too! Long live peace on eawth! Comwades, thewe's no stopping the cuwsed aggwessows, comwades! And we must supply fish without west, comwades, fiwst-class fish and skins of valuable soft gold! And we, fine women, mothews, in the fiwst wanks of men, give biwth hygenically in these conditions, comwades, and we toil, comwades, fow evewyone's welfawe! And communism, comwades, is at hand!"

Concluding, as always, with communism, she would turn her back to the audience with dignity, and to a storm of applause would return to her seat, placing her serene firm hands in her lap as though prepared not to stir any more until death.

Nikolai listened to his wife, his tow head lowered. He was never elected to the presidium. He was her husband and nothing more. He'd appeared in the village three years ago and worked on the animal farm where they bred silver and polar foxes. He fed them boiled fish and salted whale meat. Because of their vitamins he added stinging nettles and birch leaf to the food. He gave the cubs milk. He liked to hear the nervous barking of the animals when he approached the open-air cage. He tried never to reminisce about his former life. Three years ago he'd been a young fellow. And now, of course he wasn't old yet, but he wasn't young any more either. His wife was a prominent, rich, ardent and strong woman; he submitted to her readily and of his own free will so as not to think about anything, but his happiest moments came when he brought food to the open-air cages and heard the nervous barking of the polar foxes. The happiness of those moments stemmed from the melancholy that they awakened in him. Melancholy was his cherished, secret, free emotion.

He had come from Tobolsk, where he'd been born, to this land of lakes and rivers lost in the taiga. A cheerful and wild Komsomol member, who, like all village boys of his age, liked to drink a half-bottle of vodka, to have a good time, to play pranks, and to dance on the village square to the accompaniment of an accordian, he had been mobilized into a logging camp, but because of his frivolousness he couldn't bear the hardships of an unsettled life, poor food, and boredom, so he ran off home. He miraculously survived the 500-kilometer route through the taiga; he starved, was reduced to tatters, became flea-ridden, wore his feet down to the bone, and when he entered the yard of his home, his father didn't recognize him and chased him away with a stick as if he were a tramp. Then Nikolai, perhaps mortified to the point of tears, all of a sudden turned round and left the yard. His father caught up with him at the gate and asked:

"Is that you, or who is it?"

"It's me," he replied, and keeled over.

They saved his life by spoon-feeding him broth for twenty days, and then the kolkhoz took him to court for deserting the logging camp. And Nikolai, after signing an agreement not to leave, took off with a knapsack at night, went to the landing, boarded the last steamship going north from there, and lying on the hot sheets of corrugated iron in the engine room, he reached Beryozovo, and there for some reason he went ashore and after standing there for a bit, he got cold from the wind on the dock and suddenly asked the captain, to whom he'd taken a liking, to take him in the launch. Without asking him for money for a half-liter of vodka, the captain said, "Come on, then, mac, get in!" —and they floundered about heaven knows where along the brunches of the Ob until they finally touched shore. It was then that the captain said, as if apologizing, "Out you go, mac!" and Nikolai ran down the ship's ladder obediently and with a sense of doom onto the sand and, sinking up to his ankles, he made his way to the unknown village. It was toward evening on a cold dark autumn day, a sparse ominous snow was coming down from the black clouds, Nikolai had only nine rubles and some small change, and in order to maintain a sense of dignity in his own eyes, he knocked not at the first or second *izba*, but at the third, and that one turned out to be Elena Dmitrievna's house, where he found for himself shelter, a wife, countless barrels of salt fish, and oblivion.

...This time the lecture was uninteresting, but here, in the north, every event was a holiday. Even if a plane flew by, people came out to listen to the noise of the motors, and animatedly tried to guess what pilot was flying where and why. And here you could see a newcomer, listen for fun to his unintelligible mumblings, and observe how, as if to save his soul, every other minute he greedily fell upon the yellow water that he poured with a hollow gurgle from the decanter.

Nikolai wasn't aware that he'd dozed off and he was awakened by a rumble as the podium was dragged back into the recesses of the stage. Elena Dmitrievna had already risen to leave, and tying the smart kerchief that everyone envied, she was looking with a severe expression at the young fellows and girls who were hurriedly dragging the benches over to the walls and stacking them on top of one another.

"So you've slept enough?" she asked. "Let's go, then."

But he was gazing spellbound at the center of the well-worn floor that was being cleared quickly, and he experienced a sweet pang of memory. At 7½ the tape recorder made cricket-like sounds, then the switch was adjusted to 3¾, and then the music sounded like music, rising and falling in unbroken thick units, like powerful billows in a river. What sort of dance was it? Nikolai didn't know. They hadn't done any dance like that in his time.

The music washed over them again and again, and it seemed unchanging, but at every new crest it returned as though it were slightly jagged—it was simple, plaintive, reminiscent of what his father used to play on his rose willow pipe, but here there were thousands of these pipes playing and it seemed as if the pipers were becoming frenzied for some reason.

Fellows who had returned from an expedition, the doctor's assistant from the aid station, a schoolteacher, a driver from the kolkhoz launch and even the fisherman Frolka simply seized the girls wearing light dresses under dark jackets who were standing by the wall and like mosquitoes they all piled together into a heap, but left a lot of room free, and off they went, rotating their hips in front of one another, waving their arms, even if only lazily, and dropping almost to their knees. And in that squirming and squatting Nikolai again seemed to see cheerful, wild despair and rage.

"I ain't goin' just yet, I wanta watch a little," he said. "You go on..."

Elena Dmitrievna was surprised at his independence, but didn't say a word. She left the community center—grand, flat like

172

all Khants, small, and proud.

Mariana Prokofievna, an ethnographer from Leningrad, met her en route.

"Lord, how gorgeous!" she cried with a smile. "Each one better than the one before. Well, Elena Dmitrievna, if you couldn't bear to sell your deerskin suit to the museum, than at least sell this one! What do you say, Elena Dmitrievna? Do sell it, dear! We'll pay well!"

"I ain't planning to die just yet. I'll be weawing it myself," she said provokingly.

2

Nikolai didn't even understand how audaciously he'd shifted from his present-day self to his old self by remaining at the community center. Without participating, he watched the others dance, without even entertaining the thought of getting up and trying to surrender his body to the spellbinding music that made one feel an irresistible urge to move. He reminded one of someone who loiters on a bridge, voluptuously and dully staring at the whirlpools of water between the piers, scarcely seeing the glasslike eddying streams or the tossing of the brown foam, or the chip that rushes senselessly about back and forth and is suddenly carried off headlong out of sight, like an arrow released from a taut bow.... He doesn't see this because he's engrossed in himself and is contemplating something else with his inner eye: the interweaving of streams in his own immortal soul, which he usually forgets to think about, and he even finds quivering foam in it, and a small agile chip... The idler leans against the railings, and spits into the water below, follows the trail of his spit, strains his ear to hear it plop on the water's surface, and he looks like a complete and utter fool, but that is a great moment in a person's life and each of us should stop on a bridge, even if only rarely, and spit into the water with an estranged and stupid look...

Nikolai didn't even notice when the music ended and the people dispersed. That didn't have anything to do with him. He sat alone, and only the odor of the dusty floor spattered with water made him look around. The cleaning woman, dipping a birch broom in a bucket, was sprinkling water on the floor in a fanlike motion and was gettin close to him.

"But you didn't even dance, Nikolai Ivanovich," she said, halting in front of him with her bucket.

"Me? You're kidding!" he replied. He was about to add that he'd gotten old, but was afraid of being hypocritical.

He sat and gazed at the woman's feet in their worn slippers. He glanced a touch higher and discovered a thread hanging down from a hem. Then he glanced upward all the way and froze: the woman's face didn't just look attractive and kind, but was that dear face that one seeks eternally, that everyone dreams of finally seeing by one's side in life, and quietly immersing oneself in it, of resting from everything. This was the face of his only real wife.

He remembered seeing her many times before—in a store, on the street, here in the community center, and she always looked at Nikolai with sympathetic interest. She was a short and plump woman, her eyes were grey, with thick lashes—dark at the lids and light at the tips, as if pollen had been scattered on them. Her hair was also multi-hued: above her forehead at the temples it was like flax, so white that it was almost silver. But on the back of her head it was light brown, thick, heavy, as though it had been slicked down with oil. There was down on her cheeks. Once during the summer she had been standing on the riverbank with her baby, while he was getting ready to catch fish for the foxes and was attaching floats to the sweep-net. He worked with cold zeal, but from time to time, as if the devil were leading him astray, he'd dart a melancholy glance sideways in her direction, and reveling in his misery, he'd admire the whitish little hairs on her legs that moved so innocently under the sun in the wind by the river.

"Where's your baby?" he asked, following his thoughts.

She answered quickly, "He's asleep, asleep, Nikolai Ivanovich—here, behind the partition."

He fell silent, and after waiting a little to see whether he'd ask her anything else, she started sweeping, and Nikolai still didn't leave; through his nostrils he inhaled the smell of the damp dust lying on the floor. Then she carried the bucket with its heavy black water past him and at the door she glanced around as if to ask: "Should I turn off the lights or not?" He got up, but instead of going home as he should, he sat on the porch, certain that she'd come out.

She did, and hardly had she sat down beside him on the step, when quickly, hurrying again, she started speaking:

"I'll tell you something, Nikolai Ivanovich... You won't believe it, I'm ashamed to talk about it—my father sold me, you know. And not for very much, for next to nothing, I think—for vodka. I didn't want to marry at all, I hid at my girlfriends' for a whole week, but my mother was really going crazy with worry, and I felt sorry for her. My husband—he was a friend of my father's, they used to play dominoes together, he was a man twice my age. One time when I was getting ready to go dancing, my father said: 'Don't go, wait, there's something we've got to settle,' What could it be? And he says to me: 'It's time you got married.' Christ, marry who? 'Matvei Kuzmich, why wouldn't he do as a husband?' And I start bawling, 'What're you thinking of, I'm young, I still want to run around some!' And he says to me: 'You've run around enough! If you overdo the running around, like a cat, nobody'll take you in marriage!' And there and then I ran off to my friends in the dorm. But then I gave in. Matvei Kuzmich took me off to Sale-Khard, started to drink, started to beat me—he was always getting rough with me. There wasn't a time I wasn't black and blue. Once he was sitting at home, in the wooden hut, and—I was working as a fish inspector—I was hanging the fish out in the yard. A young Nenets brought the fish. What a good-looking Nenets! He came over in a sleigh. And I said to him, 'I've never been in a sleigh,'' I said. And he—he says, 'Get in, I'll give you a ride!' We didn't go more that 800 meters, it was nothing at all. But my husband saw us through the window and started beating me up. He put me up against the wall right in the yard, by the refrigerator, and started throwing weights at me—how it is he didn't kill me I'll never know. I waited until spring and then quietly ran away from my husband like I was going to the hay-mowing—and then onto a steamboat. My husband ran there, looked all over the steamboat for me, he dug around, asked everybody. Thank the lord, a policeman I knew was traveling too, and he stuck up for me—and then the siren went—ooo-oo-oo! And I was off, I didn't know where. I got out at Beryozovo, got on a launch and came here, to the taiga, to the swamp, anything to get further away. At first I almost went crazy here. I thought I'd lose my mind. I'd come home here behind the partition—and there'd be only the empty walls, I was totally alone, and I'd start moping.

But after I had a kid, I seemed to recover. And now here I am bringing up a son, working as a cleaning woman in the village Soviet."

Nikolai had expected something of the sort from her. He wanted her to have had a hard, sinful life behind her. Smooth clean girls didn't appeal to him. "Fools!" he'd judge them mercilessly. What struck him was that, like him, she hadn't disembarked at Muzhi or Kondinsk, but at Beryozovo, though she'd been sailing from the north, and he from the south. "Fate," he decided. "It's fate."

"What's your name?" Nikolai asked and took her rough hot hand.

"Augusta Ionovna," she said, trustingly quick as always with her response. "It's very hard to remember."

He grinned.

For a while they sat on the steps, then Nikolai said:

"Put something on and we'll go wander down to the river."

And boy! How fast Augusta flew home for a jacket, how quickly she came back! Throwing the jacket around her shoulders, catching hold of the lapels with her small fists, she raised her serious eyes, shining in the moonlight, silver between the black lashes, up to tall Nikolai.

"Little foxes," whispered Nikolai, "Little silver foxes..."

The village was already sleeping and the street was empty. Light clouds sped one after another in the dark sky like frightened geese fluttering their wings. The green moon was shining brightly—like a large fire-fly.

They came out onto the shore, and the dew-dampened sand scrunched beneath their feet. The hulk of the old launch, riddled with holes, which had collapsed on to its side and was bloated with sand, looked black. Leaning back against it, they stood in benumbed silence.

"Okay, give it time, Gustia, it won't be right away," he said finally, and embraced her miserably and intimately, "It can't be right away, I feel sorry for her."

"Do you feel terribly sorry for her?" Augusta asked quietly.

"Terribly sorry."

"What are we doing!" Augusta suddenly exclaimed passionately. "Have we gone crazy?"

Difficult days for Nikolai dragged by. He didn't know how to approach Elena Dmitrievna to broach a conversation. He rarely saw Augusta, he didn't go past the community center, but he would leave the animal farm, cut up whale meat, cook fish, and use a bucket to throw the thick broth into bowls. The dogs' barking would disturb, cheer, and depress him... Walking past the open-air cages, he would speak with the animals as though with himself.

"Aiiiee, you—" he'd start, "Son of a bitch, you're lazing a-bout, little cross-back,[2] you're hot... Well, well... Huh, she's running away from me, got frightened... And how can I run away from my woman, tell me?..She'll die, you know... Really. What am I? I'm young, I've got strength, but her? She took such good care of me then... I can never forget that. And then, whatever else, I tell you, she's—all right, a good woman, so what that she's on in years. That's also, you know... You can't forget that. The body, it remembers everything. She bosses me about like a master sergeant; left, about face! And bless you, you turn around! Come on, now, come here, you little whore! Eat!... And I'll tell you what else— I'm afraid of her, I am! She's ill-tempered. Though, no—not ill-tempered, but quick to flare up. What she'll do, the devil himself only knows. She's already sniffed it out, damn her, but she's keeping quiet... She's keeping quiet and keeping quiet, that's all there is to it!"

And that was true—no one knew when Elena Dmitrievna discovered Nikolai's love for Augusta. No one seemed to have seen them standing at the launch that night. And yet, in spite of that, she found out. She didn't say a word to her husband, but one evening she came to the community center to see Augusta behind the partition.

"Listen, my giwl," she said. "You ought to be a bit mowe modest. You heaw? You—who awe you next to me, who awe you? An unmawwied mothew. And you know who I am? It's hawd fow you—we'll help matewially. We won't leave you in povewty. So-viet powew plus electiwicity. But you ought to conduct youwself mowally, you heaw?"

"I hear," replied Augusta, head lowered.

"A little boy?" asked Elena Dmitrievna, nodding at the baby in the cradle.

"A boy," said Augusta, "Edik."

"We'll help," Elena Dmitrievna repeated her promise and left.

Determined and stern, she came to the kolkhoz and sat down opposite the chairman Semion Moldanov. He was her age, a local Khant.

"Let's help a giwl, is thewe money in the safe?" she asked directly.

"What girl?" Moldanov was taken aback.

"The cleaning woman, Augusta... She's got a baby. Matewial aid. We must give hew assistance."

Moldanov smoked his pipe, pondering what benefit Elena Dmitrievna could derive from this, and not understanding a thing. But he knew that there certainly was some benefit, and that he wouldn't be able to shake her off.

"All right, we'll talk it over with the management board," he said.

"What's thewe to talk ovew!... I'm deputy, I'm submitting a petition, so wwite up the document. Khatanzeyeva's petition. A sewvant of the people petitioning on behalf of an unwed mothew."

"Okay."

"Okay nothing, wwite up the statement, Semionka."

"Devil take you, we'll give her a ten."

"Be suwe you do! I'll be checking. Contwol and auditing!"

And she went home, convinced that it would turn out as she wanted.

But things weren't so good at home. It had grown empty at home and very boring. Nikolai would come back late from the farm and after eating supper would run around in the yard until dark, putting everything in order as if getting ready for a long trip or death: he built a new porch, raked the small haystacks into a large one, fixed the sweep-nets and traps. And he slept apart from her on the floor...

"Kolia, my dawling! Ow don't you love Lenka any mowe?" she asked her husband one night when the light was turned out. "Don't destwoy me, ow I'll die fow suwe."

He lay on the doormat under a sheepskin, while she sat beside him on a bench, curling up her small bare feet. Her voice sounded hoarse and sweet. She knew the power of her voice, the power of pitiful howled words. And hearing him groan painfully in the silence of the house, she spoke again, choosing her words so that there'd be few of them and they'd weigh more heavily.

"My biwch sap, my wed little bilbewwy, do you wemembew how we heated the heawth that wintew, how you and I cut the fwozen beaw meat into pieces and ate them?... Do you wemembew the obligation[3] you gave? I won't leave you, you said, nevew, you've taught me, woman, to love love!... Why did you call me a pawtwidge?"

He had, indeed!... He'd called her a willow-grouse, and they'd cut up the glistening frozen meat together... And at the mere recollection of how they'd burned the cedar logs, and how the scented tarry blue smoke had made their eyes tear, and the diluted alcohol had burned their insides with a pure white fire, Nikolai sat up with a jerk on his separate bed, clasped her bony knees, pressed his forehead against them.

"Lena," he wanted to sob out, "Thank you, little berry, for everything!" But he couldn't, and he remained silent, sitting and rocking. And she, after waiting for a reply in vain, fumblingly found his head in the dark and buried her greedy, tender fingers in his curly hair. He buried his face in her knees and froze.

"Lenka, let me go," he said, "Let me go without any nastiness, please, let me go!"

And she played with his hair, completely motionless, deathly pale, and only her fingers moved quietly, combing the back of his head, as she listened to him repeating: "Let me go, let me go..."

Suddenly, pushing his head away, she dragged her bare feet to her high bed, clambered up on it, and screeched from the depths and the warmth of the featherbed:

"Tuwbot slime! Youw wowds stink of wot, you vile man!"

And she fell silent. As though she'd suffocated in the featherbed. Nikolai listened intently, waiting to see whether his wife would start crying, and he'd have felt better if she had shed tears, it wouldn't have been so terrible, so searing... Though he was afraid of her tears, because he knew his own weak, pliable heart.

And scarcely had Nikolai left for work the next morning than Elena Dmitrievna started making preparations for a visit to the regional committee. She dressed herself in a light summer coat and put on the kerchief with roses, and placing bread and fish in her handbag, went quietly to the lake.

An airplane flew by their village daily, and when there were passengers, it would land on the lake like a tiger beetle. Toward the end of the summer the river had grown shallow, but Lake Turun-lor, seven kilometers from the village, amid red bilberry and blueberry thickets, lay like a dark blue, wave-tossed, deep and cold reservoir.

"Just you wait, you'll find out what I'm about, you devil," she swore, sitting and waiting for the plane on the bank, and without looking she gathered the red bilberries around her into the hollow of her hand and tossed the unripe crunchy bitterish berries from her palm into her mouth. And she promised herself success with the Khant hunting wish:

"Luck be with you, Lenka, may youw eyes and eaws be keen!"

4

Maksim Tarlin, secretary of the regional committee, a Khant with a northener's higher education in philosophy,[4] listened to the woeful tale of the elderly woman who had flown from the taiga village to him for help, and doodling a design of bird tracks and deer antlers on a newspaper, considered what he could say to her that would be both comprehensible and inoffensive. His face was plump and puffy: the typical meekly-submissive face of a regional committee worker; his hair was coarse, black, sticking up like a short hedgehog above his low forehead, and his eyes were clever, tired and cruelly slanting. He'd known this woman for a long time, seen her at many conferences and rallies, listened to her speeches, and he didn't know whether to be proud of her or to be distressed at her fate. A strong, ardent soul, devoted to the Soviet state, she had unfortunately grown rigid with vain ignorance. He felt a pitying brotherly love for her and was angry at her stupidity and humiliation.

"Elena Dmitrievna," he said, "Resign yourself! What can you do? He won't live with you. I can't force him."

"What do you mean, you can't? Why can't you? The Soviet family is a unit of society, have you fowgotten, then?" Khatan-zeyeva shouted, seizing the kerchief at her throat with both hands as though it was choking her, furiously pulling its ends apart.

"A unit, a unit... You've learned formulas... If he's fallen in love with her, what can I do?"

"You can do evewything, you'we the Pawty!" she cried with passionate faith and misery in her slate-black eyes.

"Listen, Elena Dmitrievna..." he was about to begin, but she interrupted him, and leaping in a frenzy, she tore the kerchief off her round head, with its hair cut short in the style of Soviet Party delegates:

"I won't live without him! I'll die!... If you—the Pawty—wefuse, then who can I go to?... Talk to him! Talk to him, do you heaw?"

"All right," Tarlin sighed and screwed up his eyes. "Have it your way, Elena Dmitrievna, I'll talk with him. But mind—I'm promising you nothing. No-thing! As for talking to him—why not talk with the man?"

And going out to the secretary's office, he ordered her to radio the kolkhoz, summoning the fur-farmer Nikolai to Beryozovo.

Elena Dmitrievna subsided, and breathing quickly, retied the kerchief tightly. She'd gotten used to having the Soviet state always meet her halfway in everything, and she in no way blamed her nation's government for the fact that she'd had to shout and cry a little, but ascribed it to the political blindness of the secretary. But having won a victory, she immediately assumed the usual, favorite, and self-important stance of a government official, of a distinguished promoted worker, and observing the rules of propriety, she magnanimously changed the subject.

"How is the plan fow fish pwoduction? We'we not falling behind yet, awe we?"

"Not very much, Elena Dmitrievna," Tarlin responded with relief. "To tell you the truth, we're doing quite well in terms of quantity, but in quality, with red fish, for example..."

But after a glance at her, he made a dismissive gesture with his hand.

"What does fish matter, though... Look, you'd better tell me this: aren't you the one that the Leningrad museum is haggling with to get some unusual national costume?"

"Yes, I am," Elena Dmitrievna nodded proudly. "But I didn't give it... When I die," she cast her black eyes at the regional committee secretary ominously, "When I die, then I'll sign the

181

costume ovew to the museum."

"Come on, come on, live!" Tarlin said with good-hearted alarm. "You're such a spirited woman, wear it in health, be happy! Leningrad will do without."

Observing the secretary keenly, Elena Dmitrievna privately noted both his alarm and the affectionate note in his voice. She was undecided as to whether she should play her main trump-card. And Tarlin nodded, smiling at her as though at a child:

"What is it, then, what is it? Get it off your chest. I'll do everything for you that's in my power."

"Comwade Tawlin," Elena Dmitrievna said in a whisper, drawing her idol-like face, flat as though it had been chiseled out of stained wood, toward him. "If my Nikolai stawts wesisting, you scawe him a little... He wan away. He wan fwom the law... He used to wowk at a timbew camp and he wan away. Scawe him a little bit."

Tarlin recoiled from her as from a syphilitic or a person with trachoma. In an instant, his tired narrow eyes flashed, like hers, with slate-black mineral fire.

"What? What are you saying? Why? And I thought of you as one of us! You can't be that inhuman! I've heard nothing! I don't want to!"

And he banged both his fists on the desk in a rage. Elena Dmitrievna took wing from her seat heavily, like a duck, and on short legs hobbled away to the door, and there stopped short like a bird shot in flight. Her fear was dreadful. She didn't understand what she was guilty of, she only saw that she'd made an irreparable false move. But, of course, old fool, stupid fool that she was, her holy duty had been to report this three years ago!... And she, Khatanzeyeva, was sheltering a criminal and had even married him. Whom had Khatanzeyeva betrayed? Her own nation, the Soviet government, for the sake of a mangy dog with burrs in its tail, for the sake of a vile turbot, for the sake of a slimy, stinking fish!

"Ay-ie-ie!" she howled in extreme distress. "Ay-ay-ee-ee!"

Tarlin stopped banging, stared at her, and finally realizing the cause of her suffering, went up to her, put his arm around her shoulders, and seated her on the couch. Completely at a loss, she drew deeper into the couch, and her little feet in their schoolboy shoes dangled defenselessly in the air.

"It's all right, Elena Dmitrievna, stop upsetting yourself, that's enough," said Tarlin. "I'll talk with him, it's all right, don't tremble, little wagtail, calm down, go to the hotel, go and have a rest, we'll call you when we need to. Go on!"

5

As soon as it got light, she got up, had some bread with fish, and set off for the regional committee office. Reaching the public garden, she sat down and waited.

She saw Tarlin passing on his way to work, but she didn't move from her seat. It was still a long time until the plane, and she sat with eyelids closed under the warm sun and sang quietly:

> "And here I, a woman, sit on a bench by the office,
> I go against shawp winds that awe like awwows,
> And the fwost is getting hawdew, so that skis awe cwacking,
> And the snows howl with pain like dogs..."

She sat for many hours in the public garden and during that time the weather frolicked and played mischievously to its heart's content. When clouds covered the sun, the wind would rise; the river Sosva, which could be seen from the hill, one moment would sparkle radiantly like scattered coins, and thrash about furiously the next, and then it would get dull grey and black like a wolf's coat. Leaves from the trees would float by obliquely, the sand would curl upward in little columns like lifeless grey campfires. She waited.

At last she saw Nikolai's tall figure as he walked, bouncing, with a map-case over his shoulder. Her heart rushed to fall like a wounded bird at his feet, quivering, its wings crackling. But she herself didn't stir. She sat and sang with eyes closed:

> "I don't have a gun, Nikolai,
> I don't have a knife, Nikola,
> And I lost my bow in the taiga, Nikolai,
> But I'll cut you with my song, I'll kill with a wowd, Nikolai!"

After waiting for as long as she thought necessary, she got up slowly and menacingly, shook out her coat and straightened it meticulously, and went, swaying like a duck, to the regional office.

In Tarlin's office she calmly seated herself on the couch. "Well, Elena Dmitrievna, I've had a talk with your husband," said Tarlin, without looking her in the eye. "I have..."

"Did you give him instwuctions, in youw capacity as leadew?"

"What instructions?... He says he's fallen in love with this woman. That's the way it is."

"So!" said Khatanzeyeva. "So!"

Doubled up and his tow head lowered, Nikolai maintained a depressed silence. Then Tarlin started impatiently tapping on the desk with a pencil, and to this small, insistent drumbeat, Nikolai unexpectedly rushed to the attack.

"Are you hoping that nastiness will help you, Lenka? Nastiness has never helped anyone yet, Lenka! And it won't help you—no way. I suffered a whole month like some accursed thing. But you dashed to the regional office to complain, and suddenly I felt better. I went to Gustia yesterday and said: well, my sweetheart, I'm leaving Lenka, I'll go to the regional office and say so—and that'll be that, I said! Here in the presence of comrade Tarlin I'm telling you—it's over!"

Nikolai's face became foxen, like an animal's, with bared teeth—and only the face of a good and honorable person can openly and sorrowfully change like that because of grief.

And Tarlin was obviously ashamed. He didn't even betray a natural curiousity, he didn't look at the couple, and hiding his eyes, tapped on the desk with a pencil. And this shame was apparently so alien to his nature that his mouth stretched into a rough and rigid line, the corners of his tight, dark lips curled downward.

"It's bad, bad," Elena Dmitrievna shook her head virtuously. "It's bad, my fwiend and comwade. Think, use youw head, what did you have on when you came to me? Did you have pants? A shiwt? Wewe you weawing a jacket? Fow thwee yeaws you ate and dwank youw fill, and now you'we exchanging a Soviet family fow a giwl with a baby? I took pity on you, I let you into my house, and now you'we leaving me, you no longew need old Lenka? You'we a dog, a dog!" And Elena Dmitrievna started crying quick little tears that flowed down her flat cheeks effortlessly and unrestrainedly.

Her weeping was so wretchedly quiet, so disarmingly human,

at such odds with her stupid, nonsensical words, that Nikolai instantly and fearfully began to doubt himself. Was what he'd started worth these tears, worth one tiny drop that trickled down without a trace, without a sob, without a sound, and that dried and then flowed afresh? Even Tarlin stopped tapping, put down his pencil, propped his temple on his hand, and lapsed into thought with a dazed and sad expression.

"Lenka, maybe we can live together as a threesome?" Nikolai suddenly asked with pure hope. (His strange question came out simply and not at all strangely.) "Maybe you can be like a mother to Gustia and me, eh, Lenka?"

"Brother, you've really lost your mind!" exclaimed Tarlin, but glancing at them, he stopped short.

Elena Dmitrievna was looking fixedly at Nikolai, and he was looking fixedly at her, and suddenly it seemed to Tarlin as though these two were in the process of pulling the sweep-net or towing a boat against the current—together.

6

The young couple awoke early, leaped up, and as though someone had flicked them with a switch, ran into separate corners to dress. Edik groaned in his cradle, arched his back, made a little bridge, goggling with his infantile bluish prominent eyes.

"Kol, take a look, where is she?" whispered Augusta.

"Just a sec," said Nikolai and carefully pulled aside the curtain that was suspended on a wire.

The house was empty, Elena Dmitrievna's bed, piled up high, shone like a snowdrift because of the light blue pique bedspread from under which a snowy starched lace sheet-trim hung to the ground.

"She's gone," Nikolai said in perplexity. "She's not here."

... The previous evening, when under the disapproving glances of the entire village, which had poured out onto the street, they had transferred Augusta's scant belongings in two birch containers, Elena Dmitrievna met them on the threshhold with a hospitable, honeyed speech:

"Come in, giwl, live hewe, don't be afwaid of anything. Fwiendship and peace. Peace and fwiendship. I'll be a mothew to

185

you, you a daughtew to me. And like all Soviet people. We'll bwing up the baby Edik. Thewe's money and thewe's fish."

Augusta smiled in confusion and rushed to start washing the whole house—floors, windows, walls. And she and Nikolai also sawed firewood in the yard until dark. Elena Dmitrievna sat without a light in the house and took care of Edik.

Augusta dashed in once from the yard, greedily drank some water from the birch ladle floating in the bucket and asked respectfully:

"He's not sniveling, is he?"

"The baby's a fine lad, he's quiet, he stawes!" replied Elena Dmitrievna in a moved voice. "I nevew had childwen myself, so I'm vewy fond of othew people's."

And Augusta ran off. They finished sawing the remaining firewood and stacked it up.

"It's time to eat supper. Let's go, she must be tired of waiting there," said Nikolai gloomily.

"What an old woman! She's some old woman! Just an extraordinary person!" Augusta almost overdid it out of generosity, but feeling Nikolai wince at her words in the darkness, she shrank, "Kolenka, what'll happen?"

"Have patience, dear," he replied, "Patience, and patience, dear Gustia, anything can happen, but you have patience, my darling!"

"Trust me! I'm a person who's been battered about and I'm used to all kinds of misfortune. If you're fated to burn, you won't drown."

It was already going on midnight when they all gathered together at the table. Augusta and Nikolai, tired, sweaty, disturbed, sedately seated themselbes side by side like well-behaved children.

"Well, we ought to dwink to it," said Elena Dmitrievna, and lightly pounded the table with the single bottle, which she had bought earlier, that stood there.

"Let's drink, Lena," replied Nikolai in a quiet voice, "Let's drink to everyone's health—to yours, to Gustia's and mine... I'll bring us some good light salted fish right away."

They drank, had some fish with bread, avoided looking at one another, but sometimes the glances of the two women crossed as they fell on Nikolai and dug into him like a deadly unremovable tick.

Augusta, her eyes lowered obstinately without a murmur, cleared off the table, the fish remains, and brushed off the crumbs and scales. And Elena Dmitrievna, full of lofty humility, watching her, subjected Augusta to the torture that from now on would never end.

Then they turned out the light in silence and went their separate ways.

Behind the curtain in the alert oppresive stillness of the house, the young couple tenderly came together, and one moment completely forgot themselves, tuned out of this world, and the next returned drowsily to it, caressing each other and whispering about the bitter fate freely chosen by them, accepting it and submitting to it in the interests of a higher justice as they both understood it.

... And now in the morning it turned out that Elena Dmitrievna wasn't home.

"Wait!" Nikolai barked gloomily and ran out of the yard.

Why his legs carried him to the village Soviet he himself couldn't say. But he ran to the village Soviet without turning off anywhere or looking back. The village Soviet was, after all, Khatanzeyevna's refuge, her large, her main house! And he was right—already through the window he saw her in the empty building at the chairman's desk. Nikolai entered the hall and stopped at the door, listening. Lenka was reading aloud what she'd written:

"Comwade secwetawy of the local pawty committee, distinguished woman Khatanzeyevna of the Bewyozovo wegion sends you Communist gweetings. I tuwn to you with a gweat wequest. The political buweaucwat Maksimka Tawlin insulted me, the faithful daughtew of a small nowthewn people, he didn't listen to me, he talked pwejudicially with my husband Nikolai. And he, the cuwsed tuwbot, has mawwied a giwl with a baby, has bwought hew into the house. And Nikolai himself wan away, is a desewtew fwom mobilization. He should be put in jail, yes, let him pewish! It's bad to commit mowal offences against the Soviet family. But leave the baby Edik with me, comwade secwetawy of the local committee. I'll bwing him up honowably as a citizen of the Union—thewe's fish, thewe's money. Matewial conditions awe fine. And I ask that you check on the cuwsed single woman, who she is, fwom whewe she came. Fowgive me gwaciously, I wemain with gweetings,[5] Elena Dmitwievna Khatanzeyeva. I infowm you also that I'll give my coat, my deewskin national costume, to the museum as a gift fwee ow cheaply. That's all!" That's what she had written in a dreadful scrawl, in ominous enormous letters on a scrap of paper. Nikolai seized the denunciation and as he read it, evading her hands, Elena Dmitrievna ran around him and shouted:

"Thief, bandit, enemy of the people—devil, dog! Give me back my complaint, give it back!"

But he finished reading, and pushing the paper in his breast pocket, he regretfully slapped Elena Dmitrievna across the face with the flat length of his huge palm. She didn't even make a sound, she even seemed to cheer up, while he stood shaking a little with misery. Then he carefully took her by the hand and led her home through the whole village. She didn't resist, but on the contrary, tried to keep up with his long strides. Looking up at him from below, she seemed to feel pride in front of the people watching.

Once home, Elena Dmitrievna wordlessly approached the cradle, sat beside it on the bench, and started rocking Edik. She sat for a long time over the child, enigmatic, engrossed in herself, then started singing:

> And youw head, Edik, is a ladle fow puwe watew,
> And youw eyes, Edik awe wood bluebewwies,
> And youw awms awe the oaws of my little boat...

1968

Translator's Notes

Published in *Tertium non datur (Tret'ego ne dano)*, M. Sovetskii pisatel', 1969. The present translation is based on the author's original manuscript. All deviations from the printed Russian version were suggested or approved by Inna Varlamova in consultation with the translator in July 1979.

1. Elena Dmitrievna suffers from a speech defect which in Russian involves the substitution of "z" for "zh," "s" for "sh," "ts" for "ch." In the English version, the defect is rendered as the use of "w" for "r."

2. The Russian here is *krestovatik*—a fox with a brown cross on its reddish fur.

3. She wants to say "promise," but uses the bureaucratic word, as is her habit (I. V.).

4. I.e., educated at the *Institut Narodov Severa,* where the level of education is below that of central Russia.

5. The Russian contains an untranslatable pun on words: *s privetom* means "with greeting" and also "cuckoo" or "crazed."

Sergei Zalygin

The Night of the Angels

A roof hung over the factory furnace, huge, noisy, and made of iron; a din could be heard, the sound of one force striking against the other; sparks flew up into the low blue of the sky, a multitude of sparks, each one spinning behind it a thread—bright and thin like a razor blade.

Then the threads broke and the freed sparks, which should have flown further into the higher regions of the sky, began to fall down gently of their own accord and, like the threads, went out.

When the furnace lid slammed shut and the resounding noise of something being poured had ceased—something with which the furnace had been filled a thousand or more times in its life—the silence was immediately filled with the call of cranes, with the noise of water falling over the dam, with the drawn-out mooing of a cow and that inexplicable rustling which is audible only in early fall and only during limpid afternoon hours.

Now, on top of the mountain, you just had to stop and take a look around, to see in the folds between the mountains narrow little streets, the village square and the factory fire tower, to see the reservoir smoothed out by the sun as if it had been ironed, to catch the sound of silence and all the noises with which this silence was filled. But his mother didn't stop, not even to catch her breath.

His mother was young, and not everyone guessed, certainly not always, that she was a mother, that the little boy named Pavlik was none other than her son. And this lack of perception on the part of mankind made the son feel good and happy; he would laugh and in such moments he liked his mother's strictness.

In such moments he understood her strictness deep in his heart and wanted it. The stricter his mother was—young, in her tightly-tied silk kerchief and her grey-green coat with a very wide belt—the more interesting it was for him to live in the world and to love her with deep understanding.

But today his mother was stricter than strict. She kept silent and in silence led Pavlik over the mountain, her palm enveloping his firmly, as if forever. But he, on the other hand, felt bewildered. He kept getting tired, and in his tiredness ached for the grown-up in him, for the man he had been unable to grow into for so long, the kind who could walk down roads and streets all by himself, vigorously swinging his arms, stopping to

193

look at the sky and then moving on.

What's the order of things in the heavens today? Which cloud is sailing behind which, which one is lagging behind, and which is racing past all the rest? What's going on up there, in the heavens, which often makes the earth feel warm and cozy? What's going on up there, which is making his mother rush so much and rush Pavlik as well?

Tripping now and then over the rocks which the narrow winding road had chipped out of the earth, Pavlik kept glancing at the sky, and although he knew his mother wouldn't want to answer, he nevertheless asked her:

"Does this mean they're there?"

"Watch your step, Pavlik!" his mother answered.

"You can't see them, but they're still there?"

"We don't have time, Pavlik!"

"Did you ever see them? Just once? Well, even for the tiniest second?"

"No one has ever seen them."

"Why?"

"They're invisible."

"And who gives birth to them?"

"No one. They come into the world all by themselves...."

This was particularly interesting because it related directly to Pavlik. He knew that his mother had given birth to him. He was even more convinced, however, that he too had come into this world basically by his own efforts. It was another matter that his mother found it somewhat awkward to talk to people about such independence on the part of her very own child. And of course, his mother couldn't speak about this to Pavlik, or else he might think too highly of himself and become spoiled.

But to his understanding only dead rocks failed to take part in their own birth, because they after all were dead their whole lives. When living beings, and people especially, are born, they know how and why they are doing this; they can't help but know and forget their own birth only for a time because of a lack of intelligence.

When someone is growing up, becoming wise and mature, he comes to enjoy recalling his childhood and loving and understanding children. And finally comes the moment when with the memory of an adult he can recall everything without which he can't exist any longer—his whole birth. And those who can't remember any of this at all have no reason to live, no reason to look and listen to the world around them. They're better off dead and gone, lying still and deep under the earth, just like rocks.

And the fact that angels were born completely on their own, whenever they felt like it, was also fascinating and nice to think about. And a great many questions arose from this sense of fascination.

"Why do people draw them, if they're invisible? In the church? On the walls? And on the ceiling, at the very top? If no one has seen them, who drew them? They drew themselves, right? Do they know how to draw themselves? They must, if they know how to come into the world all by themselves?"

"Faster, my little boy," his mother said immediately in response to all his questions. And although it couldn't be said that she rapped him on the head, she did let her head rest firmly on it.

The world was steadfastly quiet. In it hummed a single factory surrounded on all sides by speechless expanses and almost completely hidden behind the mountain. Only one little river was rippling and pouring over the dam. And the steps of only two people could be heard—those of Pavlik and his mother.

Everything nearby fell silent and seemed a mere reflection of more distant places, just like the reflection of the nearby mountains in the blue and sunlit water of the factory reservoir. But today even the distant places were a reflection of something even more distantly removed than they were themselves. And so it continued without end, so that everything that existed was simply a tracing of something else, of something infinitely remote and yet as real and genuine as it could possibly be. This tracing was filled in and colored with a great many brushes, large and small, of every possible description; and these brushes were sunbeams, nothing else.

The world was quiet—saying much, yet speechless, like a very interesting drawing. It was light and free of everything— free even of itself, exactly the way a drawing is often freed from the object from which it once had been made.

You had to be very high up to grasp in a single glance not only the drawing but the true and genuine object as well; and you had to feel boundless envy of the one who lives at such a height that he can casually see both one and the other.

Pavlik began to consider what he knew about angels.

Twice his mother had taken him to church. There he had become acqainted with the angels who were depicted on the walls and in that deep recess where the church cupola had pulled them.

There, up above, the still twilight locked in the cupola was cut by constantly quivering bands of light. This light and this quivering motion seemed to pull the narrow iron-grated windows into the church. It was painful to look up there, and it was incomprehensible how the cool and dusky recess, strongly resembling a deep pond or lake, suddenly appeared above you. To look at it intently you had to throw your head back and endure the pain in the back of your head and even between your shoulderblades.

Pavlik endured it and waited for someone to swim across the band of light, some sort of fish perhaps, maybe even two, a small roach or perch. And then the slightly reddish eye of the perch, which had turned a bit sideways, would become visible, as often happens in sunny weather when you stand by the reservoir and look down into the pool into which water and the sun's rays are pouring in and in an instant growing still, seemingly turning into a thin transparent crust of ice....

No one was swimming up there, and after a while Pavlik realized that no one would, because only angels dwelt there.

There was some kind of riddle, an undefined riddle, in the concave curves which the cupola gave to the angels' bodies. You could see the round, curly heads of the angels and the little wings that they displayed when they turned to one side like the little fish. You could see the naked little tummies and chubby little legs which, bent at the knee, supported the angels suspended in the air. But in no way could you see or learn any more from them....

Much simpler were the lower angels drawn on the straight walls. They too had outstretched wings, but were not depicted in flight; they existed not for their own sake but only so that you could stealthily glance at them and make it easier for yourself to examine more closely those who were highest up, who were at times almost invisible because of the deep recess, because of the dizziness and even nausea which this recess aroused in man.

To glance at the very accessible angels on the walls was just like asking how a fairy tale ends without having heard it through.

Pavlik didn't like such questions, never posed them to anyone and always left the church feeling the mysterious glances of the higher angels and the reproachful looks of the lower ones upon him.

At home over dinner his father asked Pavlik or his mother, it wasn't clear which:

"Did you go?"

At first his mother replied:

"Yes,..." she said, pouring soup into a plate. Then she pulled out from the table the chair on which lay the cap to his father's uniform with its tiny criss-crossed hammers.

His father had one habit, keeping his cap next to him. Everyone knew that it was silly, including his father, but all the same he invariably took up the chair with the cap, which looked very much like a gymnasium student's.

In addition, he liked to read at the table, not without some enjoyment hearing out his wife and even Pavlik when they explained to him that this simply wasn't done. Having agreed with them, he would contine to read on even more intently.

This time Pavlik answered his father as well.

"Mama went, and I did too. We both did."

"Well? And what was going on there?" his father asked again, addressing only Pavlik's mother.

"Nothing much...."

"Did you like it?"

"The choir was good. There were a lot of people."

"A lot?"

"Whether they're singing or not, it's nice there anyway."

"Aha...," said his father.

"Well," Pavlik now thought as he followed his mother as fast as he could along the rocky, uneven road, "Well, it seems that that's all I know about angels...."

Because Pavlik didn't know anything else about them and couldn't even imagine anything else, it never occurred to him that he might know much too little about them.

He really had so many questions for them—Who could have drawn them if no one had seen them? How does everyone recognize them if no one has met them? Why do we have them if they don't exist?—that these questions, this boundless interest in them, completely replaced his actual knowledge of them.

Today it was a different question that he couldn't resolve: Why didn't his mother want to speak to him and answer his questions? Why was she being so mysterious about her strictness today?

She walked quickly and refused to notice how tired he was, how exhausted he was by his questions for her and how, in spite of her presence, he was nonetheless forced to be all alone, to gaze alone at the huge sky, so inaccessible for a small boy who couldn't read books easily yet because letters didn't always form words for him.

And he was ashamed for both his mother's sake and his own. He tried to pull his hand away from hers but just then badly tripped on a rock, and his mother grasped his hand much more tightly than before.

It was in this loneliness that Pavlik caught sight of an angel's wing.

It waved to him from the heavens, white like the cloud from behind which it had appeared—even whiter, much whiter, incomparably white. It was made of feathers, not rounded and smooth ones like birds have, but rather of straight lines, which in sharp and precise detail formed fine small scallops along the lower edge of the wing.

The precision and sharpness of the lines aroused doubt and anxiety in Pavlik, but only briefly, only until he was completely overcome by the amazing whiteness of the wing, compared with which everything white that he had ever seen in his life—white sheets, white down, white snow, white birch bark, white paper and even today's white clouds—ceased to be genuinely white and became merely a reflection of the whiteness he had glimpsed in that instant.

It was such that the deep blue of the whole sky became bluer still because of it alone.

It was such that the green of all the forests cloaking the mountains remained green for all times for the single reason that it existed.

Pavlik cried out, "Oh," to someone, probably his mother, and she said:

"You have to watch your step!"

He looked up again, and the wing appeared again before

him except now he felt its white, airy movement.

He felt that he couldn't keep quiet any longer, but his mother for her part still didn't want to talk.

Hurrying and looking stern, she didn't want to utter a single word to him.

Pavlik took a breath; it was easier to go on if he did so. "Tired?" his mother asked.

"Yes," answered Pavlik, and his legs began to tremble, just like last summer when he all but drowned—almost drowned but didn't because he was saved by his fat, tall Uncle Vasily, who was somehow related to his mother.

The situation now was the same, only the other way around: then he had been drowning, and therefore was trembling; now he was trembling first, and then being forced to drown in the blue recess of the sky's cupola, where the brilliant drawing power of the white wing had pulled him.

He wanted to say goodby to his mother, to kiss her without asking her about anything else and to forgive her for the mystery of her strictness. Only after that would he glance upward for the third time, toward the heavens so as to disappear in it forever, ceasing to be Pavlik and becoming an angel whom everyone knew but no one saw.

But something pulled and hurried him along so much that he no longer had his own thoughts. She had to hurry, but he ignored this. He held his breath and in silence looked up, sensing that his willingness to disappear beyond the earth's limits freed him forever from all human contact, from the multitude of questions he had for people, from his mother's mysterious behavior and even from his newly arisen secret, which was his very own and yet so incredible.

There was the sky up above, and the white clouds were there, but the white wing had already disappeared.

Pavlik couldn't believe that it was gone. He simply thought it over and decided that when the white wing did beckon to him for the third time, he wouldn't rush to meet it and disappear from the earth, but would point it out to his mother—let her see the whitest white in the world too, let him no longer contain this secret within him. He was ready to sacrifice it for his strict mother —let her see it too, comprehend it, and ponder over the whole question as he already had. "So be it!" he said, coming to a firm agreement with someone. Having done so, he glanced once more at the sky.

Now somewhat unfamiliar clouds floated in the sky, escorting Pavlik and his mother along their earthly road. He realized that no one would now, or perhaps ever, give him a third sign from the heavens.

"Well, you made it," his mother said to Pavlik.

The place where his mother had brought him wasn't very pretty—a gentle slope with rocks protruding here and there, small seedlings, but more than anything, tree stumps, thick as well as thin ones. The blue wall of the dense forest extended right up to these rocks and stumps. A stream flowed past them, and in it, in the middle, stood a red cow up to its knees in the water, a small cow, yet full grown, because it had huge round horns.

There were no people here, but there was a hut without a fence but with a crooked black chimney-pipe. The very hut was crooked and almost black, its extremely narrow door opened inward.

A dog dashed out of this door and began to bark, and a little bit later an old woman who was hunchbacked, like in a fairy tale, came out slowly and began to scold him.

Without even saying hello, but just straightening her wet, dirty apron, the old woman said to his mother:

"I've been waiting for you since yesterday," and took his mother with her through the narrow door. Meanwhile, the dog took a stand between Pavlik and the door and gave him an angry look.

The dog was large and of different colors—a gray and yellow head, and then gray again on the trunk. And what was no joke but certainly striking was that the dog's whole snout, covered with light little spots and gray and yellow stripes, seemed to have been drawn or invented by someone intentionally.

Stepping back almost imperceptably from this snout, Pavlik sat down on a stump which had been cut unevenly with an axe. But the dog lay down, stretching out its spotted forelegs and drawing in its hind legs under its stomach. Then the dog began to flick its tail—first to one side and then the other, finally stretching it out straight back along the ground.

This done and over with, the dog wrinkled its nose and growled at Pavlik, but then quickly changed its mind and closed its eyes.

It didn't close its eyes entirely, and certainly not both, just one. It only squinted with the other eye which held within it all the hostile feelings that the dog had for some reason shown toward Pavlik from the very start.

Some time passed, and the dog realized that Pavlik was not about to enter the hut. And Palvik realized that as long as he sat on the stump and didn't budge, the dog wouldn't touch him. Then all the weariness and bewilderment which he had experienced coming here came back again.

Now he, it seemed, knew that he had lived through a state of nonbeing which did not, however, resemble death or any other kind of final end to his existence.

His weariness hampered his ability to think about what he after all had experienced on his way to this place, to this dog and this hut. There was no way he could give a name to that riddle which he had yet to unravel, or to that question which he was obliged to answer. Yet the answer to this unknown question would not leave Pavlik at all precisely because of its unknown nature. On the contrary, for this very reason the answer drew nearer and was within his reach. The answer seemed to bypass the question itself.

Earlier in his life he had at times experienced something similar; his father and fat Uncle Vasily—the one who had saved him when he was drowning in the reservoir—loved to ask him riddles and questions. Pavlik, on his part, without fully understanding or hearing them out, would jump in and give the correct answer without any hemming or hawing.

One more slight effort was all he had to make today and he would be able to find the answer for himself; everything would be clear, and he would be able to live on, to live forever, to old age itself.

He had no strength left and comforted himself with the thought that he would be able to exert this effort later, at some future time, when, for example, he entered the gymnasium or became an adult. He still had a lot of time ahead for living, and meanwhile he could rest because he was weary.

He once more began to look at the dog, thinking that it might not be really angry at him, or that it might be angry simply because it was a good dog; it wished Pavlik well, and for that reason would not let him go through the narrow door of the hut where it was so terribly, terribly dark and smelled of mold and decay, and where the ceiling was so low; only the fairy tale-like hunchbacked old woman could live and breathe there, and for only a very short time could Pavlik's mother go in and stay there.

Next he imagined that inside, in a corner of this hut, stood a well, filled with darkness that was as thick as water and in which everyone sank who entered: one person didn't sink very deep, only to his knees; another, up to his waist; and the third, up to the top of his head. Each sank as deep as he could possibly bear, but the old woman,the mistress of this strange hut, was able to sink down deepest of all, to the very center of the earth.

"Why did mother have to come here?" Pavlik asked himself a new question, but the answer to this question came easily. His mother also wanted to test herself, to test herself in his place, in place of her son. Grownups, particularly mothers, do a lot in place of their children.

It was for the sake of this test that the old woman had waited for his mother as early as yesterday. The old woman needed to test his mother because she wanted everyone to spend some time there, in that dark, deep recess, where during her long life she had probably been many a time.

"It's too bad mother didn't see the sky when the white wing flashed twice," pondered Pavlik. If she had, they would have returned home wihtout stopping at the old woman's. Most probably the angel had wanted to indicate with its white wing that it was entirely unnecessary for his mother, and all the more for Pavlik, to undergo this test. "It seems," he thought further, "that some sort of fairy tale is being composed now in which I myself am playing a part. This is strange, because fairy tales are always about other people and not about you. Interesting,... Really, fairy tales are always written about some kind of unreal people." And Pavlik tapped himself on the top of his head and pinched his ear.

There was already much more of the unreal that there is in a genuine fairy tale in the fact that it was precisely today, after he had seen the white wing in the sky, that his mother had brought him here, to this dog, this old woman, and this hut.

... When he was going home with his mother, the old woman saw them off, but she did not say goodby to them forever, and Pavlik understood that his mother would bring him to this hut again. Perhaps she would do this soon.

His mother didn't want to; the old woman, it seemed, felt the same way, and the dog didn't want to at all. But, just the same, they would all be here together again.

Pavlik got bored, he got sad; nevertheless, he knew already that grownups often do what they themselves don't want to.

**

The two days which Pavlik had spent after returning home from his far, far away journey seemed already another life—mysterious and wearying, in no way resembling his former life.

It could be that even these two days stood apart from all other days which had been lived by people and other beings at any other time on earth.

Now the days only superficially consisted of morning, noon and evening, of hours, half-hours and quarter-hours; in fact, time held no other meaning except the hope and expectation with which it was welling from within, from its very inaccessible core.

After all, everything that happens can be repeated, can't it?

After all, everything that happens, happens for the sake of its own repetition, doesn't it? Even if for this you have to wait for a new creation of the world?

Pavlik must have known and suspected it. He must have waited with that hope and patience which remained hidden from the eyes of others and from himself, feelings which were certain that in an hour, in a day, in a week there would'nt be any need to be patient any longer and patience could be forgotten forever.

Instead of helping his mother water the vegetable garden, Pavlik could go outside and sit on a little bench by the gate of his house. Although it seemed that he was only playing with a bird-cherry twig and watching people go by, he was in fact listening attentively to everything that those passers by were talking about.

He wanted to find out if anyone had seen the white wing which had waved to the earth twice and had not waved a third time.

Suspecting that someone must have witnessed this, Pavlik pressed so hard against the bench and the fence that he could scarcely breathe. He was becoming more and more frightened.

You see, he didn't know what he would have to do when he heard these long awaited words coming not from himself but from someone else. Should he throw himself at this other person, embrace him and weep joyfully, or should he be frightened and run away somewhere? For in that fateful moment he would no longer possess all that he now alone possessed, he alone in the whole wide world, intensely coveting this secret possession.

He knew that the signs sent to him from the heavens were unbelievable, but unbelievable only because he had waited for them all his life: he hadn't lived very long yet, he still hadn't gotten used to the secret of human existence, of the existence of that person who he himself was. This waiting for someone's words or someone's signs to explain everything to him was the genuine and living essence of his life, although he couldn't put all of this into words for himself, his mother, or anyone else. Long, long ago, passers by would talk to each other in words he found familiar about things completely foreign to him: about the war and the prices at the outdoor market. As far as Pavlik could recall, they never talked so frequently about anything else; and now he could again conclude that, just as before, no one going by knew about the greatest event which had taken place two days ago, and that everyone going by was mistaken and not interested in what he should be interested in.

Of course, the war, which was talked about more and more intensely with every passing day in ever louder tones and with ever increasing fear, and about which even his mother was talking, although she never feared anything—the war was coming closer to the factory with each passing day, and that was frightening. But, then, everything frightening has one weakness: everything frightening is incomprehensible. You must understand what is frightening. You must understand fear, and then it will cease to exist. A dark room ceases to be frightening if you understand darkness, if you imagine the room without it. It isn't easy to understand all that is incomprehensible. But might it be this that the signs from the heavens had wanted to communicate, precisely how to accomplish this?

People were going past this way and that. As soon as they passed Pavlik, their faces would be erased, and without their faces they would lose even their individual step and come to resemble shadows almost completely. Without leaving a single trace in his memory, they would dissolve into huge cloud-like shadows which engulfed them all. In these past few days these shadows had become fixed at the near and far ends of the small side-street and remained motionless. Pavlik again began to play with his bird-cherry twig.

Horses would quite often go past Pavlik's house. They hauled charcoal which smelled smoky and resembled smoke compressed into tiny pieces. They hauled it to the factory where people threw it into the furnace, burned it, and threw it back into the sky as thin, barely noticeable smoke. And for all this the horses pulled through the alley large, dirty bast containers of coal and looked straight ahead with bulging, surprise-filled eyes which were lightly smoking like the coals.

It occurred to Pavlik that the signs from the wing in the heavens might be reflected completely in the horses' eyes, and he began to go out into the street and peer into their eyes.

The sky was really reflected in them, even more clearly than the earth. But all the same the horses, like the people passing by, didn't know anything either.

When Pavlik stayed alone in his little room, which was separated from the kitchen by a cardboard partition, he would lean against the door frame on which, with pencils of various colors and thicknesses, his height had been marked: how tall he had been when he was still a little boy and how tall he was now, when he wasn't really big, but wasn't small either.

It seemed to him that he must have grown an awful lot during the time he had spent outside looking into people's and horses' eyes. However, the piece of mirror he held in his hands—so that he could see both the pencil mark on the door frame and the top of his almost round head with its dishevelled light hair—showed that he hadn't grown at all.

He kept staring into his own eyes, which were greenish and serious like his mother's, and tried to figure out if they were deceiving him.

Not trusting them, he would press his hand against the top of his head and the door frame; then he would slip out from under and stand to one side and look. But his hand would again show that he hadn't grown up. This frightened him: suppose he suddenly wouldn't be able to remember why he had been born?

Would he die then without remembering this? Without even having understood those signs he had seen?

But in those moments, in spite of everything, Pavlik would force himself to feel the life flowing within him as it made a grown man out of a little boy. He would become ashamed of the childish, emotional reaction which had overcome him when the angel's wing had twice waved to him from the sky.

You have to be a bit more strict with these angels and not be surprised by their signs; you have to summon them in a demanding tone and explain everything you need.

Then he would fall asleep, thinking that if the day had brought him nothing, then perhaps it would be at night that he would meet the angels.

It seemed that he had heard somewhere that that's what happens.

There were two angels.

They carefully nudged the door open and came in—first one, and then the other.

Assuming that Pavlik couldn't see anything in his sleep, they very quickly measured themselves against the marks on the door frame.

They turned out to be almost the same height. Both were small, smaller than even little Pavlik had been when his father made the first mark on the door frame after he had put up the partition and hung the door; he had then settled Pavlik here and named the room the cardboard room.

Having measured himself, one of the angels went up to the head of Pavlik's bed, stood a while in silence and then said:

"He's asleep..."

"We'll have to wait," sighed his friend, "after all, he waited for us a very long time, and now it's our turn."

Both angels, pressing closely to each other, settled on a chair and began to breathe evenly and quietly, but Pavlik, sensing their angellically warm breathing, began to examine them with his half-open eyes.

They were little angels with naked, fat little tummies and little round blue eyes, in which Pavlik didn't notice much intelligence or strictness. They were sitting quietly, without misbehaving, and it seemed, without that melancholy feeling which any kind of waiting produces.

Pavlik very quickly sensed his superiority over them: he had many more muscles than they did, and more intelligence too.

All this made Pavlik feel good, and he opened his eyes.

Without hurrying he stretched out in bed and said like a grownup: "Hello, kids! What time is it now?"

"Hello, Pavlik!" the angels answered and amiably jumped down from the chair to the floor. But as far as the time goes, they both said nothing; they probably didn't know for sure how to answer such a question.

"So you've come?"

"Yes, we've come," affirmed the angels.

"That's good, because I have something to discuss with you..." And Pavlik told the angels in detail the whole story of how, without knowing why, he went with his mother to a hut of a hunchbacked old woman, straight out of a fairy tale; and how an angel's white wing, whiter than anything else in the world, had waved to him from the heavens. It had waved twice, but not a third time. "I propose," said Pavlik, seriously, like a grownup, "that this was one of the angels warning my mother that there was no reason to take me to the hut of the hunchbacked old woman, that it was much better to stay at home and water the garden... Or perhaps it was simply one of you fooling around in the heavens?" Pavlik asked.

"Could it have been you?" one angel asked the other.

"Or perhaps you?" the latter asked in return.

"No-ope," answered the first, "I've had a cough since last Monday and have been sitting at home; they wouldn't let me out of the house. Today's the first day I've been able to go out... Besides, our wings aren't all that white."

And the angels, as if on command, opened wide their little wings which, when folded, were hidden behind their plump little shoulders.

If in truth the wings weren't all that dark, they really weren't all that white either. In terms of color they more closely reminded you of the gray cardboard which separated Pavlik's room from the kitchen.

"Who could it have been?" the angels debated between themselves, while Pavlik continued to study them with interest and to touch their soft wings which almost resembled those of a goose. "Perhaps it was little lame Petiunka? Or Adriashka? Or Sanka Belly-Button? Or Boriska? Most probably it was Boriska." They continued to go over the names of their peers for a rather long time, but finally both came to the conclusion that it was Boriska, and decided to summon him with a trumpet blow.

"Perhaps you should call him," said the first angel to the second. "The problem is I don't have my trumpet with me. I had this cough a long time; I felt hoarse and so I left my trumpet home. In any case, I've had no use for it since catching cold."

"You're always like that!" said the second angel to the first. "Well, all right, so be it, I'll blow the trumpet." And the second angel tugged the chain hanging around his neck, pulled a silver trumpet from behind his back, cleared his throat and began to blow.

Even though Pavlik didn't have wings and as a result couldn't fly, he nevertheless wanted to fly toward the sound of that trumpet—powerful and melodious and silvery-clear. He wanted to fly toward that sound so much that an ability to fly, which he had never felt before, began to awaken him. This feeling, barely stirring at first, left no doubts about itself whatsoever after a short while. However, there was no place to fly; the angel was blowing his trumpet right next to him, and Pavlik regretted that there was no distance between him and the trumpetting angel.

The angel Boriska, however, had probably flown to such a remote place that he didn't hear even this summons, and therefore did not appear.

Pavlik wasn't very upset by this since he was taking in the trumpet music with delight and wonder and feeling ashamed of that feeling of his own superiority which he had experienced in those first few minutes when the angels appeared in his cardboard room: after all, they must be exalted, heavenly and even extraordinary creatures to be able to create such sounds so easily.

After a while, however, he conquered his feeling of shame, and, to some degree, inferiority, and, stretching out his hand to the trumpeting angel, said: "Now me!"

The angel turned the trumpet away, pulled it from his lips and answered: "It's not allowed!"

His friend also said that Pavlik wasn't allowed to, but not as brusquely, adding some further explanations.

"Do you know what kind of music is made?" he asked Pavlik. "Angelic music! Heavenly! For you, living on the earth, it wouldn't turn out right anyway."

"Now me!" Pavlik reaffirmed his desire.

"It doesn't even turn out right for us all the time," the angel without a trumpet again began to explain. "It's just today that it's coming out so well. Do you know why?"

"Why?"

"Because tonight is the night of the angels."

"Now me!" said Pavlik, and the angel who was standing empty-handed threw up his hands and sighed.

"Look, if I had brought my trumpet with me, I'd let you blow it once. But just once. And you would have failed right away."

"Now me!" Pavlik said again, completely overcoming any feeling of shame or awkwardness and realizing that he couldn't live a moment longer if he didn't get to blow the trumpet immediately, this very instant.

"You probably don't obey your mother either," the angel with the trumpet said gloomily.

"I do! And if you let me play a little, I'll always be obedient, my whole life long."

"Oh sure!" said the same angel, grasping the trumpet in his hands all the more firmly. "You're all the same—today you make promises, but tomorrow, should we glance down from there, from above, your fathers will already be pulling down your britches and giving you a spanking. Teaching you a lesson."

"As far as my father goes, the neighbors, Uncle Vasya and my mother all say that he wouldn't hurt a fly," Pavlik tried heatedly to convince the stubborn angel. "My father is a big expert at the factory, but at home he's real quiet and reads books, that's about all. Very rarely does he ever... Besides, I'm his only child."

"So much the worse, if you're an only child. Your father lets you do what you want; and your mother, after all, is only a woman, which means that she loves you more than she guides and teaches you. Mothers in general don't know how to deal with their little boys."

"Mine does! My mother's a teacher and had a lot of little boys in her class, but when I was born she began to take care of only me. Now me!"

It wasn't entirely pleasant to be talking all of a sudden about your parents, but Pavlik ignored this awkward feeling. He was ready to ignore god knows what, if only he could play the trumpet.

"Give it to him!" the angel without the trumpet said suddenly to his friend. "After all, tonight's the night of the angels, and we should be really really good."

"It isn't allowed!" the angel with the trumpet insisted all the more stubbornly.

"But what if he does suddenly become a trumpeter?" the angel without the trumpet then asked his friend. "What if he turns out to be a trumpeter his whole life? What do you say to that?"

Pavlik passionately agreed with this conjecture made about him, realizing clearly that the final and most decisive moment of the argument had arrived.

"I will be a trumpeter! All my life! I give my word of honor," he said filled with dispair and hope.

"Cross yourself," demanded the angel with the trumpet.

Pavlik hastily crossed himself, and both angels, somewhat distressed, took a deep breath. One turned red and said: "He'll cross himself again! Cross yourself again, Pavlik."

"What do you care—It's easy for you to try to talk me into it when you've left your instrument at home," said the angel with the trumpet to his friend. "You're such a good fellow, but you're so sly. Just look at how he crosses himself."

"Watch me make the sign of the cross," Pavlik said, and earnestly crossed himself with a trembling hand. "Here's the sign of the cross, I will be a trumpeter."

And at almost that very instant Pavlik pressed his lips to the trumpet, which was cool and bright like the sky; and he learned what heavenly music really was, not realizing right away that it was he who was creating it.

Listening to himself, he immediately felt that now the angel Boriska would undoubtedly hear him no matter how far away he was, that he would come on his wings and explain the whole mystery that he had wanted to convey to him through those two waves of his white wing. But even this was not the most important thing now. The most important thing now was the music which he kept creating on and on.

That feeling of superiority over the angels took hold of Pavlik once again with yet stronger delight. He realized that the angels did not exist for their own sake, but rather for the silver trumpet which they had mastered and knew how to wield. But, after all, he too knew how. Knew how better than they did.

"Forget about them, about all those signs the angel Boriska gave me from the heavens," he thought. "Just so long as I can blow the trumpet. Blow and blow!"

And in all probability the angels understood everything that was going on within Pavlik. Pressing closely to each other, they sat on a stool and looked at Pavlik in silence, in wonder, in utter ecstacy and with a feeling which even surpassed that ecstasy.

Finally the angel who had in the end allowed Pavlik to play his trumpet gave him a timid sign to stop for a moment. When Pavlik did, he asked: "You'll be our head trumpeter, all right?"

"All right!" Pavlik nodded quickly. "I will," and he began to play again.

***

Someone was saying in a very strict voice: "Quickly, quickly!"

It was his mother speaking. Pavlik recognized her, but he didn't recognize immediately the man who was sitting on a stool at the head of his bed, there where the angels had just been sitting.

For some reason this man was wearing a fur hat and a warm jacket and had a rifle over his shoulder.

It was his father. The light from the lamp fell on him at an odd angle—from below, because the lamp standing on the floor lit up the cardboard room as never before.

Pavlik wanted to ask his father what had happened, where had some things disappeared to and where had all the rest come from. But his father leaned over him and closed his lips with a kiss.

Then he stood up, kissed Pavlik's mother again without really giving her a kiss, and said very loudly in the direction of the kitchen: "Ready?"

"Vasilii isn't here!" answered a strange voice. Pavlik realized that there were a lot of people in the kitchen, that they were also wearing winter hats and warm jackets and that they all had guns over their shoulders. And that his father was their leader.

211

"Vasily? He's outside," his father said in response to the strange voice, "He's preparing the grenades."

Pavlik's father left, and by the bed in his place stood his mother, uttering the words which Pavlik had grown used to hearing the past few days: "Hurry up, Pavlik! Hurry up! Hurry up!"

Pavlik couldn't move any more quickly because he was trying as hard as he could to catch the words which barely reached him through the partition.

"So, you're evacuating yours?"

"Think it's better?"

"Into the forest?"

Different voices were asking, asking about the fate of Pavlik and his mother, and one voice, his father's, answered everyone at once: "Yes!"

But here, almost in the same instant, the voices turned again to his father: "Is it safer?"

"Better, or..."

"But mine, I..."

"I've got a mother and small children. Three of them.... I don't know what place is better. Here, or..."

"I don't know," his father again answered everyone at once. "I don't know, I just don't know. It was my wife's decision to leave here. To hide. Maybe she sees things more clearly."

Someone began to whisper loudly: "We also won't look... They've also been informed; seventeen of their people are being held in our prisons—six officers and some others."

"What else can you do?" his father said again, speaking for everyone. "There's nothing else you can do. Should they do it, it means..."

His mother was squeezing Pavlik into his shorts, but now even he hurried. Now even he knew that it had to be so because the Whites were approaching the factory with their officers and all the factory people were going to fight them. But the women and children, who would not be fighting, were going to hide from this whole war.

Pavlik cocked his ear: a hum, which reminded him of the factory, but not really, because it was war-like, like that of cannons, could be heard somewhere in the mountains. Down the next street somebody on horseback was rushing to war, and someone else somewhere not far away at all cried out because he was afraid of war.

212

Pavlik wasn't afraid.

The factory smokestack whistle blew—a strange sound at night since it was used only in the morning and afternoon— a strong and alarming sound, ready to drown out everything, every sound, every trumpet, even a silver one, and every voice.

His mother gave a deep sigh so as not to be afraid and grabbed some kind of bundle. But Pavlik breathed evenly and calmly just as before.

Uneven footsteps, many of them—and all of them uneven— were heard in the kitchen. Coughing and the sound of iron striking against wood and against something else were also heard. People quickly went out the door; it grew quiet. Pavlik too got ready to go out into the night, across the mountain to the hut of the hunchbacked old woman, to hide in the deep dark recess, to fear the dog with its muzzle that seemed to have been drawn by someone and to listen if the dog barked at the people from whom they—mother and son as well as others—were hiding with all their might.

Pavlik recalled that he had promised the angels that he would become a trumpeter, their head, but strangely enough, he didn't feel the weight of these promises.

Now he felt light and carefree.

In a moment he would place the palm of his hand in the strict, grownup and wise one of his mother. Let his mother lead him to the hut of the old, old woman; let her take him where she wanted and where she knew how to go. Perhaps the angel's wing had warned them not to go there but rather to stay home and water the garden. But what did it matter? His mother knew best what they had to do, how they had to proceed.

Pavlik felt that he had grown up at that moment, and having grown up, he understood that he was still very much a little boy.

1972

Evgeny Popov

Three Tales

THE NORTH STAR

Not long ago, over there in Sweden, they were once again handing out the Nobel Prizes for Art and one of the laureates didn't show up.[1] I won't bother to mention his surname; I'll just say he was called Vitya.

Dollars in hand, they waited for him a long time, but he still didn't show up. Neither there, nor here, nor anyplace in between—he simply didn't show up anywhere again. And no one ever heard anything more about him from anyone else because in spite of his highly public image he was a bachelor and a recluse who devoted himself completely and singularly to his outstanding work.

Here's what happened to him.

As a youth he had lived in Siberia, where he was studying the martial art of Judo and the subjects prescribed by an art institute. Then, one fine evening on the way home to his pad, he was crossing the suspension bridge over the Kacha stream when a shabbily dressed hooligan appeared from nowhere in front of him. He himself was dressed fairly modestly—his boots were just the canvas type.

The hooligan sized up the unfortunate youth (to all appearances just a juvenile) and pointing at his shabby portfolio rudely commanded, "Hey, Pfimpf, put what you've got in the case on exhibit!"

But Vitya made absolutely no reply to him. For a few brief seconds he gazed, stunned, at the solitary North Star which was pointing the way from the heavens for the prodigal human race. A flash of inspiration seized the future master's soul and he whispered to himself: "The North Star!..."

"Show us the case, you scrawny chicken wolf-bait!" the hooligan said insultingly as he moved towards Vitya. But the youth still didn't hear him; his soul was filled with an inexpressible fatigue and sweet aching. That kind of aching and unearthly fatigue which have the right to take possession of the soul of a man who sooner or later will receive the Nobel Prize. Thus it was that he once again did not reply to the hooligan.

So the hooligan began to hiss like a snake and circle around the artist. Yet the artist remained silent and didn't notice him.

"Hey, I'm gonna spill your guts now! Hey, I'm gonna string

you up!" the hooligan screamed out as he lashed at the future laureate with an unarmed but iron-heavy fist. And he would have knocked that North Star out of the master's head, but Vitya glanced around a millionth of a fraction of a second before the fist landed on his skull. And he wanted to shout that it was wrong! It's wrong to kill! It's wrong to maim! Wrong! Wrong! Wrong! he wanted to shout. But, alas, the body does not ask questions of us; it takes decisions on its own. So, by a millionth of a second Vitya ducked the blow and slammed his own head, that same thought-generating skull, violently into the hooligan's throat.

This caused the hooligan to drop and twitch convulsively, to fall silent with an intent and deadly look at the same North Star or its otherworldly light. He dropped, twitched convulsively and fell silent because he was dead.

Or he had been killed. I don't know. Neither did the artist. He cast a quick look at the former hooligan's body. Then, drawing his head back into place on his shoulders, he walked quietly away —home, to his pad, his corner which he rented from an old Tartar lady in the midst of small stucco houses and the dirt along the shore of the smelly Kacha.

Long after midnight he was still painting. The next morning he awoke an externally calm individual and he never filed reports about the tragedy on the suspension bridge. And what real reason was there for filing them? There were so many barbaric incidents like that in those remote years, and even more wild rumors. He awoke a calm individual.

I won't presume to say for certain, but it seems that his mind-reeling ascent to the top began from that day. Yet, of course, it's clear from hindsight that the ascent wasn't obvious immediately. Still, the art school was completed with honors and then studies began at the Academy of Arts, and afterwards came diplomas, party-document folders, honors, and third-, second-, and first-place prizes.

So. He'd already begun to age a bit when, by chance, one evening he turns on his transistor radio and hears—the Nobel Prize has been awarded to the artist Vitya from the Soviet Union. That, of course, made him very happy and he went out onto the balcony of his Moscow apartment. He went out for a breath of fresh air, so his joy could subside or take a proper course.

"After all, I, too, have accomplished something in this life," he said to himself confidently and was immediately overcome

218

with fear. And depression. And a cold sweat. All this overcame him, even though it was July. And once again the North Star looked with reproach and bitterness upon its prodigal Earth. And again there were the aches and writhing pains.

"What? What?" the artist whispered. "What? What?" he repeated in a barely audible voice as he stepped backwards and stumbled.

"What? What?" he kept mumbling. And then he was no longer even mumbling. For by then he had already boarded a plane silently and unobtrusively and flown off from Moscow in the absolutely opposite direction of Sweden—namely, to Siberia.

Silently and unobtrusively he walked down the airplane's ram and unobtrusively, silently, and tearfully he walked briskly towards the suspension bridge. He wept as he walked and the tears swam in his eyes, so he couldn't see anything with them—neither the newly constructed buildings which rose like mushrooms up out of the earth, nor the faces illumined with the joy of our epoch, nor even the joy itself of our epoch. The eyes of the crying man saw nothing at all.

But then the tears stopped and he noticed that there was no suspension bridge, that a new stone bridge had been built to replace it.

The tears stopped. The artist had dried up. He stood there for a while. Then, he took off his good clothes. Naked, he wrapped and knotted them in a bundle and sank them in the water. Naked, he stepped into the muddied current of the smelly stream. Naked, he stood and trembled as he uttered a word. And the word was—oh, please, don't laugh—the word was "Pfimpf."

"Pfimpf" the artist said quietly and swam slowly off. No one saw him (that is, you understand, by chance) because they didn't even search afterwards. Later, Turukhansk fishermen[2] found his disfigured corpse, but what could he have meant to them anyway?

And if you should ask how I myself ever came to know all this, well, I would have no answer for you. I would tell you something else: no one knows anything. No one knows anything. All of us have to be pardoned. I joke not. I have not yet gone crazy.

Notes

1. Outside the world of this story, the Nobel Foundation does not award prizes in the fine arts.

2. It is unclear whether the fishermen are residents of the town of Turukhanski (located at the conflux of the Yenesei and its tributary, the Turukhan) or merely from the Turukhansk District (also named for the river, but an administrative unit within the Krasnoyarsk *kraj* and, historically, a site of labor camps for political prisoners).

FREE LOVE

There was a gal of respectable parents who laid plans to bind herself post haste in the bonds of matrimony. With this goal in mind she conducted the following experiment: she gave herself to a bachelor and was just waiting to see what came of it.

However, to date the only thing which had come of it was an uncertainty. The bachelor hadn't promised anything definite and, quite to the contrary, he'd often spun her some tale about the sad misfortunes of famous people who had been destroyed as a result of married life.

It wouldn't be right to say that these comments had evoked an extremely acute anxiety on the girl's part. She was young, quite attractive and well dressed; her eye had examined the bachelor with curiosity, so she knew for certain that she would in no way come up short.

They always arranged their meeting on the telephone. There was a time when the bachelor didn't call at all. He hadn't called for sometime and then one fine day, "Hi ya, Tam! What'cha doing today?!"

So, Tamara up and goes over to his place.

And then for some reason he up and vanished again, into thin air, and didn't even answer his phone. It was then that the girl, Tamara, made up her mind. One morning bright and early she caked her lips with lipstick, put on her gold earrings and set off.

She's there knocking at the door now and there's not the slightest rustle of a response. She keeps knocking, knowing about the bachelor's shattered nerves and that he'll open up sooner or later.

Who's there?" she heard, finally, the hoarse and beloved voice.

"Me," Tamara squeaked. "It's me, Eddie."

Behind the door Eddie held his tongue for a while longer and then he opened the door to his apartment slowly, so that it creaked.

Tamara fell on him with an embrace and she acted correctly, because he otherwise might have toppled over himself. At 9:00 A.M. bachelor Eddie turned out to be dead drunk.

This didn't surprise Tamara a lot. She knew that he had a few drinks now and then. And even though she herself wasn't in the habit of drinking anything other than champagne, she somehow managed to find even this pleasing. A hard-nosed male with a glass in hand!

"Is it you?" the wobbly, but vertical Eddie whispered. "But I didn't realize that it was you."

"Why didn't you?" Tamara asked naively after she'd bussed him tenderly and in so doing lost a thin layer of lipstick.

"Because I wouldn't have let you in if I had," the bachelor replied guilelessly as he was rubbing the hairs on his chest underneath the terrycloth robe.

"Yes, I'm telling you precisely," Eddie assured her. "I wouldn't have opened the door! I'm not at home alone, just myself."

"How so, not alone," Tamara said and then paused.

"Well...what's to say?" Eddie hemmed and hawed. "Mean you don't get it?"

"No o ope," Tamara cleverly drawled, having instantaneously grasped the whole situation in horror.

"Well...she's... I've got guests," Eddie reported in a whisper and, having teetered a bit, looked back over his shoulder.

"You love her?" Tamara asked after a brief pause.

"Whatcha mean! Whatcha mean!" Eddie began whispering feverishly. "My old flame. She's up and married already! Yesterday she showed up and demanded that I put her up."

"Aren't you some creep, eh!" Tamara burst out with a guffaw, and a little tear drop fell from one of her thickly shadowed eyes.

Eddie was taken aback at first, but then he took hold of himself. "You go and wash off your mascara," he managed to say. "And meanwhile I'll try to get her presentable."

Tamara went into the washroom and gazed narcissistically

221

at her flushed reflection in the mirror as she listened to her fiance's slick-tongued speech: "Get up now, come on, eh! Zaya, get up, please!"

"Zaya!" Tamara said hissingly, shaking with anger, and spat into the shaving mug that happened to be located under her very nose.

With that the door to the washroom flung wide open and a moderately attractive though middle-aged dame flew into the wash room, too. She tottered a bit, stuck her face right into the warm shower spray, and then, once she'd unglued her sleep-filled eyes, caught sight of Tamara.

"Attention!" she said with a mock smile.

"Gleetings," Tamarochka lisped.

The woman quickly and skillfully brushed her teeth with Eddie's toothbrush. She likewise dolled herself all out in make-up, after which she said, "Don't be afraid of me, girl."

"I'm not at all afraid of you," Tamara replied coldly.

"And don't go pouting at me. I'm not here for that."

"No, no, of course not," Tamara said sarcastically as she shook hands.

"Of course not," the woman replied with conviction. "In the first place, I've still got to clear up things with my husband today. This one here put on such an act of whimpering and hand-kissing yesterday that I just up and took pity on him. All the same, earlier there really was something between us... something nice..."

With that the woman let a tear fall. Tamarochka embraced her and said: "And you know, I'm not at all angry with you, not one teensy little bit. Moreover, I understand everything."

"The old lech! Think you're somebody big! Don't you?" the woman shouted out, but then calmed down right away and said that her name was Elvira.

Having become friends, Elvira and Tamara came out of the washroom. "You're an attractive gal," Elvira said complimentarily after she had had a good look at Tamara in the light of day.

Tamara blushed a little and said, "Well, where's this fellow of ours, this lech, as you called him, Elvira?"

"Why do you refer to me so formally as Elvira? Just call me Ellie," Elvira responded.

Eddie, the lech, lay atop the shredded bed linens and stared at the approaching women in horror.

"Why are you doing it, you scum, pulling the wool over this girl's eyes?! Just bear in mind: I won't let her be shamed! I'm taking her under my wing," Elvira said threateningly.

"What's my part in all this?" Eddie mumbled. "She herself said that she's for free love."

"It was probably you yourself that did a lot of pouting and then began to pull the wool over her. I know your little sheenanigans!" Elvira shouted, and then continued, "Tammy, dear, whatcha say we pound a little sense into this nasty lech of ours, little Eddie?"

And, having burst out in laughter, the new girlfriends threw themselves jokingly onto the bed and began, jokingly, to tickle Eddie and, jokingly, to drub him with their small effeminate fists.

"Don't beat me. I had absolutely no part in it, no part," the drunken Eddie mumbled.

Scandalous! Horrible! Unbelievable!...

THE MERRIMENT OF OLD RUSSIA

It ended badly, for the old man, this extremely strange suicide story. Just that morning, you see, he had been reading in the newspaper that alcoholism had already been somewhat reduced in our country and that the main task now consisted of producing "noggins" and "pints" instead of one-and-a-half liter bottles.[1] He read this and was smitten to the point of tears by the genuine concern expressed in the article, but towards evening he went and, that's right, got sozzled again.

This distressed his wife, old Mariya Egipetovna, who received a pension of 32 roubles and took in washing from the neighboring apartment dwellers—prettyboy-lipped bachelors, in their first year of service as civil aviation pilots.

The pilots were occupied to the utmost with love; they went to restaurants and concerts and rode around in taxis—and that's why they demanded snow-white shirts from the washerwoman, with stiffly starched collars, so that a black tie piercing the whiteness would give those around to understand that this young man was genuinely neat, strong, and youthful. Having received their bundle of fresh laundry, the pilots intoned: "He, oh, he has really chaaarmed me, the fe-el-ellow, the fellow with the wi-i-ings!"

Two boozing buddies of the old man brought him home. They propped him against the door, knocked loudly on the little pane, and ran off, fearing a nasty conversation with Mariya Egipetovna. Besides that, they had a burning desire to go scrounge up some money somewhere, and do some more drinking, because they were young, like the pilots from the apartments, and had to work—one as a lathe operator, the other as a carpenter and janitor —and they wanted to get good and plastered so that nothing would be frightening.

When Mariya Egipetovna threw the door open wide, the old man didn't fall, as one would have expected, but ran through the entry flailing his arms wildly, like a rooster on a cutting block with a lopped-off head thrashes around at the last second before his fall and death-rattle.

Having run through the door, he plopped down on the handwoven mat and fell asleep. In his sleep he snored, cursed, and bubbled spittle out of the sides of his mouth.

"You old bas..." the old woman said to him, when he woke up, "old scum, alcoholic, stuffed yourself good, you bastard..."

"Don't kick me around..." he responded morosely, but timidly. "I didn't drink with your money, the fellows treated me..."

"A-a-a, the fellows! So why is it that when I go outside no one brings anything up to me, but it happens to you yesterday, today..."

"Well, who needs you, you old prostituthe?" the old man was not at all able to enunciate the last word, so therefore he repeated it again, "... yes, indeed, old prostitute, hag."

The old woman knew what recourse she had. She let down her thick grey hair whose combings left a comb full of hair and clung to the yellowed enamel of the apartment sink. She howled, she lamented, she ah-ed and oh-ed. She recalled her youth and moaned in sorrow that she hadn't married the NEP-man Struev, Grigory, she beat her head against the cast-iron knobs on the old bed, and the neighbor woman, having thrown on a vicuna wool scarf, flew across the snowy pathway towards her wailing. "Oh, Mariya Egipetovna, poor dear, so that's how God's rewarded..."

"So why're you shrieking, why're you shrieking?" slowly and mournfully began the old man, "I didn't do you any harm, when did I ever beat you, eh?"

"He beat me, beat me, how in the hell could he not have beaten me!" Mariya Egipetovna went for him excitedly.

"Hey, so I gave her a lesson once, so what, one time, that's all. She egged me on."

He waved his arm, spat and went wandering into the yard, because the neighbor woman had embraced the old woman and was whispering something in her ear.

The old man leaned with the full weight of his chest on the wicket-gate and examined the sparkling snowflakes with a blank look. It had passed, passed long ago—the time when he could recall something, count on something, have hopes.

If he had raised his head, he would have seen the moon, or perhaps even the artifical satellite "Luna,"[2] which was boozily etching the black sky with its needle-point antenna without grazing against the stars.

Then he suddenly recalled that he had stashed away a bottle of "Moskovskaya" vodka with about 300 grams still left in it.

Lurching unsteadily through the snowdrifts, he reached the little shed where cows had been kept earlier, while they were deciding whether or not to let people keep them in the city, but now not a bloominthang lived there.

He rummaged doggie-like through one snowdrift, jangled his teeth around the neck of a bottle, and began to gurgle. Oh, how good it was!

First off he began to feel sorry for the old woman. He returned home looking submissive but sullen and rolled some home-made cigarettes, but she had already bucked up a bit by then and cheered up. When she got a fresh whiff of the vodka, she started winding up the bagpipes again.

"Shut up! Shut up!" he cried out, banging his fist threateningly against the table. "You've made life miserable for me, you old hag, you've nagged me on with your endless whining, until I'm almost ready to crawl under it, then, crawl! Go on, right now if you want. To the devil's grandmother with YOU."

And again he went scampering outside. The tipsiness coursed through his veins. It was joyous. He tore the clothesline down and went straight to the shed.

But when he had already fixed everything—the noose, the little stool, the hook—dying became too boring.

"Eh-eh, no," said the old man out loud.

He cut the rope into two pieces. One piece he wrapped around his waist; from the other he made a noose and put it around his neck and hung on the wall like a large, rumpled, dishevelled and frequently misplaced doll.

Yes, indeed, you might say that he hung like a doll, in the midst of all that was going on and was about to happen nearby.

He hung there, waiting for the steps and the noise, in order to lower his head to one side, stick out his tongue and boggle his eyes.

He didn't have to wait long. The old woman, whose heart had stopped at the sight of the closed door to the shed, loitered and stamped her feet, but the neighbor woman, eaten up with curiosity, glanced into the darkness of the shed and let go with such a wail that in no less than half an hour the motor of a three-wheel police motorcycle began to rattle near the building, and through the rattle, muffled in the snowdrifts, the task-force authority Lutovinov rushed to the shed, where diverse types of people had already collected.

But the ambulance had still not arrived.

Advancing behind the yellow circle of light from his police pocket-flashlight made in China, and with his pistol drawn, he came upon the distorted face of the suicide.

The authority walked up to the corpse boldly, without wavering. But the corpse up and, that's right, embraced him around the neck, although, as I've already said at the very beginning, nothing good came of it.

The policeman, poor fellow, began to feel bad, very bad. They carted him off to a hospital in the ambulance which had arrived for the suicide. He moaned and threw up; they gave him shots and stuck the little black tube of an oxygen bag between his teeth.

So the old man got 15 days in jail. In a weak voice, Lutovinov himself requested this of his comrades when they, after throwing white hospital gowns on over their dark-blue uniforms, brought the patient chocolate and little apples and oranges which were bought with state monies allotted specially for the occasion.

The old man received 15 days in jail.

During the day they lead gramps to break up ice on "Peace Avenue" and at night they lock him up in his cell. He already has two new friends here. One is singing all the time, "Let her be one-eyed, hunchbacked, but rich with dough, that's what I'll love her for, yes, even if I do say so..."

And the other says, lisping: "Tell me what makes you go "Yuck" and I'll tell you who you are!"

Mariya Egipetovna came for a visit once. She brought meat pies in a cellophane baggy. She grieved, hushed a minute and expressed her sorrow, but not much. And, on a different occasion, the old man mumbled to his new friends during a smoke break, after he'd licked his freshly rolled cigarette:

"This ain't according to justice, spite what Pravda might say.[3] I understand. I was educated earlier. I understand everything. Back then the books still called it 'The Merriment of Old Russia.' I understand everything."

Notes

1. "Noggins" and "pints" in the Russian are the colloquial words "chistushki" and "kosushki"; they refer to one-quarter and one-half size bottles of vodka.

2. "Luna" is the Russian word for "moon."

3. No English translation can adequately render the subtlety and succinctness of the original here.

Natalya Baranskaya

The Retirement Party

A retirement party was being held in the auditorium. The narrow assembly hall was almost empty. On the makeshift stage sat three people facing another twenty or so in the front rows. The stage was separated from the hall by an arch made of three red calico strips. White embroidered slogans were woven through the red cloth. Under the arch a pitcher of water and a potted, light-pink hydrangea stood on a table covered with a plush tablecloth. At the center of the table sat a broad-shouldered man with an affable face—the director, and a plump, young woman in a bright green sweater—the chairman of the local trade union committee. To their right in an old office chair sat a thin, plain woman in a bright green sweater—the chairman of the local trade union committee. To their right in an old office chair sat a thin, plain woman with deeply sunken eyes. Across her protruding forehead fell a loose lock of a washed-out permanent. She sat perfectly still except for her thin hands which were wringing and knotting a handkerchief. The party was in her honor.

The entire accounting staff had gathered plus those few remaining senior employees from other departments who were acqainted with her. A quiet, acquiescent person, Anna Vasilievna had spent nearly twenty years bent over a desk checking and re-checking records and computations with an abacus. Only a handful of people came to know her well.

The chairman of the trade union committee spoke first. She noted that comrade Kosova was one of the remaining members of the original staff, that she had always set a good example, was never tardy, had never been reprimanded but, on the contrary, had been awarded two merit citations and that this excellent, productive clerk should be a model for others to attain a conscientious attitude toward work.

"You're leaving us for a well-deserved rest, comrade Kosova," concluded the chairman, "and we want you to enjoy it fully. The administration and the local trade union committee officially express their gratitude for the long years of honest work, and your co-workers would like you to habe this valuable gift." Removing a sheet of paper, she uncovered six teacups decorated with yellow and lilac-colored flowers.

Brief, sparse applause followed. Anna Vasilievna raised a handkerchief to her lips and began blinking, trying to hold back the tears glistening in the corners of her eyes.

Raising a fleshy hand with a glittering wedding ring on the third finger, the directory asked for attention. He rose and, leaning on the table, spoke in a quiet, mellow voice:

"Dear comrade Kosova, we're here today to see you off for a rest which, as was appropriately noted, you so well deserve. We have already heard what an excellent, productive worker you are. Now, let me add a few words about the kind of person you are...." He paused awhile and continued: "You have worked here for twenty years... more precisely twenty-one years and eight months. I've been here, as you know, only two years. Four directors have been replaced since you first came to work for us as an accountant. What does this show, comrades? It shows an enviable human quality in Anna...ah... ("Vasilevna," prompted the trade union committee chairman), "Oh yes, Anna Vasilevna—her loyalty."

He surveyed the hall, observed the attentive faces, and continued:

"Believe me, it isn't easy to say goody-bye to such a person, comrades, but as they say, the same fateful hour awaits all of us. We are not bidding farewell to you, Anna Vasilevna, but are merely saying 'until we meet again!' We still have every intention of using you whenever the need, either yours or ours, should arise."

He concluded to a loud burst of applause. Anna Vasilevna pressed her handkerchief to her quivering lips. "They don't have to say all this. They must really respect me," she thought, embarrassed and flusterd. "But I do hope this ends soon. I'm not used to this sort of thing."

The head accountant asked to say a few words. With some effort he ascended the stage, pulled out a handkerchief to clean his glasses, then shoved the glasses into the pocket where the handkerchief had been. Realizing what he had done, he quickly pulled them out and placed them back on his big nose. In a mournful, quiet voice he began:

"Dear Anna Vasilevna, we have worked together for many, many years. You're an excellent worker and a very, very dear friend..." His voice broke. He remained silent, then added in a whisper, "Forgive me, please," and went back to his seat.

Anna Vasilevna stared at him in astonishment. But at this point, a short-legged girl with a glowing pink complexion, freckles, and carrot-colored curls, jumped up onto the stage. Tilting her

head, she shot a glance at the director and exuberantly announc-
-ed:

"The local trade union committee cordially invites all of you, on behalf of Anna Vasilevna, of course, for a cup of tea. Let's all go to the accounting office. There's room enough for everybody." She glanced at the directory again and giggled. Wiggling her hips, she jumped from the stage and, running toward the door, added: "The bottom gave out in our samovar... but we'll make the tea somehow! Bring the new cups because we don't have enough!"

Everyone rose and started talking at once. Crowding around Anna Vasilevna, the party moved out of the hall carrying the varicolored teacups in a ceremonial procession.

The directory excused himself in the hallway, saying something to the effect that he had pressing business, and headed for his office. "That redhead is a ball of fire," he thought to himself and smiled.

The party did not last long. Some of the women repeatedly checked their watches while others eyed the sacks filled with their lunch-hour purchases. Anna Vasilevna also wanted to go home. She was tired and uncomfortably hot in her Sunday-best, woolen dress. After rinsing out the cups and packing the new ones in the cake box, the women put on their nylon raincoats and the whole group went out into the street. Saying their good-byes, some people went to the left, others crossed the street to the tram stop. Anna Vasilevna turned to the right.

***

Anna Vasilevna's friend, Maria Petrovna, accompanied her. Their friendship was a long and a close one. During the war both worked in the same garment factory sewing quilted jackets for the army. Their husbands were at the front and both women were widowed the same year. Maria Petrovna was left with two boys, while Kosova —all alone Maria Petrovna now had grandchildren but Kosova—no one.

"Don't be upset, Anna dear," said Maria Petrovna, meeting her friend's sunken gaze. "It's high time you started thinking about your health."

"My health—who needs it?" replied Anna Vasilevna.

"You mustn't talk like that. The Lord's ways are not always

clear to us."

Anna Vasilevna only sighed in response. She did not believe in God. In that horrifying year, when misfortune struck both women, Maria Petrovna had found solace in the church: but not Anna Vasilevna—work was her only consolation.

She loved the dull routine of her work but had never revealed this to anybody. But then, why would she? Unlike the others, Anna Vasilevna never voiced her feelings. She never complained, never cursed her fate. Regardless of the task, she always completed it with enthusiasm, rapidly and efficiently. No one could pinpoint an error faster, or find that damned kopeck which frazzled everyone else's nerves at the quarter's end. The other accountants constantly turned to her for favors: check this, calculate that, or halp finish something else. In all her years of work, Anna Vasilevna had never once refused help to anyone.

She had worked hard all her life: including this year, this month, up to this day. And now, at the age of fifty-eight, she had been pensioned off and was walking home from work for the last time. How could this have happened? But the fact is, it did happen.

Masha Panteleeva was the first to tell Anna Vasilevna that one of the secretaries had told her of a rumor that she, Kosova, would be retired. Since the secretary could not name her source, Masha advised Anna Vasilevna to dismiss the information as just another piece of office gossip. However, although Masha's advise was reassuring, from that day on Anna Vasilevna felt something ominous hanging over her, stifling her daily routine. When Antonina Rozhova, the chairman of the trade union committee, sent for her, she thought: "The rumor was true after all."

When Anna Vasilevna entered the trade union office, her heart throbbed painfully. Her throat was parched—she could barely speak. Rozhova asked her how long she had been with the accounting department and how many years she had been working altogether. Anna Vasilevna began to count. She had obtained a full-time job while still a young girl but was uncertain whether it had been forty or forty-one years. ago. The conversation seemed to be casual, not business-like at all, as if Rozhova was inquiring in her official capacity about Anna Vasilevna's well-being. But suddenly Rozhova said:

"Comrade Kosova, the administration has suggested that I

discuss certain matters with you, namely, the possibility of retirement."

"Oh! Why, Antonina dear? Has someone complained to you that I can't keep up with the younger people?"

"Now, now, nobody said that you can retire now but they can't."

"If my work is as good as theirs, then why do I have retire now but they can't."

"If my work is as good as theirs, then why do I have to retire? Would you explain that to me, Antonina?"

"Look, what do you want from me?" Rozhova snapped back. "Did I say your work is worse than anybody else's? No, I didn't make any comparisons. I'm talking about something entirely different. You've been employed for over forty years while some people haven't worked at all. We have to give them a chance sometime."

Confronted with this argument, as final as a gravestone, Anna Vasilevna fell silent. What objections could she raise? Perhaps Antonina was right! However, Anna Vasilevna still wanted to speak with the head accountant; only he could appraise her work.

"Don't bother him, Kosova. Can't you see he's a very sick man? He can't take a step without clutching at his heart. You do, of course, have the right to confer with the administration. As a matter of fact, the director said to me, 'If she'—that's you—'doesn't want to retire, send her to me.' You may not agree with his decision, in which case, you'd probably consider filing a complaint agagainst him. You can do that if you wish, but I wouldn't recommend raising too much commotion."

Anna Vasilevna returned to her desk, completed the retirement forms and took them to the personnel office. That was two weeks ago.

***

While Anna Vasilevna turned right, three others went to the left: the head accountant Yakov Moiseevich Zushkin, the accountant Lyudmila Kharitonova, and the bookkeeper Lelka Morkovkina.[1] Lyudmila, a levelheaded, calm person, was never in a hurry while the redhaired Lelka, or Lelka-carrot was forever in a rush, always running and always late. Normally she would not bother to stroll home with her fellow workers; but this had not been an ordinary day in the office. She felt sorry for Yakov Moiseevich; the old man was depressed. So she walked alongside of him, listened half-heartedly to his lamentations and to Kharitonova's sympathetic yessing, all the while engrossed in her own affairs.

"I hope Yura brought Alka home from kindergarten. But what if he's still playing and forgot about her? Should I go from house to house looking for him or get Alka myself? It won't take long to make supper. I'll just fry some cutlets and cook the macaroni. I don't think Venyamin has a job tonight. Or does he?... Can't remember now whether or not he does... getting forgetful in my old age! But if he's playing, I won't have time to iron a shirt for him. He expects to be clean, white shirt five nights a week. It's awful how he sweats. Yet people have the nerve to say, 'You call blowing a horn work!' I'd like to see them try it!... He'll raise the roof if I don't have a shirt ready!"

Lelka's husband was obsessed by two passions—clean shirts and jealousy. She cursed the shirts but adored his fits of jealousy. These impassioned displays were refreshing, romantic touches to her otherwise horribly commonplace life. Lelka thought of the director. She would definitely have to describe his syrupy-sweet glances to Venyamin... and, in passing, would add that the director placed his hand on the back of her chair and whispered: " 'Pour me some tea—it's so much sweeter when you pour it...'—No, that's not good enough. 'In your hands tea turns to wine...' No... but how about, 'Your tea and your eyes intoxicate me.' Aha, that's it!"

At last they reached Lelka's block! Saying farewell, she made another attempt to console Yakov Moiseevich: You're talking about Anna Vasilevna as if she were already dead. You shouldn't do that. What's wrong with being retired?... I think it's great! If they gave me fifty-five roubles right now and said, 'You're free, comrade Morkovkina,' I'd be so happy I'd..."

"Stop babbling," Lyudmila cut her off. "Let's get the accounting department together and visit her next week."

"That's a good idea," sang out Lelka. "Well, good-bye for now."

Soon Kharitona reached her corner. Walking on alone, Yakov Moiseevich thought back to that day in early May.

***

Following the May holidays the director of the department, Shavrov, called Yakov Moiseevich to his office.

"Hello, Yakov Moiseevich," the directory extended his hand in greeting. "Have a cigarette," and he pushed a silver cigarette case forward.

"Thank you, Pavel Romanovich, but I don't smoke," replied Yakov Moiseevich, tapping the left side of his chest with two fingers to indicate a bad heart.

"Yakov Moiseevich, I want to know if there's anyone of retirement age in your department, other than you of course!" The director smiled; he liked to kid. He knew that the department could not manage without Yakov Moiseevich and often referred to him as "the accountant of the highest merit."

"Well, what about the old ladies in your harem, huh?"

Yakov Moiseevich looked away. He had no desire to discuss this and jokingly replied: "In my harem everybody is young; the older ones are younger than the young ones."

But the director was already in no mood to appreciate jokes. Having looked at a page of notes, he took on the serious air of an executive.

"Do you have an accountant Kosova? She was born in nineteen hundred and seven. I think it's time we gave her a rest. What's her present salary?... Seventy? Well, she'll lose a little— about fifteen, eighteen roubles."

"But she's a good worker..." objected the head accountant.

"I know you, you never have any bad ones. But just in case there are a few, let's get rid of them. Now then, who is definitely eligible for retirement?"

Yakov Moiseevich kept silent.

"Come one, stop tormenting yourself," the director continued in a conciliatory tone. "As I see it, Kosova is the most suitable candidate. She deserves a rest. Let her stay home. She can bake bread for her old man and look after the grandchildren."

"Her husband was killed in the war."

"In the war?... But the war's been over for twenty years. I'm sure she found someone else long ago."

"She has no one; neither children nor grandchildren... Look, Anna Vasilevna's a hard worker, an experienced accountant..."

"Oh come on, Yakov Moiseevich, let's not argue about this." Shavrov began to drum on the table with his fingers—a sign, familiar to everyone in the department, of his growing irritation. "In one of our songs the words, I think go something like this, 'Every door is open to our youth and respect is accorded out elders everywhere.' You know we have to start making room for the young people sometime."

Yakov Moiseevich asked if the directory had already decided whom to retire.

"We'll see, we'll see," Shavrov answered absent-mindedly, leafing through a folder of papers. "So then it's settled?"

"I'd hate to hurt a good person like her if it can be avoided," sighed Yakov Moiseevich.

"Nobody's going to be hurt. Organize a good farewell party and buy her an expensive gift." The directory took out his pulled back the zipper, and fingered the bills. "Here," he was about to hand Yakov Moiseevich a three rouble note. "Ah wait, I have it. This way you don't have to give me any change." He picked out a one rouble coin from under the bills. "And don't you be stingy either!"

"No, this isn't for me," objected Yakov Moiseevich. "Let the local trade union committee arrange this affair."

"Oh well, okay," acquiesced the directory. "But you'll go along with my decision, right? From here on then, we'll take care of things ourselves. We'll even talk to Kosova without you." Saying this he dialed the number of the local trade union committee.

"Hello, Rozhnova? This Shavrov speaking. Listen, do you know Kosova in the accounting department? She's fifty-eight. What do you think of her?... Not a socially conscious person, hmm? Do you hear that, Yakov Moiseevich? Your Kosova isn't a socially conscious worker. Okay, okay, Rozhnova, drop by to see me. There's something I'd like to discuss with you.... Ten minutes would be fine."

Yakov Moiseevich stood up. He wanted to lay his hand on his pounding chest but restrained himself.

"Oh, by the way, Yakov Moiseevich, I read your request and will discuss it with Rozhnova now. We'd like to grant it but with the present backlog of work, I don't know if that would be wise."

The director was speaking about Yakov Moiseevich's application for addional vacation days without pay. The request was submitted some time ago, but Shavrov had not yet acted upon it.

"All this is rotten, revolting," thought the head accountant, descending the stairs. "I'm old, and tired of all of this.... Yes, I'm old, and tired of all of this.... Yes, I'm too old for this." Not looking at him, Rozhnova, tugging at the sweater riding up her fat sides, was already climbing the stairs to the director's office.

***

Anna Vasilevna came home, sat down in a chair and remained motionless for a long time, trying not to think of what had happened today. Finally she got up to fry some potatoes with scallions. She had not eaten since morning; at the party she was too upset to eat the cake.

Slipping off her Sunday dress, Anna Vasilevna put on a housecoat and went out into the communal kitchen. No one was there. She was glad to be alone; she did not want to talk to anyone.

After the meal and a cup of tea, she washed the dishes and returned to her room. But she could not decide what to do next: whether to darn stockings or read a newspaper. However, a sudden drowsiness overcame her, and she barely found enough strength to crawl into an old, worn-out, spring bed.

Turning out the light, she rolled over on her right side into a more comfortable position and, sighing contentedly, closed her eyes. As frequently happens before sleep, trivial concerns crept into Anna Vasilevna's head: "Will Lelka-carrot remember to revise the bill for the trimmings?... Something's burning in the kitchen; that fatso always has to stink up the apartment.... Where's my handkerchief? It wasn't in the purse—probably lost it. Pity... Was Venyamin jealous today because Lelka came home late? She'll tell us all about it tomorrow.... It's just like a novel..." But as though jolted by an electric shock, she remembered that she would not see Lelka tomorrow, now would she go to work again.

Anna Vasilevna rolled over on her back so abruptly that the worn springs almost tossed her out of bed. Fears, big and little, surged into her mind. How would she libe now? What would she do with her time? Why hadn't she bought a coat last year instead of going on vacation? She probably wouldn't be able to afford one now. How much would food cost per day?... And Anna

239

Vasilevna began to estimate her monthly budget, regretting that she had not sabed any money. However, with her salary she really couldn't have. Perhaps, if she had started earlier when her husband was alive... But they had lived together such a short time.

She had married late in life. Moreover, had she not met someone like herself, unassuming, reserved, unaspiring, she would never have married. Her late husband's first wife, disappointed in his lack of ambition, divorced him—receiving half of his living quarters as settlement—then drove him out altogether. He had to rent a corner of a room from an old woman. At that time, Anna and her mother had a large, separate room in the same flat. Anna's present lodging was just a small, partitioned part of that room: that's why the window was now in the corner.

She looked out the window; it was already dawning. "It's almost morning. I must get some sleep," she admonished herself. But sleep did not come.

In the semidarkness, Anna Vasilevna scrutinized her room as though seeing it for the first time. It was narrow and angular, wider at the head and narrower at the foot of the bed. "It's like a coffin. My God, just like a coffin!" She was terrified: the walls seemed to close in, the ceiling slowly crushed her chest until she could barely breathe.

A crow, awakened in the poplar tree under the window, cawed three times in a rusty voice. "That's a bad omen, a bad omen indeed," repeated Anna Vasilevna apprehensively. Again the tears welled up in her eyes. But the memory of the last agonizing days kept her from crying.

Anna Vasilevna's retirement was the topic of considerable discussion in the accounting department. All types of speculations were raised: some people pitied her, some quietly condemned Yakov Moiseevich, others blamed Rozhnova. At first this talk seemed to make Anna Vasilevna feel better, soothing her injury. But before long, she tired of these conversations and the whole situation became unbearable. Time stood still—the days and hours dragged on.

Soon everyone grew bored with pitying Anna Vasilevna and turned to a new subject: who would God send as her replacement?

"The administration knows who God is sending," snickered Lelka.

The staff now tried to guess what the new replacement would

be like. "It'll probably be some *femme fatale*," quipped Kharitonova. Lelka proceeded to imitate this unknown *femme fatale*. She puckered up her lips, cooed, and strode between desks on her toes without bending the knees. Spreading her fingers wide like prongs, she made a few calculations on the abacus. Then, rolling her eyes languorously, she lisped, "The sum total is one million kopecks and one hundred thousand roubles." Everybody laughed; with Lelka around there was never a dull moment. But Anna Vasilevna's heart ached. She was already forgotten.

She fell asleep in the small hours of the morning. The top of the poplar tree glimmered—the sun had risen. Birds had awakened; in the eaves pigeons flapped their wings. Chirping, ringing, squealing rose up to Anna Vasilevna from the yard. The janitress swept the sidewalk, scraping her shovel on the cobblestones as she bent down to gather up the trash. Anna Vasilevna did not hear any of this.

In the open windows radios came to life: the Kremlin chimes rang out, followed by a lively march for the morning calisthenics.... The air was filled with loud voices; a child cried somewhere, a motorcycle roared by in the street. A woman called out impatiently, "Vanya, are you ready?" People were leaving for work while Anna Vasilevna slept.

Loud ringing awakened her—the alarm clock went off. Vivaciously theumping the table with its metal legs and slowly circling around, it rang gleefully.

"Why in the world are you making so much noise?" asked Anna Vasilevna in a pleasant, sleepy voice. She had always awakened before the alarm, but the clock now indicated eight a.m. "I'm late!" she gasped and, throwing off the covers, shoved her feet into a pair of slippers. Only then did she remember that there was no need to get up or to hurry. She had nowhere to go and nothing to do.

Staring vacantly at the wall, with hands hanging limply at her sides, Anna Vasilevna sat rooted to the edge of her bed. The alarm clock continued to ring and ring as though there would never be an end to this needless ringing.

Notes
[1] *Morkovka* in Russian means carrots.

I. Grekova

One Summer in the City

When the linden trees bloom, the entire city is filled with the aroma. The aroma fills the trolley cars, the stores, the stairways. The aroma of the linden trees had also filled the large hall of the library. The windows were thrown open, and when a breeze wafted in everyone could feel the presence of the linden trees.

A readers' conference was in session. Everything was as it should be. The table covered with a green cloth. Water pitchers, flowers in vases, the microphone. There was a large crowd—about a hundred people, no fewer. At the presidium sat the writer—Alexander Chilimov. The writer's face was morose, aged, its lower half slightly swollen, with a deep, creased wrinkle between the brows. His huge worn hands were resting on the green cover and he was gazing straight ahead, at a portrait of Turgenev.

At the other end of the table, perched on the very edge of her chair, sat the library director, Valentina Stepanovna. She was nervous. There was a rasping in her throat, a burning in her eyes. When one of the speakers lost his place or hesitated, she would begin moving her lips in torment.

Mishka Vakhnin, metal worker from the instrument factory, had just left the microphone. Ekh! Just yesterday he had spoken so well, and now he had gotten all mixed up. He had called Heinrich Böll "Heinrich Buckle." He just could not manage to pronounce "existentialism." There had been laughter in the hall. Disgraceful! If they only knew him... After all, the man has his own ideas, a fresh point of view—that is pretty rare.

And the writer was bored. How many speeches like this he must have heard before....

Valentina Stepanovna's favorite stepped up to the microphone —the laboratory worker Verochka from the nearby NII. A mature girl, a clever girl—simply a marvel! Well, no need to worry about this one. But the writer keeps on staring at Turgenev—the fool, he should take a look at Verochka. Her eyes alone are worth a look. And such a fine, delicate girl, delicate as a church candle. Verochka began speaking, betraying that nervousness known as "enduring." She continuously rolled and unrolled her outline and finally threw it on the table, seized the microphone by its stand and delivered her speech at full speed, her cheek against the microphone and the cheek turning red as if the microphone were hot.

My dear, must you be so nervous? Valentine Stepanovna thought to herself. And such a fine girl! Something classical in her, something of the Renaissance perhaps. Where was it I saw that portrait—that one of the girl with a lily in her hand? Exactly like Verochka with the microphone.

In order not to add to Verochka's confusion, Valentina Stepanovna even turned away and began staring out the window. Outside, the boulevard was going on with a life of its own. A little boy in a sailor's cap was chasing a red ball. Baby carriages were rolling by, people were feeding the pigeons. Over everything there hung a large blue cloud. Soaring. Obviously, it would rain.

Verochka finished. The applause rang forth. She tore her hand away from the microphone and returned to her place, maneuvering her way nimbly between the chairs. When she went by Valentina Stepanovna, she bent over and whispered with a sigh, "Well, was it very bad?"

"No, Verochka, it was very good."

"Okh, you're always trying to make me feel better." And she slipped away.

The writer was sitting motionlessly as before, with a wrinkle between the brows. If only he would at least smile.

"Marya Mikhailovna Lozhnikova, pensioner, senior member of the library soviet, has the floor."

A small bushy-headed old woman with one stocking dangling stepped up to the microphone. A hearing instrument was hanging by a chain from her neck like a hunting horn. She spread out the pages of her outline on the green cloth. The writer shuddered. Marya Mikhailovna moved closer to the microphone, raised herself on tiptoe, and let out a metal-voiced howl through the entire room: "Comrades! Now as never before. . ."

"Not so loud!" the audience began shouting.

What?" Marya Mikhailovna asked. She resembled a siskin, bobbing her head as if pecking at something.

"Not so loud! More quietly!" voices rang out in the hall.

"I can't hear!" Marya Mikhailovna shouted triumphantly into the microphone. Well, now they are laughing again. Valentina Stepanovna stepped forward.

"Marya Mikhailovna, my dear, not so close to the microphone, and you don't have to shout so." She took the old woman by the shoulders and put her in position. Such a fragile little old lady! "Stand this way and don't raise your voice, please."

Marya Mikhailovna peered like a siskin over the top of the glasses and raised her horn to her ear. "Not so loud!" Valentina Stepanovna shouted into the horn. The whole affair was beginning to resemble a circus, and she was in torment.

"Ah, not so loud?" the old woman finally understood. She snatched up her pages and raised herself on tip-toe again. "Comrades, now as never before the educational role of literature has immense import for us. Today we have under discussion the works of the esteemed Alexander Petrovich." (Oh, terrible! The writer's name was Alexander Alexandrovich.) "These are fine works of good quality. With our very own eyes we observe in them the most progressive features of heroes of our time, of the generation of the builders of Communism. Particularly well done by the esteemed Alexander Petrovich" (again!) "are the images of the struggle against bureaucratism and red-tape for the overfulfillment of the plan. However, one cannot agree with all the images. For example, among Alexander Petrovich's images there figures the personality of Vadim who in the pages of this novel behaves negatively, commits a whole series of amoral actions—to put it plainly, he drinks. As an old teacher I ask you, Alexander Petrovich—whom and what can this Vadim teach? Can we raise our young people on such examples, I ask you, Alexander Petrovich?" She turned to the writer.

"Alexander Alexandrovich," Valentina Stepanovna prompted beseechingly.

"I can't hear!!!"

"Alexander Alexandrovich!!" Valentina Stepanovna shouted into the horn. "Aha," the old woman began nodding her head. "I understand. Can we raise our young people on such examples, I ask you, Alexander Alexandrovich?"

The writer shook his head—no. Now—at last!—he smiled.

"Excellent!" Marya Mikhailovna said joyfully. "Take a look— he is already acknowledging his mistakes. Well, I say further. . ." She again snatched up her pages. "Such examples as Vadim can only disorient our young people, push them onto the path of moral corruption. We have to show our young people authentic examples of heroism, the imitation of which... in imitating which..." She began fussing for a way to continue.

"In general, it is clear," said a fat fellow from the first row.

"Let the person speak," snapped a haggard old woman in overalls.

The old woman was still fussing, shuffling through her papers,

"He will not wait for his time... no, that's wrong... akh, yes, he presents in his hero... that's wrong again... it seems, here it is, I've found it. 'In man everything must be beautiful—his face and clothing, his soul and thoughts,' as the great Russian writer Anton Pavlovich Chekhov taught us."

"We know," said the fat fellow.

"Tsss!" the woman in overalls hissed.

"Somewhere here on another page," Marya Mikhailovna said, bustling. "I'll find it right away."Her hands were shaking and the pages scattered, part of them falling to the floor. The writer jumped to his feet and rushed to pick them up.

"Why that, why?" Marya Mikhailovna said. "You—a writer with a world renowned name—and you're picking up papers from the floor... I can do it myself, I can do it myself."

Several heads at the presidium disappeared beneath the table. The writer emerged first. His huge face was red from exertion. He gathered the sheets together and handed them to Marya Mikhailovna. She was smiling and nodding her head.

"Thanks, they're not worth the trouble. It's better I just say it, without the papers. Of course, not on the same level, but from my soul. The chief thing is that I have read your works and cried over them. And it's not easy to bring me to tears. When the woman who shares my apartment insults me, I don't cry. I choke, but I don't cry. But I read your works, and I cry. And do you remember how your Vadim walks home from his mother's funeral? You don't remember? Never mind! I'll read it to you right now. I've got it written down here... Well, that's all right, there's no need. I'll simply say that I cried. Here and in at least nine other places. I've got bookmarks placed where I cried. And for those tears, Alexander Petrovich, I thank you and bow deeply to you."

She stepped away from the microphone and bowed deeply, like a nun, before the writer. Applause thundered forth. Alexander Alexandrovich got to his feet, lumbered out from behind the table and kissed Marya Mikhailovna's hand. She pecked at his forehead and burst into tears. The hall thundered even more loudly. People got to their feet, applauded, shouted "Thank you! Thank you!" The fat fellow in the first row clapped especially loudly, like a cannon. Marya Mikhailovna returned in confusion to her place, covering her face with a handkerchief. The writer stood there, his eyes on the floor, and he clapped diffidently, softly. The gray clump of hair on his forehead danced. Finally he sat down. The audience also began to sit down. Valentina Stepanovna tapped on the microphone, the hall became quiet.

"Comrades, ten persons have already spoken. No others have signed up. Is there perhaps someone else who would like to speak? Or shall we yield the floor to Alexander Alexandrovich?"

"Call the question, call the question," ran through the hall. The writer got to his feet, huge, embarrassed, with his arms at his sides. The hall immediately fell silent. The microphone hummed softly.

"What should I tell you? In our life, in a writer's life, anything is likely to happen—both good and bad. And more bad than good, if the truth be known. You write, and you tear it up, and you write it again, and again you tear it up, and so on. And you feel you are so untalented, empty, all written out... it's hard to say how you feel. And sometimes you feel you're so useless you'll never be able to hide it. This happens. But sometimes good things happen too. Not things you'll be praised for in the newspapers—that's for certain! Whether they praise you or condemn you is a matter of chance. But something good happens when you feel someone needs you. It doesn't have to be everyone, but just someone. This is a great thing. And here you have thanked me today—it is not you who should be thanking me. I thank you, dear friends. And may God, as it is said, grant you happiness in life."

Oh, what a storm was raised! Valentina Stepanovna hastily tapped on the microphone. "Silence, silence. Alexander Alexandrovich has not finished. Continue please."

"Well, what's the use of continuing? I think I've said all I want to."

"Did you hear, comrades? Unfortunately, that is all. Permit me, comrades, to thank Alexander Alexandrovich in your name... In the name of the entire collective of library workers, of the readers' activist group and of the entire mass of readers...."

Applause, knocking of chairs, stomping of feet. The audience burst into motion, began standing, leaving, each person going his own way. Maelstroms turned in the current of people. A crowd collected around the writer—some were asking questions, some thrusting books at him to be autographed, some taking pictures. The air immediately became hot and heavy. Valentina Stepanovna knew that now the most important business would begin. The most frank, the most important discussions. At first here at the door of the hall, then in the cloak room, then on the street, beneath the pale lights of the street lamps on the embankment, on the wet benches of the gardens. And the evening would drag on and she would have no strength to leave. Everyone would be good, and everyone would be intelligent, and everyone would love one another....

No, it would be just impossible for her to stay. Lyalka would come home and there would be no dinner. "Alexander Alexandrovich, thank you! I am very sorry, but I must leave."

"Well then, leave, Valentina Stepanovna, I'll stay here and chat with your young people. Such marvelous young people you have."

"Yes, our young people are a miracle."

"Be sure and come again!" shouted a shaggy-haired young girl, heavily sprinkled with freckles.

"I'll come again. Without fail."

It turned out to have rained after all. Large puddles were standing in the streets. Yes, our young people are very fine. After a rain the linden trees smell even more strongly. Essentially, it is an offensive aroma. Sweet, clinging, luscious.... No, foul. Precisely. A foul aroma. The same way the linden trees smelled that time.... But isn't it curious how tenacious memories are? Ineradicable. So many years had gone by, the pain had gone, and here is the aroma of the linden trees—and it is as if just yesterday.

Valentina Stepanovna walked down the boulevard. The old pensioners were sitting beneath the linden trees. Old men with white nimbuses around their bald heads were plaing "goat." On the benches sat old women with their swollen legs spread wide apart. They held their pocketbooks upright on their knees, leaning them against their round stomachs. Pigeons were strutting above on the ground, children were playing in the sand.

Ahead of her worked a man in a broad checkered jacket, also a pensioner, it seemed. He was walking downcast, his carelessly combed head, a motley gray, bent to the right side. From behind there was something familiar in his gait, like a long forgotten dance. Could it be? The man turned around. Yes, it was Volodya. But how old he had grown!

"Valyusha, is it you?" said Volodya.

"As you see, it is I."

"We haven't seen each other for such a long time," Volodya mumbled. "About three years, ah? I. to tell the truth, have been strolling here almost every day waiting for you. Do you still work there?"

"Still."

"Still... And you are still the same. You haven't changed. You've even grown younger."

"That's a well known ploy. Tell a woman she's grown younger. You won't go wrong with that."

"No, joking aside, you know, I've been dreaming for a long time of running into you. You know, when you approach the end of your life... you begin longing for what was once especially dear to you. Have you ever noticed?"

"No," Valentina Stepanovna said. "I am not coming to the end of my life. You can do so if you wish, but not I."

"Well, you always were rather severe. I know you! I know you!" Volodya laughed and his long, fine still beautiful teeth flashed for a moment. Those very same teeth. Everything was gone, everything.

"Why don't we sit down here for a minute," Volodya suggested. "I'd like to have a chat with you. Especially with you. I'm lonely, after all. Don't you believe me? It's true."

"We'll sit," Valentina Stepanovna consented wearily.

They sat down on one of the pensioner benches, A tall old woman with biblical eyes who was feeding the pigeons at the other end of the bench got up, looked haughtily at them, and went away.

Volodya sat down, rubbing his hands—wide shouldered, clumsy in his jacket. His nails were not completely clean... Doesn't she look after him?

"Yes, it's been a lot of water," said Volodya. "Nowadays my thoughts often return to the past and I see that perhaps we made a mistake."

"Speak for yourself. I didn't make a mistake."

"Such a malicious one, such a prickly one," Volodya said, and he again smiled.

As if it is not bad enough that those teeth make me feel limp, Valentina Stepanovna thought to herself.

"No, joking aside, I have always missed you. And now, when I see you, so youthful, interesting, smartly dressed... Really, something begins stirring within me..."

"Such a banal person you have become," Valentina Stepanovna said sadly, drawing her heel through the sand. "Or perhaps you were always a banal person, only I just never noticed it?"

"A banal person, just so, a banal person," Volodya said gaily. "Well said. I must confess that without you I have degenerated a bit morally, and perhaps physically. Manya is a beautiful woman, a fine doctory, but she doesn't have that something in her... that something eternally feminine. Can you imagine, I am sometimes obliged to launder my shorts and undershirts myself. It's not difficult for me, of course—we have an apartment in a new building, hot and cold water, a garbage chute, we have everything. But it's somehow awkward for a man to do housework, isn't that true? Take literature—where do you find a man who keeps house. It's somehow unnatural. I didn't know such a thing with you. I remember how charmingly you used to keep house in our little room on the sixth floor. In our mansard. Do you remember?"

"I've forgotten."

"I don't believe you,'" Volodya laughed. "Women never forget."

My God! Valentina thought. That same face, those same cheeks that I loved. And so terribly! I would wake up and I'd be in love. I'd go to sleep, and I'd be in love. Always I was in love.

"The linden trees are in bloom, have you noticed?" she asked.

"Yes, a marvelous aroma."

"Well, all right, it's time for me to go," Valentina Stepanovna said. "Lyalka is waiting."

"Yes, and how is Lyalka, by the way?" asked Volodya with a somehow hungry look in his face. "Has she grown up? Is she finished at the institute?"

"In the third year."

"A beautiful girl, probably."

"To me, very beautiful."

"Whom does she look like?"

"Like you."

"And would you believe," he said thoughtfully, "I live for that. You won't believe me, of course, but it is a fact. I live for you—for you and Lyalka."

"Well then," Valentina Stepanovna said as she got up. "Live, if you wish. It is time for me to go."

He also got up. "Valyusha, would you perhaps permit me, an old man, to drop in on you sometimes for old times' sake? We could just sit over tea, have a chat, a few laughs..."

"It wouldn't be any good."

"But I am her father."

"She doesn't know you and she doesn't want to know you."

"That's sad," Volodya said.

Old Volodya, one had to be sorry for him. She asked, "And how is your health?"

"My health is fine."

They said goodbye. His hand was weak, limp, almost as if dead. When she reached the end of the walk, she turned around. Volodya was sitting there, his hands hanging by his sides. In the distance his checkered gray jacket seemed greenish.

Valentina Stepanovna climbed the stairs slowly. Don't hurry, count to a hundred at every landing, the doctor had said. There's no help for it. Now you count to a hundred. To your very death you count.

In her bag there were fresh vegetables—radishes, parsley, carrots, lettuce. They were all moist, fresh, young and green. She had not bought it at a stand but in the market. Expensive on the free market, but for just that reason good. She had to feed Lyalka—Lyalka was getting pale.

On the last, the sixth landing, she counted only to fifty and opened the door. The lock clicked—she was home.

"Is that you, Stepanovna," her neighbor Polya shouted from the kitchen.

"It is I. Well, hasn't Lyalka come home?"

"I haven't seen her. She opened her eyes at ten, ran a comb through her hair, and away she went. Didn't even drink tea, nothing. Always any old way. If she just wouldn't sleep until ten o'clock, she'd have time for everything. I..."

"Didn't she call?"

"I wouldn't know. I don't care one way or another. I was beating the rugs. Raised the dust, I did! Enough to blind the eyes. And maybe she did call. Makes no difference to me. I don't have anyone to be calling me—I don't even bother to listen."

It was always that way with Polya—you give her one word and she gives you back twenty. Valentina Stepanovna took off her coat and went to her own room. In the room it was cool. The window was open, and the white curtain billowed lightly in the wind. She sat down at the table to collect her thoughts. She always thought things out before beginning the housework. She did not think long—about three minutes. To put her thoughts in order, get them firmly in place, without any loose ends. So that she would have time for everything and would not have to hurry.

Slice the vegetables, wash them—one, put on the soup—two, while the soup is boiling, rinse the laundry—three...

She counted her moves and ticked them off on her fingers, beginning with the little finger. Lyalka was always making fun of her about this. First column halt, second column march... a battalion commander! she would tease.

"You have to think out what you are going to do. That is why I always have enough time, and you do not."

"Makes no difference, I just can't do things that way. I just can't plan."

"You can do anything you want to, Lyalka."

And that was true—Lyalka could do anything when she wanted to. Only everything came in spells. That sewing spell. She sewed herself an evening gown. Her friends came and burst out laughing. What gown? That's a pair of pants for Oleg! And then the cooking spell. Somewhere she got hold of a cookbook from the eighteenth century or thereabouts. Her colorful apron at the ready, her thin arms up to the elbows in flour. Polya would stand around, her stomach jutting forth.

"Is that any way to cook? Who cooks that way? That's sweet dough, it's sweet, that's for sure, but it should be sour, sour. And you're throwing everything in there every which way. Here you are with your powder, and there you go with the soda, and you put fancy flour in there too, it's pure idiocy. And here she is, doing everything by a book. You'd think she could at least ask a person. No, according to our way it should be sour, and it is sour, but sweet dough, that is sweet dough..."

"Listen, Polya, have you ever been wrong?" Lyalka would ask.

"No. But what do you mean, have I ever been wrong?"

"It's very simple. Has there ever been a time when you weren't right?"

Polya thought it over very carefully and answered modestly, "I can't think of any. It seems there never was a time."

And the pie turned out well—high, plump, ruddy. Even Polya after she had tried it, said it was not bad, but she immediately added, "But it's better our way."

And Lyalka's studies went the same way—in spells. A spell of fives, her portrait on the honor board—Valentina Stepanovna would be overjoyed. The next session would start off with a two. She would lie around smoking. "I don't want to study, I want to get married!"

"Lyalka, you ought to be ashamed of yourself! With your abilities..."

"I just don't know what good my abilities are. Maybe a singer is perishing in me."

And sure enough—her music spell. She bought a guitar, began playing it from self-instruction lessons. She would sing to the accompaniment of guitar—vigorously, but off-key. No ear.

"No, Lyalka, no singer is perishing in you."

"What do you mean? Is it very bad?"

"Very."

"Well then, how is it that Borka fell in love with me when I did 'Carmen' for him? Because of my singing."

"Not 'because of your singing,' but 'in spite of your singing.' "

"And you're supposed to be a mother! That's no mother, that's a beast. A real mother ought to blindly—understand?—blindly adore her child. Create a golden childhood for her. Do you understand? Now let's try it again, little mouse, do I sing well?"

"Badly."

"Okh, your honesty will be the end of you. But I love you anyway."

She would look, with her head leaning to one side, and then let out a fine squeal and start kissing. "That's for being such a good fellow! That's for being such a fine fellow! That's for being such a dear fellow!"

Well, all right. Time to get going. Clean the vegetables—one, put on the soup—two. Valentina Stepanovna went out into the kitchen, took the basin from the shelf, the cutting board from its nail. She kept everything in its place, each thing on its own nail.

255

That's not pedantry, that's simply economy of time.

She began cutting up the vegetables. Next to her Polya was doing laundry, her back bent over the zinc trough which had seen better days. The back of her blouse was dark with sweat.

"Polya, if you would just try my washing machine. It's much faster. I did a whole laundry yesterday in an hour..."

Oy, why did I have to start that? With Polya it's always the same—pull the chain and she floods. That's the way she is.

"Machine!!! I've seen your machines. There's a machine for everything. You want to blow your nose or cut wind and somebody will invent a machine for it."

(In Polya's eyes Valentina Stepanovna was the personification of the intelligentsia with all its sins and weaknesses.)

"No, Valentina Stepanovna, I don't need your machine. I wouldn't take it free let alone pay a thousand for it. It churns and churns and what it's churning for nobody knows.And you have to spend all your time keeping a watch out on it. Four minutes a-round. It doesn't know one dirt from another, white from black— everything's the same to it. Four minutes. Do I have to spend four minutes washing by hand? I take and look at each little spot in the light. Maruska downstairs did her laundry in a machine just the other day—enough to make you laugh. She put everything in at once and set it to churning. And what happened? The linen came out all different kinds of colors."

("Maruska downstairs" was the neighbor on the lower land-ing, the eternal object of Polya's judgments.)

"It's hard by hand though," sighed Valentina Stepanovna.

"For you, mother, everything is hard. You're not so young, and you've got a heart condition too. I'm the same age as you, but I'm tougher. I've toughened myself up on work. I can most likely clean anything whiter than your machine."

"Well, as you wish."

Polya again bent over the trough and, hunching her back angrily, began laundering. Valentina Stepanovna broke up the vegetables. It was quiet. Only the laundry splashed in the trough and the knife clattered on the cutting board. It's a good thing she shut up, Valentina Stepanovna thought. After all, a person has a right to silence.

No, there was no right to silence. Polya had not talked herself out yet.

"Listen, Stepanovna, I'll tell you something. Duska Savrasova has a nephew—young, but cultured. He's so cultured he's simply charming. He finished technical school. He used to go out chasing the girls—get all dressed up, comb himself like a cherub. Always carrying a transistor radio. Well, all the usual things. Duska and me used to watch him—didn't make us too happy, it didn't. He found a room and moved away from Duska's. Lived real well, only his hair started falling out. Well it keeps on falling out and so he takes it into his head to get married. Duska's got nothing against it, it didn't mean nothing to her since he wasn't living with her no more. So he got married to this woman. At first everything was all right, but then she began playing the hooligan. She puts in the whites and the grays and the colored things all together to boil—hard as it is to believe. At first he kept quiet, but then he started complaining. She couldn't care less. She got to be so brazen she'd tie up her brassiere with a string. No, he couldn't live with something like that, he got himself a divorce."

(Polya was unable to praise anyone without passing judgment on someone else. Most of the time she praised herself.)

"Tie up a brassiere with string—I'd never allow such brazenry. I might only work as a simple watchman, and I didn't finish any of your fool's schools, but I know good culture. My late husband used to drink—but I stood for it. He gets sick, and I clean it up, so I'd never be ashamed before the neighbors. I'd launder his clothes, sew them, iron them, he went around like it was Easter all the time..."

She fell silent. It was quiet. Only the sound of the laundering.

"But what I've been meaning to ask you, Valentina Stepanovna," Polya said suddenly, "Is he sick or has he just stopped going with her?"

"What are you talking about, Polya?" Valentina Stepanovna asked, pretending not to understand.

"You really don't understand?" Polya said, screwing up her eyes. "Who would I be talking about if not that Olezhka of yours? I'm not blind. After all, Stenka, it's right there before my eyes. The fellow keeps on coming around and coming around—hello there, he stops it and he's gone, like he's been flushed down the toilet. And there's just no hiding what's going on with your Lariska—don't you think I see what's going on? She paints herself up and powders herself all over, but she's still as pale as death."

Valentina Stepanovna was silent.

"You're hiding something from me, akh, you're hiding something. And what're you hiding it for? It's a perfectly ordinary woman thing, after all. You know I don't wish you and your Lariska bad. The girl grew up right before my eyes, after all. She'd come running into the kitchen not even as high as the table— Auntie Polya this, Auntie Polya that. Is it just a few times I've wiped her nose? And you off on your fancy frrr-frrr job. She comes in wagging her tail—and you're not even around. But Polya's here, where else would she be? And she's a child after all, not a cat. I feel sorry even for cats, feed them. And here you are treating me as if I've got pigs' ears."

"Polya, my dear, don't be offended. I'm not hiding anything from you, truly. I don't know anything about it myself."

"You just keep on hiding it—it's plain all the same. You can't hide something like that—it'll come out in the open. The fellow used to come around and now he doesn't come around. And the girl's not herself anymore. Mean to say you think she doesn't have any fresh eggs ready?"

"God only knows what you're saying, Polya, and with what words besides! I just can't get used to your jargon." Valentina Stepanovna threw the vegetables into the boiling, turbid soup.

"So now she's offended," Polya said. "Some sort of zhirgon. You can't get me with words like that. You're just too sensitive— more sensitive than a hair. You mean to say you didn't give birth to her yourself? You never ran around? You ran around and you gave birth to her, and there's no getting around that. And you'd be better off keeping your eye on Lariska's underthings. The girl's sloppy, throws her things all over the place, and you just take a peek at it."

"Excuse me, Polya, I have a headache," Valentina Stepanovna said, and went off to her room, off to the underground. Rinse the laundry—three... How can I rinse the laundry when Polya's in the kitchen? She's frightfully talkative. Probably because she doesn't read. It takes the place of reading for her. Should I try introducing her to books? It won't work. She'll sooner unlearn me."

In order not to lose time, Valentina Stepanovna set about

dusting the furniture. A comforting task. The hands are busy, the head is free, no one is grumbling next to you, and you can think about what you want, even about today's conference. It was all right, the conference turned out fine. No, there's no thinking about the conference, completely different thoughts creep into the head— Lyalka, Oleg.

The photograph there on the wall—Lyalka with Oleg in the woods, on skis. Oleg—tall, standing straight, dark haired with a broad chest, in a close-fitting sweater. A handsome face, in the full flush of youth. Black brows knitted over a straight nose. Next to him Lyalka—she stands all bent over as if leaning on crutches, one leg far to the side, laughing, snow in her hair...

The telephone rang. Valentina Stepanovna went out into the hall, picked up the receiver.

"Little mouse, is that you?" came that beloved, vague, husky voice from afar.

"It is I, dear. Where are you? I am waiting for you. There's salad."

"Oh, salad! That's perfect. I love salad. Little mouse, do you hear me? I love you. Do you understand?"

"I understand. And when will you be home?"

Lyalka's voice paused and said, breaking slightly, "I don't know. Soon. And no one called me?"

"No one. No one while I've been here. Shall I ask Polya?"

"No need."

"Fine, no need. And so I'll expect you."

"Agreed."

Valentina Stepanovna hung up the receiver. She had not even turned away before the phone rang again. If only it would be Oleg!

"Valyunchik, it's me."

"Zhanna! Where did you disappear to?"

"Akh, that's a whole story. Just imagine, I've fallen in love again."

"God save you."

"Yes. You can be as upset as you want, my virtuous friend, but you have to accept me as I am. Troo-la-la. Are you going to judge me, Valentina Stepanovna?"

What are you saying, judge you! I'm happy for you."

"You know, he liked my calves best of all. 'In these calves,' he says, 'is all the elegance of the age.' "

"Are you sure he's not dumb?"

"Mmmmm, I don't know, but after all, I'm not so bright myself, isn't that true?"

"Perhaps."

"I love you for your honesty. You're the same honest girl as in school."

"What are you saying, 'girl!' More likely an honest old grandmother."

"What? Already? Lyalka?"

"What are you saying? No! I was simply referring to my age."

"Yes—age. That's our nightmare, isn't that true? But we still don't want to part with our illusions, right?"

"You know I've parted with mine long ago."

"And I. But from time to time they still show up. You know that last year I swore off love completely. I made up my mind— that's enough. And here it has come flying down on me again like a hurricane. I feel something keeps building up in me, building up in me... No, Valyunchik, there's no use in my trying to say it on the telephone. Can I drop in to see you? What are you doing?"

"I'm cooking supper. I'm expecting Lyalka."

"Well, I'll drop in for a minute. I'll just sit, smoke a cigarette —and I'll be gone. May I?"

"Of course you may."

"I kiss you."

"I'm expecting you."

Okh, that Zhanna. Laughter and tears. But I love her. Our whole life together—that's no joke, our whole life. We went to school together, worked together. Suffered through the war together. If it had not been for Zhanna, we would have both fallen— Lyalka and I. The baby had already begun to get scurvy. And who saved her? Zhanna. Fruits, lemons!.. and during the war. Where from? You ask her—she laughs. I got it by honest work. She'd managed to meet the director of a warehouse. Who will judge her? Not I.

And Lyalka when she was little—what a wonderful little girl she was! Enough to make you hurt. Even passers-by on the street stopped and felt the hurt. "What a beautiful little girl!" Black hair, green eyes, severe expression and her lashes... Yes, and it's been a long time since I've seen Lyalka with black hair. Every week a new color—now like ripe rye, now like a red tree. And not long ago she came home all gray, with a lilac tint. It was an easy thing—silver dye, a bit of school ink, and that's it.

"Lyalka! Again a new color? Have mercy on me. I have a heart condition."

"You have to keep up with the times, little mouse. Catch up, exert yourself. And why talk about it? My hair? Mine. My lips? Mine. If I want, I'll paint them. You don't like it? My precious treasure! That's the nineteenth century in you."

"Lyalka, I wasn't even born in the nineteenth century. You know that perfectly well."

"Makes no difference. In your soul you're the nineteenth century. Such a cozy century. Everything as clear as with Polya. White was white, black was black. You'd want to see me pure, white, a Turgenevian heroine, with a fishing rod in my hands by an old pond. Like Liza Kalitina in *A Nest of Gentlefolk*."

"It's all untrue."

"Well, so I'm lying. You're my little child. You're my beautiful little child. And those ears, those ears! Like two cameos. And your hair. There's almost no gray. Oh, I want to squeeze you to death!"

"Lyalka, you're crazy, let me go..."

And Lyalka at the mirror—that's a picture for you too. It's so interesting to watch while she makes up her face. Her serious lips, with that air of suffering, a black pencil to the corner of a green eye, two or three strokes, and the eye comes to life—oblong, mysterious, slanted. And then the finishing of the lashes. A blunt penknife in her hand. The knife touched carefully to the lashes, and one after the other they turn up. And it had to be blunt. Once Oleg—conscientious Oleg—found her knife and sharpened it. Just trying to be helpful! Lyalka almost snipped off her eyelash. Then they made the knife dull again against the flowerpot...

"Ekh, Oleg! Why couldn't you have been satisfied?"

The doorbell rang. It's probably Zhanna. Yes, it's she. Polya opened the door and went back to the kitchen with a growl. She doesn't like Zhanna.

"Valyunchik, hello, my little sun!" Zhanna kissed Valentina Stepanovna on the cheek. "Have I made you blush?"

"I guess not. Come in."

From behind the kitchen door could be heard Polya's monologue. "Empty-headed old bag, doesn't know if she's coming or going. Off this way, off that way, and the way she puts on airs. It's time she'd better be thinking about her soul. She's in her fifties,

261

not in her twenties! And she's out chasing all the time. And Lariska just like her. The very same way."

"What's that Polya's saying? Who's she talking to? "

"Herself. She's like that. Don't pay any attention."

"And she puffs herself up all over the place, and runs all over the place, " came the voice loudly from behind the door. "She's fifty, even older, gets all dressed up, knees flapping in the breeze, and under her knees nothing but veins—like a blue ocean... And what good is it all? It's all the same—you can't jump higher than your own head, you'll never get smarter than your mother and father. Old, she's just plain old. Time doesn't go backwards, after all."

"Is she talking about me?"

"No, about herself, let's go."

Zhanna seated herself in an armchair, curled her legs up under her. And really, her legs were amazing, glorious. She took out a cigarette, lit it.

"Well, here's how it is, Valyusha. Once again I've encountered love on the path of life."

Zhanna always talked like that. How strange that it was not offensive. It became her.

"And just who is he?" Valentina Stepanovna asked.

"A sailor. A real intellectual. As you know, I'm not indifferent to gold braid. It's not without reason that women have always loved military men. The gold, caps, cloaks, mentiques..."

"And do you know what a mentique is?"

Zhanna thought for a moment. "Something like a saber?" she asked.

"Not quite. More like a tunic."

"Just as I thought—like a tunic. Akh, in our time everything is so colorless—khaki and more khaki. A sailor's uniform has always excited me. You can believe that or not."

"Oh, I believe it."

"You're eternally making fun of me. Of course, I am ridiculous. That trait—the amorousness—I know it myself. When I encounter love on the path of life I forget about everything and immediately start getting warm all over."

"And where did you dig him up?"

"Oh, that's a whole novel. We met in a ticket line. I was buying a ticket to Sochi, and he to Minvody. We started talking, laughing and he even sang 'oh, those dark eyes,' or something like that. 'And you,' he says, 'do you have to go to Sochi?' 'I have to.' 'Is someone waiting for you there?' 'No one's waiting for me, I'm as free as the wind.' 'Then,' he says, 'let's go together to Minvody.' Well, he just swept me off my feet. I had circles before my eyes. I went off to Minvody."

"Just like that? Right on the spur of the moment?"

"No, two days later. Well, of course, I had to put myself in order, trim my brows, dye my hair, do you see? It's called 'play of gamma colors.' Don't look near the part, it's grown out there. Look here. A marvelous tint. Anna Markovna made the suit for me —the arms let out, soft pleats in the skirt. I found a purse to match, the slippers are Hungarian, high heels—you know. I go off like a queen. I'm looking perfectly presentable, wouldn't have given myself more than thirty-eight years, and who should know better than you how old I really am? In general, it was a marvelous dream..."

"And how long did it last?"

"Two weeks. Ran out of money."

"Him?"

"Me."

"And him?"

"He stayed there. When we parted, he was actually in tears. He gave his word he'll call me as soon as he gets back."

"Is he married?"

"It seems so. But what of it? Valyusha, do you judge me?"

"No, honestly."

Suddenly Zhanna buried her face in the back of the armchair and began sobbing. Actually sobbing, not simply crying.

"Zhanna, dear, what's wrong? Have I offended you?"

"I have offended myself."

"God be with you, don't cry. I'm not Polya, after all. I understand."

Zhanna shook her head. Her bright chestnut locks, "play of gamma colors," came loose, and the dark hair, with touches of gray, could be seen.

"Valyusha, today I remembered Leonty Ivanych." (Leonty Ivanich was Zhanna's late husband, a general.) "I was as faithful to him as a rock. If he were still alive, nothing would have happened. He kissed the air around me. This damned loneliness! No, you don't understand."

"I am alone also, after all."

"You have Lyalka."

"That's true. I have Lyalka."

Suddenly, somehow instantly, Zhanna stopped crying. She sat up, dried her eyes and smiled. "You know, it makes me happy that I haven't lost my figure anyway. From behind you can even take me for a young girl. Isn't that true?"

"That's true."

"Well, I'll go. I've sat, smoked, had my cry... How good it is that I have somewhere to cry!"

"Always come to me, at any time."

"To cry?"

"And to laugh also."

"Oh, friendship, that's you. Valyusha, you are a true friend."

"You and I are old friends."

"As old as old can be. Come to the door with me. I'm afraid of Polya."

Valentina Stepanovna accompanied Zhanna to the door. "Parasite!" came a loud voice from the kitchen. Zhanna bravely pulled her gloves on.

"Goodbye, Valyunchik. Take care of yourself. Give Lyalka a kiss."

"Come again."

The door slammed, the slender heels tapped down the stairs. Behind the kitchen door Polya's monologue went on. "But I don't need a man. What do I need a man for? The only thing you get from a man is dirt. All you do is laundry for them, laundry... Men smell bad. Is that you behind the door, Stepanovna? Come on in, don't be timid. Don't I speak the truth? At her years to be thinking about a man—that's the last thing should be on her mind! When I was young—I was a fire! But now I don't need a man anymore. I wouldn't take one for free. The only thing you get from a man is dirt, the only thing you get from a man is the stink. Without his half-liter he's no good. I'm better off going to church. I don't need a man..."

Valentina Stepanovna moved quietly away from the door and went to her own room. She should have checked the soup, but let it be. Polya is there. It's amazing how a person can make a slave of others if she is always right.

She had to finish the dusting. And really, how messy Lyalka is! Just look at all that junk she has on her table! A purse, notes, eyebrow pencils, an elastic belt, a stocking. The road has run away with the cart. Valentina Stepanovna picked up Lyalka's purse, the wrong way, and all kinds of things came spilling out of it—lipstick, a powder box, crumpled rubles, some papers. She got down on her knees and began collecting it all from the floor. Just as the writer had picked up the papers today... One folded paper caught her eye. Against her will, she read: "Savchenko Larisa, gynecological section of maternity home No. 35... for the interruption of pregnancy... sixth or seventh week..."

For an instant the bright sky outside the window went dark, as if it had blinked. Valentina Stepanovna stood on her knees, then gathered the things and got up, clinging to the corner of the table. She put everything back into the purse. It was all senseless and impossible, completely impossible. She read the paper again. Just as before. Well, all right. It's terrible, but all right. Have to get used to it. It's terrible that she hid it from me. And I thought she had no secrets from me.

Valentina Stepanovna went out into the kitchen and turned off the gas under the soup. Polya, thank God, was not there. Then she returned to her room and sat down in the armchair. The armchair was not comfortable for her. She tucked her legs under and put her head in her hand. Somehow this helped. So that it was almost not painful to sit there. She shut her eyes. Outside children were shouting. The wind lifted the curtain and brought the aroma of the linden trees into the room.

Just the way the linden trees smelled during that cursed summer. I remember—I was standing here, and he was over there. He sat with his back to the window, and I facing him.

"Valyusha, can you really be serious? Do you really want me to leave you?"

"Perfectly serious."

"You are an idiot. You must understand, after all, that it didn't mean anything. Well, a little diversion. I was carried away. These things do happen."

"Why did you lie to me?"

"Lie! And what was I supposed to do, come and unburden myself to you? Merci. You'd have made a scandal, you'd have broken down... I valued our relationship too highly to tell you."

And that really had been Volodya who said that. Impossible. It was not he who said it, not he.

"Valyusha, you are making an elephant out of a fly. You must understand, I love you. That other woman is for me, in essence, nothing. Well, if you want, I'll break it off. Do you want that?"

How could he not understand it was not a matter of another woman, but of a lie? I said, "It's not a matter of another woman."

"What is it then?"

"It's a matter of me. I don't love you anymore. Go away."

"Look, you'll regret it."

But he left. I remember the feeling—the whole world turned upside down and fell to pieces. And right then—it was not yet too late. Chase him, bring him back. There's his cigarette, still, lit, in the ashtray. Still smoking. Why are you standing there? Go after him, bring him back. And the door slams below—and that is all.

No, there was no more Volodya! He had been divided in two. He had broken in pieces. One—the old one, beloved, my own, like my own hand. The other—new, without feeling, cruel. A stranger. And the thought—how dared this other Volodya enter my body? Murderer!

When the world falls to pieces a person is stunned. Something inconceivable has happened. It is impossible, but it has happened. And a person is unable to accomodate contradictions, and it seems to him he is perishing. Nonsense. Man is tough. Even while he is perishing he lives. He lives, forgets, recovers.

And I didn't even tell him about Lyalka. Why was that? He would feel sorry for me... One more lie. For that matter, at that time it was not yet Lyalka. I thought it would be a boy, Volodya. The boy had only just begun, there had been no final verification. I thought, I will tell him later. And so I never told him. And that there is a Lyalka, he found out by accident, two years later...

But at that time I hadn't even thought of Lyalka. I was always thinking about him. Volodya. When had it been? Had there been snow at the time or was it already spring? For some reason this seemed to be the most important thing—when had the old Volodya come to an end and when had the new Volodya begun? It was important to find this line through the past and cut off everything at the line.

Nevertheless, I went to work that day. Zhanna was sitting in the library, gossiping with the readers. There always used to be a line at her table. She noticed me and was startled. "Valyusha, what's wrong? You're perfectly green."

And I became ill. She took me off to the restroom. There were some pails of lye standing there. In one of them stood a huge brush. And the chief thing was the floor of varicolored tiles—red and yellow, as I see them now. The floor came straight up to meet me. Zhanna held my head. After a while I felt better.

"Valyusha, my dear, it's not..."

I nodded.

"God, how interesting. You will have a leetle bebbi."

Zhanna was in love with Hollywood at the time and used to say "bebbi," "darlink."

"Volodya, of course, is in raptures?"

"Volodya doesn't know."

"How is that?"

"Zhanna, you'll learn about it anyway, so it's better you know right now. There is no Volodya. We're separated."

There were tears in Zhanna's dark eyes. What are words? Tears are important.

"Valechka, may I ask you just one thing? Just one tiny thing?"

"No."

"Not about Volodya. If you say no, then it's no. I mean about 'that.' Will you keep 'that' or will you get rid of it?"

And "that" was Lyalka...

"I don't know, Zhanna, I don't know anything..."

And then a strange life began—like a delirium. I would lie around thinking. The work day would drag by minute after minute, and then I would rush home to lie down. I would arrive home, lie down on the sofa facing the back, and think. The telephone would ring—I would not answer it. Only at every ring my heart would begin beating faster. It would thunder loudly in my ears. The neighbor would knock at the door. "Telephone!"

I would not reply. Out in the hall the neighbor would shout, "Not home! Or perhaps she's asleep!"

My heart would keep on beating, but gradually it would quiet down. After half an hour—another ring, and again my heart would quicken. I never once answered it. I would only keep repeating the same phrase over and over to myself: "May you be damned, if it is you."

And again I would begin thinking. Always about the same thing—where to draw the line? On the other side was the old Volodya. He whom I had loved. On this side was the new one. He whom I had to hate. And the line kept moving one way or the other. Sometimes the new one would grow into the old one. For minutes at a time it would seem that there had never been an old one. And then I would scream at the new one as if to a living person, "What is it, do you want to take everything from me?" And sometimes the old one would begin growing into the new one... And this was worst of all. Then I would be almost ready to forgive him, bring him back... I would fasten my attention on a piece of lint on the back of the sofa. It would move continually back and forth from my breath, sway. I almost stopped cleaning the room, and eating too. I would see no one but Zhanna. I could bear to see only Zhanna. It is very important that a person does not get on your nerves. And Zhanna never gets on my nerves. She paces up and down the room, humming something. Sweeps the floor, dusts the furniture. Goes to the mirror—her curls, her lashes, this, that. Gives herself a funny wink. She is as imitative as a monkey—raises one brow and you're ready to laugh. Or she speaks about trifles in that throaty, mysterious whisper, in the manner of a Hollywood star. "The style is ve-ree ni-ice... The sleeves bouffi-que, shoulders lowered, but not too much, rather like this, just so. It forms a soft square, understand? A double-hemmed skirt to the knees, slightly fluffed below. A gusset at the collar..."

You listen to her, and it's even as if you begin to feel a little better—as if you are looking past your grief at a colorful, beautiful, carefree bird. That's how she is, Zhanna. You look at her—all put together from bits and pieces, each one borrowed from somewhere else, and somehow it's all just right. And all of it together is Zhanna. Sentimental, generous, mad, dear Zhanna.

We never spoke about Volodya. That had been agreed upon. Zhanna kept her word. How hard it must have been for her at times—one must know Zhanna to understand how hard it was for her! To keep quiet about something—after all, that is a diffi-cult thing for her. But one time as she was making up her face, even putting on lilac lipstick, she began talking. "Valyunchik, well let me just say... I'll have a heart attack if I don't. I love you, after all. And after all I'm not going to try to persuade you to go back to Volodya..."

"No."

"But one has to look to the future, isn't that true? After all, I want only your own good. You can be sure of that, that is like steel. Listen, if you've decided to get rid of it, then it has to be now, or else it will be too late."

I didn't understand anything she was saying, I didn't want to know anything. I had never had to deal with anything like this. Some sort of penal code—conspire, conceal, cover up... She had read of cases in the newspapers—both doctor and woman in court. Become a criminal, be brought to court. But without this it is impossible. Did I have to put up even with this for Volodya? Even without this I had enough worries with those others, those other two.

Zhanna arranged it all. Took me off to the doctor. Vladimir Kazimirovich. A fellow in a foreign suit. His voice was oily, like cracklings in a frying pan. And his face was swarthy, sleek, clever. Zhanna assured me that Vladimir Kazimirovich had a light hand. "You'll see, he'll do it so well that it will simply be a pleasure." And I surrendered myself, it was as if I did not even exist.

"Doubts are precluded," Vladimir Kazimirovich said. "It is a confirmed pregnancy. In so far as surgical intervention is concerned, it will perhaps not even be necessary, if the requisite measures are undertaken in time..."

This was the artificial way in which he always spoke, Vladimir Kazimirovich. Long, intricate sentences. Always skirting around the essence of the subject... Figure eights...

He prescribed "a light, painless course of injections." At twenty-five rubles per injection. Preparation straight from abroad. Not absolutely guaranteed, but it might help. I began going for the injections. He lived in a dacha in Karpovka. The dacha was a mansion. Two stories, stone, all the conveniences—gas, bath, telephone. And a garden with a ridiculous cupid in it. There were bird droppings on his head, and cupid was crying. That damned dacha! It was reached by a small street—grown over with linden trees, shady... The branches bent low over the fences and they were covered thickly with blossoms. It was then that I understood how foul the aroma of linden trees can be.

But the injections did not help. Each time Vladimir Kazimirovich would say, "If not today, tomorrow, wait and see." But I no longer believed in those injections. It seemed to me that he was leading me to the hook like a clever fisherman, taking me at twenty-five rubles per injection so as to be more sure of taking his thousand. I did not have the thousand. I borrowed it from Zhanna. But he was tender, Vladimir Kazimirovich... Each time, as he bade me goodbye, he would hold my hand in his own. And it seemed to me that I had taken hold of a toad. And then...

"Well now, young lady," said Vladimir Kazimirovich, rubbing his hands, "our course is completed, but it did not give, unfortunately, positive results. I, for my part, was careful to warn you in advance that I could not guarantee one hundred per cent success. Isn't that true?"

"What must be done now?"

"If you, as previously, do not burn with the desire... eh-eh-eh... to preserve the fetus, then we will be obliged to meet one more time in order to apply a method less pleasant, but for all that more promising."

That was the complicated way he always spoke, Vladimir Kazimirovich.

What could I do? I consented. He demanded the money in advance. "You see, a few weak-nerved little ladies have run away from me—right from the table, one may even say..."

Everything was arranged. Friday in the evening, after ten, when it had grown dark. No one to accompany or meet me afterwards. Total conspiracy. To have with me—two towels, two sheets, all sterilized, ironed on both sides. "I tell you in advance— the linen will not be returned."

Not to bring documents with me. After the operation it is to be agreed that I will not stay in the dacha more than ten minutes—is there not, after all, a chance that something could happen? "The responsibility is immense, but I do not fear responsibility," Vladimir Kazimirovich said. "I stress once again—no one to accompany you, no one to meet you."

And then it was Friday evening, already getting dark, already dark, and again I am on the train. What lay ahead—the pain, the danger—was of almost no concern to me. The whole way I was tormented by the two Volodyas. Worst of all, it seemed to me that I myself had been divided in two—I could not discern where it was I and where it was not I, and in general everything had vanished. I was surrounded by foulness, and I felt myself under the power of foulness... I approached the dacha, it was already dark. I recognized it from the cupid. I went up to the gate, turned the handle, unfastened the latch... Someone rose up out of the dark, as if out of the ground. The beam of a flashlight... "Citizen, your documents..."

Someone had come. No, it was not Lyalka's ring. Lyalka always rings loudly, insistently, happily. And this ring was faint and abrupt. Valentina Stepanovna was still sitting in the armchair, her head leaning against the rough armrest. No matter, Polya will open it. The door opened and Lyalka came into the room.

"Little mouse, are you here? What are you doing? Why are you sitting in the dark?"

"Nothing, I'm just sitting. I feel a bit ill."

"What's wrong? Let me feel your forehead. It's cold! Little mouse, you are a malingerer. I'll turn on the light, all right? There, that's better. I want to eat—I'm perishing. Where's the salad?"

"I didn't make the salad," Valentina Stepanovna said. "But listen now, sit down here."

Lyalka lowered herself to the divan. Thin, tall, leggy as a grasshopper and even in a gray-green dress, short, above the knees. Well, a grasshopper, that's her. When she sat down, her knees were raised higher than her chin. Pale, shadows under her eyes halfway down her cheeks.

"Lyalka, listen..."

Lyalka took a comb out of her hair, began chewing on it. "Well, what, do you want to have a talk with me?"

No, I simply want to tell you a story."

"Well, well."

"Well, and what happened after that?"

"After that I ran. Never in my life had I run so fast. They whistled and I ran. My legs were young, strong. Even today my legs are pretty good, they carry me."

"And did you escape?"

"As you can imagine, yes. I listened, the whistles became more faint, and finally they vanished completely. But I kept on running. I had thrown my bundle away at the start, so that I

271

was running without things, without money, without anything. And you know, it was so good to run... I felt that I was escaping from all of them—from the police, from that doctor, from the court..."

"Did they take you to court for that in those days?"

"They took you to court for everything in those days."

"Well, and what happened then?"

"After that, nothing. I ran to the station—the train was standing at the platform. It was dark, but in the train the lights were lit, huge... It was such a beautiful train and it was as if it were waiting especially for me. I rushed into the coach. Everyone looked at me—red, dishevelled, happy... The minute I got in, the train started. The controller went by—I didn't have a ticket. He didn't fine me—why, I don't know. We reached the city. I went straight to the pay phone. I called him, Vladimir Kazimirovich. I was afraid he had been arrested because of me. But he was fine, wasn't even frightened. He said, don't worry, he was accustomed to carrying out his obligations. He invited me to come on Tuesday. Friday, he said, is a busy day. And right then I cursed him."

"Oy! That's hard to believe. What was it you told him?"

"I won't be coming to you anymore. You are scum."

"And did you really say that? Oy, what a hero! And you didn't die on the spot from torments of conscience?"

"No. I even told him I'd give birth to ten just to spite him."

"An obvious exaggeration. Well, and what happened after that?"

"After that? You were born."

"What a happy little story..."

In the hall something fell, and Polya's tearful voice rang out. "What parasites! Not even at night any peace. Gabble, gabble, gabble. They sleep the whole day, and at night they keep everyone awake. Can't behave like normal people. No, I'm going to change my apartment, I'm going to change my apartment."

Fazil Iskander

Grandfather

Grandfather and I are on a wooded mountain ridge. It's a hot summer day, but it's cool and shady here. The ground is covered with a thick, somewhat springy layer of last year's leaves. Prickly beech-nut shells are scattered here and there. They are usually empty, but sometimes we find ones with the nut still in them. All around, no matter where you look, there are strong, silver beech trees and a few thick chestnuts.

In a space between some trees far in the distance is the blue spectre of a valley in the Kolkhida with an enclosing wall of sea, or rather part of a wall, because the forest covers everything else.

Grandfather is standing on a steep slope chopping down beech saplings with a "tsalda" (a sharp-nosed hatchet): some for fencing, some for new grape baskets. From time to time, he tosses the hewn branches up to me, and I pull them onto the path and gather them in a pile.

The constant chirping of birds pierces the forest air. At first their voices seem to be just singing, but then you start to feel that they are chatting back and forth, cussing each other out, laughing at each other, or, if nothing else, just winking at each other.

Sometimes a chance gust of wind reaches us from the sea, and then the shadows on the ground split and spread out, and patches of sunlight flit between them, and the chirping of the birds grows louder, as if the gust of wind is shaking it off the trees like rain-drops.

But it is all boring and uninteresting to me. I stand there waiting for grandfather. I hold his cane, a home-made staff, in my hand. He is somewhat strange, my grandfather. My interest in him flares up from time to time, but then suddenly dies. There is something about him that forces the people around him to respect him, and this respect prevents them from living the way they want to, so they often curse him for it.

I see all this and perceive it with a child's instinct, although, of course, I don't understand it and can't explain it.

At the moment, we are in the forest. He is chopping down nut-tree branches and I am watching him. He's having a hard time chopping, because he's standing on a steep slope, and the thickets of nut trees, entwined with dense blackberry vines, are downhill a little, so it's hard to reach them. Sometimes, in order to reach them with the hatchet, he has to chop up the whole wire entanglement of blackberry vines. And he chops them up. Every time he takes on a new obstacle, I hope he won't overcome it. This is because I am bored, and I want to see what grandfather will do if he doesn't overcome it. But that's not all. I sense that the people around him need to see grandfather put to shame, and they don't have very many examples of this, if any. I feel that if there were a few more such cases, maybe many of them would decide to treat him without any respect, and then nothing would keep them from living the way they want to. I feel that it would also be useful for me to have one small example of his failure at my disposal, because grandfather sometimes makes me do something I don't want to do, too. And besides, I think it would be nice to toss such a find into the adults' collection on occasion.

Grandfather finishes off the closest thickets and heads for new ones, but they're hard to reach, because the slope is steep and crumbly and he can't get footholds.

Grandfather looks around. Without letting go of the hatchet, he wipes the sweat off his red face and suddenly bends down and grabs a lone rhododendron bush with all five fingers of his left hand. Gripping all its branches with his clawed fingers, he pulls on it with his fist, the way you would pull on the reins, and now he hangs confidently over toward the fresh thickets. Short and lithe, right now he looks like a fine teenager who insists on fooling around at the top of a cliff.

Before he gets to the thicket, he has to cut down a blackberry vine as thick as a rope. I feel in my bones how hard it is for him to stand hanging on one arm and extending the other one, which barely reaches, to hack at the springy blackberry vine. The hatchet keeps bouncing back, and on top of that, the blows have no effect.

"Grandfather, it isn't cutting," I tell him from above, giving him an opportunity to retreat honorably. Grandfather silently keeps hitting the springy vine, and then, timing his answer with the hatchet blows, he says: "It will cut... It's not going anywhere... It will cut..."

And again the hatchet chops. I watch and begin to understand that it really can't get away. If it could get away, grandfather probably couldn't even keep up with it. So, it can't get away. And if it isn't going anywhere, he'll just chop at it all day, or even two days, or even more. I imagine myself bringing

276

him lunch, supper, breakfast, and he still chops and chops, because it just can't get away.

And it seems the blackberry vine, too begins to understand that it's useless to resist. With each blow, it springs back less and less and subsides powerlessly under the hatchet. Hatchet marks are cutting into it deeper and deeper. Now it collapses, but grandfather still chops and chops. Now I hope grandfather will misjudge the last blow and fall down with a thud, or even drive the hatchet blade into the rocky ground. But the vine splits in two, grandfather doesn't fall down, and the hatchet manages to stop.

I'm bored, and on top of that, the mosquitoes are tormenting me. I'm in barefeet and shorts so they've been biting me all up and down my legs. Sometimes I scratch the bites until they bleed, or I swat my legs with a sharp nut-tree branch. I lash and lash at them with a kind of frenzied pleasure.

Then I start tracking down individual mosquitoes. There, one lighted on my hand. He fidgeted around a bit, getting acquainted with the locality, thrust out his stinger, and started poking it in between my pores. At first his stinger even bent a little (he obviously hadn't hit the spot), but then he reached the blood, and I felt a slight pain as he drew it out.

And now he's sitting on my arm sucking my blood, and I put up with it all, restraining my annoyance, and I watch his stomach gradually turn pink from my blood. It swells and swells and turns crimson. But now, with difficulty, he pulls out his stinger and spreads his wings as if taking a good stretch in preparation for flight, then I get him—slap! Now there's a bloody speck on the itchy sore spot. There it is, the sweet balm of revenge! I smear it around and rub the corpse of my enemy into the wound he had inflicted upon me.

But sometimes, trying to make the balm of revenge still sweeter, I wait too long to swat him and the mosquito calmly flies away. And then in my fury, I grab a branch and flail my legs with all my strength: Go to hell, you parasites!

Grandfather notices the way I'm fighting off the mosquitoes, and I think I can just make out a disdainful smirk on his face.

"You know how it hurts," I tell him, wounded by this smirk. "You're all right. You're in trousers."

Grandfather grins and pulls a chopped off stalk out of the bushes. It resists, bends, and gets tangled up with the branches in the blackberry stickers.

"One day, Aslan comes to his friend's house," grandfather starts in without any warning. "He sees him lying on the bed. 'What's the matter with you?' Aslan asks. 'Look here, I've been shot in the leg,' his friend answers. 'I have to lie down for a while.' 'To hell with you!' Aslan got mad. 'I'll never set foot in your house again as long as I live. I thought the fever had gotten him, but he lay down just because of a little bullet.' And he left. They used to be real people in those days," grandfather says, and he throws me a long green branch. "And you—mosquitoes."

And once again he started banging away with the hatchet. What can you say to him? Well, all right, I think, I know that there used to be such a fever in these parts, and people often died from it. But why can't a person who's been shot in the leg lie down on his bed until the wound heals. I can't understand this at all. Maybe this Aslan is a famous Abrek, and what's a hailstone on the head or a bullet to him? No difference at all.

"Grandfather, who was he, a famous Abrek?" I ask.

"Who are you talking about?" Grandfather turns his hook-nosed, slightly savage face toward me.

"About Aslan, who else?" I say.

"Hell no, he wasn't an Abrek. He was a good leader, not some kind of Abrek."

And once again he started banging away with the hatchet. Again he comes up with some kind of nonsense. According to what grandfather says, an Abrek is worse than some kulak.

"Did you yourself ever see any Abreks?" I shout at him.

I talk to grandfather almost as an equal, dubiously figuring that he and I are the same distance away from middle age, even though we are on different sides of it...

"You should have a goat for every time they ate up everything I had," grandfather replies without interrupting his work.

"Your goats can go to hell for all I care!" I say furiously. "You'd better tell me why you don't like the Abreks."

"Well, why did they burn down my barn?"

"What barn was that?"

"An ordinary tobacco barn."

"Well, tell me from the beginning..."

"What is there to tell? Six people suddenly appeared. For three days we gave them food and drink. They hid in the tobacco barn. And on the fourth night, they burned down the barn and left."

"But maybe they were hiding their tracks from a posse," I say.

"Well, they themselves were worse than any posse," grandfather answers, and he spits. "We were almost deported because of them."

"Why?" I ask hurriedly, so he won't stop.

"Because the 'starshina' at the assembly in Dzhgerdy reported that we were hiding Abreks and would have to be deported, so no one else would hide any Abreks..."

"But why did he say you were hiding Abreks?"

"Because we really were," grandfather answers.

"Well, what happened then, grandfather?"

"My mama was at that very assembly, but the 'starshina' hadn't noticed her, because she came a bit late. As soon as he said this, my mama forced her way through the assembly and rode up to him and started pushing him with her horse and beating him with her damask, and she kept saying, 'Did you see my son hiding Abreks? Did you see it?!' It took three men to stop her. My mama was a wild one."

"But grandfather, didn't you yourself say you were hiding Abreks?"

"What does that matter? Everyone knew we were hiding them. And why? Because we were living way out in the country. That's why they came to us. It is our custom not to refuse entry to someone who asks to stay in your home. And if you don't let him in, it will be even worse: either he'll shoot you or he'll steal your livestock. So it turns out that it's better to let an Abrek into your house than not to."

"But grandfather," I interrupt him, "how did the 'starshina' find out the Abreks were at your place?"

"Everyone knew. How could we conceal it? But it's one thing to know and another thing to tell an assembly about it. We considered this treachery. And in our time, an informer didn't grow a fat tail for long. You may be a leader above all leaders, but if you're an informer, sooner or later you'll get your tongue pulled out."

"But grandfather," I'm trying to follow his train of thought, "wasn't the 'starshina' the most important person in the village?

Whom did he inform?"

"That's just it. He informed himself..."

"Grandfather, you've gotten something mixed up," I say. "That doesn't happen."

"I haven't gotten anything mixed up," grandfather answers. "If the 'starshina' knows and keeps quiet, or if he only talks among his relatives, by law it is considered that he doesn't know anything. But if he tells the assembly about it, by law it is considered that he knows and should punish you. So it turns out that he is an informer and has informed himself."

"Oh," I say, "but what happened then? Did the 'starshina' get revenge on you?"

"On the contrary," grandfather says, "he started to respect us. If their women are this wild, he decided, why get mixed up with their men?"

Once again grandfather started banging away with the hatchet, and I suddenly became depressed. Does this mean that Abreks aren't necessarily proud avengers and heroes? Does this mean they can set a barn on fire or kill a person for no apparent reason? Somehow, I find it bitter and unpleasant that there are scoundrels and villains among my favorite heroes. I feel that somehow this forces me to size up all the Abreks, which is, of course, an insult to the honest, noble brigands. I sadly pass before the ranks of the Abreks and search among them for the one who burned grandfather's barn. I have faith in the integrity of most of them, but it can't be helped, I have to turn out the pockets of all the knights and check them. And I feel that knights with turned out pockets, even if they appear to be honest, are no longer real knights, and they feel this themselves, and this makes me unbearably bitter.

I felt something like this once when I was taken to the theater. After a splendid show, for some reason, the audience started to applaud, and the people who lived on the stage now just came out and started taking bows. There was one person among them who was really unpleasant, and they'd killed him just a few minutes before, but now not only was he not ashamed, but he rose from the dead and stood, like a fool, among the living. He was even shameless enough to hold his killer's hand with one hand while he quietly knocked the dust off his trousers with the other.

And they all smiled and bowed together, but I felt I had been cheated and insulted. And for some reason the stupid audience smiled too, and applauded, as if to say, "It's all right that you cheated us. We really like the way you cheated us..."

And suddenly I notice a ship appearing in a space between some trees, and others appear behind it. It's a whole flotilla of warships. They slowly, slowly creep along the mirage-like wall of sea, discharging fat smoke as if it is squeezed out of their funnels. I stand still, watching them in joyful amazement. I'm especially struck by one of them: low and inordinately long, it nearly takes up the whole space between the trees.

"Grandfather, look!" I shout, coming to again, and I point my finger at it.

Grandfather watches them for a while, and then he starts in with the hatchet again.

"That's nothing," he says. "Now take the 'Makhmudia.' It was so big we could have held horse-races on it..."

"What was this 'Makhmudia?' " I ask.

But grandfather doesn't answer. He picks up an armful of the last branches, climbs up the slope with them, and tosses them in the common pile. Grandfather takes a seat at the edge of the ridge where his legs can loll comfortably on the steep slope. He takes his handkerchief out of his pocket, thoroughly wipes off his sweaty, close-cropped head, full of short gray hairs, puts the handkerchief back out of sight, and sits still, after unfastening all the buttons on his gray chest. As I watch him, I feel that I like his lithe, active hand with its stubby fingers and his round, gray head, and I enjoy the pleasure he found in wiping the sweat off his head. But I know he still has to answer my question, so I wait.

"During the 'amkhadzhira', we sailed away on it," he says, after thinking it over.

I already know what the 'amkhadzhira' is; it was when Abkhazians were forced to re-settle in Turkey. It was long, long ago. Maybe a hundred years or so have passed since then.

"Grandfather," I say, "tell me how they drove you away."

"But they didn't drive us away. We left willingly," grandfather answers.

"But they must have driven you away. It even says so in books," I say.

"They did cheat us, but they didn't drive us away," grandfather stubbornly replies, and he looks up at me. "Besides, how could you drive an Abkhazian away? An Abkhazian would go off into the forest or the mountains, because our people always give these things a wide berth. During the first re-settlement, I was just a little boy. They didn't even want to take me..."

I sit down next to grandfather as a sign that I intend to listen to him for a long time. Grandfather takes off his rawhide slippers, shakes some rocks and dirt out of them, and then pulls out bunches of a special alpine grass which is put into the slippers for padding. Now he arranges the grass in his hands and carefully, as if he were making a bird-nest, puts it back into the slippers.

"Well, grandfather? What was the trip like?" I ask, and I imagine the "Makhmudia," a huge ship, but simple like a ferry boat. It's full of refugees, but for some reason they aren't at all depressed. On the contrary, they hold horse-races from time to time, and the Turks, pompously telling their beads, watch the races.

"We sailed well, right up to Istanbul," grandfather recalls. "They fed us white bread and pilaf all the way. We were very fond of this."

"And then?"

"We got off in Istanbul, but they didn't leave us there. We only saw a Moslem mosque called Ai-Sofia."

"But why didn't they leave you there?"

"Because they told us that there were too many Greeks and Armenians in Istanbul already, and if they allowed Abkhazians, too, they said, there'd be no place to put the Turks."

"So where did they take you?"

"They took us someplace else. They let us off on the shore. We look, and the place is bare and rocky. And before, they'd told us that there are breadfruit trees in Turkey, and sugar is taken straight out of the ground, like salt. And here, not only are there no breadfruit trees, but we don't even see a simple plane tree. So we ask the Turks, 'But will you keep bringing us pilaf and white bread by boat?' 'We won't be bringing you any pilaf and white bread,' say the Turks. 'Plow the earth, raise some goats, and live...' 'Do you think we came here to plow?!' We got angry. 'We could have plowed at home. The earth was even better there, and we had spring water...' 'You'll have to plow,' the Turks reply. 'But why did you tell us that in Turkey sugar is dug out of the ground, like salt, and breadfruit trees grow?' We don't calm down. 'No,' say the Turks, 'sugar doesn't come out of the ground in Turkey. The Turks would dig all over the place, and the Sultan wouldn't allow it.' 'But this wouldn't hurt the Sultan, would it?' We are amazed. 'Of course it would,' the Turks reply. 'If the earth got dug up everywhere, it would be holey, like cheese eaten away by rats, and who would be interested in ruling a holey country?' 'That's not so bad,' we answer. 'You can fence off a hole and go around it.' 'That's not the problem,' say the Turks. 'Of course you can fence off a hole, but other sultans and even the Russian Tsar would laugh at our Sultan because he ruled a holey country, and this would be a great insult to us.' 'So it turns out that breadfruit trees don't even grow here?' we guess. 'Breadfruit trees don't grow here either,' the Turks reply, 'but, on the other hand, we have fig trees.' 'What are you talking about? You Turks are out of your minds!' we shout. 'Why did you bother us with your sugar holes and fig trees? No Abkhazian would sail clear across the sea for any fig. He wouldn't even step out of his own yard, because everyone has a fig tree growing in his yard.' 'Well,' say the Turks, 'if you are so proud and you have your own figs, what did you come here for?' 'But you told us,' we explain, 'that in Turkey sugar is dug straight out of the ground, like salt, and breadfruit trees grow. So we decided if there are breadfruit trees and we can each dig some sugar, we will live. To tell the truth, we even became Moslems because of this. Our Tsar offered to let us become Christians, but we refused.* Look, Turks, we can still give in to the Tsar.' We scare them. 'So, why didn't you give in before?' The Turks are amazed. 'We didn't give in,' we reply, 'because the Tsar's Siberia is spread out too far, and it's too cold. We Abkhazians like warm places, and cold ones we don't like.' 'But what did it matter to you that Siberia is spread out so far?' The Turks are surprised. 'Because we have a custom,' we say, 'that we have to visit relatives who've been arrested and bring them packages so they won't lose heart. And even on a good horse, you can't reach Siberia in a month. So no matter how many packages you took, you'd eat them all up by yourself on the way. We even wrote a petition through our clerk, to see if they would build a Siberia for Abkhazians in Abkhazia. We even picked

---

*After the Abkhazian uprising against Russia in 1866, peasants who were brought to trial were allowed to convert to Christianity and serve sentences in Siberia rather than be re-settled in Turkey.

out a good basin, with no exits. It even suited the police—there was nowhere to run. And we liked it. You could ride down there on a horse in no time, first with beef jerky, then with cheese, then with flat bread.' The Turks marvel at this. 'Well, what was the Tsar's answer?' 'That's just it. He didn't answer at all,' we say. 'Either the clerk didn't work hard enough on the petition, or the Tsar didn't want to move Siberia...' Now the Turks start talking among themselves, and then one of them asks, 'Tell us, in all honesty, is it true that Russians eat snow?' 'Maybe when they're drunk,' we answer honestly, 'but not otherwise.' 'Well then, settle down, raise goats, and don't wear us out any more with your talk,' the Turks decide. 'If you settle us here,' we still bargain a little, 'we might give up Islam. It doesn't mean anything to us...' 'So give it up.' The Turks are offended. 'We can get along without you.' 'But then, why did you feed us white bread and pilaf on the boat?' we try to find out. 'We like that diet very much...' 'That was politics,' the Turks answer. 'So what if it was,' we say in amazement, 'as long as there will be more.' 'There isn't anymore,' the Turks answer. 'Once you arrived, politics ended...' But we didn't believe that politics had ended. We decided that the Turkish clerks had hidden it away for themselves. 'If that's so, we will complain to the Sultan,' we threatened. 'You don't say!' the Turks shouted, 'In Turkey, you can't complain. In Turkey, they kill you for that.' 'Well then,' we say, 'we will become robbers. We have no choice.' 'Is that so!' The Turks are really frightened. 'In Turkey, you can't steal, either.' 'Well, if you can't do anything in Turkey,' we answer, 'take us back. Only see that you feed us pilaf and white bread on the way, and don't even bother to mention figs, because we will throw them in the sea anyway.' But the Turks didn't take us back, and we couldn't find the way by ourselves, because no tracks are left on the sea. Then our people lost heart and started settling all over Turkey, and some even went farther, to Arabistan, and many joined the Turkish police. And they served well, because our people like to have power over the Turks, even if it was through the police. But after a year, I started to yearn so much for home, that I got a job with a bandit on a felucca, and he took me to Batumi, and from there I walked all the way to our village."

Grandfather stops talking and gazes far into the distance humming something, and visions of grandfather's story pass before my eyes.

"That's it," grandfather says, and he picks up a slipper and kneads it before he puts it back on his foot. "They did cheat us, but they didn't drive us away from our village by force. . ."

I look at the coarse soles of grandfather's feet. They have a special, distinct structure. On each foot, the second toe is larger than the big toe, as if it fits over it. I know city people never have such feet; for some reason, only country people do. Much later, I noticed the same kind of feet on ancient pictures with biblical topics—the Christian feet of apostles and prophets.

After he puts on his slippers, grandfather stands up effortlessly and divides the branches into two piles: one, a very small one, for me, and a huge one for himself.

"Grandfather, I can carry more," I say. "Give me some more. . ."

"That's enough," grandpa mutters, and he breaks off the pliant top of a nut branch and twists it, turning it over with his strong fingers as if he were twisting a string. After he gets it good and limbered up, he pushes it under his branches, ties it in a tight knot, presses the whole bundle against the ground with his leg, loosens the knot, and tightens it again. Then he painstakingly pushes in the end of every last twig, so none of them will fall out.

While he's busy doing this, I stand and wait with his staff resting across my neck and my arms thrown over it. It feels like you're hanging on yourself. It's very comfortable.

"Once," says grandpa, breathing heavily on top of the bundle, "when they were building the Kodori road, some local people came to the Russian engineer to get a job. The engineer heard them out, looked them over, and said, 'I'll take all of you except that one. . .' " Grandpa nods his head as if to point out the rejected worker.

"But, grandfather, why didn't he take him?" I ask.

"Because he was standing just like you are now," grandfather indicates the cane with his eyes.

"What do you mean? You can't stand like this?" I ask, but in any case, I take the cane off my neck.

"You can," grandpa answers, without lifting his head, "but the only people who stand that way are loafers, and why should he hire loafers?"

"Oh where did you learn that!" I get irritated. "Look, I

took the cane off my neck. Does that mean I'm not a loafer any more? Huh?"

"Uh-uh," grandfather grunts. "That's not taken into account. Once you rested the cane on your neck and threw your arms over it at the same time, that meant you were a loafer. That's the sure sign."

Well, what can you say to him? The main thing is that even I think maybe he's right, because when I held the cane like that, I didn't feel like doing anything at all. Not only was I reluctant to do anything, but it was nice to do nothing. Maybe, I think, real loafers are the ones who get this pleasure out of doing nothing, as if they were doing something pleasant. In any case, I stick grandfather's staff into the ground next to my bundle, which he's tinkering with right now.

Now two neatly bound bundles of nut branches with long green tails are ready.

"Come on," grandfather says suddenly, and he heads toward the rhododendron bushes on the other side of the ridge.

"Where to?" I ask, and I run after him so I won't be left alone.

Now I notice that a barely visible path runs through the thickets of rhododendron. It goes along the ridge and gently drops down into the basin.

It is immediately obvious that this is the north side. It's dark. The rhododendron bushes here are especially fat and husky. Some kind of huge, chemical flowers grow on the bushes. The smell of primeval rot is in the air, and I sink up to my ankles in the loose, cool earth.

And suddenly some bilberry bushes pop out in the midst of the dark, murky green, and their light, gay green color gladdens my eyes. The tall, light bushes are generously sprinkled with raindrops of berries. So this is where grandfather has brought me!

Grandfather bends down the closest bush, shakes some berries into his palm, and pours them into his mouth. I try not to be left behind. The long, light branches, sparkling with big-eyed berries, bend pliantly at a touch. They are so delicious that I start to get greedy. It seems as if these riches aren't enough for me alone, and here grandfather keeps eating and eating berries like a little kid. He doesn't even finish stripping one branch before he's already looking around, searching for another, and suddenly—

zap!—he grabs for another branch full of berries.

But now, finally, I feel that I can't take any more. The bittersweet coating on my teeth makes them ache from the cold air when I open my mouth. Grandfather is obviously stuffed, too.

"Look," he says, and he shoves some dropping toward me with the toe of his slipper, "you can see a bear has been here. . . . And over there the bushes are even broken off."

I follow his hand and see that the bilberry branches really have been broken off in places. I look around. This place suddenly seems suspicious and unpleasant. It really is murky here, and my legs sink too deep in the damp, boggy ground. I couldn't run very well in case something happened. And over there, in the rhododendron bushes behind those chestnuts, something moved.

"Grandfather," I say, just to break the silence, "he won't bother us, will he?"

"No, grandfather answers, and he breaks off some bilberry branches, "he won't dare touch us—he's too scared."

"But why should we scare him?" I say loudly and distinctly, to be on the safe side. "We don't even have guns. Why should he be afraid of us?"

"Of course," grandfather answers, still breaking off big clusters of bilberry branches.

And yet it's somehow unpleasant and disturbing. I wish we'd head home, but to talk openly about this would be disgraceful.

"That's enough," I tell grandfather in the same loud and distinct voice. "We've had our fill. Now we should leave some for him."

"Just a minute," grandfather answers. "I want to take some to the family."

Grabbing bushes for handholds, he quickly climbs up the steep slope to a spot where there are still many untouched berries. I break off bunches for the family, too, but for some reason I'm jealous that he thought of them first. Maybe I wouldn't have remembered them at all. . .

With our bouquets of bilberries, we go back out onto the ridge. After the cold, damp footing on the north slope, it's nice to walk on the soft, dry leaves again. Grandfather straps the bouquets onto our bundles.

He puts his huge bundle on his shoulder, shakes it to feel the balance, and moves off down the ridge, supporting the bundle with his hatchet, which rests across his other shoulder. I copy what he did, only I don't have a hatchet, so grandfather's cane supports my load.

We walk down the ridge. Grandfather is almost out of sight behind the green hill of nut leaves swaying in front of me.

At first the going is easy, even enjoyable. The load hardly feels heavy on my shoulder, I step softly, the slope is not too steep, so my legs can easily keep my body from speeding up, and on top of that, sparkling beads of bilberries play right by my mouth. I could grab one or two with my tongue, but for the time being I don't want any.

But now we are coming out of the forest, and it gets hot almost immediately, and the going gets harder and harder, because it's painful to walk barefoot on the rocky path. And on top of that, the branches bite into my shoulder and some wood dust goes down my collar and stings and tickles my sweaty body. I shift the bundle more and more frequently, so my shoulder won't get numb and the load will rest more comfortably on it. But it starts aching again, and other uncomfortable branches take the place of the previous ones, and they press just as painfully on my shoulder. I pull down on grandfather's staff, as though on a lever, in order to lighten the load on my shoulder, and it really does get lighter. But then my left shoulder, the one with the cane, starts to hurt. And grandfather keeps walking and walking, and the huge sheaf of green leaves just bounces along in front of me.

Finally, the sheaf slowly turns around, and I see grandfather's savage face. Maybe he'll throw off his load and we can both rest? No, its's something else. . .

"Aren't you tired?" grandfather asks.

This question provokes me to quiet rage: It's not that I'm tired, I'm just squished by this damned load!

"No." I force this out of myself because I'm so full of bitterness I just don't want to seem pitiful and good-for-nothing to grandfather.

Grandfather turns around, and once again the huge green sheaf rustles and shakes in front of me. For some reason, I re- member grandfather's face at the instant he turned toward me, and I begin to understand that his savage expression was produced by constant physical exertion. At that moment, under the load, the wrinkles which are normally visible on his face appeared even sharper. I realize that this grimace of struggle just froze on his face, because he's been overcoming obstacles all his life.

We walk past my cousin's house. The dogs don't recognize us at this distance, and they start barking furiously. I think maybe grandfather will stop so the dogs will quiet down, but he doesn't stop. Secretly irritated with the dogs (I think I can detect this from the way his load jolts along on his back), he keeps walking.

I see my cousin come out of the kitchen and look toward us. He is a powerful giant, blue-eyed and handsome. Right now, he is standing on a hill with the sky in the background, and because of this he looks especially huge. He can barely recognize us, and he shouts:

"What do you think you're doing, grandpa? You're off your rocker—to torment a child!"

"Loafer," grandfather shouts back at him. "You'd better hold off your infernal dogs."

For a while longer, we walk along under the hill where my cousin's house stands, and he keeps watching us from above. Knowing that he feels sorry for me, I try to look even more stooped over to get his sympathy.

And the going gets harder and harder. Sweat pours down my arms, my legs tremble, and it seems as if any second they'll fold up and I'll sprawl flat on the ground.

I pick out a spot up ahead with my eyes, and I tell myself: "As soon as we get to that white rock, I'll throw off my load. As soon as we get to that bend in the path, I'll rest there. As soon as we get to. . ."

I don't know why, but this helped.

Suddenly grandfather stops by a fenced-in corn field. He bends over and leans his bundle against the fence. If only I can get to it. If only I can last that far. . .

And now he takes the bundle off my shoulder and puts it next to his.

Grandfather and I sit down on the grass and rest our backs against the fence. Sweet, blessed lassitude. The corn field is behind us, and in front of us, a huge plain with an immense wall of sea covers the whole horizon. A broad, even breeze barely reaches us from the distant sea, and it rustles among the corn plants.

"Last year they took forty baskets of corn from this field," grandfather says, "and I used to get sixty here even in a very bad year. . ."

"Good Lord, what do I care?" flashes through my mind, and I sink into a semi-conscious state.

It is so sweet to sit resting my back against the fence and feel the cool, even breeze on my sweaty neck, but then a sudden current of air will shoot across my chest or down the collar of my shirt and send a cold chill up the hollow of my spine. And it feels so strange and good to sit here listening attentively as my body keeps soaking up the coolness, and it's absolutely insatiable, and this filling somehow blends with the jaunty, even breeze, with the high, mighty sky from whence comes the drowsy, flickering sound of larks, and with the rustle flitting from stalk to stalk in the corn field behind my back.

I know grandfather is waiting for my question, but I don't feel like talking, so I remain silent.

"And why?" Without waiting for the question, grandfather asks it himself. And he answers, "Well, because I hoed three times, and they only do it twice. Even you can see that, can't you?"

Grandfather gets up effortlessly and climbs quickly over the fence. Right now, I couldn't get up for a million rubles. Still, I turn my head and watch him through the cracks in the fence.

"This should have been cut off," grandpa says, and he digs up a tall corn stalk, "and this, and this, and this. . ."

Now, even I can see that they did a bad job of hoeing. They cut off the grass carelessly at the roots of the corn and just heaped dirt over it, and now it was sprouting again. After a few minutes, grandfather jumps back over the fence with a big armful of corn stalks.

"Loafers, idlers, bums," grandpa mutters, as he ties the corn stalks onto his bundle.

Somehow, I imagine the whole village sitting in the shade listening to stories from morning to night. They all sit there with their canes slung across their necks, dangling their hands listlessly. I look down. Below us is the Sabida basin. To the right of it is a bare, green slope. We can see the black and chestnut spots of grazing cows on it. A dense forest darkens the entire basin. The green color is light only in places—these are walnut trees. They are higher than the highest chestnuts, and their tops rise above the forest like light-green hills.

"Grandfather," I ask, "where did the walnuts in the forest come from? Maybe someone used to live there?"

"Ahh," grandfather nods, as if pleased that I finally noticed them after all, "I planted them everywhere and let a grape vine grow around every tree."

It seems strange to me that grandfather, who is so small, could have planted such gigantic trees—the biggest ones in the forest. And I used to think that giants once lived in those spots, but then, for some reason, they left to go deep into the wilderness. Maybe someone offended them or something. I don't know. And now these walnuts and, moreover, the ruins of some sort of fortress walls are all that remain of the tribe of giants.

"When I came here to live, not only were there no walnuts, but there wasn't a single person here," grandfather says.

"Not even one house?" I ask.

"Not one," grandfather says, and he recalls:

"I came upon this place accidentally, and the water turned out to be good here. And if the water is good, that means the living will be good. When I came back from Turkey, my mama married me off to your grandmother, because I was too footloose. Your grandma was just a little girl then. She slept with my mama for two years, but then she got used to me. And when we moved here, we already had a child, and our livestock consisted of one goat, and that one wasn't ours. I borrowed it in order to have something to feed the baby. But later on, we had everything, because I wasn't afraid to work. . ."

But hearing about how grandfather loved to work bores me, so I interrupt him.

"Grandfather," I say, "did you ever steal horses?"

"No," grandfather replies, "what would I do with them?"

"Well, did you ever steal anything?"

"Once, out of stupidity, a friend and I stole a heifer," grandfather recalls, after thinking it over.

"Tell me everything," I say, "the way it was."

"But what is there to tell? We were walking from Atara to our village. Evening found us in the forest. We see a heifer. It was obviously lost. Well, at first, we drove it along for fun, but then we really made off with it. . . It was a good one, a one-year-old heifer."

"So what did you do with it?" I ask.

291

"We ate it up," grandfather says simply.

"Between the two of you?"

"That's right."

"But how could two people eat a whole heifer?" I marvel at this.

"It's very simple," grandfather replies. "We drove it a little farther away from the road, we made a campfire, and we killed it. All night long we cooked and ate, ate and cooked."

"That's impossible!" I shout. "How could two people eat an entire one-year-old calf?"

"We were ignorant in those days, so we ate it up. Not even a scrap of meat was left. I remember how, right at daybreak, we took the bare bones, picked clean, and threw them into the bushes, we stamped out the campfire, and we walked on."

"Grandfather," I say, "tell me about the time you displayed the most bravery."

"I don't know," grandfather says, and for a short time he gazes into the Sabida basin, shading his eyes with his hand. It looks as if he can't figure out what kind of cows those are, or can't count them. But now he sits back and goes on: "I didn't like such things. I liked to work. . ."

"Never mind, grandfather, tell me anyway," I beg, and I keep my eyes on him.

And he sits next to me, round-headed, broad-shouldered, and as small as a teenager. And I still find it hard to believe that this man planted so many gigantic trees, that he has a dozen children (there used to be even more), and every one of them is a head taller than grandfather, and still, in the end, they always give in to him. I have felt this for a long time, though, of course, I'm unable to explain it.

"Okay. If you want," grandfather suddenly comes to life, and with his back leaning against the fence, he shifts around to make himself more comfortable, "listen. . . Once I was instructed to pass on a piece of news to a fellow from our village. And at the time, he was already with his cattle in the alpine meadows. That was three or four days walk from our village. And so I went. But how did I go? First, I passed up everyone who was travelling along the road with cattle. Then I passed up all the people on foot. Then I passed up everyone on horseback. Then I passed up the people who had left with cattle the day before, and during the night, I passed up those who had set out on foot a day earlier. And the next morning, I got to the herdsmen's dairy stand before they had even had time to milk their cows."

"But, grandfather, what about the people who had left on horseback a day earlier?" I ask.

"I didn't have time to pass them," grandfather answers.

"And you never stopped once?"

"Only to get a drink of water or buttermilk at a herdsman's dairy stand. I swear on our bread and salt, I walked all day and all night and never rested anywhere," grandfather says pompously, and he rests his arms on his knees and falls silent.

And again I imagine grandfather walking along the road, and everyone who is driving cattle gets left behind, and the ones that left with cattle the day before are left behind, and the ones that set out alone the day before are left behind. But grandfather didn't catch up with those who left on horseback a day earlier. Even so, it seemed to me that they all kept looking back and whipped their horses so grandfather wouldn't catch up with them.

"Well, okay. Come on," grandfather says, and he gets up effortlessly.

And once again the green sheaf rocks back and forth in front of me. Rays of sunlight sparkle on the leaves and irritate my eyes. They are exasperating.

Finally, we come to the gate to grandfather's hourse. Grandfather opens the gate and holds it back with his legs to let me through. The dogs race toward us barking, and they don't recognize us until they're practically on top of us. Then they slow down a little and run around us. We lean our bundles against the fence.

At the noise, aunty comes out of the kitchen. She comes toward us, and even from a distance, her face has a doleful expression as she looks at me.

"He's tired out, completely worn out," she says, showing grandma, who's coming out of the kitchen, that she pities me and is condemning grandfather.

My cousins, a little boy and a little girl, are lolling on an ox-hide in the shade of a walnut tree. Now, lifting their heads, they look at our bundles with identical calf eyes. They are a year apart, one two, and one three years younger than me. The boy is a sturdy fellow with heavy eyelids, and the girl is pretty and has a round face and long Turkish eyebrows. Almost simultaneously guessing, they jump up.

"Cherry-laurels," Remzik shouts.

"Bilberries, bilberries," Zina joyfully corrects him, and both of them run toward us stamping their bare feet.

"Me, me, me!" they shout, holding out their hands toward the bouquet which I was already taking out of the bundle.

Dividing it equally, I give each of them some bilberry branches. The two dogs, Rapka and Rusty, circle around at my feet, banging their tails on the ground, and gaze up at my face. They think we have brought something they can eat, but they don't understand that this isn't fit for them.

The children gobble down the bilberries, and I feel like a grown-up benefactor.

Aunty pulls grandfather's bouquet out of the bundle and walks to the kitchen with it. She holds the branches up a little on the way just in case, so Remzik can't grab them. She carries the bouquet with an air as if it were a household necessity. Nevertheless, she can't resist, and on the way, she plucks off several berries and tosses them in her mouth, also, it seemed out of consideration of household economy: God forbid, they might be sour.

Grandfather pulls the corn stalks out of the bundle and walks over to the pen where the baby goats are kept. They had heard the rustling of the leaves long before, and now they are waiting impatiently standing up on their hind legs and leaning their front legs against the wattle fence. A thin, childish bleating pours out of them. They give little snorts from time to time. The tips of their ears and their waxy horns stick up above the fence. Grandfather tosses the armful of corn stalks into the pen, and the ear-tips and horns instantly disappear.

I feel pleasure with every movement I make. My legs tremble a tiny bit, my shoulders ache, and yet, throughout my body, I feel an unusual lightness and relief, even happiness, the way it is when you take your first step after a long illness.

Aunty brings a jug of water and a towel out of the ktichen. Grandfather and I wash up while aunty pours.

While we are washing, Remzik, having finished off his bilberries, grabs his sister's last branch and runs away. The little girl howls, and tears stream down her face as she gazes up at her mama with eyes that are expressionless and at the same time expect retribution. Once again aunty starts berating grandpa.

"I wish you'd choke on your bilberries. Why the hell did you have to bring them," she keeps repeating, and she makes threatening gestures at her son. "You're going to want to eat. You'll come back."

The sturdy little boy stands frowning on the other side of the gate. It's obvious that he isn't very happy with himself now, because he's already had time to eat up the bilberries, and now it's getting close to dinner time. The delicious smell of well-browned polenta reaches him from the kitchen.

"What's the matter with you? You promised you'd fix a new handle for my hoe, and you haven't even started," aunty tosses in grandfather's direction as she goes into the kitchen.

"Right away," grandfather says, and he goes over to the spot where several hoes and shovels are heaped in a pile. He picks up aunty's hoe, and with one blow of the hatchet butt, he knocks the blade off the handle. Grandfather bends over and takes the blade in his hand.

I walk into the kitchen and take a seat by the hearth next to grandmother. The cooked polenta hangs high above the fire in a big cast-iron pot. I stretch out my legs. The unbearably sweet, golden smell of the toasted polenta crust tickles my nostrils. It should go on the table right now, but aunty is waiting for the boss, as she refers to her husband. We won't sit down at the table until he comes.

"Well, come here, you son of a bitch," grandfather calls my cousin.

"What do you want?" I hear, after a short pause.

"Come here and turn the grindstone for me," grandfather says.

"Mummy'll give it to me," the little boy answers after he thinks it over for a minute as if giving his mama time to say something about it.

But aunty doesn't say anything.

"Don't be afraid. Come here," grandpa says, and he comes into the kitchen and pours some water into a jug to rinse the grindstone with.

My legs start to itch by the fire, and grandmother notices them. Seeing the condition they are in, she wrings her hands and starts berating grandfather. And now aunty comes over to me, bends down over my bloody legs, and starts bawling grandfather out again.

"It's nothing," I say, "just mosquitoes."

"Good heavens," grandmother says, "what on earth did he do with you, the damned fidget!"

"It doesn't hurt, grandmother," I say.

"But it's very bad if it doesn't hurt," grandmother laments. "It would be better if it did."

"What am I going to tell his mama? We did a tremendous job of protecting her child," she keeps saying, remembering that my mama is supposed to come from the city soon.

Grandma puts a teapot full of water by the fire.

"They're keening, the silly fools. They're keening," we hear grandpa's voice from outside the kitchen.

Then the rich sound of metal quiverying against the wet grindstone reaches us. Grandma sets the washbasin down next to me, pours warm water into it from the teapot, and bends over to wash my legs. I am ashamed, but I know by now that it's hard to cope with her, so I let her do it. Grandma and aunty keep on grumbling at grandpa and feel sorry for me.

I have to abandon the role of a grown lad, which is the way I felt when I entered the yard with my load. They put me in the position of an oppressed little orphan with a pitiless grandpa. I feel that this position of oppression is not devoid of its own form of pleasantness.

Although my legs really are full of bloody scratches and are a bit swollen, I don't feel any special suffering at all. It burns a little, but that's all. But I am already finding it pleasant to go along with them. It's nice to feel like I'm suffering when signs of suffering are visible, but I'm not really suffering at all.

I feel the warm sweetness of hypocrisy spread in my chest. My legs are bloody—that means I'm suffering: these are the rules of the game the adults offer me, and I take it up with pleasure.

"Turn it evenly," grandfather's voice can be heard, "more evenly. . ."

"What am I, a mill maybe?" Remzik grumbles.

Once again the juicy sound of metal quivering against the wet stone.

"Now the other side," we hear grandfather's voice.

"I'm uncomfortable. My arm hurts," Remzik grumbles, but

he still turns it.

"Lazy bones," says grandfather, "when I was your age..."

Grandma gives me a clean rag and then carries out the wash basin full of water. I can hear the water slop on the grass.

But now aunty thinks someone is calling her. She stands still and listens.

"Be quiet out there!" she shouts at grandpa, and she runs into the yard.

She goes out to the fence and listens. Someone's voice really can be heard in the distance.

"What do you want? Yoo hoo!" she shouts in her piercing voice.

Through the open kitchen door, I can see her standing there leaning forward a little, drinking in the sound.

"So chase it, chase it!" she shouts after listening to something.

Again an indistinct sound reaches us from there, and she stands still, listening. Feeling that the aerial communication has been well established, the grindstone started working again.

"My arm hurts already. I can't," Remzik complains in a weak voice.

"Well, use your left arm," grandfather says.

"I'm not left-handed," Remzik continues to grumble.

Once again I can hear the sound of metal quivering against the wet grindstone.

"Okay, we'll tell him. Okay," aunty shouts, and she comes back into the kitchen.

"What was going on out there?" grandmother asks, frightened.

Ever since the time, the year before, when her son, uncle Azis, was killed on a hunt, she hadn't been the same, and she was always afraid that something would happen again.

"It's nothing. It's nothing. Datiko's buffalo has just gotten into the corn again," aunty says, and she puts the cast-iron pot with the morning's haricot beans by the fire.

I've already heard about this buffalo a hundred times. As soon as they turn him out, he runs like a lunatic straight to the collective farm corn field, and no fence can hold him back. My uncle works as a foreman, so that's why they call us.

"If I could be young again for three days," grandfather says from outside the house (apparently he heard everything),

"I would show that buffalo. . ."

I think over grandfather's words, and I absolutely can't understand what he would show this buffalo and why he would need to be young again for three days in order to do it. Then I figure it out: grandfather would steal it and eat it up. And since the buffalo is big, it would take him three whole days to eat it. I imagine grandfather sitting in the forest over a campfire, roasting pieces of buffalo meat, and eating. He cooks and eats, eats and cooks, and so it goes for three whole days and nights. Then he gathers up the bones and tosses them in the bushes, and when he turns around, he is already an old man again: that is, his hair has turned white again, but everything else has stayed the same.

Aunty quickly and deftly sticks the beef jerky on a skewer, rakes the embers aside, and sits down on a tiny, low stool and turns the skewer over the fire. From time to time, she turns it away from the fire, because it's baking too much. The meat gradually roasts, gets covered with a rosy crust, and becomes damp from the fat which starts dripping onto the burning hot coals. In the spots where the drops fall, a blue tongue of flame shoots up. Such an aroma rises from the dried, re-roasted meat, that it is simply impossible to be patient.

"Pepe is coming!" shouts Remzik, the first to notice his father. For some reason, that's what they called him.

Aunty looks out the door, leans the skewer with the meat against the fireplace, and puts a low wooden table in front of the bench we are sitting on.

Uncle Kyazim stops suddenly right in the middle of the yard. Ahh, it's because he's picking up Zina. Somehow, everyone forgot about her. After she had cried her eyes out, she either started daydreaming or fell asleep on the green grass in the yard. Now she toddles into the kitchen beside her father.

A second after uncle, grandfather and Remzik enter. Remzik thinks he's been forgiven because he worked for grandfather.

But aunty manages to give him a quick, glancing blow on the side of the head when he's not looking.

"What was that for?" uncle says in astonishment. He is generally stern, but still, he doesn't like his children to be struck.

"He knows what it's for," aunty says.

Remzik is offended and lowers his calfish eyelids, but he can't act offended for long or he'll go without dinner.

Aunty pours her husband some water. Uncle slowly washes his huge hands, then he runs his wet palms over his face and short-cropped head a few times.

"Datiko's buffalo got into the corn again," aunty says as she pours, "and they were calling you. . ."

"What do I care?" uncle answers indifferently, and then he is silent. Then, wiping off his hands, he can't restrain himself: "Did they lock him up?"

"Yes," says aunty, and she sets the table.

"Who? The buffalo or Datiko?" I ask, because somehow it isn't clear who should be punished: the buffalo or his master.

Uncle smiles, and the others all laugh. It offends me that even the children laugh.

"He himself should be locked up for three days," says grandpa.

We all sit in a row by the hearth. Grandpa is at the head of the table, then grandma, then uncle, and then the rest of us. Aunty dishes out each portion right on the well-sanded, rosy table top. The polenta smokes profusely. Then she pours each one some haricot beans on a little plate, spreads sheaves of green onions around the table, and then even more carefully divides up the roasted meat.

I can't resist watching her secretly, out of the corner of my eye, as she portions out the meat. It really seems to me that she is giving the best pieces to her own husband and children. I know it is disgraceful to watch this, but I can't resist, and I spy on her furtively. She does the same thing with Remzik, and even though he'd done something wrong, she couldn't restrain herself, and she gave him the biggest piece of meat there was, and then, as if suddenly remembering that the scale had clearly tipped in his favor, she smacked him on the forehead with the palm of her hand, as if using it to push down the other side of the scale.

I feel that aunty knows I am watching her, and this holds her back, so she tries to hurriedly finish passing out the food.

"If I could be young again for three days," grandfather says again, with his mouth full, "I would show you what to do with that buffalo. . ."

"Well, you're our hero," uncle says sarcastically.

I know what he's referring to.

On the edge of the tobacco farm stands a huge chestnut tree.

299

Some of its branches throw a shadow on the farm, and on this spot, the tobacco is always sickly and stunted. Since the very beginning of the summer, I'd been hearing conversations about the fact that someone should cut down these chestnut branches, but for some reason, no one had done it. It's true, it's very hard to get up the tree, because you have to climb ten meters of bare trunk, and you can't get a grip on it for anything.

At first, they all decided that the farm manager, a hunter and rock-climber, would climb the tree. But at the time, he was in the mountains, so they decided to send somebody after him, because it was time to go to the mountains to get cheese anyway. The person was sent, and the farm manager came back, but when they showed him the tree, he refused to climb it, because, in his words, when he's hunting, he can scale a cliff the way a fly climbs a wall, but he's afraid to climb this chestnut, because one look at such a big tree makes his head spin. Then they asked him why on earth he had come back if his head spins even when he looks at such big trees. To this, he replied that in the alpine meadows, he missed his family so much that it seemed as if this chestnut wasn't really so high, and its branches started growing quite a bit lower. But now that he had been seen his family, he felt that he couldn't handle this chestnut and maybe he would go back, because without him there, the herdsmen would ruin all the cattle.

To make a long story short, they had to let the farm manager go, and the chestnut was left along with its spreading shadow, and no one was willing to climb it. And for some reason, everyone joked about it, or even cursed it: If it would mean climbing that tree, the tobacco can go to hell. . .

For a long time, grandfather put up with all this, but finally, a week ago, when they came to hoe this field early in the morning, grandfather was already in the tree. Leaning back against the trunk, he was quietly chopping off the branches on the side toward the farm. No one had seen how he climbed it, but judging by the fact that he came down with the help of two sharp hatchets, alternately plunging one, then the other into the trunk, they surmised that he had climbed up the tree that way, too. Not only did grandfather get no praise from them after this, but they just nagged at him for about two days because he might have fallen out of the tree and disgraced his family. People might even think that grandfather was forced to work, and on the collective farm at that. This is what uncle was reminding grandfather about now. Everyone is busy eating. Very rarely is a word thrown in. Grandfather squeezes the polenta in his fingers with greedy pleasure, bites juicily into a green onion, and keeps on savagely tearing off stretchy pieces of beef jerky with his strong teeth. Uncle eats sluggishly, as if some sorrow over an unsolved problem has spoiled his appetite forever, and he always has to force himself to eat.

I know aunty loves to eat, but she has to hide this from her sarcastic husband. She always holds herself in check. She just chews a tiny bit and then swallows the unchewed pieces straight down, so she won't make a lot of chewing movements. Sometimes I'm aghast at the huge pieces she has to swallow.

But now we've finished eating and washed our hands. Uncle, like all poor eaters, has a delicacy. He loves the dry crust which is left cooked on the cast-iron pot after the polenta is gone. Now he slowly scrapes it off and picks it out with a knife. He chomps on some himself and gives us some.

Aunty is putting her oldest daughter's lunch in a wicker basket. She was in the tobacco barn with other women and girls stringing tobacco. Zina will carry the lunch. She pulls on her little green party dress and steps into her sandals. All the same, she's going to be in front of some people.

With the basket in her hand, she crosses the yard, looks all around, and turns onto the path.

"Don't be afraid, I'm standing here," aunty says, looking after her from the veranda.

Zina disappears behind the fence, and after a few minutes, when she reaches the most frightening spot, where the path is very heavily overgrown with blackberry vines, ferns, and elder bushes, her voice suddenly rings out. Terribly out of tune, she sings a little ditty (God only knows how it made its way into the mountains) which somehow seemed obsolete even then:

They wanted to kill us, to kill us.
They did their best to do it.
But we weren't just sitting around.
We were waiting for them, cause we knew it. . .

And suddenly, not being able to bear it any longer, she broke into a run. She ran, shaking and scattering the words of the song:

The Chinese ge-ne-rals
have bold war-riors. . .

"She bolted," aunty says with a smile in her voice. She sighs and stands there for a minute, then comes into the kitchen.

I can hear grandfather tinkering around on the veranda, fashioning a new handle to aunty's hoe. Apparently he's in a good mood after he's eaten. He hums something as he planes the handle.

"He stuffed himself with meat, and he sings," uncle says sarcastically, nodding in grandfather's direction.

I love uncle. I'm sure he's the smartest person I know, and I know he doesn't begrudge the meat. He just envies grandfather's serenity. He's rarely like that himself, except maybe when he's on some binge.

But now I'm suddenly pierced with impassioned pity for grandfather. Grandfather, grandpa, I think, why do they all curse you, why. . .?

In the silence, I can hear grandfather's laborious breathing and the juicy sound of steel cutting into fresh wood: crunch, crunch, crunch. . .

Bulat Okudzhava

Lots of Luck, Kid!

This is not an adventure story. This is a story about how I fought in the war, how they wanted to kill me, and how I made it through all right. I really don't know who to thank for this. Perhaps no one. So don't you worry. I'm alive and well. Some people will be happy to hear this, and then, of course, there will be those who won't like it at all. But I'm alive. There's nothing to be done. After all, you can't please everyone.

Hayseed

In my childhood I did a lot of crying. As I grew older I cried less. Later, when I was in my teens, I only cried twice. The first time was one evening just before the war. I said to this girl I loved—and I said it with feigned indifference:

"Well then, if that's that, then it's all over..."

"...If that's it, then it's all over," she agreed with unexpected calmness, and walked away. It was then that I burst out crying because she was leaving me. And I wiped away my tears with the palm of my hand.

I'm crying for the second time right now: here in the Mozdok steppe. I'm carrying a very important message for the regimental commander. Where the hell is this regimental commander? These sandy hills all look the same to me. It's night. It's only my second day at the front. And if you don't carry out orders, they shoot you. And I'm eighteen.

Who said they shoot you? That was Kolya Grinchenko, just before I left. He smiled sweetly when he said it.

"Take care. If you don't, it's the firing squad..."

They'll put me up against a wall. But there are no walls here. They'll take me out in the fields.

And I'm wiping away the tears. "Your son showed cowardice and..." That's how the telegram will start out. But why did they send me with the message? There's Kolya Grinchenko—he's a real strong, smart fellow. He would have found the place a long time ago. By now he'd be sitting inside the warm headquarters dugout. He'd be drinking tea out of a mug, winking at the girls who operate the radios and smiling pleasantly at them.

Supposing I step on a mine. They'd find me in the morning and the regimental commander will say to the battery commander, "Lieutenant Burakov, why did you send a green kid? You didn't give him a chance to look around, get used to his place. And it's because of your indifference that we've lost a good man."

305

"Your son died in action while carrying out a very important mission..." That's how the telegram will start.

"Hey, where are you going?"

That's me they're shouting at. I see a small trench, and someone is waving at me. What the hell do they care where I'm going?

"Halt!" someone shouts behind me.

I stop.

"Over here!"

I go over, and someone pulls me into the trench by the sleeve.

"Where are you going?" they ask angrily.

I explain to them.

"Don't you know that there are Germans here! Another thirty yards and..."

They explain it to me. This, it turns out, is our advance observation point.

Then they take me to a dugout. The regimental commander reads the message, looks at me, and I feel small and insignificant. I look at my not terribly venerable, thin legs, all wrapped in leggings, and then at my sturdy army boots. I suppose all this is very funny to them. But no one's laughing. And the beautiful radio operator looks past me. Now, if I wore knee boots and a nice officer's coat... If only they'd give me some tea. I'd like to sit down at the makeshift table and then say something to the beautiful girl that would... Of course, the way I look now...

"Return to the battery," the regimental commander barks. "And tell your commander not to send any more of these reports."

He emphasizes the words "of these."

"Okay," I say, and I hear the quiet laugh of the radio operator. She glances at me and laughs.

"How long have you been in the army?" the colonel asks. "A month."

"In the army you don't say, 'Okay,' but, 'Yes, sir!'...and also, you've got your toes together but your heels apart..."

"A hayseed," says someone in a dark corner behind me.

"I know it," I say and walk out. I'm almost running.

The steppe again. It's snowing, and it's quiet. I can't even believe that this is the front, an advanced post, that there's danger nearby. I won't lose my way this time.

I can imagine how absurd I must have looked to them:

306

feet spread apart, hands in my coat pockets and cap over my ears. While this beautiful girl... They didn't even offer me any tea... When Kolya Grinchenko speaks to officers, he sort of smiles. Just barely. He never argues; he just sort of smiles. He salutes smartly and says: "Yes sir!" But I can hear him saying: "Go ahead and order, I see right through you." And he does see.

My ankle boots are good and strong. That's really fine. A heavy masculine foot and snow crunches. I wish I had a fur cap with ear flaps, then I wouldn't look so pitiful. At any rate, I'll be back soon, give my report. I'll drink a lot of tea and then get some sleep. Now I have a right to it.

I'm carrying a submachine gun across my back, two grenades on one hip and a gas mask on the other. I look real belligerent. Very much so. Someone once said that belligerence is a sign of cowardice. But am I a coward? When I had an argument with Volod'ka Anilov in the eighth grade, it was me who shouted first: let's fight it out!" And I became terrified. But we went behind the school, and our friends stood around us. He hit me first, on the arm.

"So that's it," I shouted and poked him in the shoulder.

Then we kept swearing at each other, neither one wanting to start first.

And suddenly it all seemed very funny to me, and I said to him, "Listen, I'm going to belt you right in the kisser..."

"Go ahead," he said, and put up his fists.

"Or you hit me. There'll be blood. Well, what's the difference?"

He suddenly calmed down, and we shook hands according to all the rules. But after that there was no friendship between us.

Am I a coward?

At sunrise yesterday we stopped in these hills.

"Everyone's here," Lieutenant Burakov said.

"Where are we?" someone asked.

"It's the advanced post."

It was his first time at the front, just like the rest of us, and that's why he spoke so solemnly and so proudly.

"But where are the Germans?" someone asked.

"The Germans are over there."

"Over there" we could see small hills, overgrown with patches of withered, sparse scrub.

And I thought that I wasn't at all terrified. And I was surprised at how simply the lieutenant had figured out the enemy position.

Nina

"Oh, but you're handsome," says Sashka Zolotaryov.

I'm shaving in front of a broken piece of mirror. There's nothing to shave. It's colder in the trench than outside. My hands are red, my nose is red, and the blood is red. I'm cutting myself to bits. Can I be handsome? Ears set wide apart. Nose like a potato.

Why am I shaving? We've already been at the front lines for three days, and we haven't heard a shot, or seen one German, or had anyone wounded. Then why am I shaving? Yesterday evening that same beautiful girl from headquarters stopped at the entrance to our trench.

"Hello!" she said.

And I looked at her, and I knew that I was unshaven. I saw myself in her eyes. It's as though I was reflected in them. She has such large eyes. I forget their color. I nodded to her.

"How's life?" she asked.

"I'm living," I said sullenly.

"Why are you so sullen? Haven't they fed you?"

I took out my cigarettes.

"Well," she said, "cigarettes."

"What's it to you, haven't you anything better to do?" I said.

"Let's have a smoke," she said and took a cigarette out of the pack by herself.

We smoked and didn't say anything. Then she said, "You know, you're just a small fry."

"What's that?"

"That's a fish that's just spawned."

I crawled into the trench and could hear her laughing behind me.

"Did Ninka come over?" Kolya Grinchenko asked later.

"Yes. Do you know her?"

"I know everybody," he said.

Now I'm clean-shaven. I still have some cigarettes left. I feel that she'll come. I've unbuttoned my shirt collar. That way I'll look dashing. I've unbuttoned my coat and put my hands in my pockets. And I'm standing behind the shell crates, so that my leggings won't be seen.

Who am I? I'm a soldier. A mortar man. We're the regimental mortar battery. I've risked my life. Maybe it's a miracle that I haven't been wounded yet. Come on, you radio operator you, you headquarters rat. Come on, I'll treat you to some cigarettes. Come—perhaps tomorrow I'll be lying with my arms stretched out...

"Oh, but you are real handsome," says Sashka Zolotaryov. I spit and turn away. Maybe he's laughing. But my lips are twisting.

Sashka is scraping the mud off his boots with a stick. Then he smears them with a thick layer of lubrication grease.

Will Nina come or won't she? I'll say, "Hi, small fry..." I'll have a smoke with her. Then it'll be evening. If this is war, why isn't there any shooting? Not a single shot, not a single German or anyone wounded.

"Why aren't there any higher-ups here?" I ask.

"They're in conference," says Sashka.

It's a good thing I'm tall and not fat like Zolotaryov. If only my coat fit!

Kolya Grinchenko comes over. He smiles winningly and says, "The sergeant's a beast. He makes omelets for himself, but gives me concentrates to eat." Kolya looks at Sashka and me.

"Don't make so much noise," says Sashka.

"This isn't the home front," Kolya continues. "They don't do much talking here. They give it to you in the back of the head, and it's goodbye. They won't even recognize you."

"Why don't you go and tell him that," says Sashka.

The sergeant is standing behind Kolya. He has a grease spot on his chin.

"Okay," he says.

Nobody says anything. He turns around and goes into his trench. Everyone is silent. Sashka's boots shine like the sergeant's greasy chin. My hands are sweating. Kolya Grinchenko smiles sweetly. The smell of fried eggs comes out of the sergeant's trench.

"Fried eggs are good with onions," says Sashka.

Shongin comes over. He's an old soldier. A famous soldier. He has served in all armies and in all wars. In every war he winds up at the front lines, and then he gets diarrhea. He hasn't fired a single shot, nor been in a single attack, nor ever been wounded. He has a wife who has seen him off to all the wars.

Shongin comes over. He's eating a radish and doesn't say anything.

"Where'd you get the radish?"

Shongin shrugs his soulders.

"Give me a radish," Sashka says.

"It's my last one," says Shongin.

It's a good thing there are no big shots around here. No one is giving any orders or driving you. I really carried that message. The devil only knows why...as if they couldn't have sent Kolya Grinchenko. When my father was seventeen, he organized an underground Komsomol, and here I am, round-shouldered, ridiculous-looking, and I haven't done a thing. I just brag about my noble character, which likely doesn't even exist...

Shongin keeps pulling radishes out of his pocket. The red little balls fly into his mouth and make a crunching noise.

"Shongin, give me a radish," I say.

"It's my last one," says Shongin.

I make a wager: if Shongin pulls out another radish, Nina will come. Shongin puts his hand in his pocket and pulls out his tobacco pouch. She won't come. Suddenly Kolya says, "Here's Ninochka."

I turn around. She's coming down a small hillock. With her is another girl I don't know. Nina has a light step. Her coat is buttoned up all the way. She's wearing a fur cap with ear flaps. A bit cocked, the cap, and what a cap! Hi, small fry! Everyone looks in her direction. She's coming.

"Aaa!"

That's Shongin screaming.

"Aaa!" and he falls down. Sashka too, and Kolya Grinchenko.

"Down!"

I throw myself down. This is it. Somewhere off in the distance there's an explosion. A short one. There is some rushing noise, and then everything is quiet.

Someone's laughing. The sergeant is standing at the trench entrance.

"That's enough lying around in the dirt, boys."

Silently we get up. Kolya is gone. He's running towards the hillock where Nina was. From a distance I see her get up from the dirty snow. The other girl lies there motionless. Face up.

Slowly and silently we go over there. Other soldiers too. That was our first mine. The first. Ours.

War

I've gotten to know you, war. I've got large welts on the palms of my hands, and a buzzing noise in my head. I want to sleep. Do you want me to forget everything I've gotten used to? Do you want to teach me to submit myself unquestioningly? The screams of the commanding officer—run, do, bellow "Yes, sir!" when you reply, fall down, crawl, fall asleep on the march. If there's the sound of a mine—bury yourself in the ground, dig with your nose, head, feet, your whole body, at the same time not experiencing fright, or even thinking. A tinful of barley soup—secrete gastric juice, get ready, grumble, stuff yourself, wipe your spoon on the grass. If comrades die—dig a grave, cover it with earth, fire mechanically into the air...three times.

I've already learned a great deal. I pretend I'm not hungry. I pretend I'm not cold. I pretend I'm not sorry for anyone. I only want to sleep, sleep, sleep...

Like a fool, I've lost my spoon. An ordinary aluminum spoon. Tarnished, with a jagged edge, but still, a spoon. A very important item. Now I have nothing to eat with—I drink the soup straight from the tin. And if it's *kasha*...I've adapted a piece of wood. I eat my *kasha* with a piece of wood. From whom could I ask one? Everyone guards his spoon. No one's a fool here. And me, I have a hunk of wood.

Sasha Zolotaryov makes notches on a stick. One notch for each casualty.

Kolya Grinchenko smiles crookedly.

"Don't worry, Sashka. There'll be enough dames for everyone."

Zolotaryov doesn't say anything. I'm silent. The Germans are silent; today at least.

Lieutenant Burakov goes around unshaven. I'm sure it's for show. We've not been ordered to open fire. There's some sort of conference going on. Our commanding officer's making the rounds of the mortar crews. The mortars are in the trenches, in a hollow. The trenches have been dug according to all the regulations. But we don't study the regulations.

The gunner Gavrilov comes over and sits down near me. He looks at the cigarettes I've rolled.

"Why are you smoking so much?"

"What of it?"

"The wind's blowing the sparks all around. It's already dark, they'll notice it," he says and looks about.

I put out the butt on the sole of my shoe. The sparks start flying around like fireworks. Suddenly a six-barrel mortar opens up on the German side. The shells land with a thump somewhere behind us. Gavrilov is crawling in the snow.

"You mother... I told you..." he suddenly screams. Explosion after explosion. Explosion after explosion. Closer and closer. My comrades are running past me to the mortars. And I'm sitting in the snow. It's my own fault... How will I ever be able to face them? Here comes Lieutenant Burakov. He's screaming something. And the shells keep falling.

Then I get up too, and start running, shouting, "Lieutenant, lieutenant!"

The first mortar roars, and suddenly it's more comfortable. It's as though we found some powerful, quiet friends. Then the shouting dies down. All four mortars are now firing into the air from the hollow. Only the telephonist, the young and scrawny Gurgenidze, shouts, "A hit! A hit!"

I do what I'm supposed to do. I drag the crates with the mortar shells out of the shelter. How strong I am after all! And I'm not afraid of anything. I just keep dragging the crates. Rumbling. Shouting. The sharp smell of explosives. Everything's all mixed up. Now this is a fight for you. A real battle. Clouds of smoke... But I'm making it all up. Not one shot has been fired at us. It's us making all the noise. And I'm at fault. And everyone knows it. They're all waiting for me to come and say that it was all my fault.

Now it's getting darker. My back hurts. I barely have time to grab some snow and swallow it.

"All clear!" Gurgenidze shouts.

I'll tell the company commander everything so they won't think I'm hiding anything.

"Lieutenant..."

He's sitting on the edge of the trench and running his finger over a map. He looks at me, and I understand; he is waiting for me to say I was at fault.

"It's my fault. I didn't think. You can do what you want with me..."

"And what am I supposed to do with you?" he asks thoughtfully. "What have you done?"

Is he kidding? Or has he forgotten? I tell him everything. I get it off my chest. He looks surprised. Then he just shrugs his shoulders.

"Listen, go take a rest. What's your cigarette got to do with it? We just launched an offensive. We simply had to do some shooting. Go, go!"

I go away.

"Watch out you don't fall asleep, or you'll freeze to death," the lieutenant calls after me.

In an hour we're on our feet again. We're shooting at the Germans again. An attack. But I can't see it. What kind of an attack is it if we're sitting in one spot? Is this the way it's always going to be? Rumbling. The smell of explosives. Gurgenidze screaming, "It's a hit! It's a miss!" And this damned hollow from which you can't see anything. But there's an attack somewhere else. Tanks rolling, infantry, cavalry, people singing the *Internationale*, dying without letting their banners out of their hands.

And when there's a lull, I run over to the observation point. I'll take a look, even if it's out of the corner of my eye, and see what an attack is like. I'll breathe it in. Why, the OP's nothing, just a hilltop, with observers lying on their sides, their heads slightly raised, and battery commander Burakov looking through a stereo-telescope. I crawl up the steep hill and raise myself waist high. And I hear birds singing. Birds!

Someone pulls me down by the feet.

"Tired of living?" the battery commander hisses. "What in hell are you doing crawling around here?"

"I just wanted to see," I say.

The observers laugh.

"Where did the birds come from?" I ask.

"Birds?" repeats the commander.

"Birds..."

313

"What birds?" asks the telephonist Kuzin from the trench.
"Birds," I say, and I no longer understand anything myself.

"Do you think those are birds?" the commander asks wearily.

"Birds..." Kuzin laughs.

I'm beginning to understand what's up. One of the observers puts his hat on a stick and lifts it above him. The birds start singing right away.

"Get it now?" the commander asks.

He's a good man. Anyone else would have started stamping his feet and swearing. Our commander is a good man. I would have been killed it it weren't for him. He was probably the one who pulled me down by the feet.

It's getting darker and darker. A gray dusk is enveloping the hill. I hear a machine gun firing in the distance.

"Machine gun," I shout. No one pays any attention to me.

"They're ours," says commander Burakov. "We'll start any minute now." Then he says to me, "Here, take a look."

I squat down near the telescope and look. I see the steppe. At the extreme edge of the steppe, against a background of gray sky, a settlement streches out in a line. And there, just like fireworks, multi-colored lines of tracer bullets stretch out from one end to the other. And I hear the rattling of machine guns and the staccato of submachine guns. But I don't see any people.

"Let's go, let's go!" someone screams behind me.

"Where? Where to?"

And suddenly I see—solitary figures, hunched up, running across the steppe. But only a few of them.

"That's enough," says the battery commander. "Back to the battery."

I roll down the hill. I'm running. A jeep comes toward me. A general is sitting in it. I don't know what to do: run past or march past and salute...

The general is red in the face. He doesn't see me. He's waving his arms. And the jeep is getting closer to the observation point. The commander is already standing at attention. And the men too. And the telescope, also, is standing motionless on its tripod.

The general jumps out of the jeep and runs up to the commander.

"You're firing on your own men, your own men!"

The commander is silent. Only his head moves from side to side.

Then the general looks into the telescope, and the commander explains something to him. The general shakes his head.

"There are miracles," I think to myself.

"Cease fire!" Kuzin screams into the telephone.

The battery is silent; as though everyone were listening for something. And the mortars, like dogs, sit on their hind legs and are also silent.

"What's the matter with your hands?" asks the sergeant.

My hands are bloody. I don't understand where the blood came from. I shrug my shoulders.

"That's from the shell crates," says Shongin.

They'll bandage them for me in a little while.

The sergeant turns around and goes away. He probably went to get the medical orderly. I stand there with my hands stretched out in front of me. They really must have bled. They'll bandage them, and I'll write home...

"Go wash off your hands," says the sergeant. "We're changing our position now."

The Little Bell—A Gift From Valdai

Help me. Save me. I don't want to die. Just a small piece of lead in the heart, or head, and it's all over. And my hot body, will it no longer be hot? I don't mind suffering. Who said I was afraid of suffering? It was at home that I was so afraid. At home. But now I've gotten to know a lot of things. I've tried it all. Isn't this enough for one person to know? I'll be set for life. Help me. You know, it's ridiculous to kill a man who hasn't had time to do something in life. I didn't even finish tenth grade. Help me. I'm not speaking about love. To hell with love. I'm content not to love. When you really come down to it, I've already loved. If you really want to know, I've had enough of that. I have a mother. What's going to happen to her? Do you know how nice it feels when a mother strokes the head of her child? I haven't had time to get unaccustomed to it yet. I really haven't been anywhere yet. For example, I haven't been to Valdai yet. I really must know what this Valdai is like. Someone once wrote: "The little bell is a gift from Valdai." And I can't even write such lines. Help me. I'll go through everything. To the end. I'll shoot at the Fascists like a sniper, I'll fight tanks singlehanded, I won't eat or sleep;

I'll suffer...

To whom am I saying this? Whose help am I seeking? These logs which hold the dugout together maybe? Even they aren't happy about being here. After all, not so long ago they were rustling pine trees. Remember the warm shelter when we left for the front? Of course, I remember. We stood in the open doors and sang some solemn song. We held our heads high. The troop train stood on a siding. Where? At the Kursk railroad station. We didn't get home leave. I only had time to phone home. No one was there. Only an old neighbor, Irina Makarovna. A nasty old witch. Boy, did she get on my nerves! She asked me where the train had stopped.

"Too bad your mother won't be able to see you," she said hypocritically.

I hung up and returned to the troop train. An hour later Irina Makarovna turned up at the train and shoved a bundle into my hands. And later, when we were singing, she stood among a group of women spectators. What is she to me? Farewell, Irina Makarovna. Forgive me. How was I supposed to know? I'll never be able to understand it. . . Perhaps, you're the very person one should ask for protection? Protect me then. I don't want to die. I'm saying this honestly and without shame.

There were some dried biscuits and sunflower-seed oil in the bundle. I made a vow to save one biscuit as a souvenir. But I ate it. I couldn't even do such a simple thing as that. What do I want? And wasn't it me who stood in full view when the Heinkel swooped down and everyone took cover?

"Take cover!" they screamed at me.

But I didn't hide. I walked alone and laughed out loud. If they only knew what was going on inside of me! But I can't tremble in view of everyone. No one must know that I'm afraid. But can I myself face the truth? That's what I mean. I'm my own judge. . . I have a right to do this. Me, I'm not Fedka Lyubimov. Remember Fedka Lyubimov? Of course, I do. Fyodor Lavrente-vich Lyubimov. My neighbor. When the war broke out, he'd come out into the kitchen every evening and say: "Those German bastards are really pushing... Everyone should stand up to the defense. Wait and see, as soon as my arm gets better, I'll volunteer."

"You'll be called up anyway, Fedka," they'd say to him. "It's not a joking matter. Everyone will be called up. When the country is in danger you shouldn't wait. You should join up yourself."

"Do you love your country?" he would ask me.

"Yes," I said. "I learned that in the first grade."

Once I ran into him in the recruiting office. I was delivering telegrams at the time. He didn't see me. He was speaking to some captain.

"Comrade captain, I've brought my exemption certificate," he said.

"What exemption?"

"Reserve. As a specialist I've been exempted from the service. They won't release me from my job. . ."

"Go in there and register. If you're exempt, then you're exempt. That's all there is to it," the captain said.

If you're exempt, then you're exempt. That's Fedka for you. What kind of specialist is he, a watch repairman on the Arbat? And Fedka went in and registered. He passed by me, noticed me, blushed, and stopped.

"Did you see?" he asked me. "That's the way it is. Who wants to die?"

He's probably still exempt. As though he were some well-known engineer or great actor.

We didn't build this shelter. It's a good shelter. True, it's smaller than headquarters, where Nina is, but still, it's not bad. It looks like someone left in a hurry. Somebody lost a photograph of a woman. A young, unattractive woman smiles at me from the photograph. But someone must love her. Why did he forget to take her picture with him?

"Hey, Sashka, did you get an exemption?" I ask.

"Who's going to give it to me. Not everyone can get one," Sashka replies.

"If you slipped something to the right person, you would have gotten one," says Kolya Grinchenko.

"Probably costs a lot, doesn't it?" Sashka asks.

"Three thousand. You could have sold some stuff to get the money. You could have saved up enough."

"Sure I could. My desk alone is worth three thousand."

"Then you could have given it to them."

"Akh," says Sashka and waves his hand. "Go to hell."

"Why didn't you slip them something and get exempted?" Shongin asks angrily.

"I didn't have any money," laughs Kolya.

"You blabber too much," says Shongin.

Lucky

Our mortars have been at it for eight days now. We have three wounded men. I haven't seen them. When I returned to the battery, they had already been taken away. We keep moving from one place to another, so that not only do we not have trenches, but we also don't have any communications trenches. There's no time for it. It's an attack. When it began Kolya Grinchenko said: "We're in luck, boys. Now we're in luck. Now we'll eat well. We'll live off captured goods now. We've had enough of canned goods for a while."

At that time we all believed him. But it was in vain. The artillery and we always get there last, when everything is already gone.

It's canned goods again. And it's dried biscuits again. And Kolya Grinchenko says to the sergeant, "Sergeant, this canned goods stuff is crap. Where's our front rations?"

"Do you remember, kid, how you were threatening me?" the sergeant asks.

"Prove it," smiles Grincheko.

"You'd better shut up," says the sergeant.

Now he has something on Kolya. And I see that Kolya is afraid of him. But sometimes he forgets that he's afraid, and he starts in on him again. This can be very funny.

I remember when we entered the first village—it was the same one I had seen from the observations point. It was destroyed. The huts, which were already being repaired, were full of cavalry men; they were dressing, sleeping, playing harmonicas, and, in one hut, they were even making pancakes. Well, of course, we're late everywhere. Where are we supposed to go?

"Let's go," says Grinchenko.

Sashka Zolotaryov and I follow him. We go into a hut. It's hot there. The stove is on. It's empty. Only a Cossack is there, bent over a frying pan. You can tell he's a Cossack from his uniform trousers.

"Hi," says Grinchenko from the threshold. "Welcome some guests."

Kolya really knows how to speak to people. He's really quite at home with them. He smiles when he speaks. He smiles in such a way that you can't help but smile back at him. The Cossack now turns around, and I see a face with high cheekbones and slanting eyes.

"So you're a Cossack!" says Kolya. "Where are you from?"

"What do you want?" the Cossack asks.

"You're a Kalmyk, probably, not a Cossack. A Kalmyk, right?" And Kolya says to us, "Let's get settled, boys. Oh, you Kalmyk Cossack!"

And Kolya puts his field pack on the bench. The Kalmyk picks it up and throws it on the threshold. He stands in front of the tall Grinchenko; he is so small, with his high cheekbones and wide shoulders.

"What's the matter? You don't like Kalmyks? Go away!"

"Why, you swine. . ." Kolya's face turns red.

"Go, go!" the Kalmyk says calmly.

"I've shed blood, and you're throwing me out in the cold?" Sashka takes Kolya by the arm.

"Don't be cute, Mykola."

"Take your friends with you," the Kalmyk says.

"Please, don't get mad," I say.

"Get going. . ."

Suddenly the door opens, and some Cossacks come in. There are three of them.

"What's the trouble?" asks one of them.

The Kalmyk doesn't say anything. Sashka and I are silent. Kolya also keeps quiet. Then Kolya smiles, and asks the Kalmyk, "Why are you silent, Kalmyk?" and then he says to the Cossacks, "See that bastard. . . he lights the stove for himself and sends Russians out into the cold!"

"What's with them?" the Cossack asks the Kalmyk.

"Come on boys, take off," says the other Cossack to us. And the third one says to the Kalmyk, "Come on Dzhumak, let's eat."

We leave the hut in silence. Into the cold. It's twilight. If

319

Grinchenko says something now, it'll be sickening. It seems to me that I've insulted a man. Kolya is silent. He "shed blood". . . He hasn't even gotten a scratch.

Now we're already beyond this populated point. Fire, mortars, fire! Blow, wind! Pour, you, half-rain, half-snow! Get wet, you back of mine! Hurt, you hands of mine!

What can I do so my feet won't freeze? Boy, do I need a pair of boots! Wide ones. Three sizes too large. So I can really wrap my feet. . . so my foot will be just like in a nest. I must walk some more. But we almost never walk. We have to change positions all the time. This means, get into the trucks, and get rolling. It's raining. It's coming down from the sky in a straight line. Now it's snowing. It comes in at a slant. The wind's blowing from all sides. Day and night we get soaked. Towards morning it starts freezing up. You don't feel like moving.

I'm thinking about Nina. And it seems to me that she's somewhere on one of the trucks. The telephonist Kuzin is dead. Caught a bullet right in the mouth. It was a spent bullet, a weak one. But somehow it managed to pierce him, and he died.

Conversations

This is probably the first night that we've been able to sleep normally. We're lying on the floor of an abandoned hut. We're on our coats. It's impossible to cover up. It's hot. Shongin has heated up the stove. We've really crowded into the hut. It's dark. Only the red glow of Shongin's cigarette hovers about slowly and constantly.

"Give me a smoke, Shongin," says Sashka Zolotaryov.

Shongin is silent. The red glow is flying around.

"Give me a smoke, Shongin," I say. We continue the gag, slowly, as we always do.

"He's asleep," says Kolya Grinchenko.

The red glow hangs suspended in the air, pitiful and motionless. I stare into the darkness, and it's as if I can see the smile on Grinchenko's face, and as if I can see Shongin's clenched lips and his blinking eyes.

"I want to smoke," says Sashka. "Should I wake him or not?"

"Don't wake him," says Kolya. "Let the man sleep. Take it

yourself. Take as much as you want."

"He's got his tobacco in his gas mask," I say.

"I'll give you 'take it yourself,' " says Shongin. "I'll give you some myself."

"See, you've awakened the man," says Kolya.

You can hear Shongin groaning.

We lie there and assiduously inhale the bitter cigarette smoke.

It's quiet. Then someone says in the darkness, "It'd be nice if Nina would come here. We could talk to her."

Sashka Zolotaryov laughs.

"I like plump girls," he says, "and girls that are taller than me."

"Ninka has a husband," I say.

Sashka laughs.

"I have a wife, too. Maybe Ninka's husband is with my 'dumpling' right now."

"It's war," says Kolya. "Everything has been mixed up. And then, if you want to speak about love, then in that case you can't order. . ."

Sashka laughs.

"You're a bunch of animals," says Shongin, and he turns over to the other side.

"I wouldn't marry someone like her," someone says in the darkness.

"But I would. . ."

"I had a girl, Katya was her name. What a beauty. Braids down to her waist. Now Ninka, well. . ."

"No one is forcing her on you," Kolya says angrily.

"If you don't like her," I say, "you don't have to take her. Right, Kolya?"

"Your Katya probably has a nose like a belly button," laughs Sashka. "You like 'em like that. A nose like a belly button and smelling of dough."

"You won't be laughing for long, Zolotaryov," someone threatens from the darkness.

> You're still alive, my old girl,
> I'm alive too. Regards to you, regards.
> Above your roof, let there swirl. . .

It's Kolya singing.

Suddenly the door opens. The commander's voice cuts into the darkness:

"Who's spreading pessimism here?"

And then it's quiet again.

What will happen tomorrow? Where are we going to wind up? No letters from home. There's no more room for notches on Sashka's stick. If I'm wounded, I'll be put in a hospital. I'll eat my fill. I'll go home on leave. I'll go over to the school. And everyone will see my crutches. I'll have a stripe on my chest. For my wound. And perhaps I'll get a medal, and they'll see that too. And Zhenya will come out. And she won't be laughing this time. And everyone will look at her, then at me. And I'll say to her, "Hi, Zhenechka." And I'll walk, walk along the corridor. And she'll catch up to me. "Why don't you drop over and visit me at home. I've missed you."

"At home?" What do you mean? Why, what do you mean?

"There's no reason. A lot has changed." And I'll walk along the corridor. And the girls will tell her quietly: "You fool, Zhen'-ka. It's your own fault."

"I've got a stomachache from the pumpkin," says Sashka.

"When I was a civilian, I never even saw one," says someone.

Kolya advises Sashka: "You know, Sashka, you ought to go and take a load off your mind."

"You fool," says Sashka. "A pumpkin is a good thing, only not if it's raw."

"And I like borsht," someone says in the darkness. "A thick one, so that when you put your spoon in it, it'll stand upright. I don't need any dumplings."

"And I don't have a spoon. Being without a spoon is like being without hands. They laugh at me and my piece of wood. I'm laughing myself. . . But I don't have a spoon. . . And I don't have boots. If only I had a pair of boots, we'd talk differently, Nina. . .

Nina, you're so slim. Look, here we are, you and me, walking through the city. Here's Zhenya coming towards us. She understands everything. And she's silent. She's a fool. And we're walking. And I'm wearing black slacks and a white shirt with a turn-down collar, and there's a Leica across my shoulders. And there's no war.

"And I'd like to eat some sour cream, too," someone says in the darkness.

Nina

No matter how many times I come to regimental head-quarters, no matter how many times I look at Nina, she doesn't notice me.

But her own people, the ones from headquarters, speak to her very simply: "Nina, give me the mug. . ." "What's the matter, dear, tired? . . ." "Let's have a smoke. . ." "Hi, Ninochka. . ." "Good to see you again! . . ," and they embrace her. And she—she hands them the mug, smiles, smokes, sitting on the crate, and kisses those who return right on their unshaven cheeks.

That's because they're "her own." But who are they, these "her own"? They're headquarters rats, and I come from the battery. I risk my life. My hands are cut to bits, my coat is burned, my lips chapped. But they're—"her own."

I crawl into the headquarters dugout. It's warm there. A joyous, potbellied stove is burning. It smells of bread. There's no one there. Only Nina is sitting with her earphones near the receiver.

"Don, Don, this is Moscow. Over. Don, Don, this is Moscow. How do you read me? Over."

"Hi, Nina," I say in an offhand manner.

She nods to me. It's so friendly, so nice. It's so unexpected.

"How do you read me? Is it better now? Over."

She takes off the earphones.

"Sit down, warrior. Rest up."

"No time," I say, and sit down on the boards. And I look at her. She smiles.

"Well, why are you staring?"

"Oh, nothing. It's been long since I've seen a woman smile. There are no women at the battery, you know. Sashka Zolotaryov sometimes smiles, and Kolya Grinchenko, but there are no women."

She smiles again.

"Your Kolya comes here often. He keeps telling me about his heroic deeds. I don't like braggarts."

"Come to see us. . ."

"Where?"

"At the battery."

"To drink tea?"

"We'll sit a while, smoke. . ."

"We'll sit a while, smoke." She smiles.

How daring I was when I first walked in. How daring! Even the flame of the lamp trembled. But now it's not moving.

"If you want, I'll give you some tea."

"I don't drink tea," I say ironically.

"Oh, I get it," says Nina. "You've gotten used to stronger stuff."

"Accustomed or not, I prefer it. We'll get our fill of tea when we're civilians again."

She looks straight at me, not blinking, and smiles.

"You're a strange one. Our reconnaissance men are good kids too, but they don't refuse tea. . . You're a real strange one. But I'll come to the battery, okay? We'll sit a while, smoke, eh?"

"Really?"

"Yes. . . you know, you have nice eyes."

White wings sprout on my back. White. White. They make everything light, like a rocket flare at the front. Delirium.

"I still say you're lying about the 'stronger stuff'."

She says this from afar. I don't see her. Only two large eyes. Round. Gray. Derisive.

Some people come in. They stamp their feet. They speak words. But I hear: "Don, Don . . . you have nice eyes. . . I'm signing off, Roger."

"Are you from Lieutenant Burakov?" they ask me.

"Yes, sir!"

"Here, take this. . . "

I take a piece of paper, put it in my pocket. I go over to Nina.

"You'll come, then?"

"Where? Oh, the battery? We'll sit a while, smoke. Right?"

"Come."

"But I don't smoke," she smiles. "We'll just sit, okay?"

"Hey, Ninochka, what are you doing, entertaining the handsome soldier boys?" I hear behind my back.

". . . Everything is calm, quiet, but I feel kind of bad. I have a feeling, says Shongin, "and I'm not happy about this silence. No, I'm not happy about it."

The small, scrawny Gurgenidze stands in front of Lieutenant Burakov. A drop hangs from the tip of his nose. He's waving his arms.

324

"Let me go home for four days. My house in Kvareli. I bring all kind *purmarili,* food, wine, *khachapuri, lobio.* This porridge no good."

The lieutenant laughs.

"And who's going to do the fighting?"

"I will," Gurgenidze bows. "Who will? I will. No war here now."

"And how will you get there?"

"What?"

"How will you go?"

Gurgenidze looks at the lieutenant regretfully.

"Give me leave. I'll get there."

The commander looks at us.

"Well, what do you say, shall we let him go?"

"Well, you see how it is, comrade lieutenant," says Shongin, "it'd be okay to let him go, but supposing it suddenly starts? How are we going to get along without a communications man?"

"You see how it is," says the commander. "We can't get along without you."

"Why not?" Gurgenidze becomes worried. "Sure you can. No fighting four days."

"Listen, Gurgenidze, why don't you go over to the Germans and ask them when they are going to begin. Perhaps you can even go after all," Sashka suggests.

Everyone laughs. They can't hold back. Gurgenidze tries to understand what happened. Then he shrugs his shoulders.

"Eh!" and he himself laughs.

And the drop, no longer being able to hold onto the tip of his nose, falls to the ground.

And the commander says, getting serious, "Rest. All of you. We'll be working this evening." And he goes away.

In the evening, again, nothing happens. I asked her to come to the battery. Why should she? Why? What is she going to do here? I invited her as though for a walk in the park. If she only saw my hands, covered with scabs and calluses; my hangnails, my hands which are impossible to wash clean, so deep has the dirt eaten itself into the flesh. . . I'll say to her, "Listen, why fool around? You see everything, you understand. Well, come on then and let it be simple: you and me. That I might know that you visited me. Let everybody see. Come on, what do you say? Listen, we're the same age. It's a lot of nonsense that the man must be older. I've known you for a long, long time. Well, please don't pretend that it's all the same to you. I know the reason you laugh at me is because you're embarrassed." And when I say this to her, the white moon will come out, and the snow will glisten, and there won't be anyone around us, and my leggings won't be showing.

"Why aren't you resting?" asks Kolya Grinchenko.

What am I going to tell him?

"Yesterday I made a date with Ninochka. She'll come today."

"You're still lying," I say, relieved. "Boy, do you ever lie."

"You'll see," he says. "Wait."

Kolya stands before me. He smells of perfume. He shaved. Shaved? Is she really coming? Why, of course; she smiled, and I. . .

A white rocket flare goes up over the German trenches. Somewhere in the distance a machine gun rattles, lonely and sadly, and then it falls silent.

Kolya Grinchenko blows cigarette smoke into his cupped hands. He smiles.

"Yes, Ninochka will come, we'll talk. . ."

"But she's married," I say. "You won't get anywhere with her."

He smiles and continues smoking. Then he walks off. And he doesn't say anything. If he's quiet, it means he's telling the truth. It means she will come. Fool that I was, fool. I asked, begged. One must do it the way Grinchenko said. Yes, that's the way. Embrace her, squeeze her till her bones crack so she can't say a word; so that she feels here's a man! They like that, yes. But conversations, who needs 'em? Oh, you gray-eyed Nina, you! Now I know what to tell you. . .

Beyond the dugout a jeep rumbles. And a female voice is heard. And I see Kolya heading in that direction. She's come. And I hear her voice:

"Hello, hello!" What a smile, what a smile. I can't stand it. . . "See, I came to visit you. Just for a minute, I asked the major to take me with him. Well, how are things? Well, look now, you've even got Germans nearby. Why are you so quiet, Kolya? As though there was no war here—what a dandy you are, Kolya. You even have time to shave. Listen, you have a boy here, a dark-eyed one, where is he?"

"What dark-eyed one?" asks Grinchenko.

"You know, the dark-haired one."

I hear her quiet laugh. She laughs well. Should I go over? But why should I? Why must it be me she's talking about? Gurgenidze is dark-eyed, so is the platoon leader Karpov, and so's the battery commander.

Her dark, slim silhouette swims out from beyond the dugout like a dark moon. She has stopped and is rocking back and forth lightly.

"There you are, warrior. . . We'll sit a while, smoke, right?"

She comes nearer, closer.

"Now that's really something." she says. "I have a date in the middle of the war. Why are you so quiet? Oh, oh, you probably filled yourself with that strong stuff, right?"

"I didn't drink anything. . ."

"Well, tell me something. . ."

"Let's go over there, near the shell crates. We'll sit."

"Aren't you something! Head for the corner right away."

"Why do you say that?"

"Because everyone wants it. And even more so at the front. What's going to happen tomorrow?"

"I like you, Nina."

"I know."

"You know? You're really convinced of it?"

"Why what do you mean? What do you mean, my boy? Grinchenko told me that you speak to me in your sleep."

"He's always lying!"

From beyond the dugout someone shouted. "Nina! Nina Shubnikova, let's go!"

"Well, it's time. You haven't really told me anything. Who you are, what you are, what we're going to do," she says and passes the palm of her hand over my cheek.

"Well, goodbye. It's war. Perhaps we won't see each other."

"I'll come to see you tomorrow. I like you."

"Many people like me," she says. "I'm the only one here, you know."

She runs to the car. She runs quickly and flares go up more and more often above the German trenches.

Oh, Tobacco, Tobacco. . .

Just as thunder roars out of the calm, so unexpected colors

appear in a gray morning: red on gray; saffron on gray; black on white. Flames, rusty, warped metal, motionless bodies.

Nina went off with the major to headquarters. The last rocket over the German positions is like the last flower. Nina is probably screaming into the telephone: "Volga, Volga, this is Don, how do you read me? Over!" And I have such a fat, little, peaceful shell in my hands. I'll pass it to the loader. Then the mortar will groan, sitting back on its hind legs.

I know how it's going to be. Boy, am I ever experienced now. And the palms of my hands don't hurt anymore.

And Kolya Grinchenko is sitting on the mortar base plate. He smiles pleasantly. And he sings quietly to himself:

"Oh, tobacco, tobacco. . ."

"Did you hear? The Germans broke through," says Sashka. "Infantry?"

"No, tanks."

"Are they heading this way?"

"They're behind us. . ."

"How many?"

"They say about forty."

German bombers are flying high over our position. They don't want us. They'll drop their bombs behind our lines.

"The medics will have plenty of work," Sashka says.

And Kolya sings:

"Oh, tobacco, tobacco. . ."

And then a German shell explodes on the hill, to the right of us. Our mortars send them a friendly answer. All four of them. Then another one. And again.

And behind us red balls of fire burst up. I can feel the hot wind on my back. The back of my head aches. The German artillery keeps pouring it on.

"They're onto us," someone says.

I keep bringing more and more shells. I don't stop to think about anything. Each movement is as automatic as hell. Ten steps back. Pick up a sixteen-kilo, cold suckling pig. Ten steps forward. You can do it with your eyes closed. A couple of round trips. And the fingers themselves unbutton the coat. And they pick some snow and shove it in the mouth. And suddenly I get a stupid idea: after the battle, I'll take some sugar, mix it with the snow, and I'll get ice cream. . .

Ten steps forward. Ten—back. There are fewer and fewer "suckling pigs." How much time has passed? Happy people never notice time pass. . .

A shock wave hits me in the back. I can't stand up. I fall. "Aaa, aaaa," someone screams. And then again, but weaker this time, "a-a, a-a-a-a-!"

It's me screaming. I see the backs of my comrades. They're shooting. They don't see me. Thank God, everything is okay. No pain. Why did I scream? Supposing there was a direct attack. . . But that's impossible. Why me especially? And why not? And suddenly there is an especially violent explosion. And there's a scream again. But it's not me, it's someone else this time. The way he screams—you can't help but look. I see Kolya run up to him, and then he covers his face with his hands and runs back. And before reaching his mortar, he stops and bends over.

Who was on the first mortar? I can't remember anyone. No one. Absolutely no one's left. And there's no more room for notches on Sashka's stick. The platoon commander Karpov shouts at us to change our position. And everyone's as busy as hell. Quicker, quicker! If we don't get a move on, the Germans will clobber us. The mortars are already hitched to their carriers. And we crawl out of the dugout where our position was. Where will our new position be? What's going to happen? Everybody's quiet. Now I see dark spots in the snow, a crater, and a figure in a long coat approaching us. And I don't want to think about it, but it won't leave me, and I can't get rid of it for anything.

"Number one is gone," says Sashka.

"Gone," I say.

"A lot of the boys are gone," says Sashka.

"Shut up!" says Shongin. He's sitting, hunched over.

The trucks keep moving. And I don't notice the shooting anymore. I only see Kolya's pale face. He is looking somewhere off in the distance and not moving.

"Hey, Kolya!" says Sashka. "Better say goodbye to Ninka. They'll be transferring us to another division."

Kolya doesn't move.

"Shut up!" says Shongin.

"As if it wasn't enough, now they have tanks crawling up our backs," says Gavrilov.

We pass some sort of fire. Probably a barn. Burned to the

ground. Some logs are still smoldering. Smells terrible. A smell of burning, of burning. . .but that's not the word.

From the new position we can see the firing on the enemy. Three of our mortars keep pouring it on somewhere over the hills. I keep bringing more and more shells.

But it could hit our mortar. Not number one, but ours. And I wouldn't be carrying shells. Maybe I'd be walking slowly along the fields, just barely moving, and then I'd fall. So far it's quiet here. They haven't spotted us yet. There it is again: "Retreat!" And again into the trucks. And into the night, and into the darkness.

We're stamping our feet in the darkness near the trucks. We hitch up the mortars. And somewhere up in the sky the bombers are droning on.

"Ours."

"You never see them in the daytime."

"It's better than nothing."

Second Lieutenant Karpov, our platoon commander, comes over. He's rubbing his hands and cheeks. Our platoon commander is either frozen or he's worried.

"Are we moving again?" Sashka Zolotaryov asks.

"What do you mean," says Karpov. "We're moving up, boys! Enough of this sitting around."

"Sitting around," says Shongin. "Look how many men we've lost."

"That's war," says Karpov quietly. "And what's an old soldier like you, Shongin, talking like this for?"

Everyone is quiet. Words—that's really funny. It really is war. What are you going to do? Is it Karpov's fault? Look at him; young, red-cheeked, energetic. . . Is it my fault? Kolya's?

We're sitting in the trucks. Miserable road. The truck keeps rocking like a boat. We rock from side to side. It's a good thing we're riding. Otherwise, the road would have become so muddy. You try and pull a truck through the stuff. We're riding. It's half raining, half snowing. We gradually get soaked. At first it's even nice: it's cooling after the heat. And the cold raindrops run down inside your collar comfortably. But now it's no good anymore. Enough. I know, in a minute we'll be shivering. Then try and get warm. And the feet freeze. Quickly and certainly. We're moving to a new battle sector. You can already clearly hear the explosions and the song of the automatics. And a lit-up sky swims out from beyond the hill.

"And Where is Your Daughter?"

How well everything is going. Tomorrow I'll write home. I'm alive. What's left of the battery? Two mortars and no more than thirty men. And I'm alive. Didn't even get a scratch. I'll write tomorrow. Home.

"Let's see what's there," says Sashka Zolotaryov.

Night. Some sort of a hut. The windows are dark.

I knock on the shutters. "Lady, would you be so kind as to. . . ." No answer. "Lady, I made it, I'm alive. Oh, if you only knew what it was like!" I knock on the shutters. "The boots—here; the uniform—in the closet; the sword—on the chair. . ."

"Thank you. . . But where is your daughter?"

"Sleep, sleep, sleep. . ." says Kolya.

I knock on the shutters. "Grouse? . . . Cheese? . . . Wine? . . ."

"Oh, thank you. A small piece of cold veal and some rum. I'm a soldier, lady." I knock on the shutters.

"We'll freeze to death."

"Let's go to another one."

"Knock again."

I knock on the shutters. Sashka knocks on the shutters. Kolya knocks on the shutters.

"Here's your room. Good night." "Good night, lady. But where is your daughter? . . ."

"What do you want?"

A woman is standing in the doorway. She's all bundled up.

"We'd like to spend the night here, lady."

"We made it, we're alive," I say.

"Big deal. . ." says the woman. "That's all I needed."

"Can we come in?" asks Kolya.

"It's very cold," says Sashka.

"We'll just stay overnight and then leave," I say.

It's cold in the hallway. Inside it's warm. A lamp is burning and smoking up the place. Someone is tossing and turning on the Russian stove. It's a small room. How are we all going to fit in there?"

The woman takes off her kerchief. She's very young.

"Lie down here," she says to Kolya, pointing to the corner. Kolya's got a good place. "And you, over there," she says to Sashka.

Zolotaryov spreads his coat under the table and lies down on it. Kolya undresses silently. She puts me on a bunk near the stove. I can only lie on my side. What the hell—as long as I'm lying down. The woman herself lies on a bed. A folding bed. There's a rag of a blanket on it. She crawls under it without taking off her outer coat.

I put my coat on the bunk. The blue flame of the lamp goes out. A hand strokes my hair.

"Come up here," says a quiet voice from the stove. "It's warm here."

"Who are you?"

"What's the difference. Come on. It's warm here. . ."

"Manka," the woman says indifferently, "watch out. . ."

"Who asked you," says Manka from the stove. And her hand keeps stroking me, stroking me.

"Come on over here."

"Wait, let me take my shoes off."

"Come on, what's the difference?"

Supposing they hear? . . . "Where's your daughter, lady?" Supposing they hear. . . now there's a daughter for you. . . It's warm near Manka. If I just touch her, the whole thing will be shot. Manka. . . Is that really her name?

"What's your name?"

"Mariya Andreevna."

Now there's something for you. How can. . . She has a hot, resilient stomach and small, clutching hands.

"How old are you?"

"Sixteen. . . Why?"

"Sh. . . !"

"Why? Why?"

"They'll hear us."

"Let em. . . come closer."

"Manka," says the woman, "you'd better watch it, Manka."

"Never you mind," says Manka.

Down below, Sashka Zolotaryov coughs, and Kolya says: "Lady, aren't you cold?"

And Manka wraps herself around me, and I don't know which is me and which is her. Everything is all mixed up.

"Your heart is really thumping." She laughs right in my ear. "What's the matter, are your afraid?"

And Kolya asks, "Aren't you cold, lady?"

Is that how simple it is? And will it be the same with Nina? With everyone?

"What's the matter, are you dead or something?"

"Leave me alone."

"I'm just kidding, silly. . ."

"Let me go, Mariya. . ."

"Mariya," says the woman. "Hey, Mariya, you're not Mariya, you're a towheaded fool."

"Let go of me, or there'll be trouble."

"Come on, let's just lie here, okay?"

"Let go. . ."

"Go back to your bench if you think it's too crowded here."

The bench is cool. Sashka's coughing.

"Lady, you must be freezing under that rag. Want me to cover you with my coat?" says Kolya from the corner.

. . . Someone's walking around in the hut. And he's whispering something. It's a quiet, hurried whisper. I can't make out the words. It's probably Mariya on the stove. And maybe it's the woman. And perhaps it's not a whisper, but just the stillness. But someone is sobbing. How difficult it must be in this small village. And tomorrow I'll be a laughingstock. They'll make fun of me for sure. . . Serves me right. She herself asked, begged. . . They'll laugh at me. I'll get up early in the morning and go to another hut, or to headquarters, or to the trucks. She's hot like fire, that Mariya Andreevna. She'll be the first one to laugh. Sixteen. . . Kolya calls them "peaches and cream." But someone really is crying. Or is it outside the window?

"Who is it?" I ask.

"Don't shout," says the woman. "Lie down and sleep."

I must be in a delirium. They'll laugh at me, really laugh at me. And still, someone is crying. Could it be that it's Mariya laughing?

In the morning Sashka Zolotaryov says, "Looks like we'll be eating here. The battery commander's eating potatoes. The trucks broke down."

Sashka has already washed. He has an air of cold about him. His cheeks are just like children's cheeks, crimson. He's had time to find out everything. And Kolya is sleeping. And the woman and Mariya are gone.

"What's going to happen now?" I ask.

"Nothing," says Sashka. "We'll wait for some new equipment, and then we'll start again."

"And the trucks have broken down?"

"Completely."

"Is the kitchen operating?"

"What kitchen?"

Sashka takes out three packages of powdered peas from his field pack.

"Here's what they gave us. We'll cook it. Better wake Kolya. Get up Mykola!"

And suddenly the woman comes in. She takes off her kerchief. And I see that she is very young. And beautiful.

"Get up, Mykola," says Sashka. But Kolya sleeps.

"What are you waking him for?" the woman asks. "Let him sleep—he's tired."

She speaks very severely. And she keeps looking at Kolya.

"Give it to me, I'll cook it," she says, taking the powdered peas from Sashka.

We're sitting at the table. We're silent. We're eating the pea soup. With wooden spoons. But I don't have a spoon. As soon as we leave this place, I'll get my piece of wood. . . For now, I'll use the wooden one. I haven't had a spoon for a long time. . . We eat the pea soup; there's no bread. Kolya eats slowly. Occasionally he looks up at the woman. She's sitting directly opposite him. And she looks up at him from time to time. And that's all. And I'm waiting for Mariya to start laughing at me. But she won't even look at me. It's only that I haven't really looked at her. She's pug-nosed. And she has a wide face. And a funny lock of hair hangs down her forehead. And she has several large freckles or birthmarks on her nose.

"Well now, freckle-face," Sashka says to her, "what's going to happen to us?"

"We'll get along," says Mariya.

"It's tasty soup," says Kolya and he looks at the woman. "How come you don't look alike?" asks Sashka. "You live together, you're like sisters, but you don't look alike. . ."

"But we're not sisters," says Mariya. "We just know each other and live together."

"You know, the soup's not bad." says Kolya. And he looks at the woman. But she doesn't say anything.

Suddenly Shongin comes in.

"Here we go again, another one," the woman says loudly. And Shongin sits down on a stool.

"There are a lot of dead," he says, "and wounded. They've taken them away." And he takes out his tobacco pouch.

"Are we gonna smoke?" asks Sashka.

"What is there to smoke?" says Shongin. "There's not enough tobacco for me," and he shows the pouch.

"Where did you sleep, Shongin?" Kolya asks.

"I didn't sleep," says Shongin. "There were a lot of wounded. By the time we picked them all up, it was morning."

"I'd love a smoke now," says Sashka.

"Here smoke, smoke," says Shongin, and he takes a drag. He blows out large clouds of smoke. "I just dropped in to see how you were," he says.

Meanwhile the woman is pouring milk into some cups. And Kolya says, "Listen, Shongin, that powdered stuff wasn't enough. Would you like some milk?"

"It's goat's milk," says Mariya.

"I've eaten," says Shongin. "I've eaten. Gurgenidze was wounded. I made soup for both of us."

Poor little Gurgenidze. Just a boy. With an eternal drop hanging from the tip of his nose. "It's a hit—it's a miss."

"Is he bad, Shongin?"

"Nothing much," says Shongin. "He's in the truck. The last one. They're going to take him away.

"I'm running along in the fresh snow. To the truck. Soldiers are walking around it. Gurgenidze is lying on some straw in the back of the truck. In a burned coat. He raises his bandaged head. A drop is hanging from the tip of his nose.

"I got hit," he says with a sad smile.

We weren't even friends. Just knew each other. And his red eyelids keep flinching.

"Where'd you get it?"

"I get it in the head, the stomach, in the leg. Shongin carry me on his back."

"It's okay, Gurgenidze. Now you'll rest up. Everything will be okay."

The motor turns over. Gurgenidze falls back on the straw. His hands are folded on his chest.

"What's our section?" he asks. "What number?"

"Special mortar battery, friend."

"No, which regiment?"

"229th, I think."

"What division?"

"Why do you want to know?"

"They might ask me in the hospital."

The motor is even. The back of the truck shakes.

"What division?"

"Who the hell knows," I shout after him.

The truck rumbles along the fresh snow. Gurgenidze's arm is sticking out from the back of the truck. He's saying goodbye to us. He has left, gone. And I forgot to ask him for his spoon.

"Get them together. It's time. We've rested," the battery commander says to me.

There's no one in the hut. Kolya and the woman are sitting on a log in the back of the hut. She's silent. She's resting her head on her hands. Her eyes are red. Her lips are pouting, just like a little girl's. And Kolya is smoking and is also silent.

"It's time, Kolya," I say. "The battery commander ordered. . ."

"I know," he says and stands up. And he looks at me.

I wait for him.

"I know," he says.

I go away. Let them say goodbye.

The Road

"Did you see the German trucks?" Kolya asks. "They have tarp covers and all that stuff. They're real comfy, just like at home. But our stuff. . ."

"I can't feel my feet anymore," says Zolotaryov. "I'd love to have me some boots. Fur-lined ones. To hell with the face, the main thing is the feet. Maybe I've already lost my big toe, eh? If I take off my shoes, it'll probably fall out."

I don't want any fur-lined boots. Just an ordinary pair of boots would do. With wide tops, and like boats. If I got into water nothing would happen. If I got into snow nothing would happen. Even if I stood there all night. No matter.

Steppe, steppe, steppe. When are we going to stop? There's an attack. Our battery keeps moving from position to position. First we're sent to one section, then to another. Who knows where the regiment to which we were attached is now? And Nina is there. Nina, Nina, you smiled so sweetly for me. And I can't forget you. Who are you, and where are you from? I don't know anything. Where am I going to look for you? Everything in the past has grown dim and hazy. Zhenya is somewhere in a fog, in the distance. There's only you, Nina. And why did you speak so nicely to me?

"Do I talk in my sleep?" I ask Kolya.

"Once, to Ninka Shubnikov."

"What did I say?"

" 'Sit next to me, Nina sit. We'll sit down, have a smoke,' that's what you said. Great fun."

"Did she say anything to you about me?"

And why did I ask? He'll laugh in a minute. Or maybe he'll make up some story. . .

"No, she didn't," says Kolya with a frown. "What's there to say? She's living with the regimental commander. You remember—that tall major."

I remember. I remember. I'd have felt better if he hadn't said anything. If I ever meet her, say, purely by chance—it could happen—I'd say to her. . .

"When I was serving in the cavalry," says Shongin, "now that was really terrible. I'd come back from a march, and I wouldn't be able to sleep. First I had to unsaddle the horse, then feed it, and then, if there was any time left over, then I could rest."

"The English soldiers have waitresses serving them," says Kolya, "and they get cognac with their dinner."

"You're lying, Grinchenko," Shongin mutters.

The trucks have stopped. A traffic jam. It's getting dark.

"Get down, boys. Warm yourselves."

No letters from home. I wonder what's happening there.

"Shongin, ever get any letters from home?" I ask.

He looks at me attentively.

"Of course, I do," he says, and pulls out his tobacco pouch and offers me a smoke.

"Here, warm up."

If we stay here like this until morning, we'll really catch cold. What eyes that Shongin has. They're tender and kind. Yesterday, when we were cooking the powdered peas, he came over to me and Kolya and put a handful of millet in our mess tins. The millet made the soup thick. He came over himself: "Here, boys, I'll put something extra in. . ."

"Shongin, let's have a smoke," says Sashka.

Shongin is stamping his feet up and down, warming them.

"You'll get along without it," he mumbles.

When it gets dark, you can't see the snow. It feels warmer. The platoon commander Karpov comes over. He always has red cheeks. You can even see them in the dark.

He's laughing.

"What's the matter, warriors, you frozen?"

"You'll freeze too," says Kolya. "The sergeant's warm, though—he warms himself on the truck radiator. Maybe we can start a bonfire, lieutenant, what do you say, eh?"

"No bonfires," says Karpov.

Like a guard, Shongin stomps his feet in the snow and bangs his mess tin with his hand.

Gavrilov comes over and says quietly, "Boys, there are some trucks up ahead, full of groats, and the drivers are asleep. . ."

"So what?" says Shongin.

"Nothing," says Gavrilov. "I was just saying that the drivers are asleep. . ."

"You know, it wouldn't be so bad if we could get us a potful of groats," says Sashka Zolotaryov.

And he goes off into the darkness, in the direction where the drivers are asleep. And everyone follows him with their eyes. And everybody is silent.

If it's millet, we can make some thick soup. If it's buckwheat, it's good with milk. If it's pear-barley, that's nice with onions. Will I last until morning or not? I'm soaked through and through. Supposing I catch pneumonia?

No letters from home. Where are you, military post?

I'm loading machine-gun magazines. I'm loading, and I'm silent.

"Why so sad, kid?" the sergeant asks.

I can't answer him. What can I tell him?

"Oh, nothing," I say, "just reminiscing about home. . ."

You've got it good, sergeant. You eat omelets. And we eat cold pea soup. You've got it good, sergeant. And we don't get any decent sleep for days on end.

"We've reached Rostov," the sergeant says.

. . . You have such a pleasant face. And there're fewer and fewer of us. And this Mozdok sand screeches in my teeth and in my soul. You ought to give me some boots, sergeant, or something. The artificial soles on my American knee boots have cracked. When it's cold, I shove my feet in the bonfire. And the knee boots are a beautiful red. But what's left of them?. . .

"You ought to grease those shoes, kid. Just look at them, they're no good."

. . . And what kind of shoes did I wear before I got into the army? I don't remember. Did I have stylish chocolate-colored shoes with a white edge, like ocean surf? Or did I just dream about it? I probably wore plain black shoes. And in the winter I put galoshes over them. Yes, yes, galoshes. At the last Komsomol meeting I forgot them at school. I forgot them. I came home without galoshes. And the war had already broken out, and no one noticed my loss. That's the way I left. And they were new galoshes. Shiny ones. Now I don't know. . . will I ever have another pair like them?

And when we had the last Komsomol meeting, Zhenya was sitting in a corner. While we each took our stand and swore to die for our fatherland, she didn't say anything. Then she said, "I'm sorry for you boys. You think it's so simple to fight? Wars need silent, sullen soldiers. Warriors. No need to make noise. I'm sorry for you. And you..." she pointed to me. "You still don't know how to do anything except read your books. There's death out there, death. . .and it loves young people like you."

"And you?" someone shouted.

"I'll go too. But I won't scream and suffer. What for? I'll simply go."

"We'll also go. Why are you lecturing us?"

"You must be mentally prepared. . ."

"Shut up, Zhenka. . ."

"Otherwise, you won't be of any service."

"Shut up!"

"Enough," said the Komsomol organizer. "Why are we shouting like this?" Like a bunch of kids?"

And when I kissed you at the gate so that you moaned and embraced me, what was that? Does that mean I don't know how to do anything except read books? . . .

"Tomorrow we'll go get some mortars," says the sergeant. "You can take it easy for another night, kid."

"What mortars?" I ask.

"Stay alert. We'll be getting some replacements tomorrow. You'll be teaching those babies."

"But how can I?"

"What's the matter, do you need three years fighting to teach our business to a bunch of school kids?"

Our business? My business? Does he mean the mortars? I'll be teaching?

"Okay, I'll teach 'em," I say.

School kids. But I was a school kid too. Does this mean I'm no longer a school kid? But at that meeting I was a school kid. And when everybody made noise, I made noise too. Zhenya said, "You're making noise, just like a school kid. You can't do that there. You need severity there."

And she looked at me. I looked at her, too. Someone told me that, if a girl loves you, she won't hold out a "stare." She'll blush and lower her eyes. That means she didn't love me. She didn't love me.

"Let's all go together, the entire class," someone shouted.

"Let's all go!" I shouted.

"Shut up," they told me. "Shut up, you jerk!"

Then the school director came in, and the Komsomol organizer said, "Okay, we'll continue the business of the day."

And on the agenda there was but one question: Komsomol studies.

". . .When you finish with the machine-gun magazines, come into the smokehouse," says the sergeant and goes away. . .

. . .And after the meeting we were all walking along the embankment together. And Zhenya was walking with us, but she

340

didn't look at me. It was dark and tense.

"We won't see the tenth of the month, boys," someone said. And a siren suddenly started wailing. And I found myself next to Zhenya.

"So we're school kids?" I asked.

"Of course," she said calmly.

"In other words, we won't make good fighters?"

"Of course."

"To be a good figher, you have to be broad-shouldered, right?"

"Yes," she laughed.

"And indifferent, right?"

"No," she said, "I didn't say that."

"Let's go over there," I said, pointing to a dark side street.

We were walking along the side street. It was even darker and even more tense there. And suddenly a window opened. With a bang. On the third floor. Laughter came out of the window. Then music. The phonograph was playing an old prewar tango.

"As though nothing every happened, right?"

"Right," I said.

The window closed. The music died down. And the siren started again. . .

. . . I loaded all the magazines. I'm walking to the smokehouse. It's not a smokehouse, just a simple hut where the sergeant is staying.

The sergeant is warming his hands near the stove. Our battalion commander is sitting at a table. He's writing. And the platoon commander Karpov, so pink-cheeked, is shaving near the window. Even through the white, foamy lather, you can see his pink cheeks.

Sashka Zolotaryov is standing at attention in front of the battalion commander.

"In other words, you stole someone else's millet?" the battalion commander asks.

"I stole it," Sashka says.

"You ate someone else's gruel! When you stole, did you think that someone else would go hungry? Did you?"

"Yes, comrade lieutenant!"

"Well?"

"I was hungry, too."

"You know what you can get for this?"

"Of course, I know," Sashka says quietly.

"He gave some to everybody," I say from the threshold. The battalion commander looks at me piercingly. Will he hit me? If he only hit me.

"They're a bunch of hooligans, not a battery," he says.

"They've gotten out of hand," says Karpov. "Grinchenko is their leader. They're continually talking about love and stuffing their faces. . ."

"Okay, Karpov, go on with your shaving," says the battalion commander. "I have other business."

And I want to ask Karpov where he was when we were raw troops, just beyond State Farm no. 3, when we took part in our first battle. He was eating food at school.

"About face!" the battalion commander shouts at me.

I'm walking to my place. Maybe Zhenya really is right. Maybe I really am a school kid. The winter will be over soon. Soon we'll be returning to the front lines. Then we'll see what kind of a school kid I am. . . And I'll meet Nina again. "Hi, small fry," she'll say. "Haven't seen you for a long time. Let's sit a while, have a smoke, right?"

Conversations

We've been at this destroyed village for four days and nights. There was a state farm here. A big, shredded windmill, like some sad bird, looks at us from above.

Shabby batteries, battalions drained of blood, regiments thinned out in attack; all of these have gathered here. Depots have sprung up in former dugouts, and tired commissaries, who haven't had enough sleep, distribute, give out and supply us with all kinds of goods.

The roads to the North pass through here. The offensive has gone that way. We can hear the deafening cannonade from there. New units hurry along these roads to the front. In new uniforms. Spic and span. On new trucks. And they look at us with curiosity and respect, with fear and envy.

I haven't seen Nina for a long time now. I'm already forgetting her face. Her voice. How quickly everything happens in war. . .

342

Kolya Grinchenko has had a good night's sleep and has cleaned up. He's happy again. Every two hours Sashka Zolotaryov cooks something for himself in addition to the rations. And he sleeps. His eyes are very, very small. His cheeks are even more crimson. I can't tell now whose are more crimson, his or Karpov's. And Second Lieutenant Karpov walks around like a conqueror in his sheepskin coat, cocked hat, and with a twig in his hand. He keeps hitting his boot tops with this twig, just as a calf drives away flies with its tail. His voice has become clearer, more ringing. And for some reason, we clash more with him.

"He's got nothing to do," says Kolya Grinchenko, "so he keeps poking his nose in everything."

"He's a commander," says Shongin.

"Didn't even hear a word out of him at the front," says Sashka, "but he'll start educating us soon."

"He's a commander," says Shongin. "He's got to do it."

"He'll get around to us soon," I say. "See how he keeps looking at Kolya?"

"He doesn't like me," says Kolya. "The battalion commander does, but not this one..."

"Now the battalion commander, that's altogether something different," says Shongin. "He's not about to walk around with a twig in his hand."

"He's smart," says Sashka Zolotaryov.

Second Lieutenant Karpov comes up. He's hitting his boot tops with his twig.

"Grinchenko, why are you wearing a navy belt buckle? We're in the artillery," he says to Kolya.

"Yes, sir! The artillery," says Kolya and smiles.

"Then take off that buckle and put it away as a memento."

"Yes, sir! Take off that buckle," Kolya salutes and smiles.

"I mean it," says Karpov with great restraint. "No joking around on the front."

"Yes, sir!" says Kolya and smiles.

Karpov looks at us. We're not smiling. Sashka looks aside. Shongin stands at attention, but I can't. Both legs just keep buckling under me. Now one, now the other.

"Take it off, and bring it to me," says Karpov. He hits his boot tops with his twig and leaves.

Kolya quickly takes off the belt buckle. It's a beautiful

buckle with anchors on it.

"But I didn't argue with him," he says. "What got into him?"

"He's a commander," says Shongin, "and you're a jerk. That's why."

Kolya walks off swinging the belt in his hand.

"He'll get it yet," says Sashka Zolotaryov.

Whom does he mean: Kolya or Karpov? I don't know. We also walk away. To our hut. It's warm there.

Kolya's sitting on the bench. He's changing buckles.

"I'll transfer to reconnaissance. They're okay," he says. We sit and keep quiet. Tired of sitting and being silent—of speaking. No replacements.

"Why don't they send us out a little farther; as it is, we don't do anything," says Sashka. "We'd go into some small town. . . On leave. An orchestra probably would be playing in the park. Soon the apple trees will begin to bloom."

"Karpov would surely let you have it," says Kolya.

"The apple trees will bloom without you," says Shongin, "and there are no orchestras now. What good are they. . . now? When I left for the front, there was an orchestra playing."

"That was the last one," I say. "Then everybody became a machine gunner. They all became machine gunners."

"Eh, bull. . ." says Shongin.

"Yes. No orchestras are playing now. Now they only play when we liberate a city."

. . .And when I left, there was no orchestra playing. It was autumn. It was raining. Seryozhka Gorelov and I were standing at the streetcar stop. We had rucksacks. And we had a packet from the enlistment office. And our orders sending us to separate mortar divisions.

"You'll get there on your own," the head of the second unit told us. "You're not children."

And we left.

No one saw us off. Even Zhenya didn't come. We rode through Moscow in the evening, and we were silent. And at the Kazan railroad terminal it was terribly crowded. And we sat down on the floor. And we liked it. Seryozhka smoked and kept spitting on the floor. We played at being soldiers, and we liked this game. And I kept looking around all the time. Perhaps I'll see Zhenya. No, an orchestra did not play at our farewell. There was just a piano on a raised platform, and some drunken little sailor sat down and played an old waltz. And everyone fell silent and listened. And I listened, but kept looking around all the time: maybe Zhenya was coming.

It was some kind of unfamiliar waltz, but you felt that it was old. Even the crying children suddenly stopped crying. And the sailor was rocking on his chair, and his long forelock hung down and touched the piano keys.

"Well, now we're soldiers," Seryozhka whispered to me.

The sailor was playing an old waltz. Everyone listened. Women, children, old men, soldiers, officers. . . And I was happy that I was sitting on the floor of the railway station, that my rucksack was near me, that I was a soldier, that perhaps tomorrow I'd be given a weapon.

And I was happy that I was with them, that the drunken little sailor was playing the piano. And I wanted very much for Zhenya to come and see us in this world to which we have attached ourselves and which is so unlike our homes, our former life.

And the little sailor kept playing the old waltz. It was stifling in the waiting room. But no one made any noise. Everybody listened to the music. They had all heard music before. And probably better than this. But this music was special. And that's why everybody was silent.

And the waltz went on and on. And an officer with a red armband and two soldiers from the commander's patrol were also listening. The officer—sullenly, the soldiers—wide-eyed.

"We'll, now we're soldiers," Seryozhka said.

And the sailor continued to play. And his long forelock kept flopping on the piano keys. Then he suddenly dropped his arms. They slipped down and were just hanging there, and his head hit the keys, and the piano gave forth a strange, sad sound.

Everyone was silent. And the officer with the red armband walked over to the sailor, saluted, and said something to him. Suddenly, everyone who was close by started to shout at the officer.

"What's all this, boys. . ." said the sailor. "What if the Krauts burned my mother?"

"He sits at home," said Zeryozhka. "He ought to be there, then he'd know how to walk around with an armband. . ."

"What's with him? . . ." some woman said.

And then I ran over there and shouted at the officer, "You

headquarters rat, why don't you leave the people alone!"

The officer didn't hear me. And one of the patrol soldiers said to me in a tired voice, "Go home, kid!"

. . . The front twilight crawls in through the windows. We don't put on the light.

"When I was in the cavalry," says Shongin, "we'd come back from a march, feed the horses, and then start cooking some thick millet soup."

"And today the sergeant shortchanged us again on the sugar," says Kolya.

"I'm beginning to dream about my wife," says Sashka Zolotaryov. "We won't see any passes, lads."

"When I was in the eighth grade," I say, "we had a very funny math teacher. As soon as he'd turn around, we'd start talking. And he'd give a 'D' for it, but never to the kid who did the talking."

The Road

We're setting off for the army base to get some mortars. We—that's Second Lieutenant Karpov, the sergeant, Sashka Zolotaryov, and me.

Karpov gets in front with the driver, while the three of us take our places in the back on our one-and-a-half-ton truck.

And we're off. I'm tired of this stupid sitting around in the village. It's better to be riding. Everyone's tired of it. Sashka and I smile and wink at each other.

The sergeant has settled down up front on a soft seat made of empty American sacks. He leans against the cabin with his hands on his stomach, his short legs stretched out, and closes his eyes.

"We're off, boys, don't fall off while I'm asleep."

We're moving.

Perhaps I'll meet Nina someplace. Because of the frost, the truck moves well. It speeds from hill to hill. And up ahead—more hills. And beyond those—still more. We've only got to go forty kilometers. Nothing to it. Now I'll see how they live in the rear.

The road's not empty. Trucks, trucks. . . Tanks go by, infantry. They're all on their way to the front.

"The Siberians really took care of the Germans near Moscow," says Sashka. "If it weren't for them, who knows what might have happened."

"The Siberians are all the same height," I say. "Six feet. They're specially selected."

"Fools," says the sergeant without opening his eyes. "What's that got to do with it? It was equipment that did it at Moscow, equipment. . ."

What's the use of arguing. Let him talk. I know what happened at Moscow. I was told by eyewitnesses. When the Siberians started moving up, the Germans ran West without stopping. I know. Because the Siberians stood ready for death. They're all hunters, bear trappers. They face death from early childhood. They're used to it. And us? Sashka and me, for instance. Could we do it? Supposing tanks come at us—we'd just shut our eyes. . . And not because we're cowards. We're simply not used to it. . . Could I face a tank? No, I couldn't. With mortarts it's simpler. The front lines are far from here. You can fire away, change your position. But face to face. . . it's a good thing we're not the infantry.

Suddenly the truck stops. Up ahead the road seems empty. Only far off in the distance a lone soldier stands and is looking in our direction. The sergeant is sleeping. Sashka and I jump off the truck. Second Lieutenant Karpov is asleep in the front. His lower lip droops like an old man's. The driver has raised the hood.

And the soldier is running toward us. A little soldier. You couldn't think of a smaller one. He's running toward us and waving his arms.

"Look, look," sasy Sashka. "A Siberian."

I laugh. The soldier is really very small. He runs up to us, and I see that it's a girl. She's wearing a long coat, neatly girdled. She has sergeant's insignia on her soldiers. Her face is small, and she has a nose like a button.

"How about a lift, boys. I've been standing here for an hour. All the trucks are heading for the front lines, not a single one the other way. And I have to get there desperately," she says and gestures by drawing her hand across her throat.

I help her to get into the truck. Sashka and I give her our canvas coats, and she sits on them.

"Where are you boys from?"

We nod towards the front lines.

"Has the fifteenth left yet?"

Sashka and I look at each other and shrug our shoulders. Our truck finally moves. The sergeant sleeps. He even snores, just a bit.

"That's great," says our traveling companion, and laughs. "He snores as though he were home on the stove."

"He loves to sleep," says Sashka.

When she laughs, her lips turn up at the corners. Like a clown. A sergeant! And I'm only a private! Where is she going, such a tiny one, such a slim young girl? What happened? Everyone has been taken by it, carried away, all mixed up. . . School kids crawl about in the trenches, they die of wounds, they return home, armless, legless. . . A girl. . . a sergeant. . . what's happened?

"Day before yesterday, the base was raided by forty Junkers," she says. "It was something. We were run off our feet. . ."

"And what would you have done at the front?" Sashka asks. "It's even worse there."

"I probably would have cried," she says, and laughs.

. . . What could you expect. . . of course, she would have cried. After all, even I almost cried. Before the war, I saw a movie. All the soldiers were like soldiers in this movie: adult, experienced, they knew what was what. But I don't know, Sashka doesn't know, this girl doesn't know. . . The sergeant's asleep, and Karpov. . . But they knew what's what. Yet I don't know, Sashka doesn't know, and our commander, although he's sullen. . .

"My name's Masha," she says. "I'm a sergeant in the medical corps. In school I beat all the boys."

"And you like to brag a little, eh sarge?" says Sashka.

The sergeant wakes up. He looks at Masha for a long time.

"And where did you come from?" he asks, using the familiar form.

"May I ask you not to be so informal?" Masha says calmly.

The sergeant's cap slides onto the back of his head.

"Who do you think you're talking to?"

"It's amazing how uneducated a man can be," she says to us.

I want to laugh. The sergeant looks at Masha for a long time, and then he notices her shoulder bands.

"I'm asking you, comrade sergeant, where are you from?"

The truck stops again. The driver again raises the hood. Karpov comes out.

"How are things up there," he asks us.

"While you were asleep, your soldiers froze here," Masha says.

"Oho," says Karpov. "What a nice passenger. And you, did you freeze?"

And he invites her up front.

She jumps out lightly from the back of the truck. She waves goodbye to us.

How warm it must be up front. Hot air from the radiator, soft seats, the whole road spread out before you.

Karpov climbs in after her.

"No, no," she says, "perhaps I'd better go back, comrade second lieutenant."

"Sit down," Karpov says coldly. He gets into the back of the truck.

"Why have you spread out your legs like that, Zolotaryov?" he says. "Can't you sit like a human being."

. . . We're riding. It's getting dark already. If we don't get to the base in half an hour, I'll freeze to death. Sashka is all bundled up; only his nose is visible. A big red nose.

"A man needs a bed, not the back of a truck," he grumbles, "and a warm stove, and good food, and love. . ."

"And who is going to work, kid?" the sergeant asks.

When I return home, I'll study hard. I'll go to sleep at ten. In the winter I'll put on a fur coat, so that nothing can get to me. . .

We stop some truck. We ask. It turns out that it's still some eighty kilometers to the base.

"What do you mean?" Karpov asks, surprised. "They said forty."

"You should have taken another road," comes the answer from the truck.

"He missed the road, the devil," Sashka hisses.

"We'll freeze," says the sergeant.

Masha comes out of the cabin.

"The first turn off, State Farm No. 7," she says.

"Really?" says Karpov, overjoyed.

"For your information, I always tell the truth."

. . . Not many houses have remained intact at this state farm. Not many. But when you consider it in terms of fingers and lips numb with cold, and legs as though they were made of wood— what's the difference how many houses? There are houses, and they let you in, and it's warm inside, and you can drink some tea.

Karpov picks out a house that's bigger and more intact than the others and invites Masha there.

"You'll be more comfortable there."

And he turns to us.

"And you go there, friends, where the windows are lit up."

"I'll stay with the truck for a while," says the driver. "You can relieve me later."

I can only hold out for another minute. Sashka and I run to the house. A girl opens the door for us. She's wearing felt boots and a kerchief.

"Who's there?" someone asks from the inside.

"They're ours, Mama," says the girl.

The girl's name is Vika. Her mother is also wearing a kerchief and a shawl. She looks like my mother. Very much so. She invites us in. We take off our coats.

"You wouldn't happen to have some tea?" I ask with my frozen lips.

We put our dried biscuits on the table.

"That's all we have, lady," says Sashka. "We'd be glad to. . ."

"That's okay," she says, "I'll get you some food right away."

"And Karpov has gone off after Masha," says Sashka, "and he's having the sergeant run errands for him."

We're sitting at the table. Vika is also there, and she looks at us with her big eyes. And her mother puts the frying pan on the table. Meat pies are steaming on the frying pan. Gosh, how like my mother she really is. . .

"The hospital stops here," she says. "They gave me a bottle of vodka. Drink it, boys, warm yourselves."

She has big black-and-blue marks under her eyes. We don't refuse the vodka. I drink my glass and feel that I can't catch my breath. I sit with my mouth open. She laughs.

"You should have exhaled, before swallowing. I completely forgot to warn you. Wash it down with the meat pie."

I eat it. But she really does look very much like my mother. My head is swimming. It's really swimming.

"I made it from your dried biscuits," she says.

"Another one?" asks Sashka.

"Yes, let's belt one down," I say.

She pours the vodka for us.

"You ought to take one, lady," says Sashka.

She laughs and shakes her head. And my head is swimming, swimming.

"Mama mustn't," says Vika.

"Just a little bit?" Sashka asks.

"Mama mustn't," I say, "why are you so persistent?"

She pats my head and give me another pie. My head is swimming. I'm hot. Sashka has moved far off in the distance. So has Vika. . . and Mama. . . that's so I won't be so hot.

"Are you local?" asks Sashka . . . .

"We're from Leningrad," says Vika.

"How nice," I say, "and I'm from Moscow. What a coincidence. . . What a meeting. . . at the world's end. . . I'm very happy, very happy. . ."

"If you go to Leningrad via Moscow, please give me a call at my home. . ."

Sashka is eating a pie. While he's eating, I'll sleep for a while. I'll put my head on the table and sleep.

"Wait," says Sashka, "I'll go with you."

He puts me on the coat which he had spread out.

"For some reason, I'm tired," I say.

"Sleep, my boy, sleep," says Mama. She's standing over me.

"Mama," I say, "I'm alive and well. I'll return soon, with the victory. . ."

. . . In the morning it's quiet in the room. The driver is sleeping in Sashka's place. No one home. I put on my coat. I run to the truck. Sashka is walking around it with an automatic around his shoulders.

"And me?" I ask. "Why didn't you wake me?"

"You slept so—I couldn't get you up," says Sashka. "You really drank last night. You were worn out."

"And you're walking like this? Alone?"

"I've slept enough," says Sashka. "Here, you take it for a while. I'll go warm up, and then I'll come back."

Me—I'm a scoundrel and a villain. If I were in his place, I would have tried until I woke him up. I wouldn't do more than

351

I had to probably. I'm a swine. I ought to be taught a lesson. I'm a traitor. If anyone would come for the truck though, I'd cut his throat in short order.

The sergeant comes out of the house.

"Well, kid, everything okay?"

I don't answer. He doesn't need it. He gets into the back of the truck and yawns.

"Go call the boys. We have to go."

. . . "Wait a minute," Vika's mama says to us, "I'll make some potato pies."

"Thanks, we have to go," I say.

"You and your daughter eat it, eat it to our health," Sashka says.

We go over to the truck. Masha is sitting in the truck. She smiles at us.

"I've got it right now. It's another thirty kilometers to the base," says the driver.

"That's amazing," says Masha.

"Everybody in?" Karpov pokes his head out of the front seat.

And suddenly I see Vika is running from the house. She holds out a bundle. I manage to take it on the move.

"That's the pie," she shouts. "Goodbye!"

We wave to her for a long time.

"How did you sleep, Masha?" Sashka asks.

"The lady of the house and I slept fine," she laughs, "but I don't think the lieutenant slept."

"He slept," says the sergeant.

"Well, that means you didn't," laughs Masha. "Someone kept waking us up, three times during the night, knocking on the door. 'Masha, I have to speak to you!'"

"I didn't knock," says the sergeant.

Nina

Karpov comes out of the division headquarters. We look at him.

"The replacements have already left," he says. "We missed each other. They didn't wait."

"All the better," says the sergeant. "Less worries."

We'll be getting an American armored car," says Karpov. "That's not a bad deal either. Sergeant, take the boots at the depot, load up the one-and-a-half-tonner and get going! We'll go in the armored car."

Boots! So there they are. Real boots. Now things will really begin. Boots. The way I am now, I walk around like a cart driver, with rags around my feet. I'm even ashamed. A submachine gun and rags. Now we'll do some fighting!

Karpov goes off to various sections.

"You can wrap all sorts of rags around your feet when you have boots," says Sashka. "No frost can get to you."

"And they won't let any water in," I say.

"It's okay," says Sashka. "Smear them with some lubrications grease and you're all set."

"And you can stick your spoon in the top," I say.

"To put 'em on is just sheer pleasure," Sashka says. "One pull and you're all set."

"You have to pull 'em by the boot tab," I say.

"Of course, by the boot tab," says Sashka. He goes off to look for some friends. Fellow-townsmen. I'll take a walk too. I'll take a look, see how people are doing here.

It's war. It just goes on without respite. Goes on about its business. Doesn't pay attention to anyone. It's war. My submachine gun is getting rusty. I haven't used it once.

"God, where did you come from?" I hear someone say behind me.

It's Nina! She's wearing a soldier's shirt. She has an empty mess tin in her hand. It's really Nina. . .

"Did you come for a visit?"

"I looked for you," I say. "I've been looking since that first time."

She laughs. She's happy. I see it.

"Oh, you darling... There's a real friend. So you didn't forget."

She's cold standing there. There's a frost, and it's windy.

"Let's go eat. We'll talk, okay?"

She pulls me by the hand. I'm following her, following her. We sit in the headquarters mess hall. A barrack. No one around.

"Everyone has eaten already," she says. "I was late. Let's ask Fedya for something."

"Fedya," she says into the window to the cook, "give me

some soup, Fedya. I have a friend up from the front lines. . ."

And Fedya pours a full tureen of soup for me. And Nina breaks off a piece of her bread for me.

"Well, we've managed to scrounge up a meal for you," says the black-mustached Fedya from his window.

"It's warm here," I say.

"Well, how are things going there?" she asks. "How's Kolya?"

"Nina," I say, "you know I really did look for you. I thought and thought about you. . . Why were you silent?"

"Well, we'll eat now, and then have a smoke, right?"

"Why were you silent?"

"If I didn't go out to eat, I probably wouldn't have run into you."

"Now I see what color eyes you have. They're green. I tried, but just couldn't remember what color they were. What color were they? Now I finally know."

"Eat! It's going to get cold. Do you have it tough there?"

"You know, I once even imagined how we'd meet after the war. You were wearing a rose-colored jacket, and no hat. . ."

"None at all?"

"We walk along the Arbat. . ."

"Eat. You soup's probably cold, isn't it?"

"I have to go back soon. If you want, I'll write you a letter."

"And I told the girls here: 'I've got a friend there,' I said. Dark-eyed. He's the only one, all through the war. But they didn't believe me. He's the only one, all through the war. But they didn't believe me. They laughed. But you remembered me, didn't you?"

"Why the only one? Don't you have others?"

"With the others it's something else. . ."

The black-mustached Fedya looks at me attentively. Why is he staring? Maybe he's sorry he gave me the soup. Maybe he's one of those "other ones"?

"Listen, I mean it seriously. I really did think of you. I never thought about anyone like I did about you."

"Well now, you too. . ." Her lips twist. "How nice it was then. . ."

. . . And on the edge of the tureen, a solitary noodle hangs there just like a tiny worm. A white, sad, little noodle. And Nina has rested her head in her hands and looks past me. And I see the barrack windows in her green eyes. And beyond that, green twilight approaches.

"You don't even hear any shooting here," says Nina. "We've only been bombed once."

"Listen, Nina," I say. "If you want, I'll write to you, all right? Nothing much. Just how things are. . . Otherwise I'll lose you. Where am I going to look for you then?"

What a fool she is. Doesn't she understand. What am I, some seducer or something? . . . It's war. It's not Zhenya. Then everything just seemed to be, seemed to be. But this is more real. Doesn't she see? I understand everything now. What a little fool. . .

"What do you think, that I'm like the others? If you want, I'll prove it to you. If you want, I'll write home about you right now. You can send it off yourself. . ."

Black-mustached Fedya keeps looking at me. Doesn't he have anything else to do?

"Well, we'll have another date, right?"

". . . and when the war is over, we'll go together. . ."

"Right smack in the middle of the war we have a date. The only thing that's missing is ice cream. Fedya," she says, "you don't happen to have any ice cream, do you?"

"For you, Ninochka, I have everything," says Fedya, "only the ice cream is hot, it's almost boiling."

"Before the war, when I used to go for a walk with some boy, he'd always buy ice cream for me. There was one boy who didn't. I got rid of him fast. . . We had a park in town. . ."

"Nina, I have to go soon."

"I'm sorry for you," she says. "You shouldn't be fighting. What are you going to get for it? Just don't get angry, don't. I don't mean that you can't fight. Just simply, why do you have to?"

"And you?"

"Well, I'm already used to it. Now Fedya there, he worked in a restaurant. The Poplavok. Is that right, Fedya? He made salads, cooked chops. . ."

"I have to go," I say. "Tell me, are you going to write me? It'll make it easier for me."

"I'll write," she says. "I'll write."

We head for the exit. The spoon clatters in the mess tin.

355

"Listen, Nina, that major, what was he. . ."

"Major?"

"Yes, that major. . ."

"Oh, so you noticed him."

We stop again, near the door. She stands next to me. Very close. How really small she is. Frail and thin. How defenseless she is. I'll take her by the shoulders, her little round shoulders. . . I'll stroke her head with my hand. It's okay if she doesn't explain. I didn't want to ask, I didn't. . .

"Are you feeling sorry for me, is that it?"

"No, but don't feel sorry for me either, Nina."

"What are you going to do now?"

"I'll wait for your letters."

"Supposing you don't get any? Anything can happen."

"I'll get them. You promised."

"What do you need it for, you dope. . ."

Boy, I am a dope, a real dope. I said something I shouldn't have. I didn't say what I wanted to.

"You have a bread crumb on your cheek," I say.

She laughs. Wipes off the bread crumb.

"It's time to go. They'll miss you."

"Let 'em miss me," I say. "Let 'em. It's all the same. . . One problem after another."

"How daring you are," she says with a laugh. And she strokes my head.

We go out into the lobby. I touch her back.

She pushes my hand aside. Very gently.

"Don't," she says. "It's better this way."

And she kisses me on the forehead. And she runs out into the storm, which is just starting.

. . . The armored car is standing near division headquarters. Sashka is walking around it. He looks around.

"We'll be off, right away," he says.

Fun

An armored car is a very convenient vehicle. It's just like a gray beetle. It can go through everything and get out of everything. It's comfortable and warm. The electric heater works. You can even sleep on the go.

I'm not sleeping. I'm just dozing. What's going to happen in the evening, when we catch up to our battery? Maybe there'll be a big battle. Maybe we won't find anyone alive. . . We'll arrive, and I'll wait for Nina's letters. . . And Sashka is sleeping. Really sleeping. And Karpov is sitting next to the driver; he's either sleeping or staring motionless at the broken road.

. . . And the sergeant has brought the boots. But what if I don't get any?

"Comrade lieutenant," I say, "if the road was good, we'd probably really move."

But Karpov doesn't answer. Karpov is apparently asleep.

"Fedosev," I say to the driver, "now we really have a good vehicle. . ."

"But I'm not Fedosev," he says, "I'm Fedoseev. Fedoseev is my name. Everyone mixes me up with someone else. They call me Fedoskin, and all sorts of things. In the war you really can't stop to figure it out: Fedoseev or Fedosev? No time for it. I was once even called Fedishkin. It's really funny. But I'm really Fedoseev. I've been Fedoseev for forty years. From the day I was born, as they say."

We're carrying a barrel of wine. That's for the whole battery. The front-line ration.

"There's a smell of wine here," says Fedoseev.

He has protruding pink lips, white eyebrows, and his teeth are large and have gaps in them. He speaks in a singsong tone of voice. He probably never loses his temper. He makes you feel comfortable and secure.

"There's a smell of wine here," he says.

It's a big barrel. The opening is closed with a wooden stopper. Very tightly. It can't be knocked out. And even if you could, it's all the same, how would you get the wine out? At the battery they're taking on replacements now. Rookies. Young kids, probably. They're standing around, looking. It's funny. Schoolboys. Kolya Grinchenko is probably standing around in front of them. Show-off. And Shongin is probably smoking and saying to Kolya, "You just love to talk, don't you, Grinchenko!" The sergeant has brought the boots. Supposing I don't get a pair?

"Fedoseev, supposing you were to give it the gas, what would happen?" I ask.

"The speed would increase," says Fedoseev. "An increase in

speed. That's if you give it more gas. But you can't here, the road's bad. If I give it the gas, it'll shake. . ."

"Let it then. . ."

"But why?"

"It'd be interesting, when it shakes. . ."

"A pity to ruin the car. And people are sleeping. Let 'em sleep. You and I aren't sleeping. But they are. Let 'em."

What if I don't get any boots? Why shouldn't he feel sorry for me? You ought to drive faster, Fedoseev. Maybe I'll make it on time yet.

"It smells of wine here," says Fedoseev.

It really does smell of wine. A sweet aroma come out of the barrel. And I'm hungry. But we can't drink the wine; it's in the barrel. And the stopper is as big as a fist.

"We could pull out the stopper," Sashka whispers in my ear. Supposing Karpov hears of it. He'll really let us have it.

"Of course you could," says Karpov, without turning his head.

"Just say the word, nothing to it," says Fedoseev.

We turn off the road and stop near a solitary pole. We pull out the stopper. It's easy. It comes out of its nest, just like out of butter. And a cloud of wine vapor breaks through the frosty air. Stronger and stronger.

"Each one take his ration," says Karpov. "No more."

"It'd be nice to have a bite with it," says Sashka.

"We'll grab a bite at the battery," says Karpov.

Fedoseev does it very simply. He takes a rubber tube used for siphoning gas, and he puts one end in the barrel.

"Hold out your tins," says Sashka, "so you don't spill any."

The golden wine runs into the tin. Sashka takes aim. We look at him.

"It stinks of gas," he says.

"That's nothing," says Karpov, "nothing."

He takes a few gulps.

"Pure gas," he says and spits it out.

"Can't do without it," says Fedoseev. "It's the tube. Here, let me try it. . ."

We drink our samples. It's strong wine. You can feel it right away.

"Don't breathe when you drink," says Sashka.

"Gas fumes are very useful," says Fedoseev. "They prevent all sicknesses. You just have to get used to it. It doesn't bother me. Nothing to it. Here, let's have that tin...."

"Well now, pour out the rations in full," says Karpov.

"What is the ration?" I ask.

No one can tell what the ration is.

"As long as we keep drinking," I say.

"Now that sounds like double-talk," says Karpov.

I know what's going to happen. I'll drink, and the fiery liquid will go through my body. I'll feel hot, weak and strange.

"Don't drink too much, Fedoseev," says Karpov. "You have to drive."

"It's like water," says Karpov. "I could drink two liters full of this stuff and not bat an eyelash. It's like water."

"Yes," says Sashka. "This isn't vodka, buddy, it's water."

I can't drink anymore. There's still plenty left in my tin, but I can't anymore. For some reason my lips have become tight. I can't open my mouth very easily. And Sashka's chin is covered with wine. He just manages to catch a breath, and he's at the tin again. And Karpov holds onto the armored car.

"Damn it, I'm weak from hunger," he says.

"It's time to go," says Fedoseev and gets into the cab.

"A fine place to stop," says Karpov. "Right smack in the middle of a bumpy field. There's no place to put your foot. There's a more level place over there."

"You've really belted it down," says Sashka to Karpov.

"That's nothing—I can do it with pure vodka," says Karpov.

"What's your first name," asks Sashka.

"Alexei," says Karpov.

His cheeks are bright red, Sashka's too. They're like brothers. We crawl into the car.

"You want some more, Alyosha?" Sashka asks.

Karpov shakes his head. Sashka sucks the tube. Wine pours into the tin.

"Here, drink." Sashka pushes the tin at Karpov. "Drink, Alyosha. It's like water."

Sashka has short arms. They're like two stumps, and instead of a head he has a barrel. Now there's a head for you.

"But where are you going to put the stopper," I laugh, "not in your mouth?"

Sashka merely shakes his barrel and doesn't say anything.

"Where's the tube?" Fedoseev asks.

"In the barrel," says Sashka.

"It's swimming," I say laughingly.

"Swimming?" asks Karpov. "I didn't see it."

"Oh, you Alyosha," I laugh.

He's okay, this Karyou. I shouldn't have been teed off at him. He has such a hurt look on his face. I tickle his neck.

"Hey, Alyosha," I say. "Don't be sad."

Sashka has put his head on the barrel and is sleeping. Let him sleep. He's okay, too. Everybody's okay. And when they give me a pair of boots, I'll really show 'em how to fight.

"Sashka," I say, "close up the barrel. It's sickening."

But Sashka is crying. Large, childlike tears flow down his cheeks.

"Where am I going?" he sobs. "What the hell do I have to go with you for! Klava is waiting for me. . . Where are you, Klava?"

What a sickening smell. A combination of gasoline and wine. Suppose you mix perfume and peaches? It's still bad. And suppose you mix roses and shoe polish. . . If he just whined quietly and softly, soft like a mosquito, it'd be easier.

"What's the matter, kid," asks Fedoseev, "you sick?"

But I don't feel sick. It's just that the smell is sickening. And I can't strech my legs. It's crowded.

"Come and see me. I'll show you my dog," says Karpov.

"Where?"

"Eight Volga Street."

"Funny," says Fedoseev.

And Sashka is weeping big tears. He remembers his Klava. And he wipes away his tears. But I don't want to cry. Why cry? And again Sashka has a barrel instead of a head. It whirls and whirls, this barrel. There's no help.

"Because of the Krauts, you'll forget me Klavochka. . . Buy a pack of Nord for me as a memento. . . We'll say farewell on the theshold. Klavochka, buy yourself a bright kerchief . . ." is heard from the barrel, "I'll even give you money if you come. . ."

But I'm not crying. It'll be better if I just whimper. It's easier to breathe that way. Because this damned smell . . . Forgive me Nina, so slim, so small, and so strange. . . so unknown. . . forgive me.

"Where are we going?" asks Karpov.

"To the battery," says Fedoseev. "They're on their way, flying, flying."

"Are you drunk, Fedoseev? . . . Who's flying? Rockets? Are you driving us to the front lines?"

"That's right. There she is, over there."

"What do I want it for, Fedoseev?"

". . . there's nothing to do there for me."

"Better turn off, and let's have a cup of tea at my place. . ."

"I could take a cup myself, but this damned smell. . ."

. . . I open my eyes. Our armored car has stopped. Firing can be heard distinctly up ahead. My head's all fuzzy. Sashka is asleep. Karpov is asleep. Head thrown back and mouth open. We've been drinking. Repulsive.

"Why have we stopped?"

"We've arrived, but the battery is gone. No one is here," says Fedoseev. "The front has moved. We have to catch up. . . You were okay. How did you like it?"

The car moves on. The headlights are out. Very thick snow is falling. It lights up everything around us. It's transparently light like in a dream. I'm dreaming. Or am I drunk? The offensive is under way, and we got drunk. I'm delirious from the drinking; up ahead there is a white figure. It stands in our way. It has raised its arms. It holds a submachine gun in one hand, and a lantern in the other. The small yellow flame doesn't illuminate anything.

"Fedoseev, stop!!" I say.

The car stops. Karpov has awakened. He looks at the figure. He reaches for his holster.

"They're ours," says Fedoseev. "Let's find out what's up."

Supposing they're Germans? Where's my submachine gun? It's gone. It's probably under the barrel, someplace. Under the wine barrel. The figure comes closer and closer. Fedoseev flings open the doors.

"Boys," the figure shouts, "help us, quick. Some of our friends have been killed. We have to bury them. . ."

The figure comes up to the car. It's a soldier. He is completely covered with snow. One side of his coat is torn off.

"How did they get it?" Karpov asks, and he yawns.

He yawns as though he just got out of bed. He yawns and our boys are lying there, dead. Karpov is drunk.

"Bullets," I say.

"Mind your own business," says Karpov. "Where are the dead?"

The soldier waves his lantern.

"Over there, over there," he says. "All seven of them. Two of us made it. Help us, boys."

"There's fighting going on," says Karpov. "We can't be late for the battery."

"We're already late," says Fedoseev.

"We shouldn't have drunk so much," I say, and am surprised at my daring.

But Karpov looks at me and doesn't say anything. He doesn't say anything, because there is nothing to say.

"We got drunk like a bunch of swine, while the fighting was going on," I say loudly. "Let's go, Fedoseev."

We climb out of the car. Karpov too. Silently. Then the sleepy Sashka. We take the spades and a pick and follow the soldier.

"You've never seen anything like it," he says, and continues walking. "Nothing like it from the very beginning. We pounded each other for six hours. Then we went forward."

We are walking across the bumpy, snow-covered ground. No, it's not a dream. Up ahead the terrible fighting is going on. I can hear it well. Well, Ninochka, your warrior has distinguished himself. Beneath a low hillock, a solitary soldier is hacking away at the frozen ground. And the one who came with us says, "Here, Egorov, I've brought some help. Now we can do it quickly. You go on hacking. We'll all help you in a minute."

A little to the side lie the seven bodies of the dead men. They're all sprinkled with powdery snow. Their coats and faces are white. Seven white men lie there in silence. What dream is this? They're dead men. Ours. And we drank wine.

"Not a bad commander," I say to Sashka. "He got drunk and let us get drunk, too."

"Shut up!" says Sashka.

"Grab the spades," says Karpov.

"Everybody should," I smile ironically.

Sashka and Fedoseev look at me.

"I'll take one, too," says Karpov calmly. "I also have a spade."

And the seven lie there motionless, as though they had nothing to do with it. We dig in silence. An hour or two. The ground doesn't give very easily. But we manage. We'll be burying the dead in a minute. How will I be able to look at them?

"Put out that lantern," says Karpov.

Egorov puts it out. But nothing changes. It hardly gave off any light anyway. And why did Karpov suddenly think of putting out the light? . . .

It's a deep grave. And the first soldier gets into it.

"Well, come on, Egorov," he says. And I know what he means. And Egorov gives us the sign, and we follow him. Am I really going to pick up dead bodies with my own hands and bring them to the grave? Sashka and Egorov take the first one. They carry him. Fedoseev bends down for the second one. Karpov looks at me. And why shouldn't I take one? I'll take it by the feet. Ar least it's not the head. I must. Yes, me. Not Karpov, but me. I pick up the dead man by the feet. We carry him.

"Careful, boys," says the first soldier from the grave. "Don't drop them."

"Certainly not Lenya," says Egorov, going by.

"That's our Lenya," says the first soldier. "Let's have him."

He takes Lenya's body from us and carefully lies it down. Then we drag over another one, and another.

"Saltykov on top. He was young," says the first soldier. "It'll be easier for him to lie like that."

"Can't you keep quiet?" asks Karpov.

"They don't mind it, lieutenant," says the soldier, "and, naturally, I can keep quiet."

We put them all in. Carefully. They lie there in thier coats. All of them have new boots. We work with the spades in silence. We do everything that's necessary. Now even the boots are hidden under a layer of earth. And a helmet is lying on the hillock. Whose—I don't know.

We're off in the same direction again. Towards the firing. We're silent.

. . . And who has counted how many times we've changed our position? Who? And how many shells I passed to our loader Zolotaryov? And how my hands ache. . .We don't just change our position. If it were only that. We're going forward. Mozdok is somewhere behind us. Come on! Come on! Now I'll probably get a spoon. I'll have a nice new spoon. And as soon as the fighting is over, the sergeant is going to give me a pair of boots. . .That is, when it is over. But when is it going to be over? . . . Kolya Grinchenko keeps bending down. He looks through the sights. Then he stands up. He is tall.

"Platoo-oon!" shouts Karpov. He waves his twig. He stands there so pale. "Fire!"

Sashka Zolotaryov has thrown off his coat. The padded jacket has come apart. His lips are white. He just keeps throwing those shells into the mortar barrel. And he groans each time. And the mortar groans, too.

Through the shouting and the explosions, you can hear the German "Vanyusha" mortar begin to snort. And its terrifying shells land somewhere behind our battery.

"I hope they don't close in," says Shongin. He's actually screaming, but he's barely audible. "If they zero in on us we're goners."

"Retreat!" shouts Karpov.

"Thank God," Sashka laughs pitifully. "My hands are falling off. Nothing to replace them with."

The trucks come out of their covers. We hitch the mortars. And again we hear the snorting of the Vanyusha and the whistle of the shells overhead and their screech, somewhere behind us. Missed. Missed again. How sickening your own helplessness can be. Am I a rabbit? Do I have to wait until I'm hit? Why doesn't anything depend on me? I stand on a flat piece of land, and suddenly. . . you've had it—it's better in the infantry, really. . . at least there you can go into attack screaming. . . and then it's each man for himself . . . and there's no fear, the enemy is right there. But here, you're fired at, and you cross yourself: maybe. . .There it is again. Vanyusha keeps snorting more and more persistently, stubbornly. The shells keep landing more and more frequently, more accurately. Our trucks screech heartrendingly as they get out of the line of fire . . .Hurry up, damn it!

And there's that snorting again. It seems so peaceful. Again and again. And the whistling . . .

"Get down!"

Behind us, Shongin keeps turning round and round.

"What are you doing, picking mushrooms?" screams Karpov.

"My leggings . . ."

And he keeps turning and turning. He catches his leggings like a kitten playing with a ball of string.

Something hits me in the side. The end? . . . I hear running. It's to me. No, they go by. I'm alive. My dearest mother . . .alive . . .alive again . . .I live . . . I'm still alive . . .my mouth's full of earth, but I'm alive . . .. It wasn't me they killed . . .

They all run past me. I get up. I'm okay. My dearest mother . . . I'm okay. Shongin lies not far from me. And Sashka stands over him. He holds his chin in his hand, and his hand shakes. It's not Shongin lying there, just remnants of his coat . . . Where is Shongin? Can't figure out anything . . . There's his tin, submachine gun, spoon! Better not look, better not.

"Direct hit," says someone.

Kolya takes me by the shoulder and leads me away. I follow him.

"Spit out the earth," he says, "you'll choke."

We walk towards the trucks. They're already moving. Several people remain beside Shongin.

"Come on, come on," says Kolya as he sets me down.

"Everyone okay?" asks Karpov.

"The rest are," says Kolya.

. . . Towards evening we arrive at some kind of village. We stop. Is it really over? Are we really going to get some sleep? The kitchen comes up. My stomach is empty, but I don't want to eat.

The three of us are sitting on a log. I drink my soup straight from the tin.

"The Krauts are putting up a fight," says Sashka.

"It's all over now," says Kolya.

"Now we're even flying in the daytime," I say.

"Is your head all right?" asks Kolya.

"He's got a head like a rock. It can take anything," says Sashka. He laughs. Quietly. To himself.

"It's tough about Shongin," I say. We finish eating our soup in silence.

"It's easier for you without a spoon," says Kolya, "you take a couple of gulps, and it's done. But this way, by the time you get in the spoon and bring it up to your mouth, you've spilled half of it. . ."

"I saw some German spoons here," says Sashka, "new ones. They're all over the place. I should bring you some."

And he gets up and goes off to look for the spoons. I'll have a spoon too. Of course, it'll be German. But what's the difference? How long I've gone without a spoon. Now I'll have one at last.

The spoons are really good ones. A whole bunch of them.

"They're washed," says Sashka. "The Krauts love cleanliness. Pick any one of them."

The spoons are in my hand.

"They've been washed," says Sashka.

There are a lot of them. Pick any one you want. After eating you diligently lick it and put it deep down in your pocket. But a German has also licked it. He probably had big, wet lips. And when he licked his spoon clean, his eyes probably bulged.

"They're washed," says Sashka.

. . . And then he put it in his boot top. His leggings were probably soaked with sweat. And then he dipped it in porridge again and then licked it clean again. . . On one of the spoons there is a dried piece of food.

"Well, what's the matter?" says Kolya.

I return the spoons to Zolotaryov. I can't eat with them, I don't know why . . .

We sit and smoke.

"That *Heinkel* is having a ball for himself," says Kolya, and he looks up.

A German reconnaissance plane is flying above us. Our boys shoot at it lazily. But he's high. And it's already twilight. He also shoots at us from time to time. You can just barely hear the machine-gun fire.

"He's getting mad," says Kolya. "That Fascist was probably walking up and down this street yesterday."

And Sashka flips away one spoon after another. He draws back his arm and throws. And suddenly one spoon hits me in the leg. I can't understand how it happened.

"That hurts," I say. "Why are you throwing those spoons around?"

"I'm not aiming at you," says Sashka. And the leg hurts more and more. I want to get up but my left leg won't straighten.

"What's the matter?" asks Kolya.

"My leg won't straighten for some reason," I say. "It hurts very much."

He looks at the leg.

"Take down your trousers," he orders.

"What's the matter?" I say, "Why?"

I'm not wounded. It didn't even scratch me . . . But I'm already scared. Somewhere inside, just below the heart, I have a strange, sick feeling.

"Take 'em down, I say, you bastard."

I take down my padded trousers. My left leg is all bloody. There's a small black hole in my white underpants, and blood is pouring out of it . . . my blood . . . and the pain is getting duller . . . and my head is swimming, and I feel slightly sick.

"It wasn't the spoon, was it?" asks Sashka in alarm. "What happened?"

"The *Heinkel,*" says Kolya, "it's a good thing you didn't get it in the head."

I'm wounded! . . . How could it have happened? In battle, nothing. In the still of the evening. I didn't rush any enemy bunker. It wasn't a bayonet charge. Kolya goes off somewhere, comes back and goes off again. The leg won't straighten.

"It hit a vein," says Sashka.

"Why isn't anyone coming?" I say. "I'll bleed to death."

"It's all right, you have enough blood. Lean against this. Lie down for a while."

Kolya comes back. He brings a medic with him. The medic gives me an injection.

"That's so you won't get tetanus."

He bandages me. They put me on someone's coat. Someone comes and goes away. How uninteresting it all is now. I lie there for a long time. I don't feel the cold. I hear Kolya shout, "The man'll freeze to death. He must be sent to the dressing station, but that bastard of a sergeant won't give us a truck."

To whom is he saying this? Oh, that's the battalion commander who's coming over to me. He doesn't say anything. He looks at me. Perhaps I ought to tell him to order them to give me a pair of boots? But on the other hand, why do I need them now? . . . The one-and-a-half-tonner drives up. It's carrying empty gasoline barrels.

"You'll have to put him among the barrels," I hear the voice of the battalion commander say.

What's the difference where.

They shove some papers into my pocket. I can't figure out who is doing it . . . anyway, what's the difference?

"These are documents," says Kolya. "Hand them over at the dressing station."

They put me in the back of the truck. The empty barrels stand around me like guards.

"Goodbye," says Kolya, "it's not far."

"Goodbye, Kolya."

"Goodbye," says Sashka Zolotaryov, "see you soon."

"Goodbye," I say, "of course, I will!"

And the truck drives off. That's all. While we're traveling the same road we went north on, I sleep. I sleep. Without dreams. It's soft, and I'm warm. The barrels surround me.

I wake up for a few minutes when they carry me into the barrack of the dressing station. They put me on the floor, and I fall asleep again.

. . . It's a large, nice room. And there are windowpanes in the windows. And it's warm. The stove is going. Someone is pulling at me. It's a nurse in a padded jacket worn under her white uniform.

"Let's have the papers, dear," says the nurse. "We have to check you in for the hospital train. They're taking you to the rear."

I take the papers out of my pocket. The spoon falls out. Spoon? . . .

"Don't lose your spoon," says the nurse.

Spoon? . . . Where did I get a spoon? . . . I'll hold it up to my eyes. An old worn-out aluminum spoon, and on the handle is scratched the name "Shongin" . . . When did I have time to pick it up? Shongin, Shongin . . . something to remember you by. Nothing's left except a spoon. Only a spoon. How many battles he had seen, and this was the last one. There's always a last one.

And his wife doesn't know anything. Only I know. . . . I'll hide this spoon even farther down. I'll always carry it with me. . . . Forgive me, Shongin, old soldier . . .

The nurse gives me back my papers.

"Sleep," she says, "sleep. Why are your lips trembling? No need to be afraid now."

No need to be afraid now. What is now? Now I don't need anything. Now I'm completely alone. Supposing Kolya comes in and says: "We're attacking now. Now we'll have some fun, boys. Now we'll drink some cognac . . ." Or supposing Sashka Zolotaryov suddenly comes in: "My hands are falling off from all this work, and there's nothing to replace them with . . ." And Shongin will say: "You talk too much, you're a bunch of animals . . ." But Shongin won't say anything now. Nothing. What kind of a soldier am I? I didn't even fire my submachine gun once. I didn't even see any live Fascists. What kind of a soldier am I? I don't have a single ribbon or medal . . . And other soldiers are lying near me. I hear groans. They're real soldiers. They've gone through everything. They've seen everything.

New wounded are brought into the barrack. They put one next to me. He looks at me. The bandage has slipped off his forehead. He puts it one again. He swears.

"Be with you in a minute," the nurse says.

"I'm plenty sick without you," he says. And he looks at me. He has large, malevolent eyes.

"You with the mortar?" he asks.

"Yes," I say, "mortar. Do you know any of our boys?"

"Yes, I know 'em," he says. "I know everybody."

"When did you get it?"

"This morning. Just now. When did you think?"

"And Kolya Grinchenko?"

"Yes, he got it, too . . ."

"And Sashka?"

"Sashka, too. Everybody. Wiped out. I'm the only one left."

"And the battalion commander?"

He screams at me, "Everybody, I say, everybody!"

And I scream, "You're lying!"

"He's lying," someone says. "Don't you see his eyes."

"Don't listen to him," says the nurse. "He's not himself."

"He talks too much," I say. "We're going forward."

And I want to cry. And not because of what he said . . .
But because you can cry for something else besides grief . . . Just
cry, cry . . . Your wound's not dangerous, kid. You've got a long
way to go yet. You'll still be around for a long time, kid . . .